War of the Gods

KATIE CROSS

KCW

Guide to God Magic
Amulets

IGNIS

Luppentonisa. *Destroyed by Bianca Monroe in "The Lost Magic." Fist-sized amulet infused with orange and roving red, yellow, from within.*

Samthanruadanosa. *Ruddy amulet often referred to as 'red heat'. Similar to Luppentonisa in faceting, with less moving color. Currently assigned to Baxter.*

Handuinolomolokaya. *Strawberry-colored amulet, heart-shaped, lined with white diamonds.*

Arthraysecscentillium. *Oval, apricot-colored amulet with cherry edges and a yellow center.*

GELAS

Kibbukonialamonta. *Sapphire gem usually worn as a heart barrette, about the size of a pentacle coin. Currently assigned to Tipa.*

Nicomedianthekus. *The great lost amulet of Gelas. The largest of all amulets, and the first forged in this epoch of the gods. Has not been seen in two centuries.*

VENTIS

Oceanusorilianno. *Silver, with hints of gray and white streaked through, like swirling fog. Square, set against blunted metal. Was assigned to Baxter, but revoked. Currently assigned to Amorette.*

Arragaran. *Yellow heart with gentle tones of silver along the interior, the size of half a palm. Not set in metal, worn mostly as a necklace.*

Dappledonamikota—*Butter yellow amulet with a slate interior, rolls from yellow to gray.*

TONTES

Meloduncanate—*Rectangular amulet earring, one of the only amulet earrings. Gaudy in opulence and thick in size.*

Herimolodikus—*A string of smaller amulets, fingernail-sized, with alternating purple-and-slate coloring. Currently assigned to a demigod named Dana.*

Vinartaramet. *Stark purple run through with no other color. Blocky faceting.*

Alasparin—*Brilliant purple amulet set in a ring. One of the only known ring amulets frequently seen. Known to be one of Tontes' most powerful amulets.*

Lynnkestria—*Black amulet all the way through, long and flat in shape. Known as a lesser-powerful amulet. Currently assigned to Paran.*

*Central Network Council
Members*

Halifax, Council Member over the Tate Covens
Georgette, Council Member over the Chatham Covens
Massimo, Council Member over the Eastern Covens
Rosanna, Council Member over the Letum Wood Covens
Martha, Council Member over the Southern Covens
Rafe, Council Member over the Middle Covens
James, Council Member over the Stilton Covens
Clare, Council Member over the Western Covens
Talbert, Council Member over the Bickers Mill Covens
Sia, Council Member over the Ashleigh Covens.

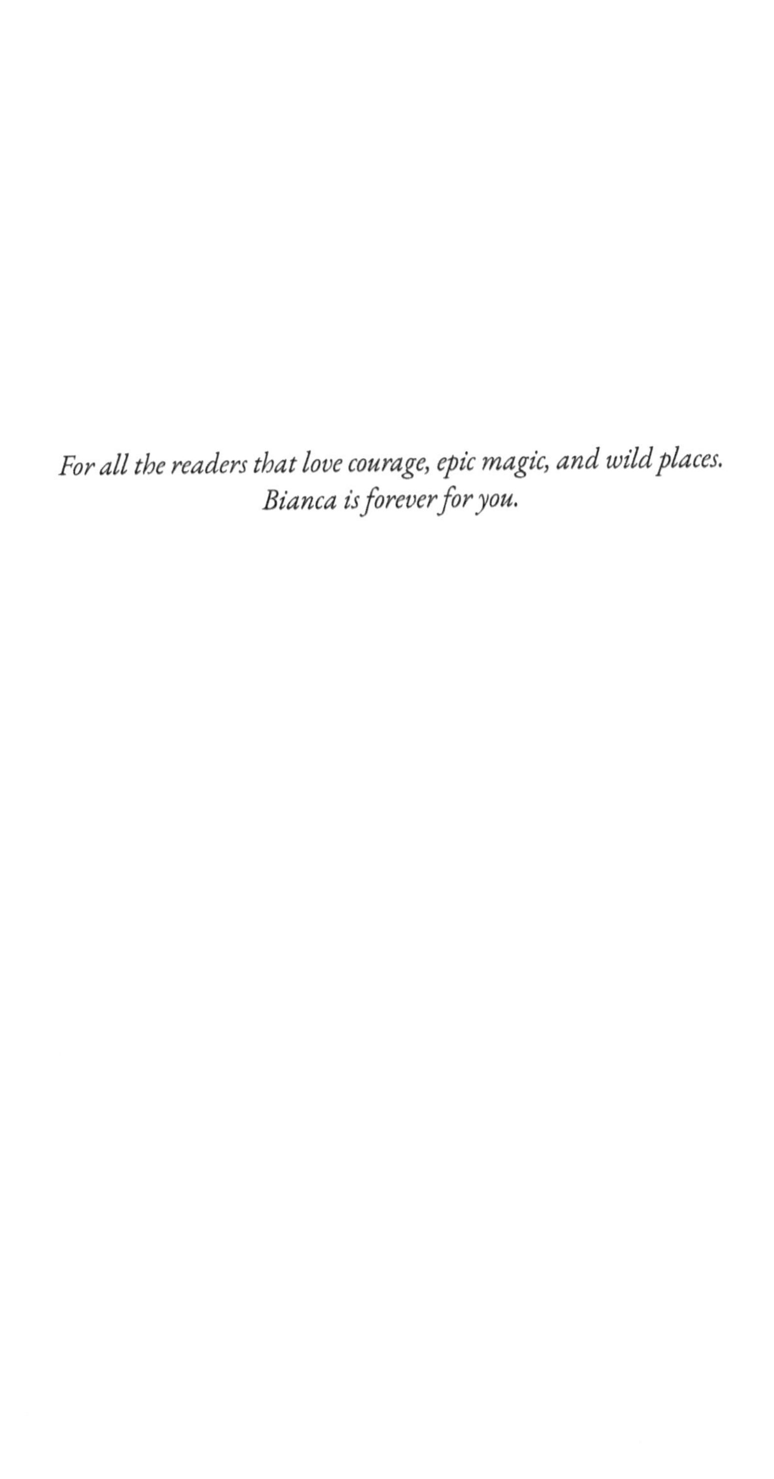

*For all the readers that love courage, epic magic, and wild places.
Bianca is forever for you.*

Chapter One

The voice of the forest called to me.

They harm the children.

I stood on a branch as wide as my cottage, head tilted back to peer into a bright upper canopy. Children?

What children?

Thick moss lay under my feet in an emerald carpet, washed with shoots of electric green. Curlicue vines supported a rainbow of differently-colored flowers, the tiny buds small as pebbles. A thin vine grew, looped around my ankle. The tree spoke again.

They harm the children.

My heart leapt back to life. Letum Wood rarely spoke with a single, determined voice. Hundreds or thousands of trees frequently whispered in looped refrains, perfectly synced. Rarely did the forest individuate.

"Who?"

The ill-fated.

"Demigods?"

A low keen answered.

Unexpected magic surged into my feet, shoved me into pressure and darkness. A transportation spell. A blink later, I stood in a different part of the forest. Letum Wood moved me with magic again.

An equally high branch overlooking rolling plains ahead supported me. A dirt road cut through waist-high grasses, a hundred paces away, to form a boundary. This had to be the edge of Letum Wood near the Eastern Network. I visited here when I worked with Marten as the Ambassador's Assistant years ago.

The sound of a pompous voice prompted a fast invisibility spell.

"Witches are terrible, terrible creatures!"

I grabbed a vine, swung to a different branch of the tree with a better vantage over the road. A line of children stood on a dirt track, squinting against the vivid sunlight. Hiccuping sobs broke from the youngest. The oldest glared in stony silence. Each child stood with their hands behind their back, probably tied that way.

"Mongrel demigods," I muttered.

Four adult demigods, recognizable by their general larger-than-life presence, positioned themselves at altering angles around the children. A clear, tactical formation meant to keep the kids from scattering. Beyond them stood a schoolhouse. The door was flung open, creaking on loose hinges.

No teacher?

I slipped Viveet from her sheath, comforted by the warmth of her blade. The Volare slid free of its cylindrical carrying case on my back and hovered expectantly behind me. Eager magic flowed from both of them. I canvassed the scene one last time, stepped onto the Volare, and sank to the earth.

On the ground, I crouched behind a trunk, which proved to be unnecessary as the demigods weren't paying attention anyway. Nor could they detect goddess magic. The Volare shrank to half its size while it hovered above the forest floor, understanding my intent and anticipating what I wanted.

As I crept out of Letum Wood, grasses parted ahead of me. Bushes crawled out of the way. I advanced in silence. The pretentious male voice from before became more sonorous as I approached.

"You are also terrible, terrible children."

A spry demigod with flaxen hair on a too-large head waggled a finger. His skinny neck, thin arms, gave him a gaunt appearance. His shoulders shook as he spoke. Light hairs sprouted from a split in his shirt past his collarbone and led my gaze right to an amulet.

A gaudy oval, apricot in color, rimmed with cherry-colored edges and a yellow-sun center. Such an amulet belonged to Ignis, god of fire. After my time in Alaysia, Baxter had given me a painting on rough parchment-like paper with all the amulets for each god listed. *Get familiar with them,* he had said with resignation. *They'll be coming back.*

This one appeared to be Arthraysecscentillium. But . . . that couldn't be right. Ignis wouldn't send his children here. He fought on the side of witches, not with his ill-reputed brothers Ventis and Tontes.

"Witches have no redeeming qualities. None at all. Fortunately, we are here to help you with that."

A bloodied body lay on the ground. Female, with dark blood staining her nose and chin. The youngest children stood nearest her, a girl and a boy, probably no older than five. She'd attempted to protect them, no doubt. Both trembled. One cried quietly, lips puckered into a frown, nose running. Tears streaked the cheeks of the other.

Two of the older boys, around twelve, glared at the demigods with locked jaws. Good. Their indignation might help us later. Rage was a mighty power when used correctly.

From a distance of thirty paces back, I circled the group,

studying the demigods. Two of the four gazed into the forest and down the road every ten to fifteen seconds. The third focused on the children as the wiry demigod spewed more drivel. Only one amulet was apparent.

"Bound to incantations," he cried, a hand to his forehead. "How do you survive with so much to learn and memorize?"

The dramatics irritated me. Viveet smoldered with greater heat as I tightened my grip, teeth gritted. Demigods were naturally stronger than witches, with or without amulets. Them having only one amulet present would tilt the odds slightly more toward my favor, but still vastly out of balance.

They had rounded up thirteen children, tied their hands, and stood them in a line side to side . . . to what end? Demigods hadn't been seen in Alkarra since the failed uprising over two months back. Certainly not since I returned from Alaysia, half dead, six weeks ago. Their elusive motivations I'd deal with later.

For now, I had four demigods to battle and thirteen children to save.

I'd faced worse.

Greater questions cluttered my mind. Was I ready to battle demigods? Had I recovered my full strength after god magic almost killed me?

Probably not.

Would that stop me?

Never.

A demigod with four braids and a slightly crooked nose bounced on her heels, head tilted from side to side in clear agitation. Her gaze darted from forest to children to road, then back again in a loop.

She muttered something in Alayslan.

The leader ignored her.

"You done yet?" the second demigod called. He frowned, bushy black eyebrows heavy over his narrowed eyes. "Let's get out of here. Set it on fire and throw the brats inside, already."

He spoke in Alkarran. To frighten the children, perhaps?

One little girl screamed. All at once, the sound calmed. Her mouth still hung open, though no noise was issued. They used god magic to silence her. Her eyes widened, big as saucers. With the demigods arguing, I slipped next to the oldest boy. He had strawberry blonde hair and bright green eyes, with freckles for days across the bridge of his nose.

"Say nothing," I whispered. "I'm Bianca Monroe. I'm going to save you all."

His neck tightened, then eased. To his credit, he didn't try to face me. Reaching behind him, I untied and loosened the ropes around his wrist, then tucked the ends into his palms.

"When I tell you to, grab the girl to your left and run for the trees. Don't stop. Don't look back. The others will come. Once you're inside the trees, the forest will hide you." I put my hand on his trembling shoulder. "Listen for my command."

A slight nod confirmed he understood.

I went to the next one.

Giant logs appeared on the ground outside the schoolroom. They crashed, sending a little tremor under my feet. A third appeared, slamming into the wall and through a window. Glass shattered in a glittering spray.

Two of the children winced.

Fury filled the face of the oldest girl when I gave her the same instructions.

"Destroy them," she hissed.

Two of the demigods squabbled in Alaysian—clearly *not* the brightest demigods from the land of the gods—while the female conjured a torch. The third male gestured toward the school-house, muttering something.

The next child confirmed understanding, which left three more to instruct. The three oldest would grab the three youngest, so seven of thirteen remained without plan. Invisibly, the Volare slid up to my side, touched my waiting fingertips at my back.

Boy twins, around ten years old, stood together. Blood stained the ropes around their raw wrists—they'd been trying to free themselves. The twins would be taken care of by my magical rug.

Five left.

"That's it!" the lead demigod cried. He sliced his hands through the air. "I'm tired of arguing. Send the runts into the fire and make sure the teacher wakes up to see it happen. Someone has to report this to their leadership."

The amulet brightened when fire blazed from inside the schoolhouse. Flames exploded out the windows, crawling to the sky.

Incantations swirled through my mind, ready to be loosed. Agitation followed, a sure sign my magic was ready to fly.

Please let this work, I pleaded.

The invisibility spell began in my mind—a quick, natural incantation I'd cast thousands of times, though never to almost thirteen fleeing children and a rug. As if the magic felt my desperation, it responded with prodigious power.

"Now!" I called.

My invisibility incantation dropped, revealing me in the middle of the circle. The children disappeared as I pressed the magic toward them. The Volare darted down, scooped up the still-visible twins, and dissipated into the invisibility magic.

Such a daunting shove of power nearly dropped me. I stumbled, catching myself with a hand on a fallen log, and shouted, "Run!"

While demigods gasped and reared back, Viveet illuminated. Shimmering flames leapt high, their heat pressing forward.

"More," I whispered.

Blue heartfire billowed, dazzling high in a shocking blast.

With a loud cry, I swung her in a wide circle and advanced. The aquamarine and sapphire flames danced along her blade, rippled the air above her like a mirage, and distorted the shocked demigods. They threw their hands in the air, stumbling back.

"My name is Bianca Monroe." I whirled to the side to fend off a pathetic advance. The demigod faltered mid step, slinking away from Viveet's daunting blaze. "Formerly known as the amulet-breaker. You may call me the Lady-witch of Letum Wood."

The female demigod pressed a hand to her pocket in a subconscious gesture to protect what lay inside.

"Luppentonisa has already fallen to me," I continued, as if I hadn't noticed her hand move. "I'm a servant of Deasylva, goddess-touched witch, and friend of Ignis. I survived the Heart of Alaysia and the presence of your gods. These children are under my protection and, by extension, the protection of the goddess of the forest. Advance if you dare."

The invisibility spell faltered. At the last second, I gripped it again. Magic drained out of me like an uncorked barrel. The edges of the spell fell apart as the children scattered, requiring the magic to cover more area. A shoe appeared here, a braid there.

With a growl, I pushed my magical energy farther. My knees shook. I forced myself to stay standing as one of the demigods advanced with a step. A snarl sent them back.

Whispers erupted in my head.

The children arrive.

We protect them.

We protect you.

"You lost your god magic!" the leader called. "I heard all about Ignis taking it back. You're not an amulet anymore. You're a witch!"

"A witch you'd be a fool to challenge. In losing god magic, I gained more power from my goddess. Will you risk it?"

My gaze drifted quickly to the side. Grasses still moved, halfway to the forest.

Ten seconds, I thought.

Ten more seconds would be enough for all the children to enter the forest. The spell would end at the same time without a second repetition. Hastily, I cast the incantation again. My brief distraction gave the female demigod an opportunity to hedge closer to my right side. Another approached on my left.

Shock and fear faded from their expressions. Disbelief followed. The female studied me through slitted eyes, then disappeared. Why they didn't use god magic to tie me up, I couldn't fathom. Such an obvious choice.

Or maybe *they* weren't the usual suspects.

"What are you doing here?" I asked the leader.

"We came to claim Alkarra."

"By killing thirteen children?"

"We're sending a message!"

"That you're too frightened to fight *real* witches?"

He sneered.

I sidestepped to the left when a demigod advanced closer to my right, but didn't take my gaze off the leader when I called, "And claiming Alkarra has worked out so well for all your siblings?"

"Our father is a weak god. We disown him. He chose the wrong side of the war."

"Disown him, but not his magic? You speak so ill of him while you skulk away with his amulet? Now, you act like you're a hero. Do you even know *how* to do god magic? Or did you steal that amulet from someone else?"

Crimson bloomed through his cheeks. "We will have this place!" he shrieked. "The time of the witch has passed! Not even the former amulet-breaker can stop the gods who crave this land."

"Watch me," I muttered.

Footsteps approached from behind. Light and quick and a breath away. The female was about to descend at my back, but she'd put herself too far away and given me a chance to hear.

Arrogant buggers.

Viveet arced in a wide, smoldering circle as I spun, blade extended. My grip tightened, bracing for impact a second before Viveet's pristinely sharp edge whacked into flesh.

The female screamed, visible now. She collapsed, arm pressed to her side, while I yanked Viveet free. Blood spurted from a slice between two ribs.

I grabbed her uninjured arm, twisted it back, and yanked her in front of me. Blood trickled down Viveet's blade and sizzled on the hot, blue runes as I held it to her neck.

"Don't. Move."

She silenced.

Black dots swam in front of my vision with the effort. The pull from the invisibility magic had become too strong. I wobbled on my feet, vision hazy.

They are here.

The children rest.

She always comes back.

She is ours.

As planned, the spell released on its own, unwinding like a sigh. Relief instantly followed. Movement out of the corner of my eye brought me back to the moment. I swung, jerking the female in front of me at the exact right moment. Another demigod leapt. Too late, he crashed straight into her. Head slammed against head. Her neck snapped back, unconscious against my shoulder, while he rolled to the ground.

The third demigod hesitated as I dropped the female, whirled around, brought Viveet into guard, and smiled at him. Viveet sizzled. Shimmery demigod blood slipped down my wrist, hot from Viveet's blue flames.

"Leave now."

With a quick jerk of his head, and a twisted scowl, he motioned to the remaining demigods present in silent command. They shuffled back, upper lips curled. Two vanished, then the female. The leader retreated last, a promise of retribution in his gaze.

I snarled.

He cleared out.

For five minutes, I waited. No secondary attack. No sound. Certain they hadn't returned, I dropped to my knees. Exhaustion crept over me as I struggled to stay conscious. The back of my head prickled as darkness swept over me. I slapped my cheeks.

"Stay. With. It."

I definitely hadn't been ready for *that*.

With deep breaths, life slowly returned to my brain. My weak muscles regained movement. I staggered back to my feet.

Shuffling grass reminded me of the thirteen children I still had to get to safety. The whirling world settled when I leaned against a tree. With another spell, I conjured a piece of charcoal and parchment.

"What's the name of your town?" I called.

Blonde hair peeked out from behind a tree, then disappeared. Hushed whispers, then a command to *be quiet* followed. The oldest boy emerged with two children on either side of him, clutching his arms. He stopped once he saw me.

"They're gone?" he asked.

I nodded.

"The town is Tisdale."

I blinked twice to clear the double-image of charcoal in my right hand and pressed the parchment onto my thigh. Lopsided, childish letters struggled onto the paper.

Tisdale schoolhouse. Demigod attack. Come now.

The letter rushed out of sight, Grandfather-bound. I tossed the charcoal to the side, dropped to a knee, and grimaced. The swirling world stirred back up again. I fought off the urge to vomit.

"Stay there," I shouted. "Help is coming."

When no one disobeyed, I scrambled for the teacher.

* * *

Guardians flooded the area.

Sniffling noses and trembling shoulders calmed. Parents transported to the schoolhouse and children ran to their open arms. An Apothecary appeared for the teacher, who hadn't awoken, yet breathed. Scarlett appeared for a few moments, but returned to the castle after speaking with Grandfather. Trouble filled her gaze.

Grandfather, Matthais, and Talmund, the Head of Guardians, stood in a circle around me while I finished my report of events. In the background, a Guardian contingent secured the area. The wobbly feeling had faded from my head, but I hid my still-trembling legs.

Grandfather studied me, as if he sensed something wasn't right. Near the end of Talmund's questioning, Grandfather pretended to tie a shoe, then stood at my side. I leaned on him, grateful for the support.

Finally, their questions eased. Children returned home. The apothecary transported the teacher away. One by one, the meadow emptied of witches and life until only Grandfather and I remained. Trees chattered lightly in the background.

Hands clasped behind his back, he turned to me. "And now you can tell me how you *really* feel."

Weak, I thought.

The extrication of god magic in Alaysia had almost killed me —I'd flirted with death, heard the voice of Deasylva, and chose to come back to Alkarra. At the last possible moment, Letum Wood crept in, healed me. Six weeks had passed since that day. My body grew stronger daily, yet hadn't returned to full capacity. The power behind Letum Wood, and my burgeoning connection with the forest, was my only confidence.

I leaned on it for life.

"Never better," I quipped.

"Which means you're tired," he drawled in a musing way. "Such magical use must have cost a great deal of energy. That's what you get for testing your limits. *New* limits, I'd wager, since the god magic left."

I cast him a wry, sidelong glance.

His lips twitched.

"I've had some experience with strong, savior-like personalities in my life, Bianca. You're all the same. A Monroe you may be through your mother, but a Graeme you are through your father. Mildred shows in your personality everyday."

"I thought it wouldn't work," I admitted. "But there wasn't time to think of something else."

"Clever enough."

The complicated strings of the plan lay in neat lines in my head after reviewing them, but they hadn't seemed so neat at the time. Gratitude that the ordeal was over further weakened me. Food, water, and sleep would restore my ability to make sense of it.

"How did you know to come here? You didn't mention it to Matthais and Talmund."

I shifted uneasily. Not many witches knew the truth of my connection to the forest, and I preferred to keep it that way. Thankfully, Talmund and Matthais hadn't asked.

"Letum Wood brought me."

"Oh? Is that normal?"

"It's happened more since I returned from Alaysia."

"Part of your growing connection with Letum Wood? I mean, Deasylva."

"I believe so."

"Hmm." Grandfather put an arm on my shoulder, tucked me into his side. "Ended well, but this has brought up a bevy of new concerns. Baxter is going to have a headache with this one."

Chapter Two

A burly pair of shoulders and inquisitive hazel eyes waited at my cottage. I strode right into Merrick's open arms. When they settled around my shoulders, I melted. Their heavy weight drew me closer to his wild scent.

"Merry meet," he murmured with a touch of amusement.

I sighed, closed my eyes.

Safe.

Minutes later, he set his hands on my shoulders and pulled away. Dirt smudged his left cheek. A red scratch brightened the skin above his brow. I reached up to touch it, surprised to find a gentle bruise around it.

"You're hurt."

"Nah." He scoffed. "A scratch."

"What happened?"

"Matthais had me listening to a Council Meeting."

"Did the Council know?"

He grinned. "Not exactly."

"Then how did you get the scratch?"

"Council Member Rosanna accidentally knocked over a statue when she ran into it."

Understanding flooded me. I bit back a giggle. "And you were standing near said statue?"

"Had to let it scratch me on the way down, or she would have seen me. I already had my back against the wall and nowhere to escape. Laugh if you want. Hurts like a bugger," he muttered.

My lips rolled together in a poor attempt to school my amusement. "I'm sorry, Merrick. Sounds rough. Why did Matthais want you in there?"

"For the gossip session afterward, of course." He sobered. "I heard some stirrings after the Council dismissed. Your name happened to be amongst them."

"The demigods."

He nudged me to the table. "Sit, B. Tell me everything." His legs sprawled in front of him as he looped an arm over the back of my chair. The tips of his fingers rested on my shoulder. I pulled my feet onto the chair as I told the full story again. By the end, consternation clouded his features.

"We've been wondering when they'd show up," he murmured. "Didn't expect it to involve an attack, if I'm honest."

"Agreed."

"Baxter should have something to say about it."

"I will speak with him tomorrow."

Merrick's hand clasped the back of my neck in a warm touch. "Glad you're all right, B."

"The forest protected me."

He smiled. "It always does."

Unable to help myself, I slipped onto his lap and laid a resounding kiss on him. Stubble prickled my palms in a gentle tickle. He hooked an arm around my waist and stared into my eyes. A wisp of hair fell onto his forehead. I reached up, tucked it away. A faraway expression overcame him as he touched my cheek with the pad of his thumb.

"Sometimes, I can hardly believe you're real."

He pressed a lingering kiss to my lips. Agony tightened his cheeks into a grimace, then faded. Residuals from when I'd returned to the Central Network, dead. The terror of such an experience had been a beast I subdued gradually.

For Merrick, it created a different horror. He contemplated more deeply these days. Spoke more frequently. Touched more readily. The experience closed the lingering chasm that three years away from each other created.

"On other topics," I said with forced brightness, "I have a gnome issue."

"What?"

"Gnomes."

"What're they doing?"

The astonishment in his voice made me laugh. I gestured to my floorboards. "Burrowing gnomes. They're in the ground under my cottage. I've heard or seen them intermittently for the last several weeks. Then again last night."

"Not good. Don't want the floor to sag if they burrow too far and deep. It'll destabilize the ground."

"Among other things," I muttered. "They're also quite loud and nocturnal."

"Smoke 'em out?"

"Tried. Didn't work."

"Huh."

"Leda sent me a grimoire on house pests, but these miserable monsters are tenacious. None of the repellent potions or spells worked. I harbor little hope. Want some dinner?"

"Is it gnome meat?"

I laughed and slid free. Merrick stood as I headed toward a small cupboard where I stashed bread and residual goat cheese. He stretched, arms elongated over his head.

"I can't stay to eat. I need to go."

Disappointment flooded me as I turned back around. "Really? Not even for lunch?"

"Matthais has another job for me to do. I need a bigger assignment but he doesn't have one yet. I'm tired of all these . . . chores," he muttered.

"I'm sure he'll have something big and stressful and fun for you soon."

"I'll see you later?"

I gifted him with my brightest smile. "Sounds good. Keep in touch."

With a saucy grin, he snaked an arm around my waist, yanked me into his hard chest, and ravaged me with a kiss. Before I could draw a full breath, he released me and faded into a transportation spell.

Giddy, I turned back to my cupboard. My elation turned to a sour frown when only crumbs remained in the cupboard. Almost a full loaf gone? A trickle of dirt on the ground leading to the cupboard, and a tiny, grubby handprint near the handle, spoke to the culprits.

A *thud-thud-thud* and maniacal chatter echoed from below. I glanced to my feet, scowled, and yanked the cupboard door open.

Time to grapple with the gnomes again.

* * *

The next day, a thin piece of ice hovered in front of me, rectangular, transparent as glass, with a scrawling design along the edges.

Sharp points at each corner resembled icicles. Fog smoked off of it, escaping in the sultry summer heat. The sides melted, dripping onto the floor in a cool kiss.

Meet with me.

No signature. Elegant script on a sheet of ice. Arrogant

assumption that I'd know exactly what to do. The clues added up quickly.

Must be from Gelas, god of ice. My supposed ally and should-have-been-enemy-but-wasn't. Also known as Gio, my Alaysian should-have-been-mortal-friend-but-wasn't, that turned out to be a god.

I watched the message liquefy, torn over how to respond. Gelas and I hadn't spoken after the confrontation in the Heart of Alaysia. Our last interaction had occurred moments before my death—and eventual coming-back-to-life. Questions about him plagued me ever since.

Alkarra lived on a battered edge of hope since I returned. Uncertainties slammed into us at every side, like a boat on a capricious sea.

When would the gods attack?

Would they attack?

What did they want?

A meeting with Gelas could answer at least some of these questions, and more. Yet . . . I didn't want to talk to a god again. Not ever, if I could manage it. Not even Ignis, though we had been friends of a sort.

Besides, my first interaction with the god of ice hadn't gone well.

After several minutes of deliberation, curiosity won the day.

"Fine," I muttered.

A glassy chunk of the ice remained, a quarter of the size of the starting note. New words appeared.

Tomorrow. Southern Network Icelands, at the southern-most tip. You'll see me there. Bring Baxter.

* * *

The furthest edge of the Southern Network never lost its ice.

Glaciers and floes blanketed the land with sharp edges and sparkling vistas. Everything glimmered, even in dull cloud cover. Today, warmth sweated the ice. Water trickled by, sloshing as it scurried toward the ocean not far away. The block of ice I stood on groaned.

"This seems safe," I murmured.

The ground shifted.

I transported further back.

The tip of my nose tingled, my nostrils burned from the chill. Despite residual warmth, more an afterthought than a climate, arctic winds flowed through.

"So," drawled a familiar voice. "You decided you missed Alaysia and wanted to play with demigods again, I hear?"

Baxter's bright, green gaze stood just behind me when I whirled around. A mussed curl bobbed above his right ear in a perfect spiral. He grinned, a lissom figure in the snowy world. Impeccably dressed, as usual, with shoes that gleamed.

"Merry meet, Baxter. How are you?"

He made a vague sound in his throat.

"That good?"

"Busy in the Eastern Network with Niko."

"Any word from home?"

His arms tightened, nostrils flared. "No."

Baxter hadn't extrapolated much about Alaysia. No thoughts about his father, Ventis, the god of wind. None regarding his demigod sisters, homeland, or his plans for a future in Alkarra.

Instead, he kept busy. Too busy. His punishing schedule would have reduced even Papa to shreds. He spent half his time in the Eastern Network, half in the Central Network, working as an Ambassador between the two good gods—Gelas and Ignis— and all of Alkarra.

"I wanted to ask you about the demigod event yesterday," Baxter said, back to the crisp tones of his business-like state.

"Care to explain the whole thing again to me over dinner? I'll buy, but we won't call it courting. I have a feeling Merrick wouldn't like the idea."

My lips twitched. "Sounds like a plan. In the meantime, what can I expect from Gelas today?"

Baxter snorted. "No idea."

"Think he'll actually come, in person?"

"Maybe."

"Does he appear when you meet with him?"

"On occasion."

In Alaysia, Gelas appeared as Gio, a thirty-something male with streaks of gray in raven hair, an attractive, quick smile, straight teeth, and a bright gaze. Gelas, god of ice, might be an entirely different being altogether.

Rarely did the gods reveal their physical form, which only made this meeting all the more intriguing.

A body appeared in the distance, striding closer. I eyed it warily, then with greater curiosity. The figure moved with a steady clip. Unhurried, but not slow. All too soon, I recognized the face shape, the hair.

Gio—rather, Gelas—indeed.

He wore no coat. Work pants lined with fur, a long-sleeved shirt parted at the chest. The black-and-gray lined hair remained, only it was pulled into a queue at the back of his head. His still-bright blue gaze held mine, similar to the ice floes that ringed the Heart of Alaysia. As Gio, he must have changed the color. The greenish-blue stood in sharp contrast to his lighter skin.

Only briefly did he regard Baxter before turning to me. Seeing my Alaysian friend Gio—usually shirtless, in shorter pants and bare feet—clad in fur-lined clothes, eyes luminous in the icy climate, startled me. At one point, Ava had even *hugged* him. Of course, she hadn't known . . .

Jikes, the gods made *everything* weird these days.

Gelas stopped several paces away, giving us ample space.

Curiosity filled his expression as he tilted his head to the side. A slow, subtle smile followed.

I tensed.

In his eyes lurked a strange mixture of the blooming coldness of the god of Icelands, and Gio's congeniality. Standing before him again felt surreal.

"Bianca."

"Gio. Ah, I mean, Gelas."

His amusement deepened into a rigid smile.

"What do you want me to call you?" I asked.

"Gelas is fine."

"Right. Ah . . . how is the Southern Network?"

"Deliciously cold."

A pause.

"Cold even in summer," I mused, for lack of anything to say. "Ideal for the god of ice."

Baxter sent me a sidelong glance. A silent question of why-are-you-being-so-awkward? I ignored him. Gelas' brow rose. Deeper hilarity appeared, though I'd given no attempt at humor.

"I forget," Gelas murmured, "how short and fallible the lives of witches are. Alkarra was once my home. The Southern Network was the seat of my throne. Even the Icelands of the North, where Selsay now dominates, call to me after all this time. The allegiance of all ice is mine."

Another inelegant pause stretched between us. I cleared my throat.

"Well, it's . . . that is . . ."

Forget this. Skirting around frustration had never been my style. Besides, the novelty of being in the presence of a god had lessened after my time in Alaysia. All attempts at polite affability faded away.

I set my hands on my hips and glared.

"Really, *Gio*?" I cried. "You couldn't have said something to me while I was in Alaysia? You couldn't have told me or given *slightly* better hints than grumping me out of your Icelands? I was in your lands. You could have told me! Instead, you were mean and annoyed."

Gelas ignored the reproach, but his shoulders lowered in relief. Underneath his icy layers existed a god amused with life in general. A young soul, perhaps. Aligned with what he wanted, but entertained by everything else in the meantime.

In different circumstances, we might have been friends.

"When you came to my glacier, you needed a firm reminder."

"It missed its mark."

"I noticed."

I waited.

No further explanation came.

"Onto more important news. Demigods were recently in Alkarra," Gelas said to Baxter in his usual clipped way. "I've heard rumors. Any further information?"

Baxter shook his head.

Gelas continued, musing now. "I would be tempted to say that it's Ignis' children rebelling against him."

"It was," I said.

A resigned sigh responded. "Ventis or Tontes may have goaded them to sow discord," he continued after a pause, "but I don't think either rebellion or general discord are fully correct. More than likely, some demigods are growing bold and stupid because my brothers are about to do something big."

"Something big?" I echoed.

Gelas nodded. "Ignis is confident, and I agree, that Tontes and Ventis are about to make a move. All has remained quiet in Alaysia for six weeks now, which means my brothers have taken pains to hide their machinations."

"How will they *make a move*?"

"Storms, most likely. Wind. Water. Thunder. At least, that's what I'd expect, but I can't guarantee."

His easygoing attitude startled me.

"That doesn't sound so bad," I drawled, waiting for the rest to come. There had to be more to it than *wind, water, thunder.* Baxter swallowed hard, oddly pale.

"Not so bad?" he croaked. "Gelas isn't talking about wind and thunder as you know it, Bianca. My father wouldn't settle for less than cataclysmic devastation."

My heart dropped to my knees. Right. Gods, and all that. "How do we stop it?"

"We won't stop their advance," Gelas said drily. "We can't. It would weaken us, which they'd take advantage of, and we'd lose the final battle. Instead, we fight them in Alkarra."

"What?"

"There's no way to intercept them, Lady-witch. They're coming for what they want. You won't prevent that."

"What do they want? Alkarra?"

Gelas' jaw tightened when he nodded, but it was vague, uncertain. "Yes, but more specifically, Ignis and I believe they'll attack Deasylva."

"I'm sorry, why would they attack Deasylva?"

Gelas acted as if I hadn't spoken. "Ventis and Tontes want to remove her presence in Alkarra before they attempt the full over-throw. Deasylva has been the wisest of the goddesses. She spent the last several millennia building up her strength through her forest. As if she knew something like this would happen," he finished with a suspicious mutter. "Her magic systems have always been more creative."

"That means Letum Wood, right?" I asked. "Your brothers want to bring down Letum Wood?"

He nodded.

"They'll try to destroy the forest first?" Baxter confirmed quietly.

A shock raced through me at the words. Filled with horror, I waited for Gelas to reply. His icy gaze tracked mine.

"Yes."

Tontes' thick, rolling voice resonated through my night-mares for weeks after I returned from Alaysia. The thought of him anywhere near my trees, or those that I loved, sent dark shudders through me.

"We stop them *now*," I commanded with a step forward. "How? Tell me. What do I have to do? I'm ready. The forest is not going to die."

"Calm down," Gelas muttered. "That's what we're here to discuss. I have a plan and need both of you to help me put it into place."

"I'm ready," I said. "I'll do anything."

At Gelas' silent inquiry, Baxter motioned for him to continue. Gelas folded his arms behind his back. His thick eyelashes tapered. He gazed into the ice floes dotting the sapphire coast.

"My plan is simple. We stop Tontes and Ventis the only way Ignis and I know how—by destroying their amulets."

I groaned. "I knew you were going to mention amulets."

Tontes had sixteen god-magic amulets. Fourteen were active and identifiable, which gave him the most power of all four gods. To render Tontes unable to fight, we'd have to destroy at least eight amulets. Nine if we wanted to be safe.

Ten if we *really* wanted to pack a punch.

"There's no other way," Gelas said, directly to me. "When the demigods arrive, that is your job, Bianca. Ventis and Tontes have this all set up. I believe their demigods are already in Alka-rra. As they make themselves known, you will obtain their amulets and give them to me. Meanwhile, Ignis and I will be figuring out, hopefully, how to destroy said amulets."

Shock kept me from replying for several moments. The simplicity of such a plan hid a dark interior. One didn't pluck a god amulet out of the hands of a demigod—or a god for that matter.

"Hopefully?"

His grim expression inspired little confidence. "Just find the amulets," he said through gritted teeth.

"It's not that easy. I can't just *find* an amulet and then steal it from a demigod. Ten demigods! We . . . that is . . . it's impossible!"

"Improbable, perhaps, but not impossible."

"How do I draw their children here so I can steal their amulets?" I cried. "They must know that we'll try."

"Of course they know, and there's no need to draw them anywhere. I already told you. They're in Alkarra or they're coming. They'll find you. You don't need to go to them. You'll waste time and energy attempting to chase them, something they might desire."

"How do you know that?"

"Because you are part of what they want most."

The blood drained from my face when I comprehended what he meant. Suddenly, the whole picture came together in a new, hideous way.

"Letum Wood?" I whispered.

He nodded. "They know you're the Lady-witch of Letum Wood, and that your allegiance is to the goddess of the forest. They are *quite* aware that they need to remove you as an obstacle."

"But what if they don't come?"

His voice hardened. "They will. I suggest you be ready. I wouldn't say no to an amulet of Ventis either, for what it's worth. The target is Tontes, however, as he holds the most power. Weakening Ventis will help us all as well."

Gelas turned to Baxter. "That brings me to your role in this, Baxter."

Baxter's teeth sank into his lower lip. He shifted, eyes narrowed in thought, and nodded to indicate Gelas should continue. Ice groaned beneath our feet. I cast a glance down, but Gelas ignored it.

"There is something Ignis and I seek in the Southern Network to help us destroy the amulets."

"What?" Baxter asked.

"Nicomedianthekus."

I sucked in a breath. "The lost amulet?"

"Yes," Gelas murmured, his voice thick with some emotion I couldn't identify. "I have my suspicions that it has been gone for so long because it was not in Alaysia all this time."

I blinked. What did that have to do with—

Oh.

"You think it's in Alkarra?" Baxter asked.

Gelas' reply sounded like a low scrape, a rasp of fear. "I do. If we had been smart," he muttered, "we would have made the amulets a little more *trackable*. When we established this form of harnessing our power, we feared our children would constantly steal the amulets, or that the gods would meddle with each other's amulets. It was meant to be a form of protection, but the inability to find our own amulets and call them back has . . . complicated things."

Baxter snorted.

"Ignis and I have been attempting to find out how to destroy the amulets," Gelas said impatiently. "Magical objects resist their own destruction, for what it's worth. It's not going well. Our theory is that only a god with a full repertoire of amulets can destroy the amulet of another."

"You have a full repertoire?" Baxter asked.

"Lacking only one."

"Nicomedianthekus," I murmured.

Gelas nodded.

"How strong is this theory?" I asked.

"To spare your witchy mind the boring details of magical

creation, transformation, and manifestation, quite strong. Almost certain."

Setting aside the inherent insult he'd just given, I clenched my teeth and asked, "Why do you think it's here?"

"Unless it's buried in the depth of the sea—which is possible, but extremely unlikely with all the searching that's been done there—then it's nowhere else. The one place I haven't had access to in the last handful of centuries is Alkarra."

My brow wrinkled. "Back up a moment, please. Who searched the depths of the sea for you?"

"Not important."

"So you want me to find Nicomedianthekus," Baxter said, and I set aside the multitude of questions that bubbled to the surface.

"It's beyond desire at this point, Baxter. We *need* you to find it. There are two other theories that we are working to prove—or disprove—about the destruction of amulets. Believe it or not, we didn't plan out to destroy each others' amulets when we first created this system, so we're wading through new magical ground."

A dazed expression filled Baxter's face. His brow wrinkled. One hand lifted with an open palm—a silent question.

"Gelas," he whispered, "how will I find it? This is equally impossible with Bianca's task—more so."

"It's not a competition." The firm lines of Gelas' face hardened. "You search *everywhere*. I have a few ideas that you can follow, starting immediately."

No question, no query. Gelas had commanded. With hesitation, Baxter nodded.

"I'll try."

Gelas' stare glittered, glacial now. "You will *not* try. You will succeed. I did not return to my lands to have them discarded to Ventis and Tontes for total annihilation. In the meantime, Ignis and I will figure out the exact process for destroying amulets."

"Is this the reason you fought so hard to return to the Southern Network?" I asked. "You wanted Nicomedianthekus?"

He dropped into a momentary, contemplative silence. "It wasn't until recently that I realized a potential connection between Alkarra and my amulet, but . . . it's part of it. There are . . . other reasons. Memories. Many of them."

Sorrow filled his voice. The moment made him entirely too normal. Like a friend I'd gotten to know, yet could never hope to understand.

"For whatever you lost here," I said gently, "I'm sorry."

"A story for another day."

"Wait!" I called as Gelas turned to leave. "Why are Ventis and Tontes doing this? Everyone, even a god, has motivation for something, right?"

Gelas sighed, and his shoulders sank a little lower. "Because Ventis hates to lose, especially to a less-powerful foe."

"Got that right," Baxter muttered.

"And Tontes loves a good hunt. He toys with his prey. He likes to come out on top after a long and challenging struggle, that's why. In the end, they want Alkarra. Deasylva is their biggest obstacle to getting it. The path is pretty simple."

Your biggest obstacle is about to be me, god of wind and god of thunder, I thought.

Gelas nodded to Baxter.

"Time to put that fast demigod mind to use, Baxter. Between the two of you rests the fate of Alkarra. I suggest you both get to work, and prepare yourself. The gods are on their way, and they like to soften their prey up before they strike."

Chapter Three

When I entered Scarlett's office the next day, rain sluiced down the windows and humidity burdened the damp air with the sweet scent of wet earth.

Hiddleston sat behind a desk off to the right. He inclined his head as I stepped inside. Dreadlocks spilled onto his shoulder, then rolled off with every little movement. Leda stood directly opposite Hiddleston and peered anxiously at me. I sent her a questioning look. She returned it with a faint smile.

The door closed behind me. Scarlett looked up from where she sat behind the desk, acknowledged me with a nod, then stood. Seeing her in command of what used to be Papa's office lent a bizarre slant to the moment.

She'd softened the room with gentle touches, starting with a pot of tiny pink flowers at the edge of her desk. A knitted quilt lay across the back of a divan near the fireplace, which added a splash of color to the otherwise gray room.

Papa had accumulated weapons and left space to swing swords and throw axes while he thought through issues, while

Scarlett had created a cozy escape to host meetings and welcome other witches.

Probably what this office should have been all along.

"High Priestess."

"It's good to see you, Bianca. Please, have a seat."

Leda gathered several scrolls in her arms and headed for the door. Her bolstering smile reassured me, despite a hint of concern beneath it. Hiddleston followed her out. The moment they left, Scarlett sighed, dropped her shoulders, and paced back and forth behind her desk. She let out her breath in a giant *whoosh*.

Amused to see Scarlett unraveled in the slightest, I waited for her to speak first. Her reddish-orange dress shone in rising sunlight from the window. Morning unfurled, along with the twitter of birds and a wall of humidity.

A minute passed. She chewed on her bottom lip and stared at the floor.

"Your Highness?" I ventured carefully.

Scarlett held up a hand, paced two more times, then halted. She carried a Network on her shoulders. While other Network leaders squabbled about semantics, she found solutions. Her new High Priest didn't know what to do with himself, yet she carried confidence and aplomb.

Only a general sense of fatigue lingered in the creases near her eyes. Papa used to have those same creases, but on him they had been the precursor to debilitating exhaustion. Scarlett hadn't faced that sort of tiredness.

Not yet, anyway.

"Thank you for coming," she said, then gestured me into a chair in front of her desk. She remained on her feet.

So did I.

"Aren't you going to sit down?" she asked.

"Yes, if you do."

A startled expression crossed her face, riddled with amusement. "Really?"

"You're more nervous than a cat, Scarlett."

A delighted chuckle spilled out of her, but quickly faded. The somber air returned to the room as she sank into her chair.

"Thank you, I think. I intentionally didn't connect with you one-to-one before the Council Meeting, and it's been rabidly busy since then." A tinge of color rose on her cheeks. "I'm embarrassed that it's taken me this long to call you in here after the meeting. I apologize. I have been tracking your health otherwise."

"Don't be. I had a lot of recovery ahead of me."

"Your exoneration is appreciated, but I wish it wasn't needed. You're feeling better?"

"Back to myself, High Priestess."

"Running through the trees, as usual?"

"The moment I could."

Sometimes faster than before, I added silently. No god magic remained within me, but an expansion of goddess magic had taken its place, and then some. Scarlett pulled me from my thoughts.

"I'm happy to hear that. Before we talk about the Sisterhood and your plans with it, may I inquire about something regarding your forest?"

The words *your forest* gave me a silent thrill. *You are mine,* I said to the trees.

Their distant keening filled my mind.

You belong to us.

With a mental shake, I brought myself back to Scarlett's office. "Of course. You can ask me anything."

"What can Letum Wood do?"

"Do?"

"You've mentioned voices from the trees when we've spoken about it. There have been allusions to magical systems at work and . . . possibly more. Sentience, perhaps? Knowledge? Is there magic *in* the forest?"

"Loads of it."

She tapped a finger against her chin. "What can this magic do?"

My reply stalled with my thoughts. An initial response of *what can't it do?* rose. Goddess magic had constraints and limitations because it was reliant on spells and logic.

Was the same true for the forest?

Deasylva's direct connection to her trees was obvious, yet the intricacies eluded my understanding.

"I'm not sure of the depths of magic in the forest," I said carefully. "It can transport me from place to place. The trees speak with me. As individuals sometimes, but mostly collectively. I've always assumed they're connected through the root system, but I'm not sure."

"What creatures are you aware of?"

"Many."

"Dragons, of course." A flippant hand dismissed those. "Reports of trolls are mostly legend, which is a relief. Forest lions, beluas, mortegas, almost thirty packs of different fairies . . ."

"Don't forget the gnomes," I said wryly.

"Gnomes, of course. Over twenty different, individual species. But what of others? Any more . . . nefarious animals?"

"I would imagine there are many we haven't discovered."

"A daunting thought."

"Why do you ask?"

Several beats of silence passed before she leaned forward, "I wondered . . . if Letum Wood had magic that we could use, perhaps it might be an advantage to us against the demigods?"

"The forest?"

She nodded.

"You want the forest to fight?"

"One could call it *fighting,* but I see it more as grappling for one's existence. Witches aren't the only ones that will lose their homes as the gods advance. Baxter has informed me of Gelas' opinion about Tontes and Ventis' plans and I'm . . . attempting to think outside our usual routines. The Network delegations will be meeting soon to form a rudimentary, initial plan-of-attack, should the gods descend unexpectedly."

My heart inflamed yet again with the thought of Letum Wood in danger. Scarlett's question created immediate discord that only made it worse. Letum Wood in danger was one thing, but expecting the forest to fight?

By sheer willpower, I kept my shout of *not a chance* trapped inside, though not easily.

Several moments passed while I comprehended the full extent of the question, and all the little details that lay behind it.

Nightmares of fire-torched trees, illuminated like out-of-control candles, recalled in my mind. Screaming saplings intruded next. I shoved them away. While in Alaysia, Tontes had threatened me with such ideas to frighten me. It worked; nightmares haunted me. I swallowed back a rise of fear that had become a little *too* ordinary.

"If we're discussing tactics that would be unexpected," Scarlett said gently, "then a fighting forest would be one of them. There's no historical precedent that Hiddleston can find in the paths thus far, so I may be entirely wrong in my hope. Such a thing would certainly give us an advantage."

"You want *trees* to fight demigods?"

"You yourself said that, during the War of the Networks, the trees had some level of involvement. They aided *you,* at least."

"Vines and branches and a few things here and there are hardly a war effort," I countered just as quickly. "Yes, the trees help and respond to me, but . . . what you're asking is for more than that."

"I know what I'm asking," she said quietly.

"I don't think you do."

We stared at each other in an impasse.

"Letum Wood is not a weapon," I stated a little too forcefully.

"No, of course not. It's a presence. A place. A . . . magic. An unconventional one at that," she murmured, "one can't deny it. Whether it's feasible to use Letum Wood or not, we obviously can't be certain yet. I was curious about your thoughts on it and have no definitive plans thus far."

The only words I could find stumbled out of me like a drunken old man. "I'll consider it, High Priestess."

"Thank you, that would be appreciated. Now, shall we talk about the Sisterhood? Council Member Greyson—your only other political support outside of me—has taken up a new residence in Carcere in the Eastern Network, where he belongs. Such a reality poses a significant problem for the advancement of the Sisterhood."

A peeved tone colored her voice. This conversation had been inevitable for weeks. I'd both welcomed and dreaded it. Without Greyson, the Sisterhood stood on tenuous political ground. Only one witch with political power believed that I could be a benefit to the Network. It happened to be Scarlett, the Highest Witch, but that lent no guarantees in these brutal times.

"I'm hopeful this doesn't sound presumptuous, Your Highness, but I hoped that the Sisterhood could be of personal use to you, as we had discussed before Alaysia. I'd rather not work for, or with, the Council."

"After all that has happened, you still desire to work directly for me?"

"More than ever."

Her shoulders sagged back a little. "That's good to hear. And Leda?"

"She's interested in a supporting role, as long as it doesn't interfere with her current job."

A brief smile appeared on Scarlett's lips. "I find no fault with continuing as we had planned before, but Greyson's removal means that we have no leg to stand on with the Council. For now, that may be all right. Too much swirling around the question of the gods to worry about the Sisterhood." She grimaced. "I'm sorry to say it."

A sinking feeling dropped through my feet. "I understand. Definitions can be fluid, High Priestess. I'm here to serve you."

Scarlett arched a high brow. "You're willing to work in the shadows? To be an unknown figure?"

"Yes."

"That's very selfless of you."

Ignis, god of fire, had censured my need for approval while in Alaysia. *Your Sisterhood will do an admirable job of proving your worth,* he had said, *since that is what you strive to do. Worth must be proven, right? The attachment to other witches approving who you are is . . . strength personified, don't you agree? But I expect nothing else so foolish from a witch.*

His words replayed back through my mind often. A gentle cadence.

A reminder.

I dropped my gaze to my hands.

"Not really," I said. "I'm not selfless."

"Oh?"

"My father taught me." I shrugged. "It's what I know. The Sisterhood was never going to be easy. Besides, this isn't about accolades. This is about Letum Wood."

"You want to protect your forest?"

"With everything in me."

She regarded me in deepening thought for a long time. I held her gaze, hopeful she could see the sincerity in my eyes.

Finally, she nodded.

"Let's focus on saving Letum Wood *and* Alkarra, shall we? Definitions and details for the Sisterhood will easily come once we've secured our land again. Thank you for coming, Bianca. I hope to see you again soon."

* * *

One moment I darted through the forest, the next moment, a pile of rough hewn logs blocked my path. I skidded to a stop, panting. The forest had whisked me away, mid stride, and deposited me . . .

. . . here.

A witch with sweaty dark hair straddled a log as tall as my waist. Papa. The damp air gave a slight curl to his hair, twisting it at his temple. Such boyish charm made me smile.

Dust and twigs and dirt coated his shirt with great detail. Rags wrapped both hands, which gripped the ends of a sharp piece of metal, like a sword with no hilt. He reached forward, pressed the edge of the metal into the bark, and jerked it toward him. A long shaving appeared, whittled from the top. He grunted, edged it closer, until a chunk of bark three paces long, and one wide, gave way.

He broke it with a *crack*, inspected it, and tossed it onto a pile. Without looking my way, he called, "Good to see you, B. How did you find me?"

"The forest brought me."

"Tell it to bring you more."

I laughed.

He grunted, braced his hands on the fallen tree, and dug the knife into the trunk for another shaving on a different part. While the process repeated itself, I twirled around.

"New place?" I asked.

"That's the plan."

"I can't say I've been to this part of Letum Wood before."

"Good to hear. I'd rather not be easy to find."

Letum Wood shifted daily. Magic. Vines. Trees. The landscape changed too much to commit it to memory, though individual trees could be recognized. In general, I had to clue in to different observations to figure out my place in the greater scheme. The age of the trees, and depth of sunlight, hinted at general locations.

The older parts of Letum Wood, central to the forest, hid the circle of the ancients—the most gargantuan trees in the tightest canopy. As the forest crawled toward the edges of the Central Network, it would often thin, or the types of trees would change. More sunlight, less clutter, varying tree types. The wood had patches, like a bunch of forests quilted together. Here it was less cluttered and more open.

Papa tossed an arm ahead of him, indicating a patch of cleared earth.

"I like this spot for a house."

He'd cleared several hundred paces square. Fallen trees littered the ground. Several of them stacked in a rectangle to map out a house, no doubt. Wood shavings, knives, hammers, and sundry items littered a bench made out of a fallen stump.

"It's beautiful, Papa."

He nodded behind the place. "There's a stream back there, for easy water access. The banks are pitched high enough that it shouldn't flood, unless we had an extraordinary amount of water, which seems unlikely."

"How long have you had it picked out?"

"Weeks. I don't get a lot of time to work on it, but I had a few hours today. Thought I'd warm up and chip away at it for a bit." He chuckled. "Literally."

"Warm up? It's blazing hot."

"Don't ask."

I opened my mouth to do just that, but closed it again. He had been elusive about where he'd been passing his time when I asked last time. He'd tell me when he was ready. Auburn curls and wary green eyes came to mind, but I ushered thoughts of Regina back out to turn my attention to matters at hand.

"Well, it will be a cozy place."

"Quiet," he countered.

"Same thing."

"Is it?"

He reached up with a forearm and wiped the sweat off his forehead, then climbed off the tree. He propped the metal shaver against the trunk as a pouch of water appeared in his hand. He drank deeply, then braced his hands on his hips.

I spread my hands. "Well? Give me the grand tour."

He snorted, then pointed to the far corner. "Bedroom. Fireplace. Table. Another bedroom. Attic."

"So complicated and intricate."

He snorted. "Not too big, I think. About twice the size of your cottage, with two rooms, partitioned off."

"An attic?"

"Why not?"

"You're going to be a grumpy old man living alone in a forest while you build your own house."

"Exactly my goal."

My laughter bounced off the trees. The saplings responded with similar sounds of delight. One leaned toward me, branches brushing my shoulder. My fingers trailed along it in a quick acknowledgment. Suffuse blue light responded, rippling through the leaves.

Papa said with satisfaction, "This is the place, B. My new home." He pointed to me. "Yours too, if you want it. I'm building a room for you, or you can take the attic. Or the chicken coop."

"Thanks, Papa," I muttered wryly. "Do you need any help? I have several million friends that might know where to find fallen trees. To avoid killing the saplings, you know. They're . . . emotional and sensitive."

Amusement flitted through him. "Are they?"

"Would you want to be murdered with an ax?"

"Fair point. I'll take whatever help I can get. Hiddleston has sourced nails for me, and a few other things from a blacksmith." He kicked the shaving tool with a foot. "Like this. Right now, I'm collecting wood to prep it for stacking. The straighter, the better."

You belong to us.

We serve her joy.

"Well," I murmured, "prepare yourself."

"For what?"

I grinned. "Help."

A giant *thud* rang behind us, followed by the clatter of rolling timbers. I whirled around to find fallen trees piling on top of each other, just outside the boundary he marked for his living space. They rolled over themselves until they settled into silence. Papa's eyes widened.

"The good gods," he whispered.

Delight coursed through me. Would the forest never cease to amaze me? Did it always have nuances to discover?

I hoped so.

"Let me know if you need anything else."

Papa laughed. "I will, thank you, B. I mean, Letum Wood." He tilted his head back. "Thank you!"

A nearby sapling shook, leaves shivering like clattering coins.

Papa stepped closer, then hooked an arm around my neck and pulled me into his side. I wrapped my arms around his waist, grateful for the quick, steady connection.

"I'm glad you're going to be so close, Papa."

"Me too."

"I never dreamed . . ."

A note of emotion touched his voice. "Me either."

The moment trailed away into a companionable silence. The gift of such freedom seemed like too much to ask for. A liberated

Papa. He could craft and live an existence of his own making. How he'd managed to pull off the impossible yet again, I'd never understand.

"Do you need somewhere to eat dinner tonight?" I asked. "I can't promise it will be the most delicious meal, but I have bread at home. Assuming the gnomes haven't gotten to it yet. A few mushrooms are just starting to emerge, too."

"Sounds delightful."

"Great! See you then."

He grimaced. "But I can't."

"Why not?"

A rigidness in his jaw gave him away. Before he said the words, I knew what would come out.

"I'm . . . eating with Regina tonight. We have a . . . *thing* that we're doing."

By force of will, I managed to say, "Oh," before the silence consumed the affable air, leaving an awkward, wrung out space. He kicked at a rock. It pattered away, settling in leaves.

"Regina is someone we need to talk about, B."

He met my gaze, but it cost him. The strange expression of his face, half uncertainty, half insecurity, startled me.

Papa nervous?

"All right," I drawled.

"I suppose now is as good a time as any. I know I haven't been around that much. Most of my time has been spent helping her with . . . a few things. She's catching up on some sleep after a long night and taking a break and then we'll be back at it."

"Don't *you* need sleep?"

He shrugged. "I had plenty and I like working with my hands. It . . . helps me sort out the thoughts in my head. Anyway." He drew in a deep breath and drove a hand through his hair. "I . . . uh . . . the gods. This isn't easy to say."

Deeper concern filled me, but I stayed silent. Frozen, like a statue, unable to comprehend what could possibly put him in a state like this.

"Papa?"

"I have feelings for Regina."

The words burst out of him. I blinked. He winced. The words looped through my mind again, merging into memories. The way Papa and Regina stood close in his office, only to break apart when I arrived. The fondness in his voice that he couldn't quite hide. His time with her the last several weeks. Though he only spoke of Regina in a professional manner, I'd sensed something underneath it.

The good gods.

He *did* feel for her.

"Say words, B."

"I don't know what to say, Papa."

"What's in your head?"

My attempt to remain lighthearted flopped like a gutted fish. "Thanks for telling me. I'm sure you'll have fun with Regina tonight. Merry part!"

His hand flashed out, capturing me before I could transport away. His stare narrowed and my stomach dropped. Oh, I'd seen that face before.

No way I'd get out of this now.

"B, we need to talk about this."

I tried to wrench my arm free. "Not today, thanks."

"We do."

"Papa, you're free to live your life." I couldn't quite meet his eyes. "I get it, and . . ."

Grasses rustled beneath his feet as he stepped closer. "This must feel weird to you. It feels weird to me, too."

He released me.

"I'm not exactly sure when it all happened," he said, a hand waving in front of him. "Slowly or all at once or both. I realized it when we worked together to out Greyson. She's . . . capable and bright, and she understands me. I love to be around her, and when I'm with her, I feel . . . happy."

He stopped, agony in his features.

"I've torn myself up over the memory of Marie, over how I feel about Regina. In some ways, I feel like I'm cheating on Marie. I shouldn't feel like this about another witch that isn't your Mama."

A long, low breath escaped him. I attempted to absorb his words, to understand the rotating emotions that thickened everything he said, but I couldn't. Everything was locked up inside, dammed together, and terrified.

"I can't even say that I feel the same way about Regina as I did about your mother. In truth, B, I'll never feel about anyone the way I felt for Marie. By the gods, though, Regina is special and I feel deeply for her."

In an attempt to buy a few more seconds of processing time, I licked my lips and murmured, "I see."

"Years and life stretch ahead of me now," he said in a whisper that sounded like a finish. "And I want Regina to be in them."

An insinuation that he had thoughts to organize lingered, unsaid, in his words. Papa hadn't exactly *stated* that he and Regina were courting, but it had been more than apparent. With Regina exiled from the North, and Papa no longer the High Priest, both of them had reasons to hide.

Papa.

Regina.

Courting.

Sure, it wasn't too great of a surprise, yet it . . . was. Papa had been skirting around their relationship for awhile and I'd let him. I didn't really want to talk about Regina. Or Mama. Papa interested in another woman that wasn't Mama set me on a strange, dark highway of puzzlement.

Disquieted emotions overwhelmed me with frustration. Despair. A sense of all not being right with the world if Papa was with anyone but Mama. Caught in the tangle of things, I shook my head to clear them.

His heart held in his eyes as he waited for my response. I reached out, touched his arm.

"I'm not upset, Papa."

Relief weakened his tension like a wave. He narrowed one eye.

"Truly?"

"I'm confused, but I'm not angry. Mama is gone. I've accepted that. You have a life that you want to create. I'm happy for you. I will just need time to think through it and see how I feel."

Something else emanated from him. Desperation, perhaps. A lost soul searching for himself. A low-level melancholy hummed in his eyes.

Was Papa . . . afraid?

"Papa, are you all right? I mean, you left the throne, the Brotherhood—"

"Not the Brotherhood."

"Are you still working as a Protector?"

He met my gaze straight on. "Of a sort."

"All right," I drawled. "Anyway, you're building a house by hand, doing something mysterious with Regina. You went from the busiest witch in the Network to . . . not-so-busy. I'm worried about you."

"I know."

"Should I be?"

He gazed out. The contemplative expression that followed reassured me he wouldn't give platitudes.

"Not yet. When Regina and I find success with what I'm helping her with, I'll be better. And when we settle the demigod issue. And I have a place to live. And when I figure out how to *not* worry about problems that aren't mine anymore." His voice bleakened considerably. "There's just a few things to get settled, I suppose."

Unable to help myself, I giggled.

Papa chuckled. "Stark, isn't it?"

"Definitely."

These concerns and more cluttered my mind, but the press of worry faded a little with Papa's words. Alkarran troubles mixed in my mind with Regina and Mama and fears I'd rather not tackle right then.

My response came out like a plea. "Give me time, Papa?"

He softened. "Of course, B. Yes, of course. Whatever you need. I just . . . I wanted you to know. I'm not hiding it, because I'd never do that. I'm . . . figuring it out. I love you more than anyone, and that will always be the case. No matter what I feel for any other witch, you will always be the best thing that ever happened to me."

He swamped me with his arms, holding me so tight my ribs ached. I returned the fraught embrace, hopeful to soothe his agitation.

"I love you, Papa."

His voice thickened. "Not as much as I love you."

The reassurance calmed a screaming girl inside that I hadn't known existed until this exact moment. Until I knew what that frightened part of me wanted to say, I silenced her until later.

Much later.

Chapter Four

Follow our path.
She always comes back.
You belong to us.
We lead you to more.

The sanguine whispers were at odds with the fast thrum of my heart as I sprinted through Letum Wood once more, thoughts abuzz with Papa, Regina, and demigods. My chest ached, but that was easier to feel than the frustration of life in Alkarra right now.

My legs flew through the forest. Vines, shrubs, branches, slipped out of my way as I hurtled down a path that appeared at each step. I didn't know where I was going, and that was why it felt so good. Leaves whipped past my thighs. Earth shifted under my feet. Each thready breath restored a missing part of my courage.

Sweat collected over my spine and dribbled down my back when I slowed. My painfully-fast breath occupied my thoughts as I leaned my palms onto my knees and doubled over.

Breath.

Breath.

Blessed breath.

My big toe had been sliced open on a rock, but a spell bound the skin back together. Dried blood flaked off the sides. I ignored it.

Because . . . breath.

My racing heart calmed. Blood thrilled through me as I sagged against a tree, gulping smaller lungfuls. At my touch, a single voice broke through the cacophony.

She touches.

She arrives.

Her heart is happy, her heart is sad.

She touches.

She arrives.

I slid to the forest floor, twitchy with fatigue.

While the tension faded, I kept an eye on the grove. Arcadian silence filled this cluttered section of the forest. Dense trees tangled together in spiny braids. Signs of dragons, scorch marks and trees cracked in half from an errant tail, were abundant in these deeper areas. Magic raised this forestland to indomitable heights, unbelievably tall, ancient, and wide.

Sitting in this halcyon spot, I couldn't fathom Scarlett's idea to use Letum Wood to fight. The demigods wanted to claim our land, so it made sense that the land should fight back. At some point, it would be unavoidable. But we weren't there yet.

As I dragged my fingertips in the loamy earth, the song of life entered my chest. Such rampant vibrancy turned to ill-will?

Impossible.

These trees had lived for thousands of years. Centuries of stacked life, magic, and potential. They recognized me, knew me, depended on me, and saved me. How could I encourage such gentle creatures to be part of a battle?

Sensing my rising emotions, the saplings keened. Startled, I glanced up. Boughs bent toward me to pat my shoulder like a friend.

You are safe, I said. *You are mine.*

The words pacified their apprehension, but not my own.

"You won't fight. I'll protect you before it comes to that, if I can. You saved me, I'll save you. We're part of each other."

A sough of wind brushed my hair off my neck. I shoved off the ground and straightened stiff legs. With my palms, I brushed the loose dirt off my bare calves and stretched.

She has found our heart.

I tilted my head back.

"Your heart?"

Sapphire magic glowed beneath my feet, warm and tingling at the same time. Delighted peals followed. Their voices lifted in a harmonious symphony, frantic and joyful, as if each tree tripped over itself to be heard. Ahead, bushes rattled. I drew closer, understanding the movement as a cue. Once I approached the trembling branches, another danced a few paces away.

Being led by the forest was nothing new, but the weighty air and silent heaviness *was.*

No sign of forest lions overhead. No hiss of leaves on dragon scales as they slunk by. In the depths of a magical forest, *anything* could wait in the treetops. Flickers of movement from still-unknown creatures had haunted me before, when saplings steered me away with painfully loud fear, or the older trees urged me to caution in a new understory. In some areas, purple ropes lay on the bark from silent beluas, like strings burned into the trunks.

Odd, but not frightening.

The eerie ambience was a different story. A lack of recent predators also made me suspicious. This deep into the forest and no fresh claw marks? No skeletons or dried blood?

A vibrant voice came to my mind. *Come,* it whispered. *Come to us. We have long awaited you, Lady-witch of the forest.*

Following the cues of the undergrowth, I wound through

tidy ground. A tonal, mild hum intensified. The lower canopy, which soared almost out of sight, cleared until I glimpsed the apex of the trees, where only dragons and creatures lived. So far away, and still no sky.

I advanced through a thinning thicket, drawn by fascination, to hunt between roots tall as hillocks. A meadow appeared, circled by twelve gargantuan trees too indomitable to comprehend. No other trees cluttered the coppice at the base of these. No bushes. Only clement green grass. Mossy rocks. Sprigged flowers clumped in waves of periwinkle. Branches occluded the dome with sweeping arms.

Protruding roots grew taller than me as I walked by. Compared to these behemoths, normal trees appeared more like twigs and leaves. An ancient weight of magic burdened the air with vitality. The reverberative song brightened from a hum to a chorus.

Then stopped.

Across the circle stood a collection of buildings at the base, tucked into roots like surfacing snakes. Moldering houses. I started toward them, but stopped when the voice spoke again.

The world of the Dragonmasters is not yours. Allow us to guide you on your path, as we always have.

A cobalt fissure of light appeared at my feet, warbled north in a ribbon-like river, away from the houses. Several paces away it paused, as if waiting. I jogged to keep pace. It halted at the base of the largest of the twelve mountainous pillars of bark, life, and age.

I reached a shaky hand out, touched the closest root. The same line bloomed beneath my fingertips, sprawling out in slow lightning. Vibrance stirred. Magic. Sap. Faculty. The feeling like a string passing through my heart followed.

You have always belonged here, Lady-witch of the forest. Speak with us now, if you will.

The depths of the voice felt like a hollowed-out cave. Fathomless. Deep. Warm-toned and affectionate.

"How do I speak with you?"

A vine rolled down the trunk until it landed next to me, ending on a loop. I stepped my left foot inside, wrapped the vine around my wrist, and pushed off the soil. When I transferred my weight to the vine, it ascended. The Volare jumped out of the case on my back, hovering just beneath.

Up and up the vine retracted, to impossible heights. I gripped it in both hands and forced myself not to look down. Instead, I tilted my head and kept a firm gaze on the encroaching canopy.

On us, the voice said. *Keep your focus on us.*

Letum Wood had always carried its own environment. Up here, a parasol of new life existed. Broad curtains of leaves the size of homes. Moss like blankets, drawn over the ancient trunks. Entire houses could fit on the edges of the bark flakes. Branches that might encompass small villages.

The vine stopped on a sprawling arm that disappeared into shadow at the end. I stepped off of it. With a twirl above my head, the vine retracted. I whirled around with a sharp breath of surprise.

A darkened doorway had been carved into the tree, filled with shadows. I waited, breath held, for what to do next.

Come, the voice said. *You belong to us.*

A tentative step, then another, closed the distance. Across the way, a tree branch groaned. A shiver sprinted down the trunk that shook my knees. Leaves trembled. The voices of my forest escalated.

She belongs to us.

She has come.

She appears.

The long-awaited day arrives.

At the doorway, I stopped. Muted light extended a few paces

inside. The aged darkness had been sitting there for too long without touch. It felt as if I'd break a glass shell when I entered. It offered a clear delineation point. I'd return from this adventure a different witch.

Who was the last witch to have entered? I didn't realize I'd asked the question out loud until the voice responded.

Sanna.

"Crotchety old Sanna?"

As you say.

Driven by greater curiosity, I stepped inside the trunk and pressed my palm to it. More voices broke through in vague whispers. Spiderwebs of light exploded through the walls, illuminating a path. They widened overhead in a zigzag, removing shadow.

I ventured further inside, moving slowly past smooth walls which revealed intricate paths in the grains of wood. The way forward plunged into the heart of the tree, disappearing around a corner. My fingers trailed the walls, where light continued to play.

"Have you been waiting?"

Always.

"I didn't know you were here."

We are aware.

"Who are you?"

We are exactly what you believe us to be. You know us. We know you. We have lived many lives with you.

My heart raced. The trees had long-since proven themselves sentient, to some degree. Whether the magic gave them life, or amplified their ability to speak, didn't matter. Though connected with Deasylva, they clearly existed apart.

We are the beginning of Letum Wood. The twelve that began the forest, back in the far reaches of time, thousands of years ago.

"During the time of Esmelda?"

As you say.

Magic bloomed beneath my touch. Information I didn't know before filled my head, given by the power. How like the trees to silently, subtly impart wisdom. At the beginning of Letum Wood, these twelve trees gave the goddess of the forest a foothold in Alkarra. The last two-thousand years had been Letum Wood's opportunity to become exactly *this*. Deasylva's plan, all along.

A latent sense of hastening filled the air. The forest wanted to tell me something, warn me.

You are almost there.

A distant flicker of light ahead brought me farther into the darkness. The hallway continued inward, then slanted to the right. My fingers trailed on either side of the narrow path, not an inch of space wasted. The walls brushed either side of my shoulder. Though the hair on the back of my neck crackled with energy, I felt no fear.

I pressed on.

The light extinguished.

The walls disappeared.

The sense of a cavernous, open space widened overhead, where a rustling sound flowed. I reached through the vaporous black, found a wall, and pressed my ear to it. Deeper tones resonated within. Life at a colossal scale. Movement. Depth. I stood in the heart of the tree, where it lived around me, burrowed inside secret shadows.

I am Arborra, the eldest of the ancients, the twelve trees who began Letum Wood millennia ago.

"Arborra."

You belong to us.

The simply-stated words held deep affection. My heart soared, tangled in the feeling of it, until I could hardly draw breath. Sacredness permeated the air. I pressed my hand to the wall.

"You belong to me," I murmured.

God magic has returned to our land.

"Yes."

You brought it?

I opened my mouth to deny it, but couldn't. Technically, I had brought god magic into the forest.

Sort of.

"I had a part in the process, yes."

We condemn not.

"I didn't know it at the time."

We know your heart.

The phrase seemed to be a dismissal—a forgiveness. I took it as such, eager to move onto something different.

"Do you remember the gods?"

Very little.

"They're coming to take back Alkarra. They want the land."

She tells us.

"Deasylva?"

A groan issued, reverberating all the way through the dark. The tree shook as I touched the wall to stabilize myself. Cobalt beams crawled through the wall in luminescent cracks. The momentary light illuminated unfamiliar textures, shapes I couldn't identify before they bleached away.

We are ready for the gods to return.

"I'm . . . you . . . I'm sorry?"

The forest has been prepared for the gods' wrath. Without Letum Wood, Alkarra would cease to be Alkarra.

Letum Wood spanned the most ground in all of our land. Most of the Central Network, some of the Northern and Southern Networks. The timbers changed, but the forest remained. The woods crawled up the foothills in the north, where evergreens and conifers dotted the mountains. Far more sparse, less lush. Woods without the same beating soul. Letum Wood slid into the swamps of the Eastern Network, where the water became too brackish and deep to sustain.

"You want the gods to return?"

Not all of them.

"Some, like Gelas?"

The god of fire can stay far away.

A rising anxiety lifted through the air, rolling like a sigh. It passed as quickly as it came, borne on the exclamations of distant saplings. The darkness hid my amusement. The trees had never liked fire. One of the first times I began to hear them had been panic over flames.

You are our caretaker.

"Yes, I think so."

We have always had one.

"Sanna, too?"

Sanna cared for the dragons, and the dragons cared for us. We cared for her because of her love for the forest, but you are different. You belong to us. None have belonged to us before.

"Oh."

Deasylva says you gave her allegiance in the other land.

"Yes."

It is the way of the goddess-touched. We speak to you today as preparation for what's to come. The forest must survive.

"I'll protect you."

We will protect each other. We have been preparing.

Prickles edged their way down my spine, filling me with courage. The presence of Letum Wood had always strengthened my hidden, feeble parts.

You are one of us. You will lead us to greater freedom, greater purpose. In you, the goddess says we will find our own path. The forest will reach its full attainment with your guidance.

"Me?"

You.

"How?"

Together.

"I don't know when the gods will attack, or what it will look like or . . . I can't give you a plan yet."

For now, it's enough that you know our desires.

With a heart-curling sensation, I whispered, "I don't want you to fight."

Fight, we must. Together.

My resolve to save the forest solidified like hardened rocks. *We* would save Letum Wood. By saving Letum Wood, we'd also save Alkarra. My soul stirred with a sigh. An acknowledgement.

A promise.

"Together," I whispered.

Chapter Five

Sunshine poured through open windows while I worked the next day, leaving a polished cottage in my wake. Freshly-washed sheets fluttered off a tree branch to dry in the wind. Bundles of dried vermillion thistle hung from the rafters by twine.

Routine, warmth, home.

The stability of my cottage soothed my soul while I thought about Gelas' warning over amulets, Papa courting Regina, and what the demigods would do next. Pattering feet on my rooftop, followed by a quick, obnoxious chatter, broke the stillness.

I froze.

The sound faded as quickly as it came.

Five minutes later, an ear-splitting scream stood the hair on the back of my neck up. Viveet slipped to my hand with a spell as I whirled around. My front door slammed against the wall with a crack.

A gnarled creature stood in the doorway. Hairy, dirty, and naked, like a recently-pulled turnip. Mud smeared a fat brown face, curled into a snarl. Two pointed fangs poked out of wide lips, while beady black eyes glared from beneath a shaggy head of hair. It toddled a few steps forward, legs too short for the squat body. In one of two equally-short arms, it gripped a spear the size of a letter opener. A screaming gnome in the flesh.

The spear pointed at me.

The gnome shrieked.

My lips rolled together to hide a giggle. Chattering, screaming, burrowing, and falling gnomes lived all over Letum Wood. They filled it with the strangest sounds. Chattering gnomes were the most common forest gnomes. They lived in trees, scuttled around branches, and threw Leto nuts at potential enemies.

Annoying creatures, all of them. They tended to eat most bugs and hunt smaller rodents, but terrorized gardens. Their particular love for garlic meant that my grandmother, Hazel, had waged an eternal war against them.

All gnomes held similar characteristics—chubby, naked bodies. An obsession with rolling or digging through the dirt. All of them were small and ornery, resentful of witches and anything that wasn't gnome. They didn't speak with words, but communicated through clicks and grunts.

I tilted my head a little.

The gnome bared its teeth and did the same.

When I made a clicking sound with my tongue against the top of my mouth, the gnome straightened. Slowly, I reached an arm to my table, grabbed a piece of bread, crouched lower, and extended it. The black eyes regarded me, then the bread.

It screamed.

Four other gnomes popped into sight from beneath my porch, cracking boards as they emerged from underneath. I gritted my teeth. Another chore to put on my list. Could gnomes do magic, or were they strong enough to break wood?

Neither answer worked in my favor.

All four new gnomes toddled closer, bearing similar weapons, in a barbaric group that muttered, grunted, and clicked. In the repetitive rhythm of their sounds, I detected a subtle pattern. A symphony to presumed chaos.

Carefully, I lowered onto my knees. They shrieked, jumped. I sent Viveet back to the holder on the wall, her blue glow smoldering away. When I put my bare hands on my knees, the gnomes visibly relaxed.

Two of them stared at the bread.

The other three stared at me.

"Merry meet."

The first to arrive—the presumed leader—shuffled forward. He made a noise like a low whistle, a dropping sound. Three clucks followed. The tiny, thick features of its face had screwed up, as if it asked a question.

One of the other gnomes scuttled toward the proffered food. It dropped the spear, picked up the bread, and exclaimed with an *oooo*. The leader smacked it on the head, barked a command, and the other gnome grabbed its spear and retreated—bread in hand. Moving slow, I nudged another piece of bread their way.

A gnome war commenced.

While the four gnomes shredded the bread, each attempting to gain control of the largest piece, the irate leader advanced closer to me. He stayed out of arm's reach. The dark color of its rough skin was due more to dirt than pigment. Underneath, he seemed to have a yellowish tinge. More gold than earthy, speckled with dirt.

"Shall I call you Goldenrod?"

His eyes shuttered.

With another scream, all five gnomes disappeared in a shocking *pop* of sound. I blinked, astonished. Crumbs littered the floor. I gasped.

They *could* do magic!

That indicated an ability and intelligence beyond anything I'd heard of before. Historical texts postulated that witches who studied gnomes never saw magical use amongst them. Not once.

A chorus of familiar voices broke into my thoughts.

Come to us.

We find the ill-fated.

She belongs to us.

I only had time to gasp before the forest whisked me away.

* * *

Letum Wood deposited me in a hushed copse of trees. I landed invisibly, thanks to Letum Wood, with my back pressed to a trunk. Bushes hid where I stood, while branches shifted ahead ever-so-slightly, revealing a gap.

And demigods.

A string of fingernail-sized amulets in a tight necklace caught my attention first. With little difficulty, I recalled the list of amulets Baxter had given me. This one was Herimolodikus, perhaps. One of Tontes' amulets known to have mid-level power.

A woman with white hair, streaked by dove gray, wore the amulets in glittering bangles around her neck. Alternating smoky purple-and-slate colors glimmered. A daughter of Tontes.

She stood near a fallen tree, freshly cut. Splits in the wood indicated broken grains from falling, yet the trunk cracked unevenly. A nearby ax must have started the process, but the tree looked as if it had been pushed over with god magic.

A tree of that size was a sapling only as thick as my arm length. Immediately, I understood it to be several decades old. Life drained from it slowly, a gradual loosening of power. Low, panicked cries with hysterical notes set my hair on edge. Saplings.

The female demigod spoke to a male with no visible amulet, but he looked too healthy to be a mortal. His golden eye color gave him away. She swept her fingers along the ground, then brushed her arm toward the higher canopy. With god magic taken from me, I couldn't understand what they said.

Other bodies bustled in various stages of busyness. Mortals, I guessed for most of them, though they looked far more healthy than Ventis' mortals. They labored around different trees. Three of them drove long, hollow spikes into the ground with giant hammers. Five mortals dug a steep trench around another tree, backs glistening with sweat.

Flecks of bark flew out of another sapling as a different demigod stood nearby. His concentration, and the manipulation of an amulet under his shirt, seemed to indicate that he attempted to drop it with magic.

Another mortal held what appeared to be a glass timer, filled with sand, and a piece of paper. The sand dribbled out of one side into the other. Once it ran out, he flipped it, and noted a mark on the page.

I watched, breath held.

Like an army, they moved together. Silent. Each methodical movement had a purpose, and every mortal and demigod had a job as they attempted to destroy Letum Wood. They tested methods to kill the forest. Saws. Axes. Potions. Magic *had* pushed that other tree over. The thought that they might try to bring down Letum Wood one tree at a time brought a dying scoff to my lips. Insane. Letum Wood had millions of trees.

Mournful wails returned. Beyond physical hearing, they rang up from the depths of soul instead of mind. A removal of life. Dying throes. At once, I understood it to be the trees, just toppled or about to be. The pathetic mewls, a desperate gasp of life and sadness.

Go in peace, I said.

The narrowing whisper washed away. Others filled its place, equal parts sober and frightened.

They kill us.

We protect each other.

The ill-fated have returned.

I pressed a palm into the tree.

I'm here.

Ferocity welled up inside. Barging into a scene of demigods wasn't going to help, not until I knew what they were doing. If they left when I arrived, we'd gain no answers. Mortals carrying giant black cauldrons of a bubbling liquid approached the demigod driving stakes into the ground.

A call from deeper in the woods must have come, because the female demigod turned, neck taut. Her lips moved.

Demigods couldn't sense goddess magic at work, so I used a spell to help me climb the tree. I scuttled to a branch that stretched toward the female demigod. The mossy arm held my weight as I walked along. Not a leaf stirred.

Vines retracted out of the way as I crept forward. Other operations with mortals revealed themselves. Attempts to saw into trees with long, floppy blades. Sharp spikes drove into trees with mallets. Boring holes through branches. More timers.

The female demigod stopped to speak to another demigod with a rectangular amulet in his ear. Gaudy and thick, it tugged on his lobe, stretching it farther down his neck than the other side. Meloduncanate. One of the only amulets used as an earring.

The female's contemplative face, attentive expression, led me to think she was the leader here.

Three amulets, likely twice as many demigods, and maybe forty mortals here. A bit too much for me to tackle alone. A slinking motion just beyond the demigods drew my eye higher. Shadows. Changing darkness, yet nothing definite to see, indicated one thing.

A forest dragon.

The resurrecting voices in my mind confirmed my growing suspicion.

The fire breathers arrive.
They protect us.
We fear them.

They protect us.

The alternating messages didn't surprise me. Tinny voices, typically the saplings, squeaked their fear of the dragons, while mellow responses came from the older trees. Greater questions stirred in my mind with their arrival.

Could the trees speak to the dragons?

By extension—could I?

The female demigod stepped out of the way of three mortals carrying glass vials that smoked. She stood below me again. For several minutes, all other mortals and demigods cleared. Alone, she stood in a slight opening between trees. Her gaze had narrowed on the ground, lips puckered in thought.

How easily I could drop on top of her, wrestle the amulet free, and disappear. Just as I crouched, a young woman and a younger male who appeared to be siblings stepped out of the trees. The smoke vials had disappeared. The two of them motioned toward a tree ringed by gray-and-yellow fumes. They curled up from the base of the trunk.

With a thought, I tuned back into the voices of the trees.

It burns.

They maim.

The ill-fated kill.

The demigod female followed the two mortals, her burgundy skirt billowing as she strode.

Another shadow moved in the distance.

Then a flash of fire.

A wash of heat brushed past from the right. Ah . . . *several* forest dragons had come.

My heart raced as the demigod female stopped at the smoking tree, regarding it with a hand on her chin. A line of wet, putrid liquid ate away at the bark, which crumbled to the ground in piles of mustard-colored ash. Her lips moved. The mortals turned to face her. My gaze darted from her, to a nearby mortal, then back to her. A plan began to form.

I didn't have much time.

The forest dragons would attack soon, I imagined. Sanna had once called death by forest dragon, *a blanket of fire or a basket of teeth*. Today, I hoped that would be true.

I transported to the forest floor, only a few paces away from the demigod female, and slipped behind a tree. The Volare leapt to life again. I climbed on top, one hand on Viveet's hilt.

The Volare inched forward a breath at a time. Though the mortals and demigods couldn't detect goddess magic, and wouldn't be able to see me, that didn't make me undetectable. Sounds would be my first mistake. Breathing too loud, exclamations. For this to work, timing needed to be just right.

My stomach clenched when we hovered just behind her, so close I could touch her hair. She quieted, then waved a hand in a dismissive gesture. The mortals turned away.

Collected parchments lay in her hand, filled with indecipherable Alaysian words. A distant shout, then a deafening crack, preceded the crash of a falling tree. A tremble rippled through the ground. A violent uproar from the nearest saplings raged through my mind. She made a noise in her throat, stepped back.

The Volare shrank, preventing the demigod from jostling into it.

I crouched.

The demigod female lifted her head, nostrils flaring. She turned to the right, nose in the air, and sniffed. The faintest hint of sulfur trickled by on a breeze. Brimstone. Heat wavered close, looming.

She tensed. I tipped my head back ever-so-slightly to see the darkness of unfurled dragon wings as they cut overhead. Fire built in a half open mouth, then disappeared. My stomach clenched. A flare of flames brightened nearby.

I jumped.

The female crumbled beneath my weight as a roar sounded

overhead. My fingers closed around the necklace as we toppled to the ground. She bellowed something. I ripped the chain free. Links disintegrated in my hand like smoke as the demigod female rolled onto her knees, back, and popped upright with stunning velocity.

She snarled at me as I removed my invisibility spell, disdain coating her angelic features. Her eyes were dark, a stark contrast to her graying hair. In the background, mortals screamed. Fire flashed from all directions, punctuated by the *thud, thud, thud* of forest dragons stomping.

"Amulet-breaker," she muttered in the common language. "You're supposed to be dead."

"What a delightful surprise for you. Please, call me the Lady-witch of Letum Wood. You're not welcome here." My voice hardened. "Get out of my forest."

Her naked neck drew my gaze momentarily. The amulet had disappeared into smoke. An illusion? She smiled, a coy curl of lips, when she saw my attention divert.

"I'm not a fool that wears my amulet in the open like the rest," she hissed. "I think we've learned at least that much."

A scream cut short came from behind. She glanced back, stepping away from me. I advanced, but she moved faster. Before I could get another word out, she disappeared.

"Jikes," I muttered.

Mortals disappeared in the trees, some of them mid-cry. Others lay on the ground, necks snapped, faces burned, bodies torn open from talons. My nose wrinkled as I turned away from the wretched sight. The demigods didn't even take the bodies back with them.

Forest dragons and I had never seen eye-to-eye. They didn't like me, and I didn't particularly care for them. After Mama died, my out-of-control emotions had led to violent magic, which made the giant lizards uneasy. They weren't overly fond of magically potent beings outside of themselves.

Though I had far better control these days, we carefully avoided each other.

In the short chaos of the dragons arrival, the trees had quieted. A dark shadow flew overhead. Forest dragons expertly navigated between closely-packed trees with such massive wingspans, it defied logic. Logic didn't matter in the world of Letum Wood. Despite tightly-packed trees, the dragons always fit.

A dragon stomped into view. The red, a smaller female dragon, seethed while she glared at me. I held up a hand in a gesture of peace.

"We serve the same goddess!"

The red snorted fire. A pile of cinders landed on the ground in front of me. I stepped back, wincing from the heat. She grunted and shoved off the earth. Her giant talons scored the soil in deep gouges as she took to the sky.

As quickly as they had come, the dragons left, devastation in their wake.

Chapter Six

Merrick's room lay in silence.

I sat on the floor, my back to his bed, and stared at the wall. The vines that I'd originally put above his door as a welcoming present months ago had started to fade. I recalled the spell and cast it, reviving the enigmatic green colors. The fresh smell of wild places drifted with it, bringing a smile to my face.

Evening breezed through his room above the Piccadilly Pub, cooling my hot skin. I leaned into it, grateful for the relief.

Chatham City bustled below with the clatter of wooden wheels on cobblestones and cries of distant newsscroll hawkers. The deepening hour, and gentle twilight, cast an easy ambience. I let the contemplative silence roll, grateful for his smell to soothe me.

The fake amulet ran through my mind, sprinting like a mortega.

Failure stung.

They'll come to you, Gelas had said. *You don't need to go to them.*

I scowled.

A sweating cup of cold water hovered next to me, floating in the air. Merrick's belongings littered the room. A random leather boot. A knife that needed sharpening. A strip of leather he wrapped around his knuckles when the Brotherhood practiced hand-to-hand combat. They eased the prickly questions when everything else felt like it shifted. Moving puzzle pieces, all of it.

I drew my knees into my chest, set my chin on top, and let my mind wander to Regina. Considerations about Papa's feelings toward her and Mama's death swirled in low eddies, like a tired tide.

The sound of boots in the hallway, and a click of the door handle, drew me away. Merrick stepped inside, stopped short, then advanced with a lopsided smile.

"Merry meet, little troublemaker."

I glanced up as the door closed. Half armor covered his shoulders. A streak of dirt ran across his left cheek. His hair flowed out in loose tendrils of a braid, cluttering his forehead and eyes. Dirt and grime coated his neck, parts of his cheek. He smelled like wet forest and wild things. Mud flecked the bottom of his pants, near shoes made of leather and laces.

I tilted my head back and smiled.

Muscles flexed as he pulled his half armor over his head and tossed it aside. He dropped to a knee, wrapped a hand around my arm, and pulled me into a hot kiss. A day's growth of stubble gently pressed into my skin. I reached up, hand on his neck. Silky tendrils of hair pressed against my fingertips. His warm touch, the rough contact, melted my insides.

Everything made sense again.

He pulled away, pressed his forehead to mine, and said with a rasp, "The gods, but I'm happy to see you. Give me a few minutes, then you'll have all my attention."

With that breathy explanation, he gathered a few things and disappeared into the hall again.

My heart flopped around, attempting to recover. To pass the time, I rummaged up a rag and cleaned his half armor. Soot and dirt came away. A little sand. With gentle fingertips, I plucked leaves and twigs free from the space between the metal plate and leather which bound it all together.

Twenty minutes later, a freshened Merrick returned. He tossed a wet towel onto the back of a chair. He paused, looked at his gleaming half armor, and tilted his head.

"Did you clean it for me?"

I nodded. He pulled me off the ground and back into his arms. Then he kissed me thoroughly again, turning my stomach into a bowl of porridge. When he finally pulled away, I felt like a snow storm. My arms looped his neck to play with strands of hair at the back. Now he smelled like soap and forest and a dozen other things that gave me a lightheaded rush.

"How was your day?" I asked.

His brow lowered in thought. "Fine. I tried to find Regina to see if she'd take over Lana's protection, but can't find her. Again. A very early, very powerful hurricane that started on the East coast is creeping toward the North. Weird stuff. Oh, and Matthais gave me a most unexpected assignment this afternoon."

"Oh?"

"I'm working with Baxter."

My eyes popped open. "Baxter?"

"I'm helping him search for Nicomedianthekus."

"You? But Baxter is a demigod. He can—"

"Take care of himself, yes. I'm there so he can focus. I can detect lies through goddess magic, find active goddess magic systems that could be hiding something, and I know Alkarra better than he does. Especially the underground black markets and more unsavory characters that might benefit from such an amulet."

I swallowed a dozen nervous questions. The thought of

Baxter and Merrick working together made me want to . . . giggle. Baxter and I had only kissed before we realized we weren't meant for something committed, but it still seemed weird.

"And how is it going?" I drawled.

He sent me a wry look, as if he knew the path of my thoughts. "Just fine."

"Any luck on the amulet?"

"Absolutely nothing. No sign of it anywhere."

"That's . . . not great."

"Tell me about it," he muttered. He tightened his hold on me, hands on my waist. Concern appeared in his searching gaze. A few wisps of wet hair tumbled free, near his eyes, from a queue at the back of his head. Hints of water still splashed his shoulders.

My stomach clenched at the sight of him.

Three years.

How had I lived three years without him?

"Enough about me. What about you, B?"

"I had an interesting conversation with my father."

"Tell me."

A squeal escaped me as he reached down, lifted me off my feet, and swept me to a small divan not far from the door. We settled there together—barely enough room for both. I leaned back against the edge, my legs draped over his lap. He put a warm hand on my ankle and gave me his full attention.

All the angst and confusion melted away when I let the words tumble free. I told Merrick everything Papa said, eager to see his reaction. A bemused expression crossed his face, fixed there for minutes. When I trailed into silence, the tale told, he chuckled. The rumbling sound trailed from his ribs, into my bones. My hand rested on his chest, warm from his natural heat. I snuggled closer.

I tilted my head back, hair sliding onto my shoulders so I could see him better. He met my gaze, but his eyes dropped to my lips. He reached up, running his fingers through strands of my hair as he studied me. His building amusement set me on edge in light of our conversation. What was he about to say?

"While we're on the subject—let's talk more about how you *feel* about Regina. You told me what your father said, but . . ."

My face dropped into an instant scowl. His lips twitched at the edges, but he wisely didn't give into a smile. I sent him a look of warning.

He ignored it.

"I know you don't want to."

Thoughts of Regina sent my mind into several spirals I didn't want to face. Not until I had a pressing reason. A prickling sensation crawled under my skin. Thinking about Regina brought other thoughts up that I didn't want to entertain. Not questions of Mama. Questions about . . . Papa.

"I don't know how I feel about it. I'm . . . not sure. I mean, I wouldn't want Papa to be alone all of his life, especially now. But to be with someone that isn't Mama?"

"It's different. And strange."

My gaze darted to the door. Five steps and I could be out of here. A spell would take me back to the forest to sprint off this angst in the paths. That would feel infinitely better than the cagey heat threatening to erupt from my chest.

"You're scared of something, B. You get a dodgy look." He pointed to me. "That one."

I scowled.

"Out with it. Now. This isn't how we work. We don't have to goad the truth out of each other. We talk. It's time you finally face whatever you're hiding from. Talk to me, B."

Resignation turned me to a limp noodle.

"Fine."

Smug *and* elated, Merrick set the cup aside and trained his intent gaze on me.

"I don't like the idea of Papa with another woman because . . . it's different. It feels like he's cheating on Mama."

"Is he?"

"Well . . . no, I guess not. She's been gone for years."

I still hated that it was true.

"Is it better for him to live alone and wait until . . . whatever comes next? Or to move on, live happily while he can?"

In a starting revelation, I realized we'd never talked about his mother, Kalli, remarrying during our three-year split from each other. Many events existed in that strange miasma when we were apart. The murky middle that left us as different witches, but still much the same.

"Did you go through this with your mother?"

He stretched an arm over his head in a cat-like yawn. I enjoyed the flexing muscles and attractive elongation of his shoulders. He lowered his arms back to the table, blinking through sleep-watery eyes. A frown marred his brow, this time in thought.

"My father had been dead for a long time, and I'd seen what it was like for my mother to be alone. To navigate the winters on her own, worry about Jacqueline or herself or me. For me, it was a relief when she found someone else. Once I proved him out," Merrick added as a firm aside. "I wouldn't have just anyone handfasting my mother."

"How did you prove him out?"

"Little chat after dinner." Merrick winked. "He passed my test right away. He loves her. Quiet bloke, but gentle. A little like my father in that regard."

A pause stretched between us.

"Am I wrong for feeling this way?"

"You know this is a normal part of the process. Think your way through it."

"What do *you* think of Regina?"

"She's like my annoying older sister."

I scoffed. He sobered.

"I love her like one, B. If there was anyone for Derek right now, I'd pick her."

The confidence in his voice didn't settle my raging insecurities. I turned away, my throat thick.

"Papa as a Protector is the only side of him that I've ever known." Tears blurred the gentle glow of light from the window. "When Mama died and Papa became High Priest, I finally had time with him as a real father. Now . . . I don't know who he is without all that. To add Regina to it? It's too much, too fast."

"We're all wondering that," Merrick said with a laugh. "The Protectors are bettin' on—anyway." He cleared his throat, shaking those thoughts free. "Think of it this way, B. You're not the only one that's scared. Can you imagine what Derek is feeling? He has no job, no wife, no house. The bloody man is definitely hiding something," he muttered as a wry aside.

Sheepishly, I admitted, "I hadn't thought of that."

"With Regina, it won't be so . . . lonely. He's not staring down the face of a lifetime by himself. At least, that's how Mother explained it. Talk to Regina, B. And Derek."

I nodded. "I will. Now, I still have to tell you about the demigods."

"What?"

"Just wait. There's more to tell."

With my legs tucked between us, and Merrick's riveted attention, I told him everything I'd seen with the demigod female, the forest dragons attacking, and my suspicions around their attempts to kill Letum Wood.

Merrick blew a raspberry. "The gods, but they're sneaky. What are you going to do about it?"

"First, tell Baxter."

"I'll fill him in tomorrow."

Relieved to have that taken care of, I sighed. "Thanks. After that? I'm not sure. *Something* . . . I just don't know what. They couldn't possibly expect to destroy Letum Wood one tree at a time."

"Why not?"

I opened my mouth to counter, but stopped. "That's . . . insane."

He shrugged. "Is it? We don't know much about Tontes or Ventis. How many demigods do they have who are willing to fight? How many mortals? What do they want over here? Maybe they could kill Letum Wood one tree at a time. Who knows? We should be ready for anything."

My already irritable mood soured as the implications rolled through my mind. "Great," I muttered.

"You should tell Matthais."

Merrick's offhand suggestion sent a crawling sensation through my back. My upper lip curled over my teeth.

"No, thanks. Our last confrontation didn't end so well."

He shrugged. "Considering that you single-handedly took on Alaysia and several gods, survived the removal of god magic, and still run through the forest today, I think his respect for what you can do might have changed a little."

"And if it hasn't?"

"Who cares? You don't need Matthais. Though, he might have some insight into strategy."

Merrick stared at the ceiling, arms on the chair next to him. I stood and walked to the window, peering through thickened panes.

What to do now?

Asking Matthais for help didn't bother me as much as the thought that he might know how to take care of Letum Wood better than me. How could he have greater insight into Ventis and Tontes when he hadn't been to Alaysia?

I sat with the questions for another moment, mired in uncertainty. While I didn't need Matthais's approval, I would admit that I wanted it. It rankled me that Ignis had been right about my desire for acceptance. *The attachment to other witches approving who you are is . . . strength personified, don't you agree? But I expect nothing else so foolish from a witch.* I *knew* he was right, and I still couldn't let it go.

My retelling of meeting the ancient trees hadn't affected Merrick with any surprise, either. Only intrigue. As if he expected my relationship with the forest to always be strangely connected and odd.

Perhaps he did.

Merrick leaned forward, forearms braced on his thighs. "Do you know anything about what your father is up to?"

"What do you mean?"

He captured my hand, braided our fingers together, and pulled me to his side again. I went willingly.

"I think something else is going on with your father and Regina, outside their relationship. I haven't been able to track it down yet, but I think Regina is returning to the North. She's rarely in the Southern Network when I go to speak to her, and your father isn't getting all that much work done on his house for how many weeks he's had it picked out."

"Papa mentioned helping Regina with something."

Merrick ran a hand through his hair. "I want to ask him, but I can't ever *find* him."

"What do you think they're doing?"

"Dunno, but they're not including me, and I think it has something to do with Geralyn. Either way, I thought I'd see if you had noticed anything. Or if you knew when I could bloody find the man. He's ignoring my messages, and so is Regina. They're avoiding me."

I shook my head. "Sorry. I have no idea."

He lay a warm kiss on me, gripping my jaw gently. He pulled away, looking in my eyes.

"I love you, little troublemaker. But sometimes, you're a bit stubborn."

My arms tensed.

I blinked.

"You what?" I whispered.

He smiled affectionately. "I love you. I always have. I always will. I know we haven't said it yet, and I don't expect you to say it back. Just . . . know that I do. If there's anything else you can feel rock-solid about, it's that."

Another kiss to my forehead, and he set me free. I blinked, frozen to the spot, rooted from shock.

The easy burr of those words rolled back through my mind. *I love you, little troublemaker.*

Like they'd always been there.

* * *

Grandfather sat alone in his circular room, sunlight warming the window panes. Despite a broiling hot day, an enchanted tea kettle on a side table kept water lukewarm. Once I crossed the threshold, I allowed the tension from worrying about demigods and Regina and Papa to release. The momentary calm that my soul sought was always present here.

Grandfather glanced up, startled, then smiled wide.

"My very favorite," he murmured, with a tap on the shell of his ear. "I'm sorry, B. I didn't hear you come in. These old ears, you know."

He crossed to where I stood and pulled me into a warm embrace. I melted like butter. The scent of sage surrounded me as I drew in a deep breath. Grandfather held onto me for several moments. When I pulled away, he gripped my arms.

Tea appeared in a cup that hovered in front of me. I eyed it in apprehension. A sweltering summer day lay on the world outside. Not even noon, and my skin already felt clammy. The last thing I wanted was a hot cuppa.

Grandfather chuckled. "I sweet-talked ice out of Alina. She

had one of her butlers send it here an hour ago. The tea is not hot. I'm much wiser than that."

When I sipped, a delicious, cool, minty concoction flooded my mouth.

"Lovely."

Grandfather's lips twitched. He stood at the window now, perusing several books at the same time while he mumbled under his breath. On the window seat, which overlooked Letum Wood, lay scattered books. Old tomes, with tattered spines and pages canted out of the side. Titles in gold-scripted font filled the fronts.

History of Ebenezer Milliferd.

Ambassadors in the West.

The Historical Implications of the Mansfeld Pact.

"Riveting reads?"

He laughed, which turned into a rattling cough from the depths of his chest. He sipped his own teacup, which hovered next to him, and cleared his throat. "They were riveting once. I'm sending them to the Great Library of Burke to find other interested readers."

"Sanako might like them. She's not a Librarian over that division, but I'm sure she could help them find a home."

"They have little to do with gods and goddesses. Isn't that her area of expertise?"

"Yes, but she surprises me all the time."

A sweep of his hand sent the books away with a spell, clearing the padded window seat. I flopped onto it, using a collection incantation to gather all the dust and send it out a window.

Grandfather lowered onto a plush seat near the fireplace, away from his desk. He stretched his legs, folded his hands onto his lap, and peered at me. The neat array of belongings on his desk, and lack of scrolls, meant he must have concluded his business for the day.

"You're coughing," I said.

"Lingering malaise."

"Have you seen an Apothecary?"

He nodded. "Yes, and they've signed me a perfect bill of health. Anyway, your letter requesting an official meeting with me today sounded a bit ominous. Shall we get that out of the way first so I can invite you over for dinner tonight?"

I smiled, unable to help myself.

"Gladly."

The story of the demigods in the forest unwound over several minutes. By the time I finished, his frown had deepened.

"Why not take this to Scarlett?"

"I tried. Leda said her schedule is *more than overbooked for the next week or so, Bianca. You can't just magic yourself into her day.*"

He chuckled at my imitation. "Surely, for this, an exception could be made?"

I shrugged. "I sent her a letter instead. By all appearances, it was only a scouting party that the dragons took care of. I didn't really find out any pertinent information beyond the assumption that they're curious about how to kill trees. It's why I came to you. You can talk to Scarlett while I can't, because something must be done. We can't lose the forest."

"The fake amulet is unfortunate."

"It at least informs us on their tactics. Unfortunately, they've learned from the other demigods who failed."

He made a noise in his throat, swamped in thoughts. One of his fingers tapped on his dark brown pant legs, gaze tapered. Several moments later, he drew in a deep breath. "I'll discuss it with her tonight. We have a meeting this evening. Surely, she will have read the letter by then. I'll see what she wants to pursue as a recourse."

"She, ah . . . she may have mentioned to me an idea to

weaponize Letum Wood. Or to . . . have the forest fight our battles, if it could."

"The forest?"

"She's looking at unconventional methods."

"Certainly is one." He tilted his head in thought. "Can't decide if it's a feasible one, though."

"*I* don't think it's a good idea."

"Why not?"

"After what I saw yesterday, it's clear that the forest didn't fight back."

He hummed in his throat, a finely-haired brow rising gently. "If not the forest, then do you have any ideas on how to stop the demigods?"

A spark of something in his expression led me to think he already knew I had ideas. I leaned closer.

"The dragons. I think they could be the answer."

"How so?"

"Have *them* fight. They're goddess-protectors, too. Servants of Deasylva, like me. Instead of the trees, Scarlett could focus on the giant lizards with a chip on their shoulder. They're practically made for this sort of thing."

"Stands to reason."

"The magic of Letum Wood is powerful, but not used for war. Though the trees are willing to fight, should it come to that."

"Are they?"

Reluctantly, I nodded. "Yes. And maybe it will come to that. If we can avoid it, I'd like to."

Grandfather's gaze tapered. "You're protecting the forest."

"Yes."

"Why?"

"Because it's my job. It's . . . who I am."

Together, Arborra had said. *You will lead us to greater free-*

dom, greater purpose. In you, the goddess says we will find our own path.

Grandfather blinked, awash in contemplation. He leaned forward. "But it's not," he said gently. "You're so much bigger than that."

Breath suspended in my chest, painfully still as his words ran through my mind. I swallowed, dropped my gaze, completely taken aback. So much lay buried in that comment I couldn't unpack.

How to . . .

That was . . .

Was I bigger than Letum Wood? Than the magic within?

My mouth bobbed open and closed again. I cleared my throat, mentally set that aside to stew on . . . later.

"The dragons?" I asked desperately.

Taking mercy, he straightened up. "Yes, the dragons are another avenue that I agree we should pursue that I haven't yet heard discussed." He cast a sidelong glance at me. "While you contemplate . . . other truths."

A quill on his desk hopped to life, scribbling notes.

"I'll relay this information and should have an answer for you in the morning." He lifted his hands in an open gesture. "Anything else?"

"No, but about that dinner invitation?"

A warm smile brightened his face. "Come to my apartment this evening, have dinner with me. It's been too long and I have a new book on flora and fauna in Letum Wood. A rare find, with paintings, that I think might interest you." His eyes sparkled. "If I'm not mistaken, it has a few tricks for dealing with gnomes."

Chapter Seven

A knock woke me from sleep.

I jerked awake to find myself at my table, my forehead pressed to my stacked fists. My shoulders ached and my fingertips tingled. The top of my head, where my fist had been resting, burned from the pressure. I blinked several times as I tried to gather my thoughts. I had clearly fallen asleep scouting for new places to find demigods.

The slanting light, slightly muted, indicated it must be near dinnertime. Grandfather would expect me any minute now.

Beneath my arms lay several maps of Letum Wood, dotted with colored ink where I'd attempted to map out demigod sightings. There hadn't been many throughout Alkarra to record. The children of Tontes and Ventis either weren't here, or had learned how to be sneaky.

A second harried rap on the door startled me again. I jumped, then rubbed a hand over my eyes.

"Coming!"

Once I opened the door with a spell, Ava spilled inside wearing a school uniform.

She panted, doubled over, hands braced on her knees. A

second before I could ask what the hurry was, Priscilla appeared in a transportation spell. A high flush colored her cheeks, hands propped on her hips. A generously pregnant belly hung low—she was days away from delivering a baby. Fatigue showed in deeply-creased eyes and pale skin.

Hands on her hips, she glared at Ava. Ava straightened up, jumped, then screamed when she saw her.

"Ah!"

"Ava," Priscilla growled. "You can't run away every time you are reprimanded. Nor can you come to Bianca's whenever you want. You can't just *leave the school*. We've been over this before!"

Ava pressed a hand to her heart. She gulped, face still twisted in a grimace. A sparkle on the edge of her jaw drew my gaze. A tear, perhaps? One she hadn't been able to frantically wipe away before throwing her body inside?

"I . . . I came to talk to Bianca," she said.

"*Miss* Bianca."

The struggle to keep from rolling her eyes was, I could tell, difficult. Ava blinked furiously instead. Thanks to god magic, Ava could speak and understand Alkarran, which had only driven Priscilla to greater educational plans.

Ava loathed said plans.

Ava, who never had to sit through a class before in Alaysia. Never experienced a testing regime, a chalkboard, a timer, nor a textbook.

Fortunately, Priscilla was equal to such a prodigious challenge. Ferocity infused her these late days of pregnancy, generating what Baxter reported as a *generalized war against my wild niece, who needs a furious woman to control her.*

"*Miss* Bianca," Ava finally growled.

Priscilla tilted her head back, staring through light eyelashes. "And did you ask for permission to leave?"

Ava feigned ignorance. "Purr-meesh-un?"

"Don't try that trick with me," Priscilla snapped. "You know exactly what I mean because we've had this discussion before. You have to ask before you leave. You can't run amok through the forest here, Ava. It's not safe! This isn't the castle. And, frankly," Priscilla tacked on with an impressive amount of haughtiness, "the castle wasn't all that safe for you to jaunt around either."

Truly puzzled this time, Ava murmured, "uh-muck?"

"Wild and crazy and not controlled," I said.

Ava rolled her eyes.

Priscilla smoldered.

"*Miss* Priscilla," Ava said in a rigid attempt at conciliation. "I was taking some fresh air. The room was . . ." she waved her hands, "too small. Too much. School is just a . . . cage."

Priscilla pinched her lips into an impressive glare. "You were supposed to be taking a test, Ava. You aren't being held prisoner. This is our fourth attempt for the same test. You know this work! You could have been done in ten minutes, but you keep *leaving*. Ten minutes, Ava. That's all I'm asking!"

Ava shrugged. "It's not fun."

Priscilla folded her arms across her chest. "Well, you can't always have fun. Sometimes you have to do things you don't like."

The disgusted expression on Ava's face expressed a strong disagreement. I had to hold back my laugh.

"You cannot run like a wild child in the forest."

Priscilla sent me a wry look that told me to be totally silent. I dropped my gaze, properly terrified. As a teacher, Priscilla put rigid Miss Scarlett to shame.

"It's not that far from here," Ava cried.

"There are dragons. Beluas. Who-knows-what-else!"

"Gnomes," I added with a glance to my roof. "Who can do magic now, it would seem."

Priscilla looked at me as if I'd lost my mind. The interruption of her bluster forced her to take a breath. She did so raggedly.

Ava's bottom lip trembled. One of her shoes had come off on the run over here, and a braid loosened on her left shoulder. Fully awake now, I put a hand on Priscilla's forearm.

"How about I chat with Ava? She'll return as soon as we're done. I will vow for her that she will take your test before she goes to bed tonight."

Ire bled out of Priscilla, a breath at a time. They remained locked in a staring contest that ended when Priscilla muttered, "Fine! I will allow it this *one time*, but not again. Ava, you must keep yourself safe."

With one last frustrated, care-burdened sigh, Priscilla disappeared. Ava turned to me with sparkling eyes. I opened my arms. She crashed into me with a sob.

There she remained for several minutes, crying against my chest, until she'd vented it all out. Finally, she stepped away, mopping her cheeks with the back of her wrist. I used my foot to hook a chair and pull it out, then pressed her into it.

"Sit," I murmured, a hand on her shoulder. A quick, silent calming blessing left her gooey against the seat, finally relaxing. "Let me get you some tea. Then you can tell me all about it."

* * *

"I'm like you! I'm an outside girl, not an inside one. We didn't have walls in Alaysia. They're . . ."

She trailed away with a shuddering glance around. Only my experience in the land of the gods helped me to understand exactly what she meant. Wide sky and open ocean, with nothing but daylight for structure.

"You want to be outside playing instead of inside learning?"

"Yes!"

The word came out half cry, half sob. She doubled over, forehead on her hands, and wept again. Leda and Priscilla had been slowly confirming that Ava's education had been minimal, at best. Hardly surprising.

A figure appeared in my shadowed doorway.

Baxter.

Priscilla must have written to him. He cut a worried glance to me, concern in his eyes. I waved him off, shaking my head. He eyed Ava, then disappeared. I assumed he hadn't left, but watched invisibly.

While Ava let her emotions take charge for a second time, I hesitated over my approach. One day, not *that* many years ago, I'd been in similar circumstances. Hated restrictions, wanted more than books and lessons. Papa trained me outdoors every time he could, but he'd been gone more often than not. That led to extensive lessons with Mama and Grandmother, in the house or the Tea and Spice Pantry. I knew this bottled-up feeling very well.

I reached over and put a hand on Ava's arm. She peered at me through a curtain of kinky hair. Her youthful face reminded me that this was about more than just school. Ava had lost her parents, her homeland, her language, and her friends. With her and Baxter here for certain now, a settling in had to occur.

A painful settling in.

Her age—almost-twelve—and all the riling, new emotions that escalated with such a time, made it worse. Jikes, but the girl was just hitting puberty. It might take *all* of us to get her through this alive.

"Ava, I know how you feel."

She straightened, filled with hope. Tears streaked her cheeks. She reached up, swiping the tears away with an impatient brush of her arm.

"You do?"

"It's hard to be inside when adventure awaits."

She nodded, then her nose wrinkled. "How come you can

do whatever *you* want? If it's so dangerous, maybe you shouldn't run around either."

I tilted my head back and laughed. "I haven't always done whatever I wanted. I had to learn from books first, just like you."

Deep skepticism showed on her wrinkled face. A long, thin finger pointed in the direction of the school.

"There?"

I nodded again. A flustered sigh escaped her as she dropped her forehead back to her arm and let out a dramatic breath.

"I can't. It's too hard."

Baxter's eye roll could be felt from across the room. Ava continued, undaunted.

"Learning makes my head hurt, and reading is so boring. I don't care about math or Alkarran history. All of it takes too long. I want to be back on the water, in the sea spray." She patted her cheeks. "With the sunshine."

"Would you want to learn more about Alaysia?"

Her growl echoed off the table. "No. I hate that place."

Couldn't blame her there.

"What are you excited about?"

"The ocean."

"Easy. Ask Miss Priscilla if you can learn more about the ocean. Nautical things, or trips to the sea, or something. Then, you can use those things when you grow up and make your own decisions. *This* education will prepare you for *that* real life experience. Do you see?"

"Yes."

"Help Miss Priscilla nudge your lessons in the way that will set you up for success later. Communicate with her. It will help."

She brightened. "Can I?"

"Can't hurt to ask. If you cooperate more, I bet she'd tweak some lesson plans."

A tentative smile appeared. "I'll try. Yes. That's a good idea."

"Also, what if we brought your birds here?"

Her voice pitched higher in surprise.

"My manulele?"

"We could bring the sanctuary to my house. When you finish your schoolwork, you can come here to see them. We'll talk to Baxter and Priscilla?"

She shot out of her chair and slammed into me, arms thrown around my neck.

"My manulele! My friends! Please!"

"We'll talk to Priscilla and Baxter, but you *have* to listen to Priscilla. Do you understand? Trust her. She wants the best for you. Right now, learning whatever you can is for the best. One day, you'll run free again."

With a shuddering sigh, she nodded. A swipe of her arm removed the tear tracks.

"I'll go back now," she whispered. "And I'll take the test."

"Thank you."

Ava sighed.

I nodded to the door. "Run back in a final taste of freedom for the day. Tell Miss Priscilla that I said you could run alone this one final time. Then, tell her you're sorry, take the test, and once that's done, I'll talk with her and Baxter about the birds."

Ava zipped out of my cottage and onto the trail in a blur. Moments after she left, Baxter reappeared. He rubbed a hand over his eyes and banged his head into the wall. This time, I didn't restrain my giggle when he screwed his eyes shut and groaned.

"I'm not going to make it until she's seventeen. I'm not. going. to. make. it."

His stark tone, each word punctuated by another thud of his head, tickled me so much I laughed again.

"Yes you will," I cried. "You have me and Priscilla and Leda. Ava just needed more women. Positive women," I added as a wry aside. The little I knew about Ava's birth mother, Christa, wasn't warm or caring.

He conceded with a lift of his eyebrows.

"She's finally adjusting to her new reality, Bax. Give her time and space. She'll figure it out. She's all spirit . . . and a bit lost. We've all been there."

A ragged sigh followed. He shoved a hand in his pocket and leaned back against the wall. "Well, thank you for helping."

"My pleasure. Can the manulele birds come here?"

"They'd die in this forest. Every creature would want to eat them."

Cavernous voices rose in my mind. Not saplings. These were deeper, more mellow calls.

We welcome all life.

She belongs to us.

We protect what she protects.

"I wouldn't be so sure of that," I murmured.

The rapacity of the forest's words startled me. Their willingness to protect something wasn't a surprise, but the intensity in which they offered it was. Outside the window, a nearby bush shook, the tips creaking against my windowpane. He glanced at it, eyebrow lifted in question.

I held up two hands. "That was not me. It's all on you, Bax. The forest took offense to what you said. The trees said they'd protect the manulele."

"How was I supposed to know? Fine. I just don't want all of the manulele birds to die and Ava to be heartbroken. I can't exactly go back to Alaysia and get more of them," he added as a bitter aside.

"I'll help Ava figure it out. The forest will do the rest."

"Then I will use magic to send their sanctuary and hedges here. Niko has requested another dinner with me tonight. I'll send them after that."

"Tonight would be soon enough. How goes the search for Nicomedianthekus?"

His lips tightened.

"Not well. Speaking of, I need to get back to it. Priscilla sent me a message and I came right away. Merrick is waiting for me in the South."

"Tell Merrick and Niko I said merry meet."

Baxter's gaze lingered on me for a moment. "Merrick's a good witch, B. You chose right. He's . . . everything you need *and* want. Something important that not many are able to find. Keep him."

The absolution of my decision to break apart the budding romance Baxter and I had, and return to Merrick, affected me more deeply than I expected.

"Thanks. That's my plan."

He gave a smile, a salute, and left with god magic. I turned to the window, where the bush remained.

"You better stave off the gnomes," I muttered to the bush.

A shudder of leaves followed.

Chapter Eight

The irritated cry of an offended chicken, followed by a bellow from a witch, drew my gaze down.

The alleys and byways of Chatham City moved below, like synchronous wheels. Bodies shuffled along too-narrow streets. Newsscroll hawkers called out headlines. Orphans darted around, hungry for someone to pickpocket.

Gritty, hot shingles lay beneath my sandals while I crouched on the roof of a tavern. Bawdy songs belted out from below, punctuated with the occasional trill of someone running scales on the piano.

I chewed on my bottom lip.

"Where are you?" I muttered.

No sign of demigods in Chatham City, at Chatham Castle, nor the Southern Network, Eastern Network, or Western Network. The *Chatterer* reported no further sightings.

I crinkled a message from Merrick that simply said, *Neither Baxter, nor myself, have heard of any new reports of demigods. They've learned from the failed demigods.*

I frowned.

How was I supposed to harvest amulets when they weren't

here? Gelas had promised that the demigods would come to me. If that was true, they weren't doing it fast enough for my liking. Too much of the last year had involved me attempting to find demigods.

A second message popped into view. I tapped the edge of the small scroll, no wider than my thumb. It rolled open in front of me.

Dearest granddaughter,

I spoke to Scarlett this morning regarding your thoughts about the dragons and she wishes to hear more of your opinions today.

If you're amenable, and to help her continue good graces toward the current Council, she requests your presence at the Council meeting, after lunch. I volunteered to write to you to ask, as she's trapped in meetings with the other Network leaders until the Council meeting begins.

Will you come?

—Grandfather

I wrinkled my nose and read the letter one more time.

Visiting Grandfather at Chatham Castle was one thing, but a Council meeting was something else entirely. While I might miss proximity to Leda and Grandfather and Reeves, rarely did I want to return to the hustle and bustle of castle life.

My dramatic return from Alaysia created a wave of notoriety I desired to avoid. Did I want to talk to the entire Council about the idea to pull dragons into the fight?

No.

Also, yes.

If such an appearance would get Scarlett's mind off of the forest and onto something else, then I'd do it, and gratefully.

I scrawled a reply.

I'll be there. Thank you, Grandfather.

—B

* * *

When I arrived at the Council Meeting, a low-level hum of tension ran like gossamer threads through the air.

Aldred stood back from a sprawling table ringed by seated Council Members, a contemplative expression on his face. His arms were folded behind his back, his gaze fixed on a painting of the forest across the room.

His tempestuous reputation had cooled after he stepped into the office of High Priest. Whether the burden humbled him, or he realized it wasn't exactly what he'd been hoping for, wasn't clear. Either way, he'd been less insufferable, more stressed, and wisely deferred to Scarlett when needed.

Scarlett sat at the top of the table in an honorary position. A crimson dress covered her strong shoulders, dropping to a skirt that faded to black. Her austere bun and placid expression revealed little as she studied a set of notes. Baxter would have been here if he didn't have an amulet to search for.

The only witch I wanted to talk to today was her, yet, I had to do it through the sieve of the Council.

Not ideal, but I'd take it.

Disorganization since Greyson's betrayal was obvious in uncertain Assistants, Council Members hissing commands, and darting looks.

Assistants punctuated the strained air with a rustle of parchment or hushed whispers. The smell of ink drifted by. So many witches in a smaller space created the general hum of political anxiety and subtle rushing, as if there was so much to do they couldn't possibly achieve it all.

Sia, the new Council Member over the Western Covens, drew my gaze when she leaned over to speak with her Assistant. Her high flush indicated stress, not to mention the fast movement of her lips. Her wide-eyed Assistant nodded frantically.

A clear divide still existed between the Council. Aldred's loyal following sat together on one side of the table, the rest scattered in various stages of stalwart independence. Each Council Member appeared eager, a bevy of hot-headed personalities ready to discuss issues and solutions. They carried a variegated array of opinions, but at least they weren't so hostile. Scarlett had subdued their growing unrest by integrating them more deeply into the affairs of security, a concession I felt she shouldn't have to make.

Near the fireplace lurked a darker presence.

Matthais.

Seeing him made my molars grind together. Did Matthais still believe me to be a pretentious young upstart? A witch with big dreams and ideas, but no way to execute them? I didn't have the courage to ask. Since I'd returned from Alaysia, we'd fallen into the habit of cordial nods and bland smiles, then hurrying out of each other's presence.

Near him stood Talmund, the Head of Guardians. A sleek, thin, but scrappy man with a fresh-shaven face and hints of gray in his blond hair. He kept one hand on his sword hilt, a distant look on his face.

A clearing of the throat from Aldred silenced various murmurs. He lifted a hand, drew the Council's attention, and motioned toward me with a flick of his fingers.

"Gentlewitches, may we begin? Miss Monroe has come by invitation from the High Priestess to discuss an idea that might be useful for Network defense. We will begin with this initial topic before diving into other matters."

Ripples of surprise followed. I braced myself. Aldred's musing tone—or the lack of annoyance in it—indicated that Grandfather hadn't extrapolated on my idea much. If it all. The Council wouldn't be likely to agree with me.

Aldred's leading presence in this meeting reminded me too much of standing before all Network delegations to answer for my time in Alaysia. It had become a tempestuous meeting, with unexpected arrivals and difficult questions.

Hopefully, today would be far more gentle.

At a nod from Aldred, I stood. A hush fell over the room. More than twenty witches stared at me. Most of their expressions held brittle expectation, as if all of them had to brace themselves to deal with me again.

"Thank you, Council, for seeing me. To get right to the heart of the matter, I believe that the forest dragons pose a unique opportunity for Network defense."

Aldred blinked.

Martha's eyes widened. Her pinched lips parted, then closed again.

Halifax's folded hands tightened.

When Council Member Massimo from the Eastern Covens cleared his throat, the interruption of shocked quiet caused a wave of change, like a breath. Several voices piped up at the same time.

"The dragons?"

"You want the dragons to fight for us?"

"An odd idea . . ."

Before they could quarrel amongst themselves, I quickly relayed my observations on the demigods' attempts to cut down trees and the subsequent attack from the forest dragons. Astonishment faded into perplexed frowns.

"As you can see, something must be done. If we don't

protect Letum Wood, then we don't protect Alkarra. The forest dragons could be a designated battalion to keep the forest safe, as well as witches. The dragons have protected Chatham City before."

Rosanna growled. "What a pain in our neck the demigods have become!"

"Hear, hear!" came a reply.

Discussion unfurled. The various threads unwound like balls of yarn from a teeming pile.

". . . never wanted to help us before."

"The ancient agreement forced them to help with Almorran magic. They're not likely to contribute again."

"Can't say it's half bad, if we can control them."

"Would this be a Guardian duty?"

"Not enough Protectors for this!"

Scarlett's lips pressed together as the ruckus expanded. She glanced at Aldred, then back to the table in a pointed, silent command. He nodded ever-so-slightly. With a lifted hand, he called, "Please, may we be productive in our discussion?"

The Council quieted.

Suddenly, I understood.

Scarlett's decision to call Aldred to the position of High Priest had been suspect for some witches. Sure, he had political aspiration in spades, but that didn't make him a great candidate. That's not why Scarlett selected Aldred.

She'd chosen him because he would be an unofficial intermediary between the Highest Witch and the Council. He had engrained himself in the majority of the Council as trustworthy. At the least, a witch to remain on good terms with. That bought Scarlett instant bargaining power Papa didn't have before. Given full reign, Aldred actually made an impact here.

Clever move.

To this role, he was oddly suited, I had to admit. The more difficult personalities on the Council, like Martha, Massimo, and

Rafe, trusted him. A penchant for the Council to listen to his directions led to a far more mollified meeting than those Papa had conducted.

Scarlett's attempts to include them into matters that weren't *technically* their business must have appeased them. Wise High Priestess, infuriating process.

Aldred drew me back to the present.

"Bianca, do you have further insights into how we could harness the dragons to our benefit? It's one thing to assume they would help us. Enacting such help is another matter entirely."

I spoke to Scarlett because they didn't hold the decision-making power over Network protection. The Highest Witch would decide.

"Nicholas and Michelle."

Scarlett's brow lifted in silent question.

"Nicholas and Michelle are foresters that have an established relationship with the dragons. If you—I mean, the Network—were to speak with them, I believe they'd be able to help with a strategy to engage the dragons' interest and work with them. Perhaps in conjunction with our Guardian force?"

Talmund's nose wrinkled. Matthais held his stony expression, hands folded in front of him.

"The dragons are likely to be motivated to protect the forest because they live in it. It's not the same thing as asking them to defend witches, though . . . maybe some dragons would be amenable to that," I added.

Halifax, a wheezy old man with a bristling white mustache, lifted an arm. He spoke into the quiet, shattering it.

"Have any other such demigod parties appeared since that one?"

"No."

"Any before?"

"Not that I'm aware of."

His gaze tapered under his bushy eyebrows. "And you say that the *forest* took you there?"

Incredulousness stained his tone, which sent a wave of hesitation through me. It was one thing to have Merrick and Papa and Leda and Grandfather understand my connection with Letum Wood, and another one to have the Council privy to it. Could they use it against me?

Probably.

Would they?

Definitely.

"Yes." I lifted my chin. "The forest took me there."

"Hmm . . ."

A flutter of surprise moved through his gaze, then out.

"It's not really our business to protect the forest," Martha squeaked. "Can you imagine trying? The sheer amount of land it covers makes it nearly impossible. Frankly, this isn't our responsibility."

"Isn't it?" I countered. "Doesn't Letum Wood cover most of the Network?"

Martha frowned. Her knuckles turned white as she clutched her handkerchief more tightly.

"Support from the Council should be mandatory for such a drastic measure to move forward," said a rich female voice.

Attention shuffled to the left where Georgette, Council Member over the Chatham Covens, sat next to Massimo. Hair piled on top of her head in an elegant, dark knot. She wore a luxurious dress fashioned out of layers of rare *linea* fabric in shades of blue-gray, just like my eyes. Her subtle, but elegant, style made me think of Stella. The sharpness in her snapping, green-eyed gaze made me think of Mabel.

"If such a plan were to happen at all," Georgette continued. "Dragons as a fighting force sounds like a tactical and logistical nightmare. The potential for endangerment of the general populace is high, particularly in Chatham City, Ashleigh, and smaller communities. This would need to have heavy consideration, not to mention testing, before such a thing moved forward."

"If Nicholas and Michelle helped, much of that could happen very quickly. The dragons are intelligent creatures. It's a matter of communication, more than anything."

"One witch and a few dragons against an untold number of demigods?" she scoffed. "You of all witches should see the fallacy in that. Please, tell me I'm not the only one."

Georgette spoke with a slicing tone aimed at Scarlett, as if she expected a fight. Leda's already pinched face hardened. Scarlett gave a vague head tilt to the challenging tone, a gentle acknowledgement, but non-answer.

"The dragons don't like witches," I said over a rising tide of objections similar to Georgette. "Dragons don't pose a threat to us, and we'd only use them when the gods come."

Across the table, Halifax winced. The *Chatterer* newsscroll, and nearly all Council Members, still used the phrase *if the demigods return*. My stronger verbiage made many of them uncomfortable.

"If!" called Council Member Rafe, of the Middle Covens. "We're still working with conjecture. We have demigods, but have yet to see the gods arise in Alkarra."

"You shouldn't be talking to us, Miss Monroe," Clare, Council Member over the Western Covens, stated. She held up two hands in a stopping gesture. "This conversation has nothing to do with the Council, and everything to do with the Highest Witch, the Head of Guardians, and the Head of Protectors. Take it to them."

Unlike sleek Georgette, Clare was a subtle woman with manicured clothes, her hair tucked in curls around her head, and an intelligent gaze. A traditional, conservative counterpart to Georgette's more progressive, non-traditional ways.

Matthais' gaze bore into me. I met it, saw no invitation to do as Clare mentioned. Talmund adjusted his weight, the leather of his boots creaking. Neither disagreed, nor volunteered. A damning quiet, all the same.

Replies to Clare's declaration parried back and forth: disputes, agreements, and questions. They bandied amongst themselves and utterly ignored me.

"Firmly not in our power to protect."

"Let the forest take care of itself."

Not a single conversation agreed upon more than one point before opinions spiraled into other paths. I held my silence, transfixed by the flapping tongues and utter lack of *anything* concrete.

After several minutes, Aldred's voice rang across the room, easing the cacophony.

"There are other ideas to present while our Head of Guardian and Head of Protectors are here, so let us wrap this up. I call for a vote for who on the Council shall support the idea of using dragons to fight in our battles against the demigods. You have two minutes to discuss before I call for a vote and we move on."

A sharp look from Scarlett compelled him to quickly tack on, "With full understanding that our High Priestess has final say regarding Network security, of course."

Satisfied, she leaned back in her chair.

Aldred blithely avoided direct eye contact with me as Council Members leaned closer, speaking quietly. Assistants fluttered to their sides. Quills scratched notes. Papers rustled. My hands relaxed in a blatant lie against my own thrumming tension.

If they opposed the idea, Scarlett would be unlikely to approach the dragons. If she did draw the dragons into the fight —or attempt to—tension would form within the Council. To avoid such a thing, her focus might rivet back to the forest, which put the trees in greater danger.

Exactly what I didn't want.

In what seemed to be an interminable time later, Aldred consulted a pocket watch, cleaned the face of it off with a handkerchief, and slammed it shut with a loud click.

"Deliberation has finished. Indicate your support of yay or nay so the High Priestess can make her determination with information gleaned from the Council."

He pointed to Rosanna. She shook her head.

No surprise there.

Georgette, another no.

Massimo leaned back and said, "Undecided." I fought the urge to roll my eyes. Better than no, though not by much.

Aldred canvassed the Council while I tallied the results in my head. Meanwhile, Scarlett observed with a contemplative expression on her face. Every now and then, Leda leaned forward to pass a message to Scarlett, or Scarlett would spin to ask her something.

When the tally settled, I felt no surprise.

Four against.

Four ambivalent.

Two yes.

Aldred met my gaze with a bland stare.

"Thank you for presenting your idea, Miss Monroe. We will continue discussions from here and let you know if we have any questions."

Frustration rippled through me as Aldred's Assistant stepped forward to escort me out. I glared at his outstretched hand before he touched me, which he quickly dropped to his side.

"Wait!" I held up a hand. "One question, please?"

Reluctantly, Aldred nodded. Rafe lifted his eyebrows in vexed irritation. Georgette stared, face inscrutably blank.

"If not the dragons, then what *will* you do?" I asked. "If the demigods have plans to destroy Letum Wood, you can bet the gods are behind it. Whether you like it or not, they are coming.

Wisdom dictates that Ventis and Tontes are preparing. The scouting party of demigods at least supports *that*. We need to be ready to defend the forest, and so defend Alkarra."

Silence.

Georgette's voice rippled through the tomb-like air. "You seem to have a special connection with the forest, Miss Monroe. Perhaps *you* can do something about its safety? Meanwhile, we have witches to protect."

My body hardened at her dismissive tone. Life breathed back through the room. Papers shuffled as witches moved on, ignoring me. My curled fingers, cramping from their tight clutch in a fist, opened.

Aldred nodded once, face implacably calm, then spun to face the rest of the room. "Now, requests from the Eastern Network have come for Guardians to build retaining walls against the surging storms. Unrelenting hurricanes plague their borders."

As I spun to go, Georgette's voice rang through my mind.

Perhaps you can do something about its safety?

Oh, I would.

Chapter Nine

Leda stepped onto a trail that started at my back door and wound into the trees.

Her skirt rustled as it trailed down my steps. Her petite, aged boots left slender tracks in her wake. I followed, the cool dirt firm against my bare feet, while Leda continued a debate which had started minutes before.

"I'm just saying that Scarlett isn't wrong for the position she's taken with the Council."

"She's dependent on Aldred to manage her relationship with them," I cried. "That holds a potential for weakness based on whatever action he takes. He's too aligned with the Council, anyway. That's all I'm trying to say."

Leda glared prettily. "He's not, Bianca. Besides, she's put more time into the Council than your father ever did."

"Right, and now look at Georgette. She's power hungry and obvious about it."

The comment earned an eye roll.

"Georgette is straightforward, not hungry. There's a difference, believe it or not. I'll concede that there's a reliance on Aldred that could backfire one day. For now, we have a war with gods to get through and the Network is in crisis mode. Scarlett's relationship with Aldred and the Council has created more productivity and harmony, which we need. That productivity has opened Scarlett's schedule to work with the other Networks to plan for a potential war with gods, at the least."

A beat of contemplative silence passed before Leda added, "Georgette has a point about the dragons, though. It's a logistical nightmare."

"No one said that when they defended Chatham City from the Clavas."

"Because they had a forced obligation. No such binding compels them now. Besides, witches weren't even sure forest dragons still existed a few years ago. They'd been out of sight for so long, they were believed extinct. It's only recently they've stirred back into sight so often."

"Maybe Deasylva will demand protective help from them, if we're not going to work with them."

She arched a brow. "Maybe?"

I faltered.

"Deasylva," she continued in a low drawl, "in whom most witches *still* don't believe?"

"That doesn't make her unreal."

"Then ask your goddess."

I scowled. Unfortunately, it wasn't that easy. Leda sighed. "Bianca, don't be obtuse. You just don't like Georgette because she didn't implicitly agree with you."

"That's not true."

"Georgette is infuriating, though," she muttered. Leda's irate huff delighted me. At least we had some common ground. She eyed me askance as she dodged over a purple mushroom.

"The entire Council is infuriating. I don't understand how you deal with them every day. Did they say anything after I left?"

"Absolutely nothing about dragons. Or about you," she tacked on mercilessly.

I growled. Any lingering hope dissipated, but it hadn't been very strong anyway. Leda lifted her chin, patting hair back into place behind her ears.

"What now? You put your suggestion forward to the Council and they stomped it into the ground, as expected."

"Do you really want to know?"

She hesitated. "Do I?"

"It's hard to tell."

A slowly-forming plan hatched in the depths of my concerns for the forest. Simple, as the best plans were, but not easy. It involved a conversation with Nicholas, perhaps an approach to the dragons with him. With two small children at home, he'd be the witch I'd work with the most. Michelle would stay with the girls.

Once I pulled the dragons to our side? I'd go to Scarlett—without Leda's permission—and tell her my plan.

First, however.

Dragons.

"Georgette did me a favor, if you think about it," I said to Leda's waiting quiet. "She basically gave me permission to do what I wanted to protect Letum Wood."

"That's *not* what she meant."

"If she wants to clarify that, that's her business, not yours. Meanwhile, I'll take matters into my own hands. If the Council has an issue with what I come up with, I'll remind them of what she said. Might be better anyway . . ."

Leda sighed. "That's what I'm worried about."

A world of opportunity lay at my feet and my instincts circled the dragons. If the Council wouldn't call Nicholas and Michelle and ask them to do it, then I'd do it myself. The easiest next step.

Short of *finding* the dragons myself, anyway, which seemed like the worst possible idea. A shudder skimmed through me. Last time I stumbled on dragons in Letum Wood, the red had almost eaten me. Only Nicholas's timely intervention kept me from the blanket of fire and basket of teeth.

Forest voices lifted in my mind, like they'd just woken up. Their unusually shrill tone stopped me. My hand clamped around Leda's upper arm. She spun with a glare. Her irritation faded when I held a finger to my lips, too aware of how still the forest had become. The hair on the back of my neck stood up.

They come for you.

They are many, hiding in darkness.

You belong to us.

They are many, hiding in darkness.

A skein of moss drifted in front of my face. My eyes crossed as I viewed it. In Letum Wood, not surprising. In a quiet magical forest unusually bereft of life?

Bad sign.

I sucked in a sharp breath and tilted my head back. Pearlescent, shiny teeth in a wide mouth gleamed aloft, dripping saliva. Ratty mane. Full chest, darkened with a mat of hair. Long, lithe legs crouched on a branch thirty paces overhead, near the juncture of the tree and the branch. Groups of coiled muscles looked ready to leap as it panted. A foul odor tinted the air.

A forest lion.

With a tug, I pulled Leda behind me and released her arm. My hand went to Viveet, who had already warmed in anticipation.

"Transport, Leda."

She paused, breath held. The fact that the lion hadn't pounced yet was a good sign. She eyed it, then me. Several seconds passed in which nothing happened.

"What is it doing?"

The lion stared, chest rhythmically rising and falling in the deep heat. With a half-purr, half-growl, it settled back on its haunches. No dried blood on its paws or lips indicated a recent meal. Not even a slightly pink tinge to the fur around its snout. So why didn't it attack?

What *was* it doing?

They are many, hiding in darkness.

You belong to us.

We protect you.

A shuffle of movement overhead drew my gaze higher. Leda sucked in a sharp breath. All the way up the tree, forest lions lounged on branches. They licked their paws, faces. Some peered at me. Others lolled on their backs, anchored to branches by their overly-long tails. One appeared so slack it might be dead.

"Twenty," I murmured.

"That's the biggest pack I've ever seen. Forest lions live in smaller packs, I thought. Six or seven."

"At most."

On instinct, I braced my weight more evenly through my feet, pushing the work into my legs. More firmly held now, I tightened my hold on Viveet, eyeing the calm, strange collection. Not only did they populate on the same tree, they didn't move. Didn't growl. Hardly a sound.

"Are the trees protecting us somehow?" Leda asked. Curiosity, more than fear, stained her tone.

"I'm not sure."

"Can they communicate with the animals?"

We speak to all.

They are many, hiding in shadows.

They give allegiance.

"Allegiance?" I murmured. "To whom?"

They are many, hiding in shadows.

Tension strained Leda's voice when she asked, "Well?"

"They aren't clear, but I think . . . I think the lions aren't going to eat us. Normally, the trees just warn me and I stay away from lion packs. I didn't even think the trees could interfere until recently, but they *must* be able to communicate with animals."

"Something is stopping them from attacking."

"I don't know what," I whispered helplessly.

A roar overhead—the lion at the very top—made Leda gasp. She shuffled back a step, startled, and grabbed my arm. I tensed and pulled Viveet out of her sheath just enough that she blazed with light.

One forest lion scowled, turned, and leaped blithely to another branch. It slunk into the mossy canopy. Another followed, then another. One at a time, they faded into the depths of Letum Wood until all of them were gone except for the one closest to us. He glared, then snorted.

He disappeared with magic.

* * *

Sheer shock, and a transportation spell, took us the rest of the way to Miss Priscilla's School for Girls.

Leda and I stood outside the old gate, which still hadn't been fixed. The rickety, squeaky thing didn't clasp, and no amount of magical fix-it spells seemed to last long. As if the cantankerous old metal repelled our attempts in a desire to be difficult. Leda stared at the old manor, brow furrowed, but didn't appear to *see* it.

I shared her befuddlement.

"Did we imagine it?" she asked breathlessly.

"No."

"The forest lion . . ."

"Used magic."

The gnomes skirted through my mind. Gnomes having magical abilities seemed like a fluke. An oversight, perhaps, because no one studied the gnomes all that deeply. Their deep loathing of witches made it almost impossible.

A pack of twenty forest lions, none attacked, and one of them transported?

Not an oversight.

"Something weird is happening in the forest," I said.

"I can see that."

I drew in a deep breath and reached for the gate, but didn't pull it open. Instead, I turned to look at her.

"Do you think—"

The squall of a crying baby stopped my words. My jaw slackened. Leda gasped. A pause of silence, then another lusty cry.

"Was that—" I cried.

Leda laughed. "Did she?"

In a blink, Leda was gone. She reappeared on the porch a second later, flinging open the door. I leapt over the fence and darted across the overgrown lawn. By the time I navigated through the halls and toward the tinny sounds of a cry, Leda stood just outside the dining room.

I skidded to a stop next to her.

The good gods.

Priscilla had the baby.

She sat on a rocking chair in the dining room, near a hearth with no fire. Her pale face was peaked, her eyes bruised with fatigue. She wore a fresh, white nightgown. A tiny bundle filled her arms, burrowed in what appeared to be a soft, downy blanket.

Niko knelt next to Priscilla, one hand on the child. They murmured back and forth in *Ilese,* the language of the Eastern Network. The lyrical sounds reminded me of a lullaby, and the baby began to calm.

Niko smiled at her, adoration in his eyes. The sound of Miss Celia humming in the other room filled the quiet, though I couldn't imagine how they hadn't heard us barreling into the school.

Leda shifted her weight to step inside and a floorboard

groaned. Priscilla and Niko looked up. Priscilla beamed. Niko smiled and swept to his feet, surreptitiously wiping at the corner of his eye with a bent knuckle. Heat and warmth and delight and shock flooded me in a languid sweep, bringing goosebumps to my arms.

The baby had finally arrived!

"Leda, Bianca." Priscilla's head rested back against the rocking chair with a little sigh. "I'm so glad you've come. Please, do you want to meet our son?"

My eyes widened. A gasp curled in my throat.

"Son?"

Leda's smile stretched wide. Clearly unable to help herself, she hurried across the room with a cry of, "Oh, Priscilla! You had the baby. A boy!"

A calm, though exhausted, smile lingered on Priscilla's face. While Leda cooed over the child, I remained back, gaze on Niko. He leaned over, murmured something in Priscilla's ear, and pressed a quick kiss to her cheek. He spun, caught my gaze, and paused.

I tilted my head toward the hallway in silent question. Despite my eagerness to see the baby, I'd never pry him away from Leda in the next fifteen minutes. She might not want children of her own, but she'd make the best aunt in the world.

Niko nodded.

I stepped out first.

* * *

Niko laughed, running a trembling hand through his hair, and said in disbelief, "It's only been six hours."

"Six hours?"

He shook his head, rubbing his hand over tired, bloodshot eyes. "No, more than that. A day. Two? I can't remember. She was in labor for a long time then . . . he was here. It's all . . . so strange. How do you say it in the common language? Ah. *Surreal.*"

"I can't imagine, Niko. I'm so happy for you. Especially because, well . . ."

I faltered, uncertain how to say it. Priscilla hadn't been sure she'd let Niko know about the birth until after. Clearly, she'd overcome her objections to let him be here for the experience. A story lurked somewhere in all these unknowns, and I couldn't wait to hear all about it. Whatever pushed her to allow Niko to be part of the birth of their child, it appeared to be the right decision.

He blinked at me with a bleary gaze. "For all our history, she had mercy on me. Allowed me to be here for his birth. Priscilla sent a message and I came right away."

Tears swam in his eyes. He swallowed the emotion back, his voice husky. "Bianca, I cannot . . . I cannot tell you how this feels. The love in my heart. I . . . he is my *son.*"

His reverence touched me deep in my heart. I pressed a hand to my chest with a quiet smile.

"He looked perfect to me."

Tears brightened his gaze. "A boy. My son. Tommaso."

I reached out, squeezing his hand. "Congratulations."

He startled me by tucking me into a tight embrace, crushing me against his chest with an exultant laugh. He smelled faintly of chamomile and calendula, herbs my grand-mother Hazel gave to every new mother. Celia's doing, no doubt.

When he pulled away, another exultant cry bubbled out of him. "I am the luckiest witch alive. I must go, declare the good news. I . . . I have a *son.* Tell Priscilla I'll return? I want to help her tonight. She needs rest. So much rest. I will be here. A few things I must do first. Another hurricane has come."

"Another one?"

"This is the biggest we've seen." He grimaced. "Terrible

timing, isn't it? On the southern coast. There's another in the north. There is fear they could merge, but . . . no. It will be fine."

Oddly terrible timing, in fact.

"Isn't it a little early for hurricanes?"

"Very. There's flooding everywhere and this one is not showing signs of stopping. I must go back, help my witches. It's difficult, but I'll make it work. For my son! I'll be back!"

Unable to pierce his haze of joy, I nodded. "I'll let her know."

"Tell her not to bathe him without me?"

"I will."

Delirious with joy—and perhaps lost sleep—Niko left. I stared at the spot where he'd been standing, flooded with questions. Who would he tell? What did this mean for the Eastern Network? The ruling High Priest just had a child with a woman that wasn't his wife.

Implications would follow.

A dozen realizations occurred with that one, namely around Priscilla. Was she safe here? Would anyone in the Eastern Network attempt to harm her and the baby? I frowned at the thought.

No, Niko would never let that happen.

Before I could transport after Niko to ask, I glanced toward the doors to the manor. A hunch urged me to call out in broken *Ilese*, "Reveal yourself, Guards. I know you're there. If you don't, I'll find someone else to protect her."

One East guard appeared at the door. I lifted an eyebrow. With a vexed sigh, he tilted his head to the left. When I stepped farther away from the manor, another East Guard stepped into view from around the corner. On the back door, no doubt.

I nodded, relieved.

Time for the important stuff.

I hurried back into the house, eager to see Priscilla and meet Tommaso. Leda sat on a chair next to Priscilla, baby in arms.

Priscilla spoke quietly. Fatigue, an occasional grimace, crossed her face every now and then. Celia bustled into the room with a bright smile and tray.

"Oh, there you are, Bianca," Celia called. "Just the girl I wanted to see. Do you know where I can find a witch hazel bush?"

"Yes, several."

She beamed. "Can you have me some by tomorrow?"

You belong to us.

We care for yours.

Startled by the intervention of the trees in my mind, I could only blink at first. Celia sent me a strange look—no doubt confused by my stymied silence—before I shook my head.

"Of course, Celia. I'll bring some to you this evening."

"Wonderful, thank you!"

We care for yours, the trees whispered.

I gazed outside, stalling mid-step. Since when did the trees pay attention to my conversations? Had they always? That line of thought derailed my progress across the room until the tray that Celia carried clattered onto a small table next to Priscilla. Celia murmured a few things, tutted at the baby, and bustled off.

Priscilla turned to me with a smile. "Please, Bianca, come meet Tommaso, though we have been calling him Tomas."

Leda passed the tiny little bundle to me. He felt weightless in my arms. A wrinkled, red face peered out of the folds. Black hair ruffled out the top in silky strands. Leda tucked the blanket away from his left cheek, hooking it under his jaw, so I could see him better. He yawned, plump, tiny lips stretching wide. How miraculous that something could be so tiny, yet perfect.

"Priscilla, he's wonderful."

"I'm so grateful that's over," she admitted with a sheepish smile. "It's the worst thing I've ever gone through. The greatest, too," she added quietly.

A wince crossed her face as she readjusted on the chair.

"Well," Leda said. "We never know what you're going to do, Priscilla. We leave you to test Ava for a few days, and come back to find you had a baby. You're quite efficient."

Priscilla chuckled. Slowly, I settled onto an empty chair near Leda—not at all sure how to hold something so fragile. When his wet lips smacked, I couldn't help the irresistible urge to touch the downy skin of his face with my knuckle.

"Niko was there the whole time," Priscilla continued. "So supportive. Amazing, really. He already loves him so much."

Leda eyed her, wary.

"And how do *you* feel about Niko being here? He certainly had an adoring gaze on you today."

Priscilla sighed. "I'm relieved that he's not ignoring the baby. It *will* be easier with his help. He's sent food and clothing and . . . little Tomas will want for nothing. Absolutely nothing. As far as Niko? I can't trust anything I feel right now. All I know for certain is that I feel tired, and sore, and everything hurts."

Leda smiled. "Wonderful. Don't worry about Niko. You have years to fret over that situation. For now, you rest. If you need any help breastfeeding Tomas, my mother has raised nine children now. She'll be here in a spell if you need it."

"Oh, that's a great comfort, thank you."

I opened my mouth to ask if she'd told her parents, but diverted at the last second. Better not to remind her of who *wasn't* here.

"Does Michelle know?" I asked instead.

"Yes. She helped me through the worst of it."

Leda squeezed Priscilla's hand. "We're all here for you, Cilla."

Fatigue tugged at Priscilla's face when I passed the baby back to Leda for one last snuggle, relieved to have him transferred safely out of my arms. Tomas wasn't the first baby I'd held, but he certainly was the smallest. Leda cooed a few things and passed him back. She stood, lips pressed primly.

"Priscilla, you did wonderfully. Thank you for letting us visit. We'll be back to check on you soon."

Miss Celia hurried back just then.

"I must be aging more than I thought," Celia said with a faint laugh. "There was a witch hazel bush right outside the back door! Can you imagine? It's like I asked for it and it popped up. Don't remember seeing it there, but with all we've had going on . . ."

She trailed away. Leda sent me a questioning look that I ignored. Another rise of whispers elevated in my mind, then calmed back down.

You belong to us.

We are yours.

Later that night, I stared at the shadows shifting on the ceiling. Merrick lay on his back on the floor, eyes closed, breaths even. Often, he appeared in the middle of the night, so silently I didn't know he was there. Tonight, he'd simply settled there without a word of explanation.

Whatever he feared, sleeping on the floor near my bed settled it. I gave no opposition, grateful for the presence of another life. Merrick, in particular. My mind meandered through Priscilla, Letum Wood, the forest lions.

Finally, I slept.

Chapter Ten

D awn stained the world with muted umber, bringing Letum Wood back to life early the next morning.

I stood at the entryway to Arborra's heart and drew in a deep breath. The other ancients, indescribably massive, populated behind my back. They were no less daunting a second time.

The thinning darkness revealed crossed branches of trees. Deep lattices painted with emerald and ebony. Moss clung to the bark, which smelled earthy. Dense heat lay on the world already.

I stepped inside the tree.

My fingers trailed the wall, illuminating a path of light that faded slowly. A low hum reverberated, resonating each time my finger crossed the line of a life ring. The melody rose up and down, warbling a faraway heartsong.

The warm darkness beckoned me, illuminated by racing bloodlines of aquamarine magic, and led to the space in the middle. An odd area of utter darkness, yet so full of life it brimmed.

Questions haunted me as I strode closer.

What if the demigods harmed Arborra or any of the others?

Could Deasylva survive such an onslaught? These trees had seen *all* of life in Alkarra. Or thousands of years of it, anyway. Because when did Alkarra begin? The gods could wreak their powerful havoc here, and then where would we be? The thought made me shudder.

You are distressed, Arborra said.

"A little."

You have spoken with your leaders.

A hardened trickle of sap pressed into my palm along the wall. I leaned into it, seeking an anchor. No sticky residue remained where the bump had crystallized. The glowing lights waned. Stillness in the pure black center returned.

"I spoke with my leaders to see if they would work with the dragons to protect Letum Wood."

This has caused your distress?

"Yes."

Tell us of the ways of witches.

"Well . . . no one thinks that my idea is a good idea."

I propped my back against the wall. Light bloomed beneath me, momentarily brightening the murky space of the chamber. Not even the magic seemed to penetrate the blackness on the other side, like a dark veil, drawn against the world.

The dragons will protect their goddess.

"I know. I just . . . I think we could be more powerful if dragons and witches worked together to protect Letum Wood. The gods have so much power and so do the demigods. Dragons alone wouldn't be able to protect *all* of the forest."

We have power as well.

"What do you mean?"

We are mighty. If the witches will not work with the dragons, it will be time for us to fight.

"You mean the trees?"

Yes.

Other murmurs and hums escalated in assent. The other

ancients. In the far reaches of my mind, I might have heard the same from far away. Echoes from without.

"How would the forest fight?"

As you have seen before.

Memories of the War of the Networks surfaced. They clarified quickly, and with greater detail than I expected, entering into my mind like smoke. Assisted, no doubt, by the forest, who likely had its own recollections to share.

Clavas had descended during the battle over Chatham Castle. Wraith-like creatures born of darkness. Vines found the Clavas, destroyed them. Roots strangled. Branches whacked.

Later, when I helped repair the injured parts of the forest—back when I first began to really hear the voices—the protection of the trees became more clear. They had provided shelter for the fleeing innocent and wrathful justice to the Clavas and West Guards who fought for Almorran magic.

"You helped witches to fight," I murmured. "You fought Clavas, who didn't hold their own magic. Not demigods with amulets. Not selfish gods with rage issues. This is so much bigger."

We are strong.

"It's too risky. This isn't your fight. The Council is the problem. They're the ones that won't come together and make a cohesive plan." I sighed. "I don't know. I just think that it's not a great idea to pit trees against demigods. I don't . . . I don't like it."

I couldn't handle it if something terrible happened to Letum Wood, I thought, but didn't want to say the words out loud. Speaking them made it irrefutable, and I wasn't ready for that either.

Could trees understand these kinds of intricacies? What really mattered after thousands of years of life?

The dragons burden your mind.

The observation, drawn straight from my thoughts, didn't

bother me as much as it should have. Nor surprise me. Of course the forest knew what I thought. After all we'd been through, it nearly owned my soul.

"The dragons and I haven't understood each other in the past. To work with them would be . . . difficult."

We are aware.

"I'm . . . nervous, that's all. But it seems like the right path forward."

We will protect you.

"I know," I quipped wryly. "That's what concerns me the most."

We trust you as we love you, but we cannot rely on your strength forever. We will fight. Allow us the honor, should it be required. This is our path as much as it is your path. We win together, not apart.

A long, halting moment stretched in the air, thrumming with my thoughts. Certainly, Arborra was correct. Alkarra—no, I—would be stronger with them than without. The thought turned my stomach, but so did reality.

Did I cling to my protection of Letum Wood *too* tightly? Had the time to loosen my hold a little bit come? Reluctantly, I admitted a grudging assent.

It's not like I could *stop* the forest.

Marten's observation haunted me. *You're so much bigger than that.* The same dissonant chord struck as I attempted to understand. How could *I* be bigger than Letum Wood? My very positioning in Alkarra revolved around my role as the Lady-witch of Letum Wood. The forest defined me.

For all intents and purposes, I *was* the forest.

"I hear you," I said to Arborra. "I don't like it, but I hear you. When the time comes, we'll . . . come up with a plan. Together."

Delight brightened their ancient tone with a modicum of inflection. *Our independence is all we ask.*

"In the meantime, we'll trust Scarlett. She'll do the right thing."

The trees will follow. The forest is yours to guide.

Arborra's voice betrayed a hint of uncertainty, but glancingly so. In my own medley of emotions, I might have imagined it.

With false firmness I said, "Whatever happens, we'll figure something out."

Chapter Eleven

An article in the *Chatham Chatterer* caught my eye the next morning.

Seven Day Hurricane Strengthens in the East.

Seven days?

Quickly, I skimmed the article while lacing up my sandals, startled by some of the descriptions. *Fallen houses. Damaged cities. Fleeing witches. No sign of stopping.* The stormy season for the Eastern Network typically began in a month, then worsened in late summer, early fall. A week-long storm of this magnitude, especially now, was . . . unprecedented.

Certainly *not* accidental.

On a hunch, I grabbed a knife and dragged it down the edge of the article. Doing so sacrificed the entire *Chatterer* scroll, which meant I'd have to buy another one, but it was necessary. After I cut the article out, I tossed the damaged parchment into the fire and set the article on my table.

I flipped the article over and scrawled across the back, *Is this Ventis and Tontes' doing?* I magicked it to Baxter, my stomach heavy with dread.

This storm was a beginning, if anything. It had the god of

wind and the god of thunder written all over it. Like shifting shadows, the gods were the type of problem that you saw best when you didn't look directly at it.

Shuffling feet sounded on my porch, followed by a voice from behind.

"Morning, B."

A hand grabbed my waist, spun me around. I collided with Merrick's chest. My hands landed on his shoulders as he tightened an arm around me. I smiled and twined my arms around his neck.

"Morning, Merrick."

His lazy, searching kiss lit a fire inside me. Too soon, he pulled away, eyes sparkling.

"How are you?"

"Better now. Busy in the South?"

"Busy with nothing," he muttered and stepped back. The gravity in his eyes drew my attention. He appeared entirely too somber for such a beautiful summer day.

"What's wrong?"

He shook his head, perplexed. "The mystery of your father. Just tried to find him again. Can't see any sign that he's been back to his new place. The protections he put there are still active, unbothered."

"I haven't heard from him."

"Same here, nor Regina," he murmured. "She's not responding to my letters, and I can't find her in the Southern Network, where she's reputedly staying. Alina hasn't seen her in several days."

"Have you asked Grandfather?"

"Not yet. I'll go there next."

"Do you need to find Papa for help with something?"

Trouble brewed in his expression. "Not sure. I have suspicions but haven't been able to confirm them. It's fine. I'll figure it out. Just wanted to see if you'd heard from him."

I shook my head. "Sorry, Merrick. No."

A forced smile appeared, fleeting in its power. Concern drowned out his attempt at levity. "Well, that's not the only reason I came. Want to go for a run, little troublemaker? I've missed you."

"Always."

Affection warmed his gaze, and I remembered again how it felt when he said, *I love you. I always have. I always will.* The same thrill rushed through me now. An insatiable power in the words.

Such words stirred up varied emotions, incomprehensible in their depths. Of course, I loved Merrick. I always had. I'd known it for ages. Yet, every time the words formed on the tip of my tongue, my mind sped back to that awful day. The day he came back.

Then left for years.

My plan had been to tell him then. Let him know the immeasurable depths of what he meant, but everything had crashed. I sent those heavy thoughts away when he reached down, threaded his fingers through mine, and brought me back to the present moment.

"A run?" I asked, in an awkward attempt to reorient in the moment. An amused sparkle lit up his gaze.

"Yes," he drawled. "You want to run?"

"Yes, I do."

He tugged me toward the door, but I stopped him when a familiar piece of parchment appeared in the air.

"Just a moment."

I reached for the message. Below my penciled question, Baxter had already replied.

I'm meeting with Gelas today and will check, but I'm inclined to think you're right. They're beginning their advance.

Stay alert.

I passed it to Merrick. He skimmed the article, then the writing on the back.

"You think he's right?" he asked.

"I know he's right," I muttered. "That's what's so scary. Let's run. I have things to figure out in my head."

* * *

Twenty minutes later, we trotted through the forest at our usual, steady clip, our breath hot and sticky in the rising heat. Shadows waned across the trail, stretching over our path as bushes bent back, grasses parted. Sweat trickled down the side of my face. Despite being hot and out of breath, I enjoyed the release of running with Merrick again.

Here, everything made sense.

"Leda saw Priscilla again yesterday, and said she's still doing fine," I said through gasps for air. "Priscilla called Leda's mom for help with breastfeeding. Ava is also helping a lot, apparently. The baby is healthy, so far."

"Think Priscilla will fall back in with Niko?"

The question stirred up hordes of others. "I don't know. I think it's wise that she's not making any decisions now."

"True. I'm glad that she survived the ordeal, and the baby too."

A voice pierced my mind with a razor-sharp note of panic.

Fire.

I skidded to a stop.

We burn.

Save us.

Deeper notes of hysteria rose from within, more audible now. I tilted my head back. No smoke here. No visible agitation from this part of the forest. The distance of the voices seemed to indicate they called from farther away.

I focused my mind into the tones, so vague they were little more than harried whispers. A part of the forest I had not visited much, perhaps.

Fire.

We burn.

The ill-fated return.

"What is it, B?" Merrick asked. He stood next to me, hands on his hips. His breath came fast and thready as he doubled over.

"The forest says there's a fire."

"Where?"

"Not sure."

Merrick braced himself. I reached out, grabbed his arm, and called, "Take us there."

Letum Wood whisked us to the perimeter of the forest near the Western Network. To my left lay endless dunes of sand. Rolling vistas, distinctly separate from the trees, filled the skyline with lurching sepia.

To my right, Letum Wood crackled with fire.

Smoke choked the air, growing from tangerine licks of light that drew my gaze to the overstory, where brilliant flames consumed the trees in greedy swaths. The inferno licked along each trunk to spread to the next in a swell of destruction.

"I'm going to jog north a bit," Merrick called with a heavy frown. "See if I can find anyone."

I nodded vaguely, waving him off. My gaze dropped to the ground, where a flicker of movement near trees drew my eye. The spot hadn't been swamped by the flames yet, it was just to the south of the growing fire line.

In a thought, I transported there.

A familiar string of small amulets on a tight chain appeared in a flash, glowing bright and brilliant. The female demigod with snowy hair stood just within the tree line, studying the copse of trees ahead. She turned so her back faced me.

I lunged.

She disappeared.

The ground rushed up to meet me and my chin struck a root. The metallic taste of blood filled my mouth. A call in the distance, a whistle, then a rustle of leaves followed. Stunned by the fall, I shook my head and shoved back to my feet. By the time I straightened up, no demigods were visible.

"Jikes," I muttered.

Had she known I was there, or did I have the worst timing ever?

Dizzy, and thoroughly annoyed, I pushed back to my feet. A roar sounded ahead, yet it wasn't animalistic. The signature of a growing, blazing inferno.

Flames swung through the trees like wild monkeys, igniting everything they touched. Terrified screams from saplings punctuated my thoughts in wild staccatos. The deep reverberations of older trees were almost inaudible, yet strangely calm. Their terror filled me, paralyzing my ability to think. It zipped into my bones, made my teeth chatter.

Be calm, I said. *I'm here.*

Coughing, I held an arm up to cover my face and transported back to where we landed. The shrill shrieks weren't so intense here, where the worst of the hysteria had faded, taking the edge off so I could think and move.

Merrick strode toward me with a heavy frown. He summoned a scarf, tied it around his mouth and nose. Another appeared in his hand, which he passed to me. My eyes watered as I tied it over my face, burning from the acrid smoke.

"Looks like the western edge of Letum Wood," he called over the blaze. "I don't see the river, so we must be standing a little south of it. We need to call in the Guardians. Foresters live not far from here, on the interior."

Giant gusts of wind scattered pebbles and sand into my face, feeding the conflagration. Cinders whisked around, and I couldn't help but think of the god of wind. The firm push of the air current, blowing the fire directly into the deeper heart of the forest, revealed the end game: Ventis fed this beast.

While Tontes attacked in the East with history-breaking hurricanes, Ventis pressed forward here.

The game of gods had begun.

"Go for Baxter," I called over a surge. "Bring him here. We need to see if Gelas or Ignis can stop this before it grows worse. I'll stay here, see what I can do with the trees to help."

Merrick hesitated, then disappeared with a nod.

Left alone, I pressed a hand to a tree.

I'm here.

We save each other.

I always return.

I'm not leaving.

Soothing voices rippled my message out. Their frantic chatter calmed to a low, painful warble. I jogged along the tree line, attempting to see how far the fire extended to the north and south. No visible demigods, the rotten cretins. They started a fire, and left it for Ventis to drive into the heart.

I should have seen that coming.

Wind buffeted me at every step, slowing my progress. A billowing, black cloud escaped out of the top of the canopy, chugging high into ominous shapes. The wind bullied those around too, thinning them into a general haze lower in the air.

The firestorm grew each second, expanding into a monstrous, living thing. Heat made it impossible to get much closer. Inside, the trees continued to cry, though the sounds lessened to a low keen as the fire rampaged over them, leaving husks in its wake.

Baxter and Merrick appeared at our original starting point as

I hurried back, coughing. Baxter's gaze fixed on the inferno, then hardened. I jerked the scarf off my face.

"Can Ignis stop this?" I cried.

"Ignis is otherwise occupied," he shouted over the wind.

"Doing what?" I screeched.

He shrugged helplessly.

Questions cluttered my mind at *that*. Now wasn't the time to dive into Ignis and his schedule, but I'd return to that later, for certain.

"Use god magic! You have Samthanruadanosa."

Baxter hesitated. "I'll try, but it may already be too big to stop entirely. See how it's growing? There's an unlimited supply of wood to burn. My father knows I'll try to help, and with Ignis's amulet. He would have planned for it, which means he wants me to waste the power I have. We need to go at it with a plan, a strategy. Otherwise, there's no hope. We'll need all the help we can get."

His dark curls mussed as he ran a hand through them, at a loss.

"I'm going for Talmund," Merrick said, yanking the scarf off his face so we could hear him better. "We need to amass Guardians to evacuate the area east of the fire. It's moving so quickly there may not be much they can do."

I nodded. Merrick left as I gazed back over my shoulder. Indeed, Ventis chose a strategic spot. All of Letum Wood for him to lay siege from here. The fire would continue to surge under the wind, consuming everything. Already the currents shifted, blowing the fire to the south, the north, and hard east, which would eventually press against the ring of ancients.

Baxter's words replayed through my mind.

Unlimited supply of wood to burn.

What if there wasn't?

Arborra, can the forest survive a fire? I asked.

If there is control. The dragons do this all the time.

Then I have an idea. You still want a chance to fight?

We desire to save ourselves.

Then brace yourselves.

Whispers escalated.

We serve you.

You serve us.

We protect each other.

I put a hand on Baxter's forearm, forcing him to look in my eyes. "Find Gelas and ask him if he can help right now. See if Samthanruadanosa can . . . suck up the fire, or something. While you do that, I have another idea that might slow it."

He nodded. "I'll be back."

Chapter Twelve

Twenty minutes later, I returned.

Merrick and the Guardians littered the boundary of Letum Wood. The conflagration had already moved on from here, leaving smoldering forestland. Most of them charred on top, some burned to the roots. Heat billowed through the air, percussively hot.

Clouds swirled in noxious, leaden piles. Trees screeched in the back of my mind, my skin puckering from the unearthly sound. Pieces of my soul crumbled with each voice that extinguished, silenced in the burn.

With all my focus, I set them aside. I had to, no matter how nauseating the losses.

Merrick nudged Talmund with an elbow as I jogged to where they stood. They both turned toward me. I met them halfway.

"Is it still heading east?" I asked.

Talmund nodded.

"Has it moved north or south?"

Talmund squinted, eyes bloodshot from ash. "Offshoots, it appears." His voice grew hoarse. "But most of the wind has been pressing east. For all we can tell, it's driving straight through, like an arrow. Like it has somewhere to go. We can't be sure because we can't get that high for long."

"Any sign of Baxter?" I asked.

Merrick shook his head.

I tilted my head to the side, the column of my neck cracking. "That's fine. I know what to do. Tell him to find me as soon as he returns. If he has help, we'll take it. In the meantime, I think we can slow the advance."

Talmund frowned. "How?"

Merrick sighed. "Better not to ask. What do you need, B?"

"Time, and more fire."

Talmund reared back. "Are you serious?"

"Very."

"What are you going to do?"

"Let the forest have its chance to fight back," I said, as if it should have been obvious. "Talmund, recall your Guardians here. There's nothing they can do. Merrick, will you stay in case Baxter returns? Baxter can bring you to me as soon as he's back with the amulet. The god magic will find me."

Merrick nodded, but gave me a wary eye. "All right, B. But don't do anything stupid."

I winked.

He scowled.

Before either could protest, I commanded the forest to take me away with a thought. Magic fissured through me in a warm purl, then yanked me away. Moments later, I sprinted through the low bracken of the forest, due east, just ahead of the fire. The roar of it chased me.

Hurry, hurry, it seemed to say.

Smoke ringed the trees as it crawled along the ground. It choked the air, my throat, coated by a sheen of ash. I cleared it and continued to run, leaving all that behind me. Any minute now, the right spot would appear.

Given enough time with these gale-force winds, all the forest would be scorched to brittle ash. Arborra's gentle guidance, the quiet voice, croaky with age, replayed through my mind. Hopefully, the forest knew what it was doing.

We save each other, I said to the trees as I sped past. *Help is coming.*

The chattering panic hushed. I brushed my fingers along a trunk as I hurried by. Only a few more steps and I'd be right where I . . .

Magic twirled me away mid step, depositing me gently at the exact position Arborra had told me about. A cleft in the trees, rent by rocks. Not far from the fire, but enough space to give a natural break. With a sharp breath, I studied the rock formations that ran like a straight line through the forest.

"This will work," I whispered.

Trees shivered overhead.

"Get ready. The fire is coming."

You save us.

We save you.

We protect each other.

My stomach ached when I gazed west, back toward the fire.

We save each other.

Roots appeared out of the soil, thin, dark cords that reached away from the rocks, wrapped around trees, burrowed deeper into the ground. Trees shifted, rending the earth into deep furrows. Deeper voices, ones I'd never heard before, elevated to greater sound. The older trees. Saplings moved out of the way, nearly crushed as the larger trees slid across the ground. Dark earth churned in the wake of the displaced behemoths.

All the way along the line of rocks, trees gave way.

"Keep going!" I called.

The separating arbors divided the forest in half, leaving mulched soil behind in an umber scar. *The fire will not burn through dirt,* Arborra had said. *A break can stop its progress on the ground.*

It wouldn't be enough for the canopy, but it would be a start.

"Take me north," I called.

The magic rushed me north of the fire, where the plume built high overhead. Trees continued to do the same here. Dark lines of churned earth would be impossible for fire to break, unless it jumped from branch to branch. A quick check confirmed that the trees south of the fire did the same.

"C'mon Baxter," I murmured. "We still need your help."

The forest quieted. My hair shuffled in a gust of wind as it twined through the trees. In it, a whisper.

Ventis.

Lady-witch of Alkarra, you cannot win. Try if you must, but all will fail in the end.

With a shiver, I transported away.

* * *

Letum Wood brought me closer to the burning band to wait for Baxter. I stood to the east, in the direct approach of the flames. Wind buffeted here in escalating power, a dark harbinger of doom.

Radiating heat turned the air into wavering lines. Sweat streaked my body. Ash littered my hair. Smoke clogged the canopy, creating an early, orange darkness. I pressed a palm to a tree.

You belong to me.

The hysterical saplings calmed. The thickness of the trees created a wind break. The wind would be faster at the tops of the trees, where the conflagration turned to a monster. That gave us hope for stopping it on the ground.

With any luck, Baxter would be able to do the rest.

As if I brought him with my mind, Baxter appeared. Relief crossed his face when he saw me.

"You're safe."

"So far. I have a plan."

"Merrick mentioned that."

I grabbed his arm.

"Read my thoughts with the god magic. Can you do what I'm imagining?"

Baxter's gaze turned long, paused. In my mind, I pictured what we would need to finally stop the fire all the way at the very heights. Showed him memories of how the trees moved to create an earthy perimeter, then my hope for a wall of ice. It would extend past the canopy, to prevent the fire from jumping over.

He sucked in a sharp breath, nodded. "It's brilliant. Yes, I can do it."

"Do you have enough magic?"

Baxter touched his chest where Samthanruadanosa, his god magic amulet, lay beneath the fabric. Crimson and burnt orange glimmered, not yet blazing bright.

"Let's hope so."

"How big can you make it?"

"Not sure. Haven't tested this amulet's limits yet, but we'll find out soon enough."

"Magic from the god of fire can create ice?" I quipped, amused.

A pause.

"Yes," he finally murmured.

Though he didn't specify, I had the impression he answered directly from Ignis. To my surprise, I missed the quick connection with the god, and his occasionally snarky comments. Like having a friend—a very snoopy, powerful friend—in my head.

A change in the roar, and a blast of heat, brought me back to Alkarra.

"The fire is almost here."

Baxter frowned into a growing gust of wind as it twirled by. Hazy smoke filled the wood with vapors. A darkening glower appeared on Baxter's face. "Your trees will still burn."

An ugly choice, but the only choice if we wanted to save the forest. My throat thickened as I whispered, "They will."

Baxter straightened, chin high, throat taut. His stark whisper startled me. "I'm sorry."

"Baxter, this—"

"Is from my father, and I'm sorry. I have to say it, even if you don't think I should say it. I'm sorry he's doing this. I wish I could stop him. That I had any ability to reason with him. I haven't spoken with him since the Heart of Alaysia. I'm not sure we ever will speak again."

I reached out, touched his shoulder. "No one holds you responsible. Not me, not the forest. We'll stop this together."

He nodded, but tension radiated through him.

"Arborra says that fire is good for the forest floor. The undergrowth here will come back next year. Some trees could survive, if only their tops are charred. Maybe, with magic, it won't be so bad."

The magic, Arborra had promised me, *can repair some of the broken ones. Time will do all the rest.*

The creaky, aged voice gave some comfort as fire ravaged all that I held dear. Releasing trees to death doubled my resolve to stop the gods for good. I burrowed my toes farther into the soil.

No more, I promised.

Baxter opened his hands and closed them at his sides. "Let's get this started."

Flickers of burnt orange and crimson hinted through the clustered green boughs. Rising hysteria from the forest lifted the hair on the back of my neck. The saplings panicked. The older trees rooted into new positions. When a burst of wind shoved burning cinders into the air, I braced myself.

"Five minutes," I called over the roar. "If that long. We can't do it too soon, or Ventis will change wind direction. While you're doing the god magic, I'll protect you so you can focus."

His half-open mouth sealed shut. With a nod, he gave way. Heat swelled closer. Ash thickened, making it nearly impossible to see. My eyes stung.

A wall of roaring flames sped closer, fed by insatiable winds. The fire monster raced, crawled, and chewed through the floor. Not even Arborra's calm assertions that fire wasn't our enemy could calm the frenzy.

Fear resurrected.

"Two minutes!"

Baxter braced himself.

Cinders, soot, and clouds filled the air. I jerked the scarf back over my mouth, where my breath stained the fabric in rings of black that tasted like char. A familiar taste, after my time with Ignis. I yanked the Volare off my back and loosed the top.

It climbed into the air, then settled at my hip.

"Begin, Bax!"

Samthanruadonosa lay visible on Baxter's chest, gleaming in plumes of red and orange. Yellow tinged the edges, like a revolving flame. A whiff of cold air interrupted the surging heat. Ice crackled on the ground beneath Baxter, climbed higher in panes of glass. The Volare widened, then scooped Baxter and me onto its tapestry.

"Hold on!" I called.

Baxter clung to the edges with a gasp. He glanced at the Volare, to me, and then shook his head. The Volare darted higher, hurrying through the bracken. I ducked a branch that rattled in the wind.

In our wake, ice sprang from the ground like frozen shards of blue teeth. The soil dissevered into cracking white panes that surged into the air.

"Keep the ice growing behind us!" I shouted over my shoulder. Wind sent us wheeling to the side as the Volare rushed toward the top of the canopy. The Volare twirled, enclosing us before we slid free. The floe of ice clambered behind, as if we pulled it from the jaws of Alkarra like the ice giants of legend.

"How thick do I make the ice?" Baxter shouted.

"I don't know! Wide enough it can't melt?"

Tears from the sooty air streaked his face in gray lines. Fire careened through the undergrowth in wild abandon, matching the blaze overhead. Cracks, groans, and bursts of cool air chased us higher, higher, higher.

The Volare climbed, vertical. We clung to the edges. Baxter shouted something. Heat emanated from Samthanruadanosa, which resembled the burning heart of a fire. Pleas for help echoed in my ears from the saplings below. My heart wrenched.

"Does Samthanruadanosa have enough power?" I called.

"For the moment."

"Keep going. We're almost to the top of the canopy."

Time seemed to suspend as we darted up, up, higher than all the limbs and forest towers. The smoky air began to thin. I yanked the scarf to lay around my neck, limp and wet. With blithe power, the Volare dodged the massive branches that overtook the upper forest mantle and sky. A murky black darkened everything. My hair fluttered behind me as we claimed the sky.

We burst above the tree line.

I dropped to my stomach and peered over the side. The white glacier rose in the air to cut the dark ground in half. On one edge, sweltering flames. On the other, lush forest. My stomach clenched as we raced higher. The ice followed.

"Veer out!" I shouted.

The Volare zipped to the side as the ice sheared past. Wind slammed into us, we wheeled back. The edges of my rug shuddered. Magic glued me to the carpet, but Baxter flailed with one arm. The vertical edge stalled, allowing me to kneel again.

Hands gripping the edges, I scissored my legs around his waist and shouted, "Hold on!"

The Volare folded into a tunnel, closing us inside. Against torrents of wind, it pressed over the top of the glacier, dodging to the other side, where all lay calm. I bent my head down to watch the wall continue to rise, lifting from the forest.

"Keep going, Baxter!"

Samthanruadonosa vibrated on his chest. His eyes were closed, lips thin. The Volare unwound, opening to give us space again. I clung to the edges as it sped to the west, out of the way of the sprawling ice flow. The ice climbed higher.

Higher.

I stood, feet firmly planted despite the rippling edges. Baxter's eyes flew open. He sucked in a sharp breath.

"It worked."

"Keep growing!" I called. "Farther along the north and south now."

Without the trees to protect us, wind buffeted the Volare in wicked torrents. I sent spells with goddess magic—not at all certain they even worked—to drop water on flames that encroached.

The sight over the currently-burning forest made my stomach lurch. A billowing plume lay over Letum Wood in towers of white and gray. The monstrous cloud bubbled overhead, a sooty underbelly hovering over hungry flames. Fire at the edge, near the pillar of ice, stalled along the blue-white wall.

"It's working!" I shouted.

With an arm, I pointed to the barrier. Baxter followed my gaze. Winds attacked the ice with gale-like power and intensity, but behind the barrier nothing moved. No flames over the top, which stood at least a turret's length over the forest.

Baxter held onto the amulet. "I don't know how long it will hold," he shouted. "I can feel the magic draining. It won't last much longer. Ignis has returned. He says that he can stop the flames to save the trees now that we've contained it."

"How?"

"We have to be closer to the fire."

The Volare sprang to action. We dashed back onto the fire side of the wall and into the terrible winds. Water sluiced down the barrier in waterfalls, quenching the closest flames.

As if he sensed his inevitable demise, Ventis poured more power into the tempest. A surge shoved the Volare back, nearly ripping us off. The edges attempted to curl as we tumbled closer to the ice wall, end-over-end.

With a shout, I commanded, "Down!"

The Volare twirled in a final attempt to do as I said. The ice wall closed in. Five seconds and we'd slam into it. Bone, breath, all would shatter.

Four.

The Volare struggled to recover, too controlled by the wind to move itself. A hole appeared in the ice wall.

"Fly through it!" Baxter called.

Three seconds.

The airstream bullied us higher, out of the path on the wall.

"I can't create the hole in the wall forever," Baxter cried. "The amulet is draining!"

Two seconds.

The hole disappeared. Baxter gasped, face pale. The light that had been an amulet ebbed away. In last-minute desperation, I issued a goddess magic spell that created density—meant to sink things into water—and pressed it onto the Volare.

At the last second, the Volare dropped. The underbelly skimmed down the wall of ice, racing out of the currents as fast as it could go. Down the face of the ice wall we plunged. My teeth rattled from the speed as we dove back into the safety of the forest.

"To the heart of the fire," I gasped. "Take us as close as you can without burning."

Trees, branches, leaves whipped past as the Volare peeled away from the wall. Water streaked out of my eyes. I yanked the scarf over my face, but it did little good against the soupy smoke. Soot and ash thickened my hair, which hung limp in my face. My throat itched, ravenous for water.

A burning heart center of fire smoldered ahead.

Baxter stood on the Volare. "We have to throw the amulet into the fire."

"What?"

"It's what Ignis says!"

"But—"

"He said to stop arguing with him and do it before it's too late."

The Volare hesitated, clearly in tune with my emotions. With a growl, I flung a hand. "Go! Stay as low and out of the wind as you can."

The Volare darted into the truculent interior, where noxious smoke billowed. I stood next to Baxter as charred, smoky remains skated by. The deepest parts of me yearned to acknowledge the terror, agony, and pain, but I stuffed them aside for later.

Wind screamed in the treetops as the Volare expertly navigated Letum Wood. The air simmered. My body felt wrung out, dried from the inside. Sweat trickled all the way down my back, saturating my ragged dress. Cinders had scorched several spots into black holes. Burned patches smarted on the back of my hands, my cheek. Sparks collided in the air as we slowed to a stop, twenty paces off the ground.

I'd felt the depth and ferocity of fire before, when Ignis had allowed me to understand our connection. It unleashed here, surging in a holocaust.

Baxter jerked Samthanruadonosa off his neck and flung it into the air. It arced away, disappearing into embers.

The Volare slipped sideways so I could touch the closest tree. *The amulet is mine,* I said. *The forest requires the magic. Protect it for me, please?*

Moments later, a gentle voice. Calm. Quiet amidst the upheaval. *So mote it be.* Luminescence spread under my fingers in haste, then faded down the trunk in an easy streak of light blue.

I turned back to Baxter.

"The trees will guard the amulet."

He nodded, lowered back to the Volare with the petrified expression of a parent releasing their child. The growl of the fire began to fade. The anticipating trees quieted. A crackling sound came from the left.

"Go!" Baxter cried. "Ignis says to leave."

The Volare winged out of the upper canopy and into the sky. Wind trickled by as the wall of ice began to crumble in great chunks, dropping to the west, where the fire still burned. Glacier-like chunks broke free and dropped out of sight.

Sizzling followed. Steam built in the air.

I whipped around as the roar ceased to bellow. Smoke retreated. Like a vortex, flames disappeared from their dance at the top of trees. Their wild ribbons retreated.

Peace returned.

Charred, smoking trees remained, like blown out candles. Torched arms settled into black.

"Take me," I whispered.

The Volare obeyed, closing in on an older tree half-burned on the western side. Its voice reached me before I placed my blackened hand on it to hear a single voice.

The fire retreats.

Flames die.

Saplings are gone.

The forest remains.

I sank to my knees. Baxter put a hand on my shoulder, voice raspy from smoke.

"We did it."

"This time."

Grim-faced, Baxter sighed.

"Tell Ignis thank you?" I asked.

"He accepted."

My legs dangled over the side of the Volare as it swept us back toward the Western Covens. A line of black stretched ahead, almost into the horizon, where the fire had pillaged and destroyed. Hot as flames, a tear dropped down my cheeks.

My forest.

My soul.

* * *

Disbelief altered Talmund's tone.

"You . . . did it."

"Several of us did it." My entire body ached, exhausted from the back-and-forth of the winds on the Volare. Dodging *Chatterer* journalists hadn't been easy while I helped Talmund understand what to do with the soused fire area.

Namely, nothing.

The forest would take care of the rest.

Baxter sent a cup of water my way. With a grateful look, I gulped it down. Samthanruadanosa hid behind his clothes again, returned by the forest just after we arrived to the edge of the Western Network. If Baxter's soot-stained skin and bloodshot eyes were any indication, I probably looked like a nightmare.

I *felt* like a nightmare.

"Well." Talmund lifted both arms. "You did well, Miss Monroe. I . . . I guess we're done here, gentlem—er . . . witches."

Talmund strode toward a contingent of waiting Guardians. Baxter watched him go, bemused.

"Ignis told me you would figure out a plan."

I rolled my eyes. How like the god of fire to throw me into a problem to observe how I solved it. He'd done it plenty of times in Alaysia.

"Is that why he was so *busy*?"

Baxter shook his head. "No. He didn't tell me why he couldn't help at first. He was just . . . absent."

"Does that happen often?"

"Lately, yes. I believe he's attempting to figure out how to destroy the amulets, but, believe it or not, he doesn't feel it necessary to inform a demigod—and not his own—of his schedule. Anyway, thank you for your help."

"Baxter, thank *you*. Without you and—"

He held up a hand. "Stop. It's literally the least I could do. With . . . well, it's my pleasure to help Alkarra."

Dozens of dark words lingered in what he said. I nodded, accepting all of them.

Baxter faded into magic, revealing a set of worried hazel eyes, filthy hair, and sooty clothes. With relief, I rushed into Merrick's waiting arms. He wrapped them around my shoulders and kissed the top of my head.

Char darkened his skin. He smelled like burned oil. His shirt was torn across the shoulder, and a streak of blood lay underneath.

He pulled back to touch my face.

"You're all right, B?"

"Fine. You?"

A half-smile crossed his lips. "I've seen better days." His voice was thick as Baxter's. Tear streaks marred his face, and his bloodshot eyes burned a wild red.

"Where did you go?"

"To help the Guardians clear the forest of witches, ahead of the fire."

"Noble."

He rolled his eyes, then glanced at the Volare lingering back. As always, the fibers of the rug remained unharmed. No deep burns or gouges, only a fine layer of dust and ash. A good plunge into a river would pull it right back into shape.

"I see your friend helped?" he murmured with amusement.

"Always."

His nose wrinkled. He looped an arm around my hip, pulling me close. "Needs a bath."

I laughed. "So do you."

"If you have a moment," he drawled, "I have an idea."

"Oh?"

"Allow me to transport you, little troublemaker?"

I pressed my palm to his.

"Sweep me away, Protector."

Chapter Thirteen

Crashing water welcomed us.

I opened my eyes to emerald luxury. A roaring waterfall tumbled over giant stones, plummeting into a river that eased out of sight in a lazy warble.

Trees sprawled overhead, casting dappled light. The pristine water revealed rounded rocks on the bottom. The cool lake beckoned my parched throat, hot skin. Behind it, mountains ribboned out of sight in towering rock walls.

"Where are we?" I asked.

"The North."

"Are you allowed to be here?"

He grinned, already wading into the water fully clothed. "Let them come find me."

The clear pool, untroubled by the sloshing foam at the bottom of the waterfall, cut into ripples as he eased under the water and back up. Hair slicked back, mossy eyes bright against darkened roots, he beckoned with a crook of his hand.

"Scared of the water, little troublemaker?"

Roaring fire still burned through my ears, a frightful disaster I'd rather forget. I reached out to touch the mist with my fingertips. The velvety soft texture eased by in a cloud, scampering past. I reached down to untie my sandals.

"How do you know about this place?"

"My father."

The water deepened as he ducked under, disappearing for several moments. When he resurfaced, char and dirt sloughed off his arms, darkening the pool.

Second sandal freed, I tossed it aside, scrambling after him. The cool liquid slipped around my ankles, calves, and knees. I dove under, luxuriating in the sensation as it wrapped my body. Heat dissipated. Coolness returned. I stayed beneath the water until my chest ached.

A hand clamped around my arm and tugged. I surfaced to find Merrick a breath away. He pulled me close, where my toes barely touched. Water lapped around his shoulders, wiping the stains free.

I coiled my arms around his neck, pressed a fast kiss to his lips. Wet cords of hair snaked around his dirty forehead. I pushed them back with a hand, enjoying the languorous way he smiled. His levity faded into concern. Arms wrapped my waist, he closed the space between us.

"I'm glad you're all right, B. I worried about you."

"Thank you for not trying to stop me."

He snorted. "There's no stopping the Lady-witch of Letum Wood."

I grinned, hands cupping his face. He leaned closer, devouring me in a kiss hot as the inferno. I tasted heat and fire. We drifted in the water, tight in each other's arms, for minutes. When I pulled back, he grinned with swollen lips.

"You don't talk about your father that much," I murmured. "Why not?"

A contemplative expression filled his face. "I don't know. I think about him all the time."

"He was important to you?"

"Very."

"What's your favorite memory with him?"

He leaned back, wetting his hair in the water. I swallowed a billowing attraction. Merrick affected every part of me: heart, spirit, soul. One look from him could bind all my organs together for hours.

While he fell into thought, I sank back into the water, grabbed sand with my fist, and surfaced. I sat on a rock and scrubbed the sand into my skin. Slashes of black rubbed free.

"My favorite memory of my father," he murmured, stealing sand from my outstretched palm. "There are so many. The ones I think of the most? The days when he showed me the North. He was proud of his Network, his work as a Master. We transported everywhere, to places like this."

His head tipped back, regarding the foliage.

"I have so many places to show you," he murmured.

"I can't wait."

"He became a trainer for incoming Masters." Merrick shoved the hair out of his eyes. "He taught Regina."

I perked up.

"Really?"

"Really. She was a mess at the time, I hear." He scoffed. "Doesn't surprise me."

His quick clip would have made me laugh, but any mention of Regina made my throat tighten.

"He wasn't much older than her," he continued, oblivious. "He'd only been in the Masters a handful of years when she popped up, but he was a natural teacher. A natural at everything, really. One of those witches that prospered at whatever he tried."

"I didn't know that."

"The entire North mourned when my father died."

He dipped under the waterfall. It crashed against his shoulders before he disappeared beneath. He popped to the top a few paces away. His laid-back air as he swam around mesmerized me.

A jungle-like forest lay at the top of the rocks, about thirty paces high. It stretched out of sight beyond. I wanted to go to one of the trees and press my hand to it. Did Deasylva linger here, as well?

"You like to swim?" I called as I scooped more handfuls of sand onto my clothes to scrub the grime free. Soot and ash ballooned out with each pass. I might have to turn the clothes to rags after this.

"Yes, but it's too cold to swim near Balmberg most of the time and I haven't seen any lakes in Letum Wood yet."

For several minutes I scrubbed, he swam. By the time he tired of it, I had peeled all but my dress off. Stockings, shoes, scarf, lay scattered across the sand under the warm sun. My skin smarted from being scrubbed clean. I worked soft, gray soap that I had summoned from home slowly through my tangled hair. Little bubbles flowed into the lake as I rinsed them free.

Merrick watched as I gently worked a bone comb through the tangles.

"You're a wonder, B."

Startled, I met his gaze. He grinned. He'd pulled his shirt off, thrown it on a nearby rock. It lay in a wet pile.

"Thank you?"

He chuckled, then strode out of the lake. Water streamed off his chest as he lowered himself onto the rock next to me, luxuriating in the sun. I brought my knees to my chest and wrapped my arms around them. He closed his eyes, set a hand on the middle of my spine, and lay back. A chill slipped over the day. I glanced up, felt Merrick do the same.

Shadowed clouds blocked the sun. Dark, ominous things that appeared almost black. Merrick's fingers tensed against my skin.

"What is that?" I asked.

"The storm from the Eastern Network," he muttered grimly. "It's been making its way across the North."

"Are we that far to the east?"

"No."

"But—"

"It's been growing without stopping. Covers half the North, most of the East. It'll cover all of Alkarra, at this rate, within a week or two."

"Jikes."

He nodded.

The elation of our hidden sanctuary dissolved in a distant growl of thunder. Merrick sat up and glowered at the sky. I tipped my head back.

"I don't want to return. Once I go back, there will be questions from the Council about the forest, and Scarlett may want me to ask the trees to fight now, and . . . Arborra and . . . I wonder where my father is? He'll be upset he wasn't here to help. I think . . ."

My thoughts trailed off, into exhausted meanderings that didn't make sense. Merrick fisted part of my dress in his hand, then released it.

"Don't think about it, B. Right now, it's you and me. That's all that matters. Give yourself an hour to *not* be the Lady-witch of Letum Wood. For an hour, be mine."

The invitation was too powerful to ignore. I lay next to him on the rock. My hair sprawled in wet strands behind me as I settled onto his shoulder. He curled an arm around my back, pulled me tight to his side.

I closed my eyes.

Sleep pulled me under.

Chapter Fourteen

Y ou trusted us and the fire has been stopped. You can see
our power?

Arborra's voice had a soothing ring as I leaned
against the wall of her heart center, regarding the maze of light
that populated from my touch. Cool vapor saturated this calm,
easy chamber in which to escape.

"I see your power."

Do you trust us?

"I do trust you."

A powerful gift.

Nightmares of charred Letum Wood played back through
my mind. I shuddered. Prevention would be our only guarantee .
. . if such a thing was possible. Besides, the trees had proven valu-
able and powerful yesterday. I couldn't discount that they were
ready and able to help.

The question was how?

*Many saplings died. We mourn them, but the forest continues
on. With time and magic, the older trees will recover.*

"I wish we hadn't lost any."

All are in agreement, but their loss is not wasted. We are empowered to help more now. We have learned. We grow. The forest craves the ability to care for itself. For all our lives, Deasylva has appointed other witches to care for us. The time for Letum Wood to stand on its own has come.

"Caring for yourself is different than fighting a god, perhaps being utterly destroyed."

Is it?

"I thought so," I muttered, "until you asked it back. You wouldn't happen to remember a god magic amulet named Nicomedianthekus, would you?"

Murmurs replied in waves, indistinguishable for language. A collective feeling of the forest speaking, then fading, filled Arborra from the inside out. When I focused on one tone, one voice, I could *almost* hear what they said. Minutes passed, as if Arborra asked all of the forest and all of the forest replied.

Arborra's response elevated above the others.

None recognize such a name.

"Unfortunate."

We remember the gods' love for the land. Their ruthlessness with justice. Their ability to lie for what they wanted. Tontes, above all, remains a blight on history.

"Why?"

He was close once with Sarena, goddess of sand and dune. Deasylva had always been Sarena's favorite, and Tontes hated our goddess for it. Sarena left and our goddess has been elusive since.

"Can a goddess leave?"

We know not where she went.

"Interesting."

That deeper intricacies lay between the gods and goddesses didn't startle me. Frustration lay in the stories, however. Beneath the paltry details we knew worked powerful beings we couldn't predict. According to Papa, understanding an enemy was only as powerful as knowing their motive.

But how to understand a goddess?

A vengeful god?

Everyone wanted something, which applied to Ventis *and* Tontes. Unfortunately, we wanted the same thing. I pushed away from the wall.

"Do you know how to destroy their amulets?"

No.

My lips pushed to one side of my face.

Can trees obtain amulets?

"I don't see why not. We'll need your help, if demigods come to Letum Wood at some point."

Then we are willing.

I would have laughed at this absurd conversation if thoughts of gods didn't have me so distracted.

"The gods are actively attacking. Hurricanes in the East and North, the fire here, and who-knows-where-else."

The cold lands?

"The Southern Network? I haven't heard of any troubles so far."

The trees in the cold lands speak to us. They are one with us, though distant. They tell us of searching and missing and remembrances and the god of cold lands and ice.

Searching.

Missing.

Remembrances.

We are stronger and more resilient than you thought. Do you agree?

The eagerness made me smile.

"I admit that you are. I thought . . ."

The words trailed away.

Silence followed.

Arborra wouldn't reply until I'd finished my thought, but I wasn't sure how. With a sigh, I slouched against the wall.

"I thought that fire was the end. That trees couldn't be healed or recover from flames. The saplings have always been so afraid. Years ago, even, when West Guards set fire to towns. The first voices I heard feared fire."

Fire is frightening, but beneficial. It does not uproot us, which is our ultimate end. Some saplings have gone to the lands and lives beyond, but many will stay. It's their path. Deasylva has plans for all her creations.

My hand rose to my chest, closed in a fist. The trees we lost would never come back. Their absence lingered like a wound on my soul. A scar. A fractured portion. It brought to light a bigger problem than I wanted to admit. The same problem that circled my head, only in Grandfather's voice.

My absolute, irrevocable tie to the forest.

You are so much bigger than that.

The question no longer remained whether Letum Wood would survive. It had changed to whether *both* of us would survive. How much of Letum Wood could die before I felt the effects?

Would *I* survive Letum Wood's devastation? Unlikely, but supposition made for a terrible friend.

"Why do the saplings speak so much, but the older trees so little?"

The saplings have much to learn.

"Can I speak to the older trees?"

Why couldn't you?

"Sometimes I want to ask them questions or know what they're thinking, but they're so quiet. It makes it seem like only the saplings fill Letum Wood."

You have only to ask.

I frowned. "Is it that easy?"

You are the Lady-witch of Letum Wood.

The loaded statement meant something—an allusion to my title ascribing to me a power that I hadn't used. The thought made me uncomfortable, but I wasn't sure why.

I straightened away from the wall, fingertips brushing the

sides. Prisms of light chased across the space to fade into the obscure darkness on the other side, where no light touched.

"I'll try that."

Promise and determination strengthened Arborra's voice, a resolution I had no real power against. *We have also been preparing for this moment, Lady-witch. Should you wish to protect us, you will not hamper our chance to rise to our potential.*

"As an army? You wish to destroy instead of create?"

We wish to live.

Their words arrested my thoughts. I released a long breath, bothered by how deeply Arborra's desire affected me. Tied into all the other intricacies, my connection to the forest had become a tangled web.

"Battle is not what you think it is."

We have seen more than you.

"I know."

We are prepared.

"I'm aware. You will fight next to me, Arborra. I promise."

It's all we ask.

Chapter Fifteen

A letter waited at my cottage the next day. Sticky with heat and sweat from a quick run with Merrick, I tapped the scroll on the edge. It rolled open as I dumped water on my face from a cup, allowing it to drip to my porch.

Blinking through the drips, I read the letter twice. A third time. For two minutes, I stared at it while water pattered the floor.

I read it again.

And again.

Bianca,

If you would be so kind, I would appreciate a twenty-minute audience with you at 11:30 tomorrow morning.

Sincerely,
Aldred
High Priest of the Central Network

Aldred?

What appeared to be a genuine signature accompanied it.

Double curious.

Goat bleated outside in plaintive sounds. My second goat, aptly named Other Goat, replied. His much lower voice distracted me as I attempted to wrap my mind around how to respond.

Yes? No?

Not a chance in Halla?

Why would Aldred want to speak with me, anyway? The fire, presumably. It had only happened yesterday, yet I'd successfully dodged missives from *Chatterer* journalists, a few Council Members, and a nosy witch complaining to me about the smoke. Why they would send complaints to me, I couldn't fathom.

Shock compelled me to answer right away, though I was sorely tempted to ignore it. A pencil popped into the air. I snatched it, scrawled my response, and sent it back before I could refuse.

I'll be there.

Curiosity drove me, more than anything. Assuming he wanted to talk about the fire, that letter should have been from Scarlett. I shook my head to break the thoughts apart. Well, I'd find out soon enough.

With a fresh towel, I headed toward the wall where a basin of cold water awaited. A new *Chatterer* scroll lay half-open on the table. Blinking headlines drew my gaze as I passed, stopping me.

Storm Rages Across East, into North. Thousands Flee.

Below it, another.

Two-Day Windstorm in West Buries Three Towns.

Fires in the Central Network, storms in the East and North, and sandstorms in the West. What about the South? In all the gathering tragedies and updates, only the Southern Network had been immune so far.

They tell us of searching and missing and remembrances and the god of Icelands and chill.

The head of the Sisterhood had reason to find out. I plucked a spare piece of parchment from a cupboard against the wall, wrote a quick note, and sent it to Alina. Hopefully, my connection with the Southern Network High Priestess still held some power.

Meanwhile, I had a meeting to prepare for.

* * *

My fingers tapped a nervous staccato against my leg as I waited outside Aldred's door.

Guardians stood on opposite sides of the hall, near a twirling staircase that led to the Hall of Council Members. The elegant marble gleamed from a fresh washing. Paintings of previous Council Members cluttered the walls and quiet salon. Viveet lay against my hip with reassuring weight.

The office door swung open, welcoming me with the earthy smell of cigars.

Though High Priest for almost two months, Aldred still hadn't transitioned into the new High Priest's office. The spacious, open place would accommodate his work and meetings with greater comfort, but Aldred tolerated change at the speed of cold molasses.

He conducted his work from the Council Member hall, as if he couldn't quite let go of who he used to be.

A vague fog lingered in the air over a desk, likely from a cigar. Several chairs clustered near the hearth, and a smaller desk was tucked into the corner. Thin windows streamed hazy light.

Not a hint of clutter lingered in stacked papers, alternating vertical and horizontal placement, nor quills and ink bottles neatly arranged in lines and cubbies.

Aldred stood behind his desk, peering at me through half-sized spectacles. He peeled them off as I entered, dropped them onto a parchment held open by two stone weights, each black as pitch. The door closed behind me.

"Welcome, Miss Monroe."

"High Priest."

With a chubby hand, he waved me into a seat across from his desk, then lowered into his own. Reluctantly, I sat on the chair, poised at the edge. My feet were firm on the floor, ready to flee. We hadn't spoken while I recovered from Alaysia and I didn't look forward to it now.

Aldred folded his hands in front of him and fixed a concentrated stare on me. His eyes sagged into his cheeks, which hung from a small-boned frame gilded with too much weight. He wore a freshly-starched white shirt, an unbuttoned vest. Crumbs from lunch lingered near the left side of his desk.

"First order of business." His hands spread, as if to encompass the room. "This is old news but . . . I am now High Priest and you aren't happy about it."

He paused.

I gave a hesitant nod when I realized he expected a response.

"I accept the fact that we may never see eye-to-eye, Miss Monroe, and I do so with gratitude. My opposition against your father was rooted in concern. There were witches in power that would follow him anywhere and trust him blindly. Greyson is a perfect reminder of why we must be vigilant."

I suppressed a flinch. To his credit, he lacked his usual cloying disregard. The directness and sincerity in his tone gave him some advantage. I couldn't help but respect a witch that drove right to the point.

"Ah . . . thank you."

"Secondly, thank you for your work in Alaysia. You provided information that will be critical to our safety and success. I wish you further improvement of health. You appear hale and hearty again. I am honestly glad to see it."

I leaned back in the chair.

Was this a ploy?

He held up both hands. "I seek nothing but to clear the air. There is no political motivation that could drive me to ask you here, you must see that."

He hesitated, fumbling for a second with his thumbs.

"Bearing the mantle of High Priest has been more significant a weight than I ever imagined. I respect Derek now more than before. My only regret is not that I opposed him, but that I didn't speak more frankly with him one-on-one."

Unable to form a reply, I simply nodded.

Aldred straightened. "Finally, to my main point. Scarlett asked me to speak with you about the fire in Letum Wood yesterday."

He paused again.

I said nothing.

With a sigh, he continued. "Scarlett didn't want to subject you to another Council interrogation again. Not after . . . "

He left the delicate implication that such a meeting wouldn't go so well a second time hanging in the air. The lift of his thin eyebrows told me all I needed to know—he didn't agree with Scarlett saving me from the Council. Arguably, he wanted me to face them.

My silence continued.

"I agreed to get your report of the event." Aldred leaned back. "Scarlett is dealing with refugees from the Western and Eastern Networks, as well as the allocation of help and resources during disasters like these that are happening all across Alkarra. In the meantime, she continues to plan for an attack from the gods with hopes of a united Alkarra."

"Are other Networks participating in said plans?"

"Most. With that behind her, I can happily take such a report off her plate."

"It's more than a report, Your Highness. It was an act of war from the god of wind."

"We are aware."

"Are you?"

He nodded, unbothered by my tone. "Very aware. To be frank, Miss Monroe, I have a feeling you don't want to discuss the fire with me either."

"You would be correct."

Surprise crossed his expression. Relief, too. He must take any interaction on my part as a good sign.

"What questions do you have?" I asked.

"Many. Before we get to the intricacies of the fire, might I interject some business of my own?"

The hair on the back of my neck lifted. I tilted my head to the side, gaze tapered. Sweat popped out on his forehead under my consideration. If he read my suspicion, he gave no sign, only a neutral expression, almost impossible to evaluate.

Jikes, had I underestimated Aldred all this time? Perhaps he played a better political game than I expected.

With a wave, I indicated he should continue.

"First, it's of no benefit to the Network or the Council if I were to support you publicly at this juncture, but allow me to say, from the privacy of my office, that I think you're onto something with the dragon idea."

Shock rendered me momentarily speechless.

"Oh?"

A noncommittal shrug removed any true support such a volatile statement would have lent. I had a feeling he meant to throw me off balance. To encourage, but not fully support. He wanted me to stay on the path of the dragons, but didn't want to say it in front of the Council.

Snake.

Aldred couldn't afford to churn the water much more than he already had. For such a leader to champion an idea of mine would upend the Council. In a glance, I understood this meeting for what it was.

A nudge *and* a judgment.

My curiosity spiked.

Aldred leaned forward, chair creaking under his weight. A finger lifted in the air. "But," he drawled, "I think you're focusing on the wrong place. You said something interesting in the last meeting about the forest speaking to you. I'd like to discuss that more before I take your report on the fire."

My entire body clenched. He lifted an eyebrow, and I cursed myself for being too transparent. Aldred hadn't asked a question, so I had no answer to give. He waited for me, then realizing I had no intention of speaking, rolled his eyes.

"Allow me to ask some questions?" he muttered.

A thrill sprinted through me at his annoyance.

I smiled.

He frowned, shifted in his chair. A handkerchief appeared in one hand, blotting at the accumulating sweat on his brow. "You speak with the trees?"

"Yes."

"And they respond?"

"Most conversations, they start."

The lines along his cheek deepened. "Interesting. They're sentient, then?"

I nodded.

"Scarlett wondered if the forest could fight. I believe she posed such a question to you?"

"Yes."

"You said no."

"Correct."

Aldred tilted his head to the side. "Allow me to review something else from a slightly different angle." He tapped a finger on his desk. "You were born in Letum Wood, correct?"

I nodded.

"You lived there until . . . well, you still do?"

Another nod.

He tapped at a different spot on his desk, as if drawing an invisible timeline. "And when you returned from Alaysia, you died, for all intents and purposes. Then you were brought back to life when the forest came into the castle and restored your breath. Also correct?"

Anxiety built in my chest. However he meant to draw all these questions together, I couldn't see just yet. Like a trap closing overhead, I could feel air escaping. Safety fleeing. Yet I couldn't walk away.

A bare whisper replied. "Yes, Letum Wood used magic to heal me beyond what an Apothecary could have done."

Aldred hummed under his breath. He leaned back and peered at the ceiling, as if in deep thought. His fingers rested on his belly, twirling around each other. The room had become oppressively hot in the last several minutes.

"Interesting," he murmured. "Considering that the forest speaks to you. One could almost say that you have a . . . *connection* to Letum Wood. A clear and obvious one. I mean, it saved your life. Also correct?"

I stared at him.

Undaunted, Aldred pressed on. He leaned his forearms into his desk. His voice remained mild, light, as if he reviewed notes from a meeting that didn't really matter instead of facts from my life that I strove to keep private.

Ignis, all over again.

"What makes this doubly interesting is your insistence that the forest *cannot* fight. Your protective stance against a magical entity that might, when you consider size, power, and general reputation, win a war for us."

"You think I lied?"

"No. I think you're scared."

I tensed.

Aldred smiled, and it reminded me of a cat. "I think you're a young woman attempting to prove herself by protecting Letum Wood. That's what I think. I also think that you *protecting* the forest will lead to the demise of our very world."

"Our world?"

"Scarlett trusts you wholeheartedly. You know this. You said the forest wouldn't fight, and she took it in good faith. Her mind has turned to other ideas now. However, I do not agree because I do not trust you wholeheartedly. Again, we come back to my point about your father—it is never wise to have full faith in a single leader."

My fingers curled into my palms, itchy with heat. Magic zipped under my skin, reminding me of the volatile days after I lost Mama. When the magic had consumed me with feral abandon. When I could barely *think* because the emotions and power were too much, too strong.

Those days had passed.

With a breath, and the wisdom of knowing that such things weren't bigger than me, I calmed myself. A full ten seconds slid by before I found my voice again.

"You're entitled to your opinion, High Priest."

"As are you. In this case, I think your opinion is based on emotions, not facts. And I think it's wrong. As the self-declared Head of a Sisterhood that doesn't exactly exist, I wanted you to face the appropriate level of critical advice. The good gods know you'll receive plenty more of it in the future, should the Sisterhood ever actualize."

"Noted twice."

He laughed. "Come, Bianca. You can be as angry as you want—I anticipated your wrath. You dole it out freely enough.

But you've never been a fool. Allow me to respect you, at least, for that."

The sneaky, underhanded compliment wasn't lost on me. I could only blink at him, trapped between the desire to rake my nails across his face and then see what he had to say. Only the reputation of the Sisterhood saved me.

"Please," I muttered between gritted teeth, "explain your opinion."

Yellowed teeth flashed in a momentary grin. He relaxed, arms resting on the chair at his side.

"Glad you asked. Shall we dive into historical precedence first? Let's discuss more recent history. The War of the Networks. I don't need to tell you all the ways the forest participated in the battle for Chatham Castle and—"

"One instance," I snapped, "doesn't make the forest ready to fight a god."

He held up two fingers.

"The Dragonmaster massacre."

"The dragons were *massacred*."

You twit, I silently added.

His chin wobbled as he shook his head. "Ah, but did you know that historical records indicate the forest attempted to prevent it? The lost diaries of the Dragonmasters have been found. They state these facts implicitly."

My mouth dropped. "What diaries?"

He waved a hand. "Found in the Great Library of Burke, if you look hard enough. We haven't even discussed the defense of Council Member Katarina Belgonne, when a pack of forest lions tried to kill her. A classic example of trees intervening to murderous effect. Or do you remember the five day war during the reign of Marcella? Letum Wood surrounded and protected an entire village from fire, curses, and dark magic. That doesn't even describe the near-death experience of Antoinne, High Priest centuries ago, saved by vines when a murderer wanted to hack him to death with an ax. The historical implications are there, believe me. Ask Hiddleston, if you like."

"I don't need to," I muttered, agitated by the lack of knowing *who* he spoke about. Antoinne? Marcella? How could Aldred know more about the forest than me?

More importantly—did I *need* to know this?

"I think you do need to ask Hiddleston, because I can still sense your skepticism. Would you like more precedents?"

"No. Make your point, High Priest."

Aldred regarded me through narrowed eyes, completely unbothered by my challenge.

"Accuse me of whatever you like, Miss Monroe," he said quietly. "Taking the throne from your father, bamboozling Scarlett. You may call me a weasel, an old man. Whatever you say, I don't care. The one thing that holds true through my entire life is my love of our Network. There are few things about this land that I *don't* know, and you can challenge me on that. My antagonization of your father came from a place of historical footing. Adoration of rulers can lead to absolute power, and absolute power corrupts absolutely."

Not for the first time, I had no idea what to say. I turned away to gather my thoughts back together. The urge to stand and pace distracted me. I opened my clenched hands, rubbed the moisture on my pants. My poorly-concealed agitation kept his attention.

Ugly as it was, Aldred had completely unseated me.

Mostly because I had little defense to give. Perhaps his words struck so deep because they rang so true.

"You want me to turn Letum Wood into an army?" I asked. "Is that what you brought me here for? Your own motivations are suspect, High Priest."

"I can accept that. Willingly, in fact. I should be questioned as much as anyone else. I brought you here to provide a different perspective. The Council isn't blind, Miss Monroe. We see the advancing gods. The fire, the dust storms, the hurricane growing across the entirety of the Eastern Network when it should be fading. Events beyond what science and belief dictates possible are upon us. Alkarra is in uproar and we *need* Letum Wood to fight.

"Meanwhile, you're being selfish. Scared. A coward. If there's anything that the supposed Head of the Sisterhood should never tolerate, it's those three traits. You pride yourself on cleverness, but I see only fear. I'm concerned you have no one else that will tell you these things, which is why I readily volunteered to call you in today. That's all I have to say on this matter."

Aldred returned to his bored expression. Two quills popped in the air, parchments appeared beneath them.

"Please, state your review of the event in Letum Wood." His gaze flickered up to mine. "Remember to be thorough. A Head of some Sisterhood would be called to *many* such reports in the future. Details mean everything."

Grateful to focus on something else, I recited what I'd already been practicing in my head, though I had no idea such a thing would be required. Something about organizing it in my brain had held vast appeal. Aldred didn't look at me once. His lack of attention helped me warm into the flow of it.

When I finished, I stood. The quills lowered back to the desk. The scroll came together. Without a word, I turned to leave. Aldred stopped me at the door.

"Oh, and Miss Monroe?"

I hesitated, but didn't turn around.

"I assume that you haven't approached the dragons yet?"

My teeth grated when I muttered, "No."

"May I make a suggestion?" He waited until I gave a bare nod. "Tread carefully. Whatever you are, Miss Monroe, it is not a leader of dragons."

Chapter Sixteen

Gently, I rapped my knuckles on a partially-open wooden door. Inside, Grandfather sat at his desk, head bowed. His hand trembled as he read a letter, peering over the top of a pair of glasses.

Papa's voice spoke quietly from behind the door, startling me.

"Come in, B."

How he knew I stood on the other side of the door, I could only wonder. Perhaps, after all his years in the Protectors, his instincts had become that honed. Grandfather lifted his head. A warm smile wreathed his face.

"Bianca. Please, come in."

I slipped inside and closed the door. Papa slouched on a chair off to the side. He winked with a familiar smile.

"DIdn't expect to see you here," I said as I sank into a chair next to him. Papa gestured to Grandfather with a nod.

"Just came to get an update on the Network at large. Can't stay long. Sounds like Alkarra is a mess right now, as expected."

"Merrick has been looking for you."

"So I've heard."

"Are you going to tell him where you've been? It's about to drive him mad."

Papa's lips twitched to hide a smile. "No. Tell him to be patient. Matthais and Baxter have enough work for him, he doesn't need to poke into mine."

"You're doing Protector work?"

"No."

I sighed away my irritation. No reason to press him. Papa would tell me when he could. After all we'd been through, I trusted him enough to know that.

Grandfather set the letter aside with a sad shake of his head. "A giant mess, all of it. Alkarra is on the verge of disaster, and only a united front will get us through this, I fear."

Papa's jaw clenched.

"What's happened now?" I asked.

"The storm continues in the East and the North." Grandfather tossed his glasses aside. "As it gains more ground, it gains more power. Flooding everywhere. Mudslides in the mountains. Fires in the Central Network. Windstorms burying cities in the Western Network. Alkarra is falling apart at the seams."

"It's the work of the gods."

Grandfather's lips twisted into a sour expression.

"I just . . . I wish we could know more of what to expect from them." He hissed out a frustrated sound. "It's all so unknown. Where will they attack? *How* will they attack? Scarlett believes they'll attack the forest first, based on information from Baxter about the goddess of the forest."

"Letum Wood *is* Deasylva's power."

"Yes," he murmured, offhandedly. "So they say."

"If the gods were smart," I drawled, musing now, "they would attack more than just the trees, but the circle of the ancients."

Papa frowned.

"Deasylva's circle of power. I think all the gods and

goddesses have one." My gaze tapered. "Prana does, for sure. She took me there a while ago."

The unexpected trip into Prana's kingdom with Sanako weeks ago had been unwelcome and terrifying. I shuddered, recalling the cool ocean, the fish swimming past.

"The gods have circles too?" Papa asked.

I shrugged. "I believe so."

Grandfather's thoughtful silence followed. "Circle of the ancients. Interesting."

"If you ask me, the gods will attack there."

A distant whisper resurrected in my mind.

It is, Arborra said, *as you say.*

Grandfather leaned forward, scribbled something on a piece of parchment. It whisked away moments later.

"I have informed Scarlett. No doubt she'll share this information with the other Networks as they continue to plan an Alkarran response. This helps immensely." His concerned gaze met mine. "Thank you, dear girl. Send any other tidbits my way. It all helps."

"I heard of a fire that attempted to crack open Letum Wood," Papa drawled. His gaze darted to me.

"Tried," I said with a blithe smile. "Didn't succeed."

He lifted an eyebrow.

"Calamities on the rise, Baxter searching for Nicomedianthekus, but not a word from the gods," Grandfather said. "Why not?"

"The disasters *are* their words, if you ask me. The gods won't lower themselves to announce anything to mere witches. They don't care about us, they care about themselves. Whatever message they want to send will come to us through destruction. We're the pawns, Grandfather."

He frowned. "Of course. I shouldn't have assumed they'd play by any rules similar to ours. Thank you for that reminder."

A grim reminder to give.

"Any idea yet what weakness we can exploit in the gods?" Papa asked. Not a burr of teasing filled his tone, which was entirely too grave for my liking.

"We know that amulets are their greatest weakness. Lose enough of them, they'll have no power. If there is another way to weaken them, I haven't found it yet."

He snorted. "Defeat a god by stealing his magic. Not an easy mission, Head of the Sisterhood. Best of luck. If anyone can accomplish it, you can."

I glared.

He grinned.

The room fell into quiet, interrupted only by the wash of a nearby *Chatterer* scroll switching new headlines every few seconds. The quiet gave me a better chance to think about what Aldred had said.

The more I pondered it, the less I wanted to.

One thing I knew for certain—I couldn't discuss it with Papa here. The less he knew about Aldred, the better.

A petite knock at the door startled me out of deepening thoughts. Papa's frown erased as Regina peeked inside. A smile brightened his face, illuminating all the way to his eyes. His knees twitched, as if he held himself back from standing to greet her.

Dark red hair, more auburn than not, spilled off her shoulders as she leaned in. Her gaze landed on me with a startled blink. I managed a quick smile, then looked away.

"Regina," Grandfather said with warmth. "You're always welcome here. Come to take this scoundrel away, are you?"

She smiled in her usual, reserved way. "I suppose one of us has to claim him."

"Let it be you, then," Grandfather said with a laugh.

My teeth ground together.

Grandfather continued, oblivious. "Derek and I are all done here, Regina. I had a few updates to give, but we've finished with that and are simply bemoaning difficult days. Bianca and I have a few matters to speak about, I believe?"

He sent me a questioning look. I nodded. Did I imagine Regina's spine stiffening?

"Thank you, Ambassador," she said. "I hope to have him returned for good very soon."

For good?

Soon?

Papa leaned close, chucked me on the shoulder with a gentle touch of his fist. He pressed a kiss on top of my head as he stood. "Take care of yourself, B? Let me know if any more fires pop up, will you?"

"You're busy with your own life," I parried back.

More tension filled my tone than I meant to convey, but I couldn't take it back now. A funny expression crossed his face. Before I could interpret it, he straightened. The door creaked as Regina stepped back, into the hall. When she was gone, I breathed easier.

Papa left with another nod, the strange look cleared into something far more focused. Whatever the two of them did together, I had my suspicions it wasn't easy, nor safe.

I turned, then startled when I found Grandfather staring hard at me. His hands were folded in front of him, eyebrows held high. The door thudded to a close behind Papa, ensconcing us in the safety of Grandfather's circular office.

"So," he drawled.

"Please, Grandfather. Don't bring up Regina and my father. If there's one thing I *don't* want to discuss right now, it's the two of them."

He lifted a placating hand. "I won't, except to say that I'm here when you *are* ready to talk about it."

Relieved, I could only nod. Grandfather leaned forward, arms resting on his desk. "What can I do for you, my dear?"

"How do you let go?"

He blinked. "Pardon?"

I cleared my throat. "I mean . . . when you *know* you should do something but you don't know how to do it because you might be . . . afraid. . . of that thing. Or the things that follow that thing."

"Ah." Understanding flooded his expression. "I see. What is it that you *should* be doing?"

"Letting Letum Wood fight."

His brow rose so far I almost laughed. "What are you referring to?"

Quickly as possible, I reviewed Aldred's advice. Try as I might to fight it, I didn't want to acknowledge that, unfortunately, our as-yet-unproven High Priest had a point.

A big one.

"The thought of bad things happening to Letum Wood frightens me. The forest will have to fight—I know that. I accept it. We'll fight together, in fact, but . . . I don't like it."

He nodded. "Understandable. You have a special connection that most witches will never know or understand."

"There's a distinct possibility that my life is tied to the forest."

"How do you know?"

"I don't. It's a hunch."

Grandfather's musing face softened a little. He regarded me, head tilted to the side, when he murmured. "These are the problems of adulthood, you realize?"

"Adulthood is the worst."

He laughed. "Yes, it's very difficult, but you're doing a fantastic job. Let me give you the secret."

"Please do."

"You trust."

"In what?"

"The forest. In its will to live, in its desire to learn and grow. The only way we learn and become a better version of ourselves is to stumble. So . . . you let the forest stumble. The more you hold it back, the more difficult it becomes. Basic teenager arithmetic, if you ask a parent."

"But . . . something might go wrong and it'll die anyway."

"It might."

I blinked. "So . . . I just let it die?"

"I have my doubts it will be that drastic, whatever happens. *You* certainly have done many things wrong, yet here you are. Consider your mother and father and what they went through, sending you to school with Miss Mabel. Yet, they trusted you."

I opened my mouth to counter, then closed it. A sparkle in his eye told me he'd anticipated such a thing.

"Didn't Letum Wood rally to your side during the fire?" he asked.

"Yes. Perfectly."

He leaned closer. "It will do so again. You have powerful instincts, my dear. Sometimes, they can work against you and to the detriment of the things you love most. Trust yourself and the forest. It's the only way this will work."

"That's . . . scary."

"The best things in life often are. Don't think too hard on this one, B. Let yourself feel it, and the opportunity will come. Soon, you'll understand what to do. Trust yourself first, and all the rest will follow."

"Is it that easy?"

Another laugh. "It's that *simple.* Easy is an entirely different word, my dear. Use it very carefully. Now, if you're not busy, will you come to my apartment? I have some new herbs for you to try. They help with burns. I'm concerned you may be facing more of those very soon."

* * *

Little Tomas smacked his lips, arched his back, then settled into my arms with a breath. His cherry cheeks, smooth as velvet, returned to their slack, sleepy state. Priscilla cast him an amused glance from where she sat across from me.

"How is motherhood?" I asked.

A rueful expression crossed her face. Grooves formed in her brow as she thought about her reply.

"Having a baby is a . . . challenging experience so far," she said, voice thick with bemusement and fatigue. "And exhausting, mostly."

Her pale skin, freckled and creamy, held bags under her eyes. Stress lines tugged at her lips as she leaned back, yawning into a hand.

In the corner, Ava sat at a desk. A parchment sprawled in front of her while a quill moved busily across the top of the page. Every now and then, she'd growl when a blob of ink splattered from the tip, but her focus remained true.

Priscilla followed my gaze, then whispered, "I don't know what you said to Ava, but ever since she last saw you, she's been so much more focused. She asked me if we could tailor her lessons around the sea, so I have. It's changed everything."

I smiled. "She just needed to know why learning mattered."

A thoughtful expression followed. She shook it off. When Tomas gave a little mewl of sound, stretching his thin arms above a head of wispy hair, I handed him back. She accepted him with a coo and a warm smile.

When her gaze returned to me, concern filled it.

"I have a favor to ask," she murmured. "That's why I sent a message to see if you could come."

"Anything."

"Can you check on Niko?"

"Why?"

She worried at her bottom lip with her teeth. "I haven't heard from him in days, what with the storms ravaging the East and North. He was sending messages, and came to see Tomas as much as he could, but . . . I haven't heard in awhile. I'm worried. The *Chatterer* reports are so frightening, and the storm so big."

Outside, a gray mat of clouds had moved in overnight. No rain, no wind, just silent, steady sky cover. Both of us glanced at the window, then back, and shared a dark look of uncertainty.

Tears filled her eyes, sparkling in the muted light. She attempted to blink them away, but one dropped down her cheek. She wiped at it with the back of a hand and a pathetic chuckle.

"I'm sorry, I'm so emotional these days."

I reached across the space, grabbed her hand. "No apologies. Of course I'll go check on Niko. I can go now. I was just going to wander around Chatham to see if demigods had appeared anywhere. Nothing to report."

"Really? I didn't expect you to take off so soon, but I'd be so grateful."

I nodded.

Relief rippled through her. "Thank you, Bianca. I don't even care if you talk to him, I just want someone to see that he's all right. I can't stop thinking about him, and I'm worried. Celia took the *Chatterer* away so I couldn't read the headlines anymore, which has helped."

"Probably wise."

Tears brimmed in her eyes again. "I have made no promises to Niko, but I have finally seen him return to the man I once loved. I don't want Tomas to grow up without his father. Niko loves him so much and I . . . I appreciate the support and help he's given."

I stood. "I'll be back shortly, Priscilla. I'm sure everything is fine."

Ava glanced up, smiled from across the room. I returned it. Voices from the forest stopped me.

The ill-fated have returned.

They attack.

We shall respond.

I tensed with their words, immediately attempting to find out where. No further information followed. I opened my mouth to tell Priscilla I'd check on Niko later, but stopped when Priscilla tipped her head back, gave me a watery smile.

"Thank you, Bianca. I'll sleep so much better tonight." She laughed. "What little sleep I do get, I mean."

Hope and relief had finally returned to her face. I paused, torn, when more trees joined the others.

We protect you.

You protect us.

We have power.

"I totally understand," I said to Priscilla. "Put concern out of your mind. I'll be back with a full report soon."

Fear compelled me out of the school, into the trees. I darted across the grounds and out the still-broken wrought-iron gate. Once out of sight of Priscilla, I skidded to a stop.

"Where?" I called, head tilted back.

Arborra replied. *The demigods return. They are near a small town, prepared to fight. What they want, we cannot be sure.*

"Take me there."

We can protect them.

I paused, breath suspended. All the forest seemed to hold still while I considered Arborra's declaration.

"What will you do?"

Stop them. Obtain the amulet, as you so thirst to do.

Grandfather's advice sprinted through my mind. *Trust yourself and the forest. It's the only way this will work.* A painful lump formed in my throat, but I swallowed it back. Of course the forest could stop the demigods.

Hadn't it before?

"Do you have a plan?"

We do.

Indecision warred with fear. What if trees were hurt? Witches? What if the demigods escaped? If another amulet got away . . . Reality brought me out of my spiral of anxiety even more quickly. Hadn't the demigods disappeared—with their amulets—with me attempting to stop them?

More than once.

If situations like this continued, demigods might come in numbers greater than what we could handle. Since the dragons and the Council still hesitated in their respective support, I had to lean elsewhere. There was nowhere else *to* go but Letum Wood. Besides, getting rid of the demigods would be more than enough to prove capability. If I allowed Letum Wood this chance to fight, I could also check on Niko.

With a wave of my hand, I said, "Then save the town. Grab an amulet or two, if you can," I added as a wry aside. Then I said firmly, "I trust you."

As we trust you.

A symphony broke in my mind, so loud I jumped. Trees wove together in musical refrains, a joyful chorus. I laughed, half-startled, half-amused.

"Bloodthirsty, are you?"

We protect you.

You protect us.

"Tell me if you need help, Arborra? I need to go to the East. I'll return."

With my heart pounding in my throat, I issued the incantation to take me to the East. The distance would test my connection with Letum Wood in new ways, and my trust in *all* the ways, but I leaned into the unknown, as Grandfather had encouraged me.

Letum Wood could do this.

I believed that now.

Chapter Seventeen

Wind sliced across my face.

Seconds after my feet touched sand—more appropriately, sea—rain saturated my clothes. The sandy beach near the castle lay under waist-deep waves that surged with icy fingers, clawing toward the land.

I gasped, shoved hair out of my face. Water coated the world. Waves. Whitecaps. Wind and sand and sky.

A nearby scream jerked me to the left.

Only twenty paces away, a woman attempted to run through the water, arms held out. The wind whisked the cry from her lips —I only heard it by sheer luck. The high-pitched hysteria sounded oddly like the unearthly wail of the storm itself.

Ten paces from her arms, a small child flailed in the water.

With a gasp, I disappeared. Magic brought me closer—I landed within a pace from where a mop of curls had been. No sign remained now. Frantic, I scoured the top of the water. The woman disappeared, battered by a wave that took her feet out from beneath her.

Heart racing, I scrambled through the waves. A spell to call the child to me brought a sea-shell right to my face, slicing open my cheek. I ignored it. A flash of color appeared briefly to my right. Across the way, the mother surfaced with a gasp, sputtering, dozens of paces back now.

Desperate, I lunged.

Another spell shoved me through the water at greater speed —oh, how I missed the ease of god magic!—and toward the spot. Waves and currents buffeted from every side, like a maelstrom of rage. My chest burned, my lungs begged for air when something brushed my hand. I grabbed, pushed my feet against the sand, and shoved out of the tempestuous water.

A limp body came with me.

Waves rushed over my head as I pushed the child into the air. A boy, no more than three, I'd wager.

I transported higher on the beach, out of the waves, turned the child over, and thumped his back. Head pointed down, water ran in rivulets down his thick curls.

"Breathe!" I cried. "Breathe!"

I rubbed his chest, opened his lips. Every healing incantation I could think of poured out of me, every blessing that came to mind. Eternities passed while I waited for a sign of life. A shriek pierced the air above the howling wind. His mother. I waved an arm, calling her closer. She stumbled onto the sand, sprinting and tripping her way over.

"Please!" I begged the little boy.

A shudder.

A cough.

A tremor of movement shook his shoulders, arms, and legs. Water rushed out of his mouth and nose all at once. He hacked, gagged, and then vomited. I pulled him to his knees, rubbed a hand on his back. Limp in my arms, the groggy lad let out a cry, calmed, cried weakly again.

Rain drove into us like sharp needles when I cradled him to my chest. His eyes lolled, lips gaining more color. The bluish tint began to recede. His mother skidded to a stop in the sand with a scream. Hair pasted her forehead and neck in wet ropes.

"He's all right!" I shouted over the wind in broken *Ilese*. "He's breathing."

She collapsed at my side. I passed the boy into her arms. He broke into quiet wails, stuttered with coughs and choking. She spoke incoherently, lost in sobs, while I grabbed onto her arm and pointed to the vague outline of the castle in the distance, barely visible through the storm.

"*Castello!*"

Child clasped tight, she nodded. The blasting wind nearly knocked her over when she attempted to stand. Sand ground into my cheeks, collected in my eyelashes as I grimaced and put an arm around her. She stumbled into me. The ocean surged closer with each passing moment.

Magnolia Castle lay several hundred paces away, surrounded by water. The lower level must be half full with this high of a tide. The ocean had advanced so far. If my suspicions were correct, magic would protect the interior.

With the wind so strong, we wouldn't make it by walking. This witch must not be able to transport, or she would have already done so with her child. If I left with the boy, I risked losing her to the storm.

Nothing for it. I had to do what I'd never done before: transport three witches at one time. Myself, two others.

It *could* be done. Whether it was wise or safe remained another question entirely. Yet, nothing about this situation was safe. No matter what I chose, life and danger lurked in the fringes.

"*Castello*! Transport."

Shock widened her eyes.

I issued the spell.

The magical demand nearly drowned me by itself. In a flash, it felt as if all my reserves bottomed out and whipped me away.

The pressure of transporting tripled, as if I was attempting to shove too-large of a burden through too-small a hole. With all of my willpower, I held onto the magic, kept the spell alive in my mind. Only the short distance saved us from getting lost.

Seconds later, we dropped.

With a cry, I landed on my back. The woman and boy thumped next to me with a groan and another plaintive, weak hiccup.

I sat up.

We'd landed inside the main foyer on the second floor of Magnolia Castle, right where I'd wanted to go. Shadows burdened a dark chandelier overhead and darkness coated the walls. I collapsed back down, relieved and magically fissured open. The spell had been quick and intense, but still drained me.

Having never required so much of the magic before, I let my heart settle.

The woman cried quietly, clutching her son to her chest. He blinked in a sluggardly way, lips faintly pink. With a spell, I wearily dried our clothes, the floor, our hair, then summoned a towel and a blanket. The mother quieted when I draped the blanket over his back. Shock glazed her eyes as she peered at me.

I gave a gentle squeeze of her shoulder.

Tears wetted her cheeks. "Thank you," she murmured in *Ilese.* I nodded, then pushed to my feet.

"Allo?" I called.

The sound rippled in the empty room, almost devoid of light. My dried dress whirled around my legs when I spun around to encompass the area, then settled. I sucked in a sharp breath.

"Jikes."

The reason for the subdued light became apparent. Behind us, wall-length windows that usually looked out on the sea now lay under water. The sea had consumed the lower floor of Magnolia Castle.

Ocean surrounded us.

I stepped closer to the windows, eyes wide. My fingertips touched the glass pane, peering into the swampy darkness. The top of the water lapped around the highest edge. Every now and then, a wave crashed into the wall with a foamy slap.

"The good gods," I murmured.

The witch approached from behind, face slack. A twig stuck out of the back of her head, giving her a wild appearance. The boy had calmed in her arms, shuddering in between breathy cries. She clutched him, wrapped in the blanket, and whispered, "*La mer.*"

A distant voice wound down a nearby staircase.

"Allo? Allo?"

The woman turned, called in *Ilese*. Moments later, a candle preceded a female in a bustling dress. Based on her lacking surprise and a sense of resignation in her tired features, I assumed we weren't the first ones to appear like this. She stopped, peered at us, and waved a hand.

"Come," she said in *Ilese*. "We go."

* * *

The Eastern Network fared worse than expected.

Bodies crowded the upper floors of Magnolia Castle. Flickering candle light and soft sighs slipped from beneath doors. Other parts of the castle lay in near silence. Servants cluttered the halls, skittering around with harried expressions. Only candlelight gave a sense of daytime to the place. The storm had blocked out the sun in a disorienting display of power.

"Niko?" I asked.

The woman that we followed huffed. Thankfully, she spoke the common language. "In his apartment."

"Can you tell him that Bianca Monroe would like to speak with him?"

She cast me a look, then shrugged.

Minutes later, she escorted me to the middle of his darkened office. I stood alone, listening to the roar of the storm, while the bustling servant ushered the mother and child farther down the hall. The mother only had time to shoot me a look of deepest gratitude before the servant whisked them around a corner. I silently wished them well.

Barefoot, I made my way to the window.

Arborra?

A mild, distant whisper replied. *We fare well. The ill-fated are gone.*

My heart thumped. Not just for what Arborra said, but the distance at which we could speak. Deasylva's magic stirred in brilliant, restless power in response. I pressed my palm to my chest, awed by the quickly-restoring magic. Transporting three witches should have tired me out all day.

Already, the ability returned.

It almost reminded me of . . . Ignis.

Waves surged, brought by gale-force winds and thunder that rattled my teeth. Yet, Magnolia Castle held against the onslaught. Fronds whacked into windows. Sand skittered against glass panes.

Necce, the city, pressed up against the flowing grounds of Magnolia Castle, would fare far worse. In winds such as this, roofs would be stripped free from homes. The sea would back through canals to flood lowlands. Crops, plants, trees, would disappear under water and tempest.

I stared at the wild storm, at a loss.

"The East has weathered many difficulties," came a purring voice behind me. "But none such as this."

I whirled around. Niko stood back there, flanked by darkness and muted candlelight. Shadows danced across the black-and-white tiled floor behind him. None of the torches were lit on the wall, nor were the candles in the chandeliers overhead. A single candle floated next to him, swamped by the sickly-green hue of the storm outside.

"Niko."

He inclined his head. "Miss Bianca. I heard you saved a woman and her son."

"News travels fast."

"It's a small castle."

"She needed a little help."

"She is my cousin." Deep tones of remorse lingered in his words. "You saved her firstborn boy. Her husband died last week, and she came here for refuge. Her power is weak with so much loss, and her transportation wasn't as precise as it should be. She landed in the sea, not knowing it had come so high. Thank you. You have my deepest gratitude."

"I'm sorry for her loss, and I'm grateful I could prevent another one. Your gratitude is unnecessary, Niko. I would have done it for anyone."

A half-smile appeared. "They are calling you the Lady-witch of Letum Wood now."

"They?"

He shrugged. "Everyone."

I peered outside. Though I tried hard to keep it locked away, I'd inadvertently brought Alaysia here with me, even in title. The thought made me uncomfortable, though I cherished the name. With a lift of my hand, I motioned outside in a bid to change the subject.

"Priscilla sent me to check on you. She's worried about you."

A gaunt expression crossed his face when his lips pressed into a grim line. "What day is it?" he rasped.

"Third day of the week."

He blinked, astonished. "It cannot be."

"She hasn't heard from you in three days. She's worried. I told her I'd come. I had no idea . . ."

Niko lowered into a chair, head in his hands. "Of course I

didn't mean to worry her. I . . . I simply didn't realize how much time had passed. I have been trying to save Necce and witches and the castle. It's . . ."

He trailed away.

"I'm sorry, Niko. She's not upset, simply worried."

"My son?"

"Beautiful. Healthy. Both of them are doing just fine."

Relief brought tears to his eyes. He blinked them back. "He is my greatest miracle."

Niko stood, this time on firmer emotional ground. "Please, give Priscilla my apologies. I simply—"

I put a hand on his arm. "She'll understand. She was concerned for you, Niko. That's all. She wanted me to make sure that you were all right."

"She cares that much?"

I nodded.

Interest cluttered his eyes, then faded. Accepting what I said with a nod, he gestured outside, to whipping winds and bleak, gray rain. Powerful magic was the only thing that lay between the interior of Magnolia Castle and the ocean. Window reinforcement spells, for one. Spells to prevent the collapse of walls and foundations, for another.

The ancient magnolia trees outside the castle continued to stand. Their branches were just visible above a wave every now and then. White petals freckled the raging sea.

"My witches move inland," he murmured, "though there isn't going to be much help there for a long time, as rain and flooding are everywhere. The next highest ground is the Northern Network, but the storm extends there."

"As if someone knew how to make this as lethal as possible."

"And Geralyn closed her borders to all lower Networks," he muttered.

I sighed.

"Letum Wood is a little higher than the East." I chewed my bottom lip. "Above the marshes on that side of the Eastern Network, at any rate. What if you send your witches into the forest?"

The lack of surprise—or revulsion—in his expression made me think that this idea must have already occurred to him. That, or Niko improved in his political alacrity every day.

"My witches are . . . quite afraid of Letum Wood."

A hint of amusement colored his tone, dampened by the macabre background of Alkarra in this moment.

"Can't say that I blame them."

He chuckled through his nose. "Coming from any witch but you, that would not be as funny."

I cracked a wry smile, then sobered. When I turned to face him, he matched me. The distance had closed, lending my first real view of his face. His dark eyes, like coffee grounds, held a great deal of weight. Fatigue. An inexhaustible . . . something . . . lurked in the background of his morose voice.

Arborra, will you protect witches from outside the woods?

The question had only just been issued when a response came.

Send them.

"Send your witches to my forest. Letum Wood is expecting them."

Niko laughed, incredulous. He sobered when I gave no response.

"You are serious?"

"Very."

For a second, he floundered. His brow lowered. "Your Council would not approve. I cannot send refugees into Letum Wood without speaking to Scarlett first. It's political suicide in a tempestuous time. Scarlett has given refuge to my Council but . . ."

"It might be an issue with the Central Network Council,

but they don't really care about the forest. You know Scarlett would stand up for you, and so would I."

At that, his amusement deepened.

I scowled.

"It's not enough, Bianca."

"The Council doesn't need to know. We'll keep your witches close to the Eastern Border, anyway. I guarantee their protection."

Niko blinked, then tilted his head to the side. His voice was a mere murmur. "Bianca Monroe, are you suggesting that we subvert your leaders?"

"No. I'm suggesting we save your witches. You have the permission of the forest—that's all you need. If you *were* to send your witches into Letum Wood, say through the village of Poitier, then they might find a natural wooden archway there. Two trees that grew together to form a sort of arbor."

With my hands, I drew an archway in the air. Niko didn't take his gaze off of me as I continued.

"Vines grew around the arch. If you see it from either side, it looks like a doorway. Should they go through there, there would be trails that would lead them into safer places to stay. Your witches would be on high ground, far from the heart of Letum Wood where the dragons lurk, and they'd be there with the blessing of the Lady-witch of Letum Wood."

I paused, searched deeper. The magic responded to my call, and voices from far away lifted.

We protect you.

You protect us.

"They're waiting," I said confidently. "My forest will keep them safe. The Lady-witch of Letum Wood promises it."

"And the Council?"

"Let me deal with them," I muttered.

He paused, quiet in contemplation for several moments. Flashes of lightening and growls of percussive thunder rent the air. The windows buffered some of the sound, but memories of the Heart of Alaysia still rambled through me, all the same.

"How can I repay you?" he asked.

"No repayment. Alkarra is one land. We need to unite, fight for each other. If we have any hope of surviving, we'll forget about Network borders and work together. This is us against the gods."

"I will send messages to the Coven Leaders attempting to keep the peace." He paused, jaw tense, then said on a breath. "Tell my son I will see him soon. And tell Priscilla . . . tell her that I appreciate her. I look forward to being with them both again."

Chapter Eighteen

rees surrounded the quaint forest town of Niffe, which boasted few residents—fifty, on a busy day. Thirty on an average day. Ten different buildings lay inside the circle of trees. A bakery, an apothecary, and several homes. Such a quiet, calm place for demigods to attack, just like the schoolroom on the edge of the forest.

Trunk to trunk, the forest formed a nearly-impenetrable wall. Vines, branches, roots, all manner of forest items, conspired to pack the arbors as close as possible, creating a barrier that I crossed only because trees shuffled to the side when I touched their bark.

A rustle in the branches overhead caught my attention as I stepped back out of the circle. A lone, male forest lion lounged not far away. He panted in the thick air, long tail wrapped around the trunk where it rested. His bushy mane lay limp, streaked with darkest brown to lightest yellow. He ignored me, gaze fixed on the town.

I crept by, eyeing him warily.

Inside the safe bubble, witches peered out of their homes. A few brave souls ventured out. Smoke ringed the ground outside the wall of trees where demigods had attempted to burn the homes. Wet earth, and the air, heavy with humidity, had stopped and suffocated their attempts.

Other violent means lay scattered in disarray. Axes broken in half. Shattered saws. A shoe had been left behind, and so had a shirt. Not Alkarran, by any appearance, but the rough home-spun of Alaysia.

Chatterer journalists milled around, speaking to any witch they could find. A few kids scampered from house to house, stumbling over exposed roots that hadn't been there before. Grooves formed in the ground where trees had once been but had moved to form their protective stance.

Amidst all the proof, I could only think of Aldred.

Turquoise light rimmed my fingers when I trailed my hand along a trunk. With Arborra in mind, I silently asked, *What happened?*

Dozens of stories bubbled to the surface, all of them bright images. Given from the trees that surrounded me, I realized.

The ill-fated came.

We protect yours.

They will not return.

We have power.

Demigods I hadn't seen before appeared in the mental retelling. One square amulet—larger than I expected—amongst a group of nine. The amulet was stark purple, through and through, with no hints of other colors.

Vinartaramet, for sure, with its signature, deep color and lack of movement.

Based on the flashing recollections, the attack on Niffe had been an awkward, uncoordinated affair. Another desperate gasp of attention.

An attempt to do . . . something.

You protected them, I said with warmth, allowing the forest to hear my delight. *Thank you, my friends.*

Thrilled voices joined. Branches shivered, the leaves twirling. I smiled, unable to help myself, and straightened up. A quieter voice broke through the rest.

For you.

Light raced through the earth, zipping in a line from my feet, through the forest floor and to a tree not far away. I padded closer to find a chattering gnome at the base of a tree. A larger-than-normal oak, with knotted branches twisting into the sky like gnarled fingers.

I hesitated a few steps away. The gnome squeaked. It held a javelin in one hand, a blunt stick with the other. Dingy leaves tied with old roots draped its body. Dirt smudged its fat face, the eyes nearly lost in deep cheeks. It muttered under its breath, a steady, current of unintelligible gibberish that stopped the moment I approached.

I paused.

The gnome tilted its head, issued a screech, then leapt in the air. The leaves around its waist suspended high, fluttering, then the gnome disappeared with a pop. A glimmer caught my gaze right where the gnome had been standing, cradled in the juncture of several roots. I sucked in a breath.

"An amulet?"

On top of the bark, nestled in bits of wood and leaves, lay a butter yellow amulet with a slate-colored center. Light glinted off the outside surface. A Ventis amulet named Dapple-donamikota, if I recalled correctly.

We protect you.

You protect us.

We have power.

"How?" I whispered, hoarse. "How did you do it?"

Letum ivy sprouted from the ground, crawled around my ankle, and wrapped halfway up my leg. With the touch, I felt a zip of power, then understanding. The tree, in combi-nation with vines, managed to trip a demigod, steal the amulet, while one of its branches pinned the demigod to the ground.

The burrowing gnome had taken the amulet underground until now. I reached out, touched the amulet. The smooth facets felt like silk under my fingertips. Within the complicated slants and cut of the gem, clouds moved. The roiling lemon color faded to dark gray, then silver. I regarded it with surprise.

So intricate and complicated. Deathly beautiful, in all the most frightening ways. If it didn't belong to, and represent, a most vindictive god, I would almost long to own it myself.

"Thank you," I whispered.

More voices surged with delight. Excitement lay in the air, palpable.

"You did well."

We protect you.

You protect us.

We have power.

"Were any trees hurt?"

The question dampened enthusiasm, but only slightly. More darting blue light led my gaze to the side. A tree cut halfway down, hacked by the demigods. White chips of bark spewed on the ground around it, near a destroyed ax head. I pressed my fingers to the fresh spot. A dying cry issued from the tree. More keen than word, until it slowly wound down, snuffled out.

My heart ached with it.

Despite the fading tree, the rest exulted in their victory.

"Bring me to you, Arborra," I commanded.

The forest obeyed.

Moments later, I stood in Arborra's peaceful heart center, amulet hanging at my side. The darkness was a welcome, cool place. The light brightened more than ever, giving life to the excited hum below the surface of the forest. The tonal voices, so deep they were nearly indistinguishable, joined a steady song.

We have done well, our Lady-Witch.

"You have."

You are pleased?

"Yes. I will take the amulet to Gelas. You have made a significant, positive impact."

Delight ran through the trees in bright choruses. Their voices modulated on their own. The forest and I had become so in tune that rarely did I feel overwhelmed by the power anymore.

"I went to the East and made a promise on your behalf. That's what I asked you about from afar."

Press your hand to the wall. Tell us about the witches.

Hesitantly, I obeyed. Familiar strands of light slipped from my fingertips and into the trunk. Memories. Like miniature will-o-wisps, cavorting from my mind to Arborra's ancient heart. Arborra made a low, keening sound.

We see what you have done, Lady-witch. The promise given to the witch in the distant land of the sea. The promise you made for us to provide safety.

"Will you still take the witches?"

Gladly.

"I'm happy to hear that."

We desire more tasks, more ability. To house witches is little. The forest is ready to fight. With you as our leader, we can save Alkarra and our goddess.

With a hand pressed to the bark, I whispered, "I know you want to fight. I sense your eagerness, but we don't create the battles. This time, we have to let them come to us, and they will continue to come. Watch for demigods?"

This, we can do.

"We need more amulets."

We will be ready.

"You are the seat of Deasylva's power. Your strength and presence provides hope of witches surviving the war of the gods. You serve us best by remembering that."

As thus, Arborra murmured, *we must wield our power and under the right authority.*

I straightened. "Authority?"

Your authority.

"Deasylva is your authority, Arborra. Not me. We're in this together."

This is who you are.

"I disagree."

Often.

My lips rolled to suppress a smile. A tree with a sense of humor?

Yet another delight.

All levity faded away. "I'm grateful for your work, for the amulet. The witches you saved are also grateful. I'm . . . sorry for those we lost."

We have accepted this path. We know that all will not survive. When will you accept it also?

Nightmares resurrected in my mind. Screaming saplings. Raging infernos of fire, ripping through tree tops. The billowing clouds that left only devastation and char in their wake. It formed a pit deep in my stomach. I pressed a hand to it, lost in the helpless sensation.

"That is not an outcome I will ever fully accept. The fight is here, Arborra. Continue to do what you have done. Protect witches, find amulets, defeat demigods. Until the gods make a final push, it is all we *can* do."

We shall.

Arborra's voice retreated. Light faded. I remained in the pulse of the center of Letum Wood, lost in a tree.

And in myself.

* * *

Bianca,

Your message was received, and with glad tidings. Gelas and Ignis will hold the amulet until Nicomedianthekus is found, at which point they will destroy.

Any obtained amulet is a win. Gelas will meet with you in two days, at Zamok Castle, so you can deliver it.

As you're probably aware from Merrick, no updates on Nicomedianthekus. We continue to scour Alkarra, to little avail.

I can't help but think we're not on the right track.

Baxter

* * *

An army of rapscallion weeds infiltrated my garden, and I declared war with a pickax and a shovel.

My tender shoots of green-and-purple lettuce fought for life and sun. The obnoxiously pink rapscallion weeds littered the ground, crawling like ivy, but with leaves as big as my arm. Thick vines wound around anything they traversed, then twisted in a crushing grip. They blocked sunlight for the seedlings and sucked up all the nutrients. My winter stores of dried greens would suffer prodigiously, and I wasn't about to let that happen.

Though I wouldn't say no to all the dinners Miss Celia might spell my way should I not have enough to eat . . .

Thunder grumbled as I yanked another rapscallion. Broiling clouds lingered. Thin, but dingy. No rain so far, but promises lingered on the horizon. Meanwhile, panicking witches bought out food in the stores and retreated to country estates in preparation for Tontes' arrival. Ventis swept the clouds farther over the Network with every passing hour.

"Nasty buggers," I muttered as a rapscallion wilted in my hand, turned gray. The color leached into the ground in pearls of a thin, pink liquid. They sizzled before disappearing into the soil. Another rapscallion sprang up immediately in the exact spot the other had occupied.

Fantastic.

My fingers dug into the rich earth to search for its root source while not disturbing my greens. A few paces away, Goat wandered her rickety pen. Other Goat chased her. She bleated to avoid his untoward advances. I chuckled again.

Springtime next year, I hoped for a new baby goat and more milk. Leda had sent me a spell from a grimoire on food preservation that would keep goat cheese mold-free through the winter.

With an incantation, a burst of flame eliminated the new rapscallion start.

"Ha! Got you," I muttered.

Dirt stained my fingertips, and scorch marks decorated my skirt by the time I finished eliminating the rapscallions. I sat on the porch, barefoot, my skirt pulled up to my knees with my favorite spell, though I normally used it while running. Honeysuckle thickened the air. With the clouds came a cooler day, and I relished the lack of intensity.

"Bianca?"

My eyes flew open. Michelle stood a few paces away, holding onto little Sanna's grubby three-year-old hand. Sanna squealed, then threw herself across the yard and into my waiting arms. I clasped her little body close.

"Sanna!"

She jabbered incessantly. Thanks to practice, I understood every third word, which helped me gain enough context to figure out she'd found a new flower that her baby sister, Isadora, had attempted to eat.

Michelle shuffled forward a few steps. Baby Isadora was

strapped to her chest, facing out. Isadora giggled, drooling down a bright smile.

"Merry meet," I called as Sanna made herself comfortable in my lap, barely stopping for breath before another story flew out. Michelle gave an uncertain half smile.

"Sorry to bother you. Is this a bad time?"

"No. Have a seat."

She eyed my filthy dress, the streaks of char on my arms, the dirt along my fingernails, then the towering pile of brittle stalks at my back. Growing amusement lifted the edge of her lips.

"Rapscallions?"

"You deal with them too?"

"All the time." She settled next to me. "They tend to find my lettuce. Most of the spells in grimoires don't work."

"Nothing was as effective as my righteous indignation and rage."

"Fire too, I presume?"

I laughed. "Figured that out after too long."

"I'm still not sure who won, just looking at you."

"Today, I am victorious."

"Wait until tomorrow," she said with a tired smile.

My joy deflated.

Michelle chuckled as she positioned herself on the stairs. Sanna wriggled her way off my lap and into the dirt in front of my porch. Several flat rocks scattered the area off to the side. She propped them into a pile, chattering about worms as she stacked all four on top of each other. Isadora gurgled, amused by the sound of her own lips.

I brought my legs up to my chest, resting my arms on top of my knees. "How are you? I'm glad you came by. It's been a while since we've spoken."

The first hint of nervousness appeared on her face. "Nicholas doesn't know I came. If . . . if possible, I'd like to keep it that way."

Concern had me on guard immediately. I straightened.

"Everything all right?"

She hedged a smile, a hand held up. "Fine. He's fine, I'm fine, the girls are fine. Nicholas would never harm me. It's nothing like that."

I relaxed back.

Michelle frowned into the forest. "I wanted to talk to you about the dragons."

Shock rendered me momentarily speechless.

"Me?"

Michelle chewed on her bottom lip for a moment. "Yes. The dragons have been . . . well, unusually agitated lately. Nicholas said that they're wanting to fight the gods. He's told them what's happening with the storms in the East and the flooding in the West. Reebis demands updates every morning."

"Reebis?"

"The red one."

"Oh. Really?"

She nodded uneasily.

"All right," I drawled, "but what does all that have to do with me?"

"Reebis wants to meet with you."

My mouth opened, but I didn't know what to say. She held up a staying hand and kept going, as if the words would get locked inside should she stop.

"Nicholas has told her no so far. Mostly for safety, I think."

"He doesn't trust Reebis?"

Michelle shifted. Her gaze dropped. In the face of her discomfort, understanding flooded me.

"Oh. He doesn't trust me."

"It's just that the god magic and . . . and then there's Alaysia and . . ."

She paused. A manulele bird darted behind us, buzzing through the air with fast, near-silent wings. Sanna shrieked when her giant tower collapsed into a pile, then destroyed the rest by jumping on it with her bare feet and cackling.

Oh, she fit her namesake, all right.

Michelle sighed. "Honestly, he's been so busy attempting to stockpile food and weapons that I haven't had a chance to dive into it with him. Whatever the dragons are, or aren't, they have never been fond of you. But it's more than that. He's avoiding the problem, which means he's afraid of something."

"Being the leader, perhaps?"

"Failing, I think."

"Failing who? The dragons?"

"Anyone. Me. The dragons. The Network." She shrugged. "He doesn't think a witch should lead dragons."

"Who says we need to lead them?"

She shrugged. "Dragon history?"

"If there's anything that I've learned in the last several years, it's that we don't have to do things the same way as other generations. We're new. Times change. The whole point is working together. Dragons, witches, the forest. Alkarra," I tacked on, thinking of Magnolia Castle. "Dragons can lead dragons, but work *with* witches."

"I agree."

"I've been . . . well . . . I've meant to speak with you and Nicholas about the dragons, too. I just haven't made it happen yet. Maybe I've been nervous," I tacked on. "I told the Council we should ask the dragons for help, but they weren't excited about the idea."

Michelle sighed, as if none of that surprised her.

"Reebis came to me this morning and asked me to speak with you. She's never done that before. I'm . . . not supposed to tell Nicholas. Not until after I speak with you, anyway."

I reared back. "You can speak with the dragons?"

"It's new."

The disquiet with which she said it spoke to greater uncertainties.

"Wow."

A bare, tired nod echoed my sentiment.

We sat in the calm for a moment, each lost in thought, until I said, "I'll meet with her."

"Thank you."

"When?"

"Tomorrow morning. Listen, I think you'll be fine since Reebis requested it, but I can't say it will be safe. Nor that Reebis will be . . . welcoming. They aren't exactly happy to need you."

"Understood."

Her teeth sank into her bottom lip as she thought, brows furrowed into deepening grooves. Absently, she ran the tip of her finger over baby Isadora's toes. Isadora kept herself busy chewing on a fist.

"The gods are coming, aren't they?" she whispered, head tilted back to the hidden sky.

I nodded.

Her lips turned down. She pulled in a breath through her nose, then let it out. "It's scary," she murmured. "How do I protect my girls? How do I protect my family?"

I reached over, put a hand on her arm. "There's a lot to lose when you have a family."

"I don't want to lose my husband to a war."

"You won't."

"I'm not strong like you."

"You absolutely are."

Michelle's small eyes sparkled. She blinked the moisture away and gazed into the forest. "How are we going to get through this, Bianca? It all feels so big, so impossible."

"Grandfather says the answer is in trusting each other to do the right thing. It's worked for me so far."

Her jaw tightened, then released. "Give Nicholas time? He'll come around. I know he's capable of doing something great, even though he tells himself that he isn't. There's a bigger world out there for him, for me, for our daughters. I want all of us to experience it. I'll talk to him, you talk to Reebis. When the gods come, you save a spot for my husband. He, too, will do the right thing."

Chapter Nineteen

For all the dangers I'd faced in Alaysia and Alkarra, standing before the forest dragons daunted me more than any demigod.

With Arborra's help, I stood in the middle of the forest, facing an emerald wall of lush vines that spiraled around trunks. Darkness stretched over the ground while a haze of light lingered above. Undergrowth cluttered the earth, thickening the forest with verdant leaves.

Unknown spaces soared overhead, while fog crawled along the floor. The muggy air left my hair limp on my shoulders. Trunks existed as thick as houses in this part of the forest—perhaps not far from the ancients.

When I touched the closest tree, a spiral of light blue glowed beneath my fingers, then faded.

I sent a thought out.

Arborra?

Other trees stirred to life, but their undercurrents hummed too low to understand. No saplings here.

The dragons await, Arborra said. *We have brought you to their current nest. They are not pleased.*

"Reebis asked to speak with me."

Nevertheless.

The distinct impression that the forest dragons had arrived filled my chest, though I saw nothing. Eyes from without bored into me. The hair on the back of my neck rose like hackles. Letum Wood quieted, holding a metaphorical breath. The strange silence resounded like an empty echo.

"Reebis?"

Silence.

The macabre reality made me want to giggle. What would Sanna have to say about this twist of fate? Nothing kind, that was for certain.

The dragons had always been uneasy with my power. Whether they were jealous or wary, I couldn't be sure. Now, after my allegiance had been given to Deasylva, I brimmed full of it. Without god magic to hold the goddess magic in reserve, it crashed around like a waterfall at times.

"I want to speak to you about fighting the gods, the demigods. I know you fought the ones that were cutting down trees—I saw you. I need to speak to you about them. More are coming, and we need your help."

Apprehension thickened the air, made my heart bang. I didn't fear for my life—the forest would protect me. Arborra had promised as much, and the trees always paid attention. Now that it had a funny way of whisking me around without warning, I leaned into the safety with gratitude.

A snort, and billow of heat, drew my attention to the left. A gliding shadow slipped between tree trunks in the distance. Something black stirred amongst the trees. The trunks were wide enough here to hide the bodies of the forest dragons. Though it had never been confirmed, forest dragons seemed to hold the power to blend into the trees, magically unnoticed whenever they wanted.

Considering Deasylva's power, I had little doubt it held true.

The end of a tail flickered a brilliant crimson. A serpentine voice entered my head.

You have approached.

I leapt back with a hiss of surprise. The ground shook when a giant body landed not far away. My head jerked to the right to find a glowing pair of yellow eyes peering at me from fifty paces away, set in a black-and-crimson face.

The red.

Reebis.

Amidst the dappled shadows, vermillion streaked through her scales in simmering hues, like the hottest ring of a burning coal. The glittering colors appeared bright against the forest backdrop.

A lithe body, tucked wings, and hornless head became more apparent. She had smoother facial features—not angular, like some of the males. Her snout was more aquiline instead of blocky. The lack of horns, and the graceful neck, gave her a more feminine appearance.

She bared bright, yellow teeth.

Right, then.

Feminine *and* deadly.

As far as forest dragons went, Reebis wasn't the biggest—not by a long shot. She was, however, the spiciest.

"You spoke to me." I touched my temple with my hand. "In my mind."

Reebis snarled and ducked back a step, as if she didn't like the reminder. Yellow eyes reappeared, closer.

Deasylva has gifted you with the ability to speak with the dragon, Arborra said. *It will, perhaps, make this easier.*

"Great," I muttered.

Can witches not understand basic communication? Reebis asked, voice brimming with disdain. She slipped noiselessly closer. Her body, elegant in its power, came into view again. Her wings were broad, almost translucent when she unfurled them, run-through with cherry streams. Her scales had a triangular shape.

"I was surprised to hear your voice in my mind, that's all."

I braced myself. By sheer willpower, I kept my hand off Viveet's hilt. My fingers itched to hold it. Reebis stopped moving to leer with self righteous indignation. She stood at least thirty paces away, wrapped around a large tree as she studied me. Heat made the sticky air oppressive.

Her full-moon gaze tapered into slits.

Your allegiance has been given. I sense Deasylva in you more fully now. You are a servant of the forest goddess, like the dragons.

"Glad we're on the same team."

I shuffled forward another step. Reebis snorted. Her heat emanated in waves that brought a sheen of sweat to my skin.

The god magic is no longer inside you. She slithered closer, her giant talons scoring the earth as she moved. I held my ground. Sunlight brightened the air as a ray fell to the forest floor, warming the loam at my feet.

"That particular god magic is destroyed."

Why did you have it at all?

"That's a long story. I'm happy to tell you."

She paused.

Sniffed.

Beyond the red, another shifting shadow. Hints of unnatural canary appeared in the trees, then removed. Glints of sapphire, silver, and magenta followed. The hair on the back of my neck stood up as I gazed around. Though not all of them revealed themselves, dragons surrounded me. Their collective heat changed the air.

I leaned back, putting weight on my right foot. My legs bent slightly, funneling power into my thighs. My left elbow shifted back, opening the way for me to grab Viveet the second I needed to.

Reebis swung back to me with a hiss. Flames sprouted from her lips, flowing toward me. Heat pressed me back. Sweat popped up on my spine, trickling down, as I ducked away.

"If you don't want to hear, that's fine. You can just say no."

We have no ties to witches, no obligation to protect.

"I'm aware."

Yet, you desire our protection.

I almost said *I never said that,* but it wouldn't be entirely true. Though I hadn't said as much to Reebis, I had said it to other witches. No telling what the dragons knew.

"You don't have to protect witches. You could protect the forest."

She hissed again.

A long pause filled the air. Though she said nothing, I had the distinct impression that several conversations continued in the background. Steam leaked between her clenched teeth. Her tail flicked back and forth, dangerously close to my knees now. I suppressed the urge to step back.

Are you the leader of witches?

"Definitely not."

Why is your leader not here with you today?

"Because she's busy."

Not a total lie, at least. The Council *had* told me to figure this out myself. And Scarlett would have sent me alone, no doubt, given the bustling affairs of the Network right now.

Is your leader a servant of Deasylva?

"Ah . . . I'm . . . not sure."

Does she desire to protect the forest as well?

"Of course."

If dragons will fight with witches, would you plan this fight with the leader of witches?

"Maybe."

Reebis paused, then replied with deepest animosity. *You believe dragons should risk their lives for a witch who has not declared herself a servant of the forest, and you have no say in her plans. Does this witch know you're here?*

I swallowed a building pressure in my throat. "Not yet."

Reebis threw herself back with a half-scream. Choking smoke issued from between her teeth, filling the air with an acrid, charred scent.

You waste our time!

"It's not a waste! The demigods are already in Alkarra and the gods are coming. Soon, there won't be much of a choice. You're going to fight for your lives—or your whelps' lives— either with or without us. We would be stronger together."

Her glinting, red nostrils widened, then narrowed.

Dragons would be safer on their own.

"Maybe."

Reebis snarled. In a flash, her neck unwound and body leapt, coming within a breath of my face. Heat fractured the air as she loomed close, overwhelming me with her size, her fire, her presence.

I recoiled with a wince.

Witches have given us little reason to trust them over several millennia, and our oath to the High Priestess Esmelda was filled with our blood. We owe you nothing.

"I agree."

Reebis slipped back. Cooler air replaced the inferno, and I breathed deep. My skin flared a bright red from her fever. She eyed me.

You agree?

"You owe witches nothing, but you owe Deasylva something."

A deep hesitation stole over her. She turned away.

The dragons want to fight, for the presence of the gods and demigods is uncomfortable. Their magic is . . . foreign. Destructive. It does not belong. We will rid the forest of their presence on our own.

"Not on your own, Reebis. They're too powerful. They're trying to overtake all of Alkarra. Don't you speak with Deasylva?"

At this, Reebis paused. *That is not part of this discussion.*

"Forgive me, but I think it is."

We have our own qualms with the goddess.

"Get in line."

Reebis tilted her head, clearly not understanding. I sighed.

"Plenty of witches feel the same way. This is about Alkarra, the forest, and our lives. No oath is required, just . . . *help.*"

Another dragon growled from the depths of darkness. Slivers of slate gray appeared in the inky depths of the wood, shifting. The ground trembled when something very large moved.

A burning pair of eyes, a snap of unfolding wings, preceded a slate-colored dragon as it came into view. His thick horns, boxed face, tense jaw, and massive wings created a powerful presence. I blinked, swallowed.

Reebis shuffled back a step. *You speak to Elis,* she muttered. *He is the leader of dragons.*

Another draconian voice, distinctly deeper, followed.

Forgive Reebis her passion for our protection. We desire nothing but a removal of this enemy from without. Dark are the days when others impose on our forest and, by extension, our lives. When the time comes, the dragons will fight.

I hesitated, unduly awed by the wise, yellow-moon eyes that stared hard at me. How old was this dragon? How many lives had he seen?

"Thank you. I'm not sure when that will be. Or what it will look like. I—"

The dragons will work with witches to destroy our common enemy. Nicholas will help us understand how that must happen.

* * *

Thickening clouds obscured the light.

My legs dangled over either side of the Volare as I leaned on my palms, tilted my head back, and regarded the broiling sky. The buzz of a run still thrummed through my veins. A necessary move after my dragon discussion, which ended as quickly as it began.

Raindrops gently plinked on my face. Their coolness, more persuasion than a drop, relieved the heat from my exertion. At my fingers, a *Chatham Chatterer* rolled itself back together. I scooped it up, tucked it into my shirt.

The headline caught my gaze again.

Rain Across Alkarra.

Massive clouds bubbled with belligerent underbellies, quiet promises of doom and despair. Thick fog lingered in parts of the forest, where humidity made the air ponderous. My clothes lay wet against my skin.

The Volare shuddered.

Slowly, we lowered back into the forest near my cottage. Streams, swollen with water from the North, bustled past. At the forest floor, I stepped off the Volare. It spun around in a tightening, speedy spiral that flung all the water free. Then it rushed into the cottage, where it settled in front of the fire. Goat and Other Goat bleated from their pen, as if they sensed something wrong.

I stayed outside, my gaze still directed at the sky.

Nothing felt right.

A fat raindrop landed on top of my head with an audible

splash. Thunder followed in a low, hesitant stretch of sound, carried on a breath of wind. Memories whisked me back to Alaysia. To the beach where Tontes killed Daemon, to the Heart of Alaysia, where Ventis' gusts never truly ceased.

The gods already attempted fire and wind in their softening advance of Alkarra. What gashes, flooding, and scars would lightning and rain create? Baxter's warning replayed through my mind.

My father wouldn't settle for less than cataclysmic devastation.

The saplings and trees said little regarding the rain. To them, this would be nothing more than a sleepy, quiet day with welcome moisture. Goat made a wavering cry. Other Goat replied, so I re-secured their shelter with a spell. Plenty of water in their trough, and grasses in their lean-to.

I stepped back into the cottage, then moved inside with one last glance back over my shoulder. With Alkarra weakened almost everywhere else, the true push on Deasylva had just begun.

I felt it in my uneasy bones.

* * *

That night, Merrick crouched at my hearth, where he stacked several logs into low-burning flames. An occasional snap, crackle, and pop issued from the branches, breathing a light scent of smoke into the air.

Steady rain coated the cottage, falling from a rumbling sky. Lightning flashed every now and then, and an early darkness fell on the world. Dinnertime, and already the world lay dark.

I set two empty tea cups to the table, near a sachet of tea. Goat milk, cakes made of oatmeal and crushed Leto nuts, and fresh water from the creek waited on the table.

Merrick glanced up, a musing expression on his face. "Baxter is an interesting demigod, isn't he?"

"What do you mean?"

A collection spell removed accumulated dust from the floor, sending it out the door in a whirl. Mist scooted into the cottage, dissipating with the heat. The thrum of rain on the roof fell harder, so noisy my ears hurt. I glanced overhead.

Several thumps came from below the floor—burrowing gnomes seeking more shelter, no doubt—but they silenced before I had to stomp on the floorboards. They might be frustrating and annoying creatures, but they were excellent bounty hiders.

With comical hand gestures, a few uncertain grunts, and a *lot* of hope, I felt reasonably sure they knew what I wanted when I gave them the amulet to hide until my meeting with Gelas in the morning.

Instinct, more than sense, ruled here.

"It's been interesting to help him search for Nicomedianthekus," he continued. "He's smart. Really good with tactical strategy. Strong, too."

"Benefits of being a demigod."

He scoffed.

"How goes the search?"

Merrick leaned back, arms clasped over his chest. "We've been to a lot of places where the amulet isn't. Wealthy houses, a museum, a few gem mines. Baxter thinks it's somewhere in the Southern Network. Gelas is inclined to agree. Alina has been helpful, but it's all supposition. It's not in Zamok Castle, for sure," Merrick muttered. "I've memorized that place by now."

Tall, turreted, and built of stone, I recalled the Southern Network Castle with a shudder. Thinking of it brought back chilly memories of cold winters, dreadful politicians, and frost. Plenty of places existed where an amulet could hide in its walls.

But for how long?

If Nicomedianthekus had been missing for two-thousand years, a large gap of time existed in that span. Zamok Castle had only been around for several hundred years, so the timeline didn't come together.

"Gelas and Ignis have so far failed to destroy the Tontes amulet that Derek obtained from Dayla in the battle at Gimsteinar," Merrick muttered.

"Which builds a stronger case for Nicomedianthekus being the answer to destroying amulets."

"If we could find it."

A grim expression crossed his face as he brooded at the flames. Another *thump* came below the floor. I glanced at it with an annoyed eye roll, and forced the agitation to pass. They hid the amulet, so I could tolerate their wildness.

For now.

Merrick straightened, studying the fire as if he'd lost something in it. He turned, one arm propped on the shelf above the hearth. Firelight illuminated him in the darkening night, causing an eruption of butterflies in my stomach.

"When do you take the amulet to Gelas?" he asked.

"In the morning, at Zamok Castle."

"I'll go with you."

I smiled. "Then it's a plan."

He studied me, then strode across the room, pulled me into his chest. I went willingly, head tipped back in a smile. When all the world disintegrated around us, *this* made sense.

"That's a weird way to spend time together," he muttered, but amusement filled his gaze. I twined my arms around his neck and reveled in the feeling of his body pressed against mine.

Heat and strength.

Power and certainty.

If there had ever been a moment where I recognized what these butterflies, the security of his arms, my eagerness to be at his side meant, this was the one. Breathless, I reached up to touch his face.

"I love you, Merrick."

The words flowed from me, like a melody that had always been mine to sing. Words that were mine to own. Not a breath of hesitation, no question, accompanied them.

He blinked, struck silent for several moments. Only the tightening of his arms around my waist told me he heard. I held back a smile, my fingers playing with the soft hairs at the nape of his neck.

Finally, he whispered, "Do you?"

"I always have. I always will. I just . . . I think I was afraid that if I said the words then . . . I don't know. You'd leave again." I pressed my palm to his chest. His heart beat a firm staccato underneath my touch. "When you came back that one night, I had planned to say it."

"Then I left."

Anxiety filled me at the thought. I soothed back the darkness that came with such memories, letting it go to fade into the night. Such grief and fear wasn't needed here.

Not anymore.

"Then we started our own necessary paths for the next three years," I said.

A vague almost-smile ghosted his lips, giving him a haunted appearance.

"And we're back where we belong. I think I just needed my feelings for you to make sense in my head. Now they do."

"What helped it come together?"

"Something Grandfather said about trusting myself, trusting others." I drew in a deep breath. "I'm learning that, if I want to really lead a Sisterhood, I'll have to say no to some things, and yes to all the *right* things. Part of saying *no* is trusting someone else, and knowing when to say *yes* is all about . . . this."

I tapped my fingers over his heart. The dull reverberation

echoed through my delicate finger bones. Merrick reached up, trapped my hand in his. He pressed a gentle kiss to my knuckles and gathered me closer—if such a feat were possible.

"I love you too, B."

He sealed the statement in a melting kiss. I faded under his touch, energized by letting those words dance freely in the world for a long time after. They set something into the world that could never be taken back. An irrevocable altering drew us together. Neither of us would be the same after such a statement.

Not ever.

Thunder and rain continued overhead, slamming into my roof as if it wanted to tear the cottage apart.

Maybe it did.

Didn't matter.

Merrick held me safe in his arms

* * *

While rain continued to sluice through Letum Wood, Merrick and I escaped to the Southern Network.

Warmth came late here, but swept in with ferocity. Under its beguiling power, the Southern Network gardens unfurled with majestic glory during the longest days of the year.

The sky opened in an azure hue that stretched horizon to horizon, drawing my gaze to the herbage that speckled the landscape with varying bushes, flowers, and hedges. Pomelo poppies, with centers wide as pinecones, bobbed toward the warm sun. Not a snowflake or hint of cold lingered in sight. Longer days and short nights brought new life to a cool world.

A string of flowers trailed in a breeze. I drew in a deep breath as we slipped past it, curious about its scent. Floral and light, with subtle notes of something sulfurous. Summer warmed the air, which lay dry and silky.

Sounds of the ice castle bustled overhead. A maid shook out a blanket and a rug. The edges snapped, dust billowed. A gardener coughed. The zing of a trowel hitting rock broke the air.

"Where are you meeting Gelas?" Merrick asked. The air behind me lay empty thanks to his invisibility spell.

"Not sure," I murmured. "Gelas tends to just . . . appear. Why are you invisible?"

"Just in case."

"Just in case what?"

"I should have been."

Before I could make sense of that, I skidded to a stop.

Down the path, near a fluffy bush of yellow-and-light green leaves, waited Alina. She stood in the middle of a trail made out of crushed rocks. The path twirled toward Zamok Castle, which glimmered in hues of white and silver. The tall turrets and steep rooftops reminded me of the forest north of here.

"Bianca Monroe."

"Alina."

If she'd held magic, I would have attributed her silent presence to a spell. She had none, however. Only her prowess and training as a Shieldmaiden brought her here in such strange quietude. She wore a simple maroon dress, with elbow-length sleeves and a slight train in the back. Her straight black hair feathered around her shoulders.

"I'm glad you came." She turned. "I've been waiting for you. Gelas is this way. Follow me."

* * *

"Things have been better in the South than the rest of Alkarra," Alina said as we strode together. "Believe it or not."

"Why?"

"Gelas's direct protection, I think." She shrugged delicately.

"Not that I wish ill on any Network, of course. For once, however, I'm grateful that we have a chance to . . . catch our breath. We'll take any advantage and protection we can."

The thought had occurred to me before, but it didn't quite fit. Would Ventis and Tontes ignore a part of Alkarra because they feared Gelas? No. There had to be another reason. Though silent, I could still sense Merrick behind me.

"Whatever is keeping you from disasters," I said in an attempt to be gracious, "I hope it continues."

Alina stared ahead as we meandered slowly down the path, toward the castle. Her neck was rigid as stone. Lacking natural disasters or not, her stress over her Network must be prodigious, no matter how firm an act she put forward.

"How are things, Alina?"

Her gaze cut to me, then back in front of her. "Busy. We're attempting to prepare for a demigod—or god—attack, but it's difficult as magicless witches."

The words *magicless witches* rolled off her tongue, as if she didn't mind saying them. Alina's transition out of magic had been a difficult one. Something in the way she held her shoulders made me believe she'd accepted it. Come to terms with it, perhaps. A story lurked beneath her calm patience, instead of the fiery frustration I'd perceived from her before.

"Tipa lives in Zamok Castle," she continued, "and that has been a great help."

"Really?"

Thoughts of Gelas' daughter, Tipa, caused me a moment of concern. Why would a demigod want to live in Zamok Castle? Had Alina invited her?

Alina eyed me askance, as if she sensed my building questions. "Yes," she said crisply. "I rather like her. I find her trustworthy. She communicates with her father on my behalf, and Gelas has . . . helped us with the things we need. Better supplies for our Guardians, food in the tribes, that sort of thing."

"I'm glad it's been useful. She's . . . interesting."

"She's fierce and independent, something you normally appreciate."

"I love a confident woman. Tipa and I just . . . didn't have a great start to our . . . acquaintance."

Alina thought that over with a pause, then continued.

"I'll be announcing a High Priest soon. His name is Lev, and he's served on the Council for decades."

"Congratulations. A High Priest should lessen your load, I hope?"

Alina barked a laugh, oddly feminine despite the harsher sound. "One would hope."

"Will you be the Highest Witch still?"

"Of course," she drawled in amusement. "You think I'd hand over my position of power?"

"I sincerely hope not."

"My Council and I have pulled together a sort of . . . charter . . . that dictates a new version of Southern law that allows the power of a woman to hold precedence. Change isn't powerful unless it's available to more than ourselves. Future generations will need the initial work."

"No one better to do it than you."

"Lev is a good witch, with a strong reputation amongst the tribes. He's older than me by a great amount and has more political experience. He'll strengthen my weak points."

"An ideal co-leader."

Alina chuckled low again. "We'll see. This way. Tipa says that Gelas waits in the gardens for you."

We turned, cutting across a patch of ankle-high grass. A maze-like structure of hedges lay in front of us, the same height as me. Flowers broad as my palm dotted the front with long, thin petals rolling open. Some remained closed in curlicues.

"Did Gelas ask you to bring me to him?"

"Yes."

"Do you deal with Gelas much?"

"Weekly, at least. Daily through Tipa. Mostly as he searches for the amulet, but we have had . . . other discussions."

I froze.

What in the name of the good gods did *other discussions* mean?

Alina stopped, peering back at me in silent question.

"Really?" I asked.

She turned to me, an arch brow raised. Her expression remained inexplicably neutral. Not a single nuance could be perceived in such a face. She kept going. I scrambled to catch up.

"The god of ice," she said quietly, her voice low, "has vested interest in this land. He's expressed as much to me. I would be a fool not to take advantage of strategic alliances."

"He has physically revealed himself to you?"

"Yes, once or twice."

"Spoken?"

"Extensively."

"Interesting," I said, for lack of anything else to say. Gelas could still have ulterior motives, though I couldn't imagine any right then.

Alina lifted her chin as she said, "We're waiting to announce Lev as the High Priest until things are . . . more stable."

"Oh?"

"Safe, I should say."

The darkening of her tone set my instincts on edge. "You're not safe?"

"I'm quite safe now. When I announce it? Well, I'm not sure. Men of the Southern Network don't like change. Most of them like Lev, though, and I trust him. He's seen many trials and has slipped into his magicless state with far more grace than myself. He will rule with me in fairness. Whether that transition will go smoothly or not remains to be seen."

"If you need help—"

"You will know."

A rustle in the bushes came ahead of us. I tensed, clasped Viveet in my hand. A lithe figure stepped out. Familiar, slanted eyes regarded me, then Alina. Thin shoulders, slight frame, but a handsome expression. I relaxed.

Andrei, the Swordmaker.

Magic prickled against my palm where I held Viveet. A warming. A shot of . . . sentience, almost. It disappeared as quickly as it came, leaving me to wonder whether I imagined it or if Andrei's presence sparked such a reaction.

Viveet had always responded to my touch, but never with anything that could be construed as more than magic. Much of the Ensis magic didn't make sense—like many magical systems at work in Alkarra. Of highest question regarding the magic was how *much* Viveet seemed to know, care, or love.

Her response to Andrei indicated a depth I hadn't expected.

Alina called softly in *Yazika*, the language of the Southern Network. Andrei nodded. I didn't understand the words, but they calmed the startled expression on his face. His heightened shock dropped into something warmer, yet guarded.

Alina continued her path without breaking stride. Clearly, she'd expected such a confrontation to happen. Each step closed the space between us and Andrei. He shuffled back to make space for us on the graveled trail. Somewhere behind us, Merrick continued to follow.

"Andrei has come to see me," Alina said. "We meet out here every day. I didn't warn you because he sometimes can't show up. Since you met him after he restored your sword, I figured it was safe for you to see him here." She cut a sharp warning gaze to me. "I trust your discretion. Others need not know of our . . . relationship."

"You have my silence."

"It seems," she said quietly, eyeing me, "that I trust you more than caution might dictate."

At that, Alina stopped walking. Andrei stood close enough to touch, but they didn't move toward each other. A connection between them had been apparent when, months ago, I took the remnants of Viveet to Alina and she promised to turn them to Andrei. Until his moment, I hadn't contemplated what their relationship might mean. Friendship had been implied.

Yet something in the way she watched him told me they were much more than that.

Andrei studied Viveet at my side with a little smile. His kind eyes lifted to mine. He nodded once with pleasure. "A good sword."

I smiled.

Alina motioned toward an outer ring of gardens, where a lone figure stood at the edge overlooking the tundra. Immediately, I recognized the cut of Gelas' shoulders, his dark hair streaked with white.

"Gelas is waiting. This is where we part."

"It was good to see you, Alina. Let me know if you need help."

With a nod, she veered to the right. Andrei followed, a metallic scent drifting off him. I steeled myself and turned to the left, toward Gelas. He didn't move as I approached, intentionally noisy. I stopped to his right, a few paces away.

This wide area had no hedge, bench, or decoration. The grass faded into dry tundra, giving way to open spaces and distant sky. White peaks lingered in the far, far west, mere bumps against the horizon. Woods swooped here and there, sometimes thick, sometimes sparse. A rabbit popped out of a burrow in the ground, then disappeared again.

I reached into my pocket, pulled out Dappledonamikota.

He held out a hand.

"Thank you."

"It's not a Tontes amulet."

"Nevertheless, it will help."

Relieved to have it out of my responsibility, I only nodded. His long fingers curled around it, then clasped it in his palm.

It disappeared.

"Ignis didn't want to come?"

"This is my land," Gelas drawled. "I didn't invite him."

"Is it your land?"

After a pause, he said, "Soon enough. To your question, Ignis insinuated that it would be better if you and he didn't see each other again."

"Probably true."

Gelas turned to face me. Given the chance, I'd almost say he appeared . . . tired. Could a god lose energy? His zest? Gelas certainly appeared as if he had. Lines filled his face. His lips were thinned, pulled down at the edges. The tension in his body sent a prickle of concern through me.

"Are you ready?" he asked before I could speak. "The final advance has come. Ventis and Tontes won't relent."

"No, of course I'm not ready."

He chuckled darkly. "You're honest, at least."

"Are you ready?"

"No."

"Then we're well matched."

Gelas darkened considerably. At that moment, I longed for my friend, Gio, to return. The man with openness and bright smiles. The easygoing laugh. This version sent waves of uncertainty through me. Whatever we faced wouldn't be good.

"I hear that refugees from the East are taking shelter in the forest," he asked. "Is that true?"

"Yes."

The skin between his eyebrows came together. "Send them here, if you need to."

"Why would I need to?"

"Because the forest is about to have something else to focus on besides keeping witches safe. Prepare yourself, Lady-witch of

Letum Wood. The gods are here. You have no less than eight amulets, nine if you're wise, to steal before we have a hope of saving Deasylva and all of Alkarra. The goal is to cripple Tontes, not just remove his power. Opportunities to find more amulets are about to be plentiful."

Chapter Twenty

A day's worth of continual rain left pools of water connected by morning light, forming a giant pond outside my cottage in the low areas. Grass stems stuck out of the pristine water, harassed by more falling rain.

Goat and Other Goat splashed through the water, muddied from hoof to belly, while I moved their pen to higher ground on the other side of the cottage. Water soaked my hair, my clothes. The rain fell relentlessly, thrumming like knuckles on the roof. A grumble issued from the sky every now and then, but the worst of the thunder had faded overnight.

We protect yours.

You are safe.

When I touched a nearby trunk, my mind zipped farther away, to the edge of the Central Network. The storm raged there, too, where witches from the East hunkered below trees. Shelters of old branches, thick with leaves or needles, littered most areas. Campfires, children scampering, saturated blankets thrown over boughs for extra reassurance. Despite the weather, the picture appeared cozy enough, with small fires to keep warm.

"Any sign of demigods?"

The ill-fated are not here.

We watch, we wait.

"Thank you."

The trees shook.

I turned back to my task. When Baxter moved the manulele birds to my house, he'd put protective god magic over the area to keep the birds safe from predators, but not from rain.

Ava and I attempted to save the tiny birds' homes. She used a pickax and shovel to create drains away from their bushes to a downhill area, while I scooped bucketfuls of water away from the hedges.

So far, it appeared to be working.

Manulele birds fluttered near my shoulders, their feathers a gentle caress on my cheek. A light murmur from my throat and one of them released a warble. I grinned, unable to help myself. So small, yet so indignant.

When a frustrated growl came from behind, I cast a wary glance to Ava. She stood near the far hedge, brow furrowed, glaring at a hole. One hand lifted to a spot in the green pillar, where a manulele bird peeked out. The bright feathers, soft underbelly, disappeared.

Ava frowned.

"You all right, Ava?"

At the sound of my question, she startled, then relaxed. I extended a small burlap bag filled with seeds to her. She managed a grateful smile as she accepted, then turned back to her birds.

Sticks rested in a shallow trench of honey nearby, where a waterskin filled with seeds lay on top. She picked open the sewn edges of the bag, grabbed a clean end of the closest stick, then shoved it inside. After she withdrew a seed-coated stick, she rested it on the hedge, just outside the bird's hole.

Instead of eating, the bird hopped to her shoulder and burrowed into her neck. I pressed back a giggle. She looked like an aviary. Birds touched every available spot on her body. Those that couldn't land, fluttered.

"Ava?"

"Hmm?"

"You all right?"

"I'm just tired."

"Baby Tomas keeping you awake?"

She shook her head. "No."

"Can you hear him crying?"

"No."

I paused, giving her a moment to extrapolate. She didn't, so I pressed on.

"Not sleeping well?"

"No."

"Why not?"

She shrugged. Another stick plunked into the birdseed, emerging speckled with various seeds. Some were black and tiny, others oblong and fat. Manulele birds flocked to her, but ignored the nourishment.

"What is wrong?" she murmured in a loving tone. One bird landed on her chest, gripping a button. It rested against her heart, burrowing close.

Ava looked at me in astonishment.

I shrugged.

"Something is wrong with the manulele, Bianca. They have never done this. They act . . . afraid."

"I can see that."

"Can birds have fear?"

"Maybe?"

Ava glanced overhead. "Any owls? Have big animals bothered them?"

"No. Baxter's magic is still working. Even the gnomes have left them alone."

She placed a stick of seeds on a trench of water, then set her fingers in the bag. When her hand emerged, fifteen birds landed across her fingers and her wrist. Their attention brought a gentle smile to her face, though concern lay under it.

"All the creatures are being strange," I murmured. "The gnomes keep coming to my house and asking for bread. I leave out water dishes for them. It's not normal."

Ava gave no response, clearly lost in other thoughts.

I nudged her with an elbow.

"Want to talk about whatever is bothering you?"

Her troubled gaze fluttered to mine, then away. "No, but the ghosts inside . . ."

She curled a hand protectively around a baby manulele no larger than the space between the knuckles of my thumb. It chirped, happy inside her palm.

"I'll tell you, but please don't tell Priscilla?"

"What is it?"

"I . . . I have dreams at night."

"Oh?"

"Bad dreams. Dreams of . . ."

"Alaysia?"

She shuddered, then nodded. Her lips pressed together, tight and firm. The other hand clutched the birdseed bag so hard the knuckles turned white.

"Is it about what happened in the Heart of Alaysia?"

She nodded.

"It was pretty frightening, wasn't it?"

Ava said nothing.

One of her only Alaysian friends, Daemon, had been killed right in front of her by Tontes. Had she not returned to my side moments before, she would have drowned with him. Then demigods captured her, held her prisoner, and four gods warred over all of our lives.

Any child would be traumatized.

"Tontes is in my dreams, my mind. I wake up sweaty and

afraid." She gazed away, cheeks burning. "I get scared at night. When the dreams come, it feels like nowhere is safe. Not home, not Alkarra, not Letum Wood. I'm worried about my birds and Baxter is so busy."

"Have you talked to him about the dreams?"

"He's too busy."

"He's not too busy for you."

She grunted, but didn't argue the point. "They're just dreams," she muttered. Her furrowed brow indicated she didn't have herself convinced yet, as if deeper issues lay in the recesses.

"What would make you feel safe?" I asked.

Ava's brow created deep grooves. "A weapon. Not a sword. Not arrows." She swiped an impatient hand through the air. "Derek taught me both of them and no. They weren't my weapons. Not those. Something else. Something smaller. Faster, but still . . ."

"Dangerous to someone who wants to harm you?"

She nodded.

"I have other ideas. We'll find weapons for you to try. Papa would love to give you a tour through all his others. You've only seen the beginning."

A spark of hope appeared in her eyes.

"Let's finish with the birds," I promised. "We'll go inside and find something."

Fear lightened to relief in her gaze.

"Thank you."

"Is there something else?" I leaned closer, driven by the feeling that she hadn't said everything yet. "Anything else you want to tell me?"

Ava hesitated, met my gaze. With a blink, she turned away. Back rigid, knuckles white. Her tone was flat when she said, "No. Nothing else."

Ava turned back to her birds, scattering seeds along the ground with long whips of her wrist. A singsong tune came out of her, like a warbling bird song. Some of the manulele thrilled to it. They stayed close, fought to be near her. The unlucky few that couldn't cling to her clothes spun in dizzying circles, attempting to peck others away. Those she scolded with a grunt, a tap of her fingers to break them apart.

Trust, Grandfather had said.

The thought sank deep.

* * *

A house lay in splinters.

I tilted my head to the side, staring in wide-eyed shock. Rain cascaded down my hair, past my shoulder blades, over my spine. Streams of it grazed my temples, falling like waterfalls to my soaked shoulders.

An oak tree lay on its side. Branches straggled out, crushed, twisted, bent. Roots, like hairy limbs, sprouted from the ground. Mud coated all of it, driving past the fallen majesty in tunnels of free-flowing earth. Standing water stood as high as my knees after three full days of torrential rain.

"What happened?" I called over a peal of thunder.

The panicked saplings exploded in my mind.

We fall.

We fear.

The rains do not stop.

With practiced control, I quieted them. A few reassuring phrases sent the worst of their anxiety into calm again. The voices were high, tinny.

The tree had toppled, obliterating a forester house. Bright green shutters poked out from beneath it, cracked in half. The tree had fallen to the edge of the house, revealing hints of what had been a home.

"Were witches inside?"

We fall.

We fear.

With a growl, I attempted to push my thoughts past the saplings. They were not helpful. Behind them, older trees would speak, if I were lucky enough to hear them.

I wrapped a hand around one of the trailing branches of the fallen tree and searched for signs of magic still inside. Rain poured down the twigs, dripping to the lake below. A faint pulse of life still lived. Roots existed in the ground, which meant magic remained active, but not for long.

No witches, it said. *No witches.*

Relief gave me a moment of pause, but it was short-lived. The fall had embedded the tree deep in the mud, which meant we'd never recover the house or any possessions inside. I shoved a rain-soaked lock of hair out of my eyes. Breath misted in front of me. The steady moisture cooled everything.

"Jikes," I muttered, at a loss. "You're supposed to bring me to the demigods!"

The ill-fated are not here.

We protect you.

You protect us.

"There are no demigods anywhere?"

The ill-fated are not here.

"They didn't push this tree over?"

The ill-fated are not here.

The wind.

I growled.

The dark side of a magical forest often surprised me. Gigantic creatures. Hungry predators. Vines that crawled around your neck at night and choked you slowly. Spots where magic didn't work, and others where nothing *but* magic lived. All of it was frightening and unpredictable.

These drenching rains were something else entirely.

Swollen streams. Flooding lowlands. Mudslides and falling trees and dying, water-logged bushes. Entire meadows had been flooded in landslides last night, whisking saplings, bushes, and any familiar landmarks away.

Though I expected the worst, I'd still underestimated what so much water could do in Letum Wood. Mistook Tontes and Ventis' brute-force personalities and tactics for impatience. The long-term game of wearing the land down in order to conquer it hadn't occurred to me.

Until now.

"How do we fight this?" I murmured, palm pressed to a tree. A hope for sloping, blue letters filled my chest with a fluttering sensation. It died away when no answer from Deasylva came.

The stronger trees held deep roots—they didn't panic yet. The ancients would be safe against most major ills. The saplings held the greatest fear, and had reason to fear. Many of them fell, born down under the combined wind and rain.

Beneath the screeching panic of the saplings, new voices arose.

The saplings give way in the wind.

We must fight this enemy.

We are stalwart.

"How?" I shouted, arms spread. "How do you want to fight endless rain for days on end? I'm open to ideas!"

Silence replied.

It falls.

We fall.

To the enemy, we must fight.

"If the demigods aren't here, no one will fight. Not even you. Stupid gods of wind and thunder!" I threw a stick into the fallen oak. "They know exactly what they're doing! They're weakening the forest, denying us a chance to steal their amulets by holding their demigods back, then they'll attack. You'll get your chance, all right?"

The buzzing energy fell into silence.

Frustration seethed through me as I sloshed away from the

house. My rage began to ebb. This situation had nothing to do with Letum Wood, but I still felt annoyed by everything all the same.

"I'm sorry!" I called. "I'm . . . frustrated."

The cry of a baby stopped my rampage away from the destroyed home. Shocked, I lifted my head and gaped.

"Oh!"

I shifted back, prevented from falling only by the presence of the Volare behind me, off which rain trickled in rivulets. A man, a woman, and a baby stood under a hastily-created lean-to near a tree. They studied me with great suspicion.

Right.

Who could blame them? I'd just screamed at the *trees*.

Water-logged hair and bright red noses indicated they'd been outside for some time. The woman bounced her child, patting it on the back. "I'm sorry about your home," I cried over the falling rain.

The man stepped forward. I didn't move, allowing him to study me. "You're the forest lady?" he called. "The one that they say talks to the trees?"

Jikes, what a reputation.

Reluctantly, I nodded.

He waved to the fallen tree. "What're we supposed to do now? Our home is gone to this confounded rain. The newscrolls say it's the god of thunder and god of wind, but that's idiotic."

"It *is* the god of thunder and the god of wind causing this."

The man blinked.

"There are resources at Chatham Castle," I continued, too tired to have *this* discussion again. Several had already occurred over the last day. "You can go there. They'll find shelter for you."

A scowl crossed his expression. "Don't want to go there." His filthy face and missing teeth likely meant he'd rarely—if ever —left the forest.

I gestured around us. "You're free to go somewhere else, but the whole forest has started to look like this. You won't find shelter in Letum Wood. All the refugees from the East are transporting to the South now. Do you want to go there?"

His frustration deepened. The baby let out another squall from beneath a pile of blankets. With a thought, I sent the Volare to the three of them. It elongated and widened, then hovered overhead, repelling the water. The woman jerked away, then stopped. A small smile appeared on her face when she realized her shelter.

The trees stirred.

Now wasn't the time for social norms. I tilted my head back and shouted over the thundering rain, "Can you help them or not?"

A pause, then, *We know the way.*

We shall guide.

We save you.

Relieved, I turned back to the forester. "The forest has a place for you to stay so you don't have to leave. Don't be afraid."

A path formed at the man's feet, shimmering at the top of the water. Watery lines twisted into the bushes, leading away from the fallen tree. He glanced down, saw the path. Shock glazed his features.

I nodded to it.

"Get out of the water, avoid the younger trees. You can get food from the castle, because there's nothing left to forage here anymore. Good luck."

Reluctantly, they obeyed. Minutes later, I stood alone again, regarding a forest that had nearly become an ocean. My lip curled over my teeth when a rumble of thunder broke the sky. A signature from Tontes.

"Get out of here," I muttered.

Lightning crackled in response.

* * *

Twenty minutes later, I peered out of a window. Raindrops raced down the panes, chasing shadows. They merged, split, disappeared, and faded into the same murky gray from which they'd come. Letum Wood lay in a vague haze of green.

I stood against the far wall of Scarlett's office, where no Underassistant would run into me, nor Guardian detect as they strolled past. With Leda in charge, magic ran rampant through Scarlett's office, which kept me safe from notice. No one knew I was here. I planned to keep it that way.

Rain intensified the solemn shroud that lay over Chatham Castle. The fireplace, bright with simmering coals that kept a pot of tea warm, belied a sense of fear in the air. The grim expression in Hiddleston's eyes matched everyone's turbulent emotions. Scarlett was nowhere to be seen.

Underassistants scuttled in the background. Leda issued flash flood reports, updated journalists with new warnings for the *Chatterer,* and passed information to Talmund through messages.

A lull of silence had fallen over the room for several minutes, giving me ample space to observe, catalog facts. I chewed on my cheek, lost in thought, while I waited for more updates to report from different parts of the Network.

I wanted to know what happened in Alkarra beyond what the *Chatterer* updated, but I didn't want to talk to anyone.

"A bridge has dropped near Stanton," Hiddleston called as he perused a small scroll. "The swollen river wiped the edges out and it collapsed. Most witches are trapped in Stanton now. It was the only way out, aside from transporting."

"Is that where two adults were reported missing after attempting to cross the river?" Leda volleyed back, rubbing a hand over her forehead with a grimace.

Hiddleston's dreadlocks swayed as he shook his head.

Leda scowled. "Blessed be. Update the board please, Shianne. There isn't time to review each warning out loud anymore, so you'll need to work as you receive them. Only report those with casualties, or impacting areas with populations greater than one hundred."

"But I'm so far behind," a young woman wailed. "There's no time to track them for the *Chatterer* and update the board!"

Leda sucked in a sharp breath. Rage brightened her pretty features, driven there after hours of struggling to contain the flow of updates, no doubt. Hiddleston held up a hand to Leda, crossed the room, and spoke to the whiny woman in hushed whispers.

Leda's bunched shoulders dropped in relief. "Daisy?" she called to a short, raven-haired witch surrounded by piles of envelopes. The woman looked up, saw Leda's flushed neck, and immediately stood.

"Yes?"

"Please update the board while Shianne works with the *Chatterer*? It will be your responsibility now."

"Of course."

Daisy hurried to a wall-sized paper—no doubt conjured by magic. She plucked a message out of a basket near the end of Leda's desk. Grids, ink, and pieces of parchment covered it. Organized chaos, of course.

Leda turned back to her work, muttering under her breath in a murderous rage. I slunk out of her crossfire by retreating to the hall. She'd go positively wild if she caught me listening in.

Once in the hallway, the melee worsened. Council Member Assistants rushed back and forth, darting across the hall, shouting questions. Guardians sprinted up and down the stairs, delivering reports with clanking swords and harried breaths. Other witches—most I didn't recognize—cluttered any available space.

Still invisible, I pressed my back to the wall to avoid a passing Council Member, then froze. I stopped a gasp at the last moment.

Michelle, baby Isadora, and little Sanna appeared only a few paces away. Water dripped off their drenched clothes. Sanna's teeth chattered, her lips frosted a darker tinge. They hurried to Scarlett's office and stopped at the doorway.

"L-Leda?" Michelle called.

A breath issued from inside, then Leda rushed into the hall. She grabbed Sanna, clasping her close.

"What's wrong?" she cried. "Sanna, you're so cold."

Michelle swallowed, her pale expression white. Baby Isadora wailed when Hiddleston appeared in the doorway. A blanket popped into his hands. He handed it to Michelle. She immediately pulled a sopping wet one off Isadora and wrapped the new one around her. Hiddleston took the wet one, then conjured another for Sanna.

"Flooding," Michelle finally managed, on the verge of tears. "A mudslide headed toward our house. The dragons warned me just in time. We left. I . . . I wasn't sure I could transport them, and then I did and . . . Nicholas is with the dragons now and . . ."

Leda's lips parted in wordless astonishment.

"Mudslide?"

No, that didn't make sense. Letum Wood had rolling hills, flat places, gradual slopes, but Michelle and Nicholas didn't live near an incline. Their part of the forest was flat, steady, with a stream that had never failed. The back of my neck prickled.

"Did your house . . ." Leda trailed away. The question died when Michelle shook her head. A sob scraped out of her throat.

"Gone," she wailed. "It's gone!"

I stopped the invisibility spell. Leda glanced up in confusion as I rushed to Michelle's side. Before I could ask, three other bodies appeared in the hallway, nearly transporting on top of Sanna and Leda.

Celia, Priscilla, and Ava. Tomas slept in Priscilla's arms, bundled into a tight knot of blankets. Raindrops sprinkled Celia's shoulders and gray hair. She gripped a basket stuffed with cloths, herb tinctures, and rolled-up clothes for the baby. A terrorized expression filled Ava's face.

"The school," Priscilla gasped. "It's flooding. A stream is flowing right through it. Swept out the windows in the north wall and the dining hall, in minutes."

Leda's head snapped to mine. A dark feeling filled my gut. "Is the flooding so bad over there?" Leda asked.

I shook my head.

She hesitated, mouth half open. Her breathy voice whispered, "Is it . . ."

Letum Wood broke into my thoughts. I held up a hand, turned my head to the side slightly to hear over the commotion in the hallway.

The ill-fated have come.

We protect you.

The ill-fated have come.

"Demigods," I hissed. "They're in the forest."

Leda paled. "Bianca . . ."

"Don't do anything just yet. Let me figure out what's going on."

Chapter Twenty-One

Rain drenched me as I crept through a water-laden forest floor, skirt pasted to my legs. I drew it higher, where it clung to my thighs, leaving my knees open to the chilly air. Raindrops plunked around my ankles. Twigs, bits of moss, and blades of grass skimmed past my calves, like fairy wings. I slipped forward a few more steps, silent and invisible.

A melody of voices brightened over the storm, a blur of singsong and desperation and panic. Frightened saplings cried over the deeper bass of the older timbers.

They attack.

We are ready.

Send them to us.

The ill-fated have returned.

Flashes of fire, and a voice, drew my gaze beyond the trees. Through branches and trunks, the back eaves of my cottage peeked out of the hazy mist. A witch—no, a demigod—appeared on my back porch. Their allure tugged me closer. I gritted my teeth in annoyance, sending away the urge to close the distance.

Demigods in *my* cottage? My sanctuary?

Not.

Happening.

Thunder crackled overhead as I slipped through the downpour, swinging around the back to denser copses. Saplings had attempted to slide closer together, braiding branches and limbs. Four trees had fallen, but were caught by the intricate webs of other trees near them. Several tilted, precariously close to crashing. They leaned on each other.

I touched them as I passed.

I'm here.

I save you.

You save me.

With Arborra in mind, I said, *Prepare yourselves. The time for us to work together has come.*

Arborra replied, blunting the chatter of the saplings.

We are ready.

I rounded a particularly thick cluster of trees to find more demigods or mortals. The front porch came into view when a flash of lightning illuminated empty ground.

"Where are Goat and Other Goat?" I whispered.

A tree replied, *We save yours.*

The urge to ask how nearly distracted me, but I set it aside when more bodies spilled out of my house. They filled the porch now, ten strong. Amongst them moved a familiar, feminine figure. The female demigod with salt-and-pepper hair. Her amulet, Herimolodikus, a collection of smaller amulets on a necklace, glowed on her chest. The dark tones faded to lilac, the edges a deep pomegranate.

My fingers gripped Viveet.

Mortals must be with the demigod. Too far away to make out whether their eye color was golden or not made it hard to tell. None of them drew me closer with inexplicable allure, and hers was the only visible amulet, which meant nothing.

Demigods hid amulets all the time, but I had a feeling *she* was the leader.

Most mortals in Alaysia had had a sickly, gaunt appearance, which made it easy to tell them apart from demigods. These showed no such difference, having strong shoulders, and powerful scowls. Above all, they appeared well-fed and skilled, with a plethora of weapons around their belts.

Mortals, certainly, but cared-for mortals. Trained, even. No obvious fear of the woman, either. Without a doubt, this demigod had sent the mudslide to wipe out Michelle's house and a stream to take out Priscilla's school. The lay of the land wouldn't have allowed such things to happen naturally.

They looked for *someone*, and I had a feeling that someone was me.

The female demigod spoke in Alaysian. The rain subdued her words, blurring the sound. Hand gesticulations swept around, encompassing my cottage and the area. She pointed straight ahead—almost to me—then made a whooshing sound, like a flood about to come.

They're going to flood the area. I pressed a hand to the trees. *Burrow your roots as deep as you can.*

A crack broke overhead as the forest moved into action. Trees shifted. Branches swayed. The earth trembled, shifting below my feet as roots burrowed down. The top of the water rippled and swayed. The demigod female stalled at the new commotion, glanced over a broad shoulder. All the mortal eyes swung around to observe the changing forest.

Deeper melodies arose from the harried cries of the saplings, who couldn't burrow to firmer ground.

What do you require? Arborra asked.

The amulet that the leader is wearing is our goal. The purple gems on her neck is the source of her power. To stop them, we need that magic.

We understand.

I'll handle her if you work together to distract the rest. I can't battle that many. Can you help me by dealing with them?

Yes. We are ready.

I braced myself, cobbling together a final plan of attack. The female demigod spun to fully face the forest, a dismissive hand waving. The register of her voice dropped—I couldn't hear her words anymore. Time passed rapidly. The mortals began to move away from my porch, sloshing into the water.

I pushed away from the tree and crouched, Viveet in hand.

I protect you, I promised the buzzing forestland. My heart hit a dull thud in my chest, anticipating the fight ahead.

We protect yours, the trees echoed.

* * *

The first mortal didn't see me coming.

I tackled him from behind and shoved him below the water. When he surfaced with a gasp, I wrapped my arm around his neck and fisted his shirt in my other hand. He stilled, nose barely out of the water, when he felt Viveet's blade tucked below his jawline.

The time he took to gasp in a breath gave me the chance to silence him with a spell. Roots twisted out of the ground, gripped his chest, lashed his wrists, then bound his hands together.

"Hold still."

He disappeared.

My body jolted. Viveet dropped into the water as we both fell. My knee slammed to the ground. Water slapped my face as I attempted to hold my unexpected weight. My other knee hit a tree root, sending a shock of pain into my hip. I suppressed a curse as I resurfaced. Viveet's bright glow dimmed when I scrambled out of the water, knees stinging.

No sign of the mortal through the glimmering fall of rain.

"How did you do that?"

Muddied and thoroughly unnerved, I advanced to the east, where the demigod had disappeared only moments before. The mortals had fanned out around my cottage, fading into the trees. I waited a few breaths before following the demigod to let the mortals disperse, lest they come to her aid and surround me.

Every now and then, cracks, bonks, and thunks sounded through the forest. Saplings screamed with each sound. Shocks hit my heart with a little crash of pain.

The mortals didn't attempt to be quiet, which only confused me more. Did they want to be found? I circled around the back of my cottage, lost in the dreary landscape. Fog skimmed over the top of the gathering water as I hurried to find the demigod.

A glimpse of unnatural white in the trees drew my gaze. I cast a curse and the sound of violent retching filled the air. A deep voice called out from somewhere else, and more vomiting responded. I kept going. Shuffles in the trees followed before the ghastly sounds stopped.

Interesting.

Had *that* mortal also been taken away?

Take me to the leader, I said.

Magic yanked me away in less than a blink. One moment I stared at the side of the cottage, the next I stared at the woman. She didn't see me—the invisibility magic remained. The speed at which it happened reminded me of Ignis. Perhaps I could use the forest more than I thought.

Thank you.

A shiver of anticipation thrilled my blood, given from the magic.

We protect you.

The female demigod stood on higher ground several paces away from a stream that gushed water like an open artery. Once a quaint brook that trickled at the height of my calf, it now cut through a culvert in a river. Tilting trees branched over it, as if reaching for each other.

As I stood there, the water rose.

The demigod smiled.

Arborra, get rid of the mortals. As soon as you fight back, they'll leave, I think. Doesn't matter, I just want them gone.

As you wish.

Gushing waves now spilled out of the forest to funnel down this culvert, as if the demigod drew the water to her. White waves crashed over a petite ridge nearby, slamming their way down the hill. The dirt on the other side of the culvert expanded, swelling twice as high in seconds.

The changing landscape nudged the culvert downhill, diverting it . . .

. . . right to me.

The forest moved me to a different spot, but the water still barreled toward my cottage. Frantic attempts to counter its flow with goddess magic proved pointless. No incantations in my repertoire could fight such a force.

Saplings cried out, upended. Roots snaked through the air like wild whips, lashing to branches of the toppling trees before they crashed. Boulders appeared out of the ground and bubbled higher as the demigod raised the earth into deep ridges.

Vines wrapped around my waist and yanked me away from a crashing tree. As I scrambled back to my feet, the earth continued to churn higher. Walls formed. The flooding water slammed into the hard-packed, magic-built partition and bounced off. It slid around the hard corner and pounded closer to home.

Heart in my throat, I resisted the urge to turn my attention and throw goddess magic at my house. The force of such water-fury would obliterate the place in moments—any magic I used to save it would be wasted.

Instead, I turned back to what I could save.

Only the reality that this could be my last chance to get *this* amulet held me to the spot.

The demigod whipped around, assessing the rocks, the dirt, the changing landscape with pleasure. Trees electrified around me like a skirt. The climbing dirt and altered landscape brought screams. Yelps. Horrified cries. They confused my mind, running through it in chaos and fear. Each tree that died felt like a rent in my heart. A physical pain.

I swallowed back the misery to get a better grip on reality. If I didn't let the saplings go, the entire forest could die.

Arborra, I commanded, *tell your saplings to silence.*

One at a time, the shrieks faded. They ebbed into quiet, until I held my own mind again. Finally free to think, I sheathed Viveet, commanded the Volare to stay safe in its case on my back, and transported to a branch above the demigod. When I tugged on a vine, it released.

Magic allowed me to turn my thoughts to the forest, a sharing of plans. Merging ideas. Like the Volare, the branch responded to my mental commands. It lowered, bringing me closer to the demigod. I clung to the vine for balance as my bare feet slid down the branch, slippery from saturated moss.

The branch tipped, tipped.

Stopped.

Hold onto me with a vine, I commanded. Another vine slipped around my waist and tightened with a firm grip.

Lower me as silently as possible.

With one hand on the vine, I silently rode the branch down, a careful gaze on the top of the demigod female's head. Though invisible, demigods had extra-powerful hearing. One errant noise and she might magic away.

She had both hands propped on her waist, studying the vista. The steady rush of wild waters as she directed them through her chiseled funnel must have been controlled by magic. Her attention didn't falter.

Once I hovered three paces above the demigod, the branch halted on my silent command.

The crash of the water filled the air, wiping out sound. At this rate, depending on *how* she structured the land by the cottage, the forest in this area would be completely ravaged.

I summoned a pair of magic-reinforced manacles from where Talmund kept them in a storage room in the Wall. They arrived to my pocket without a sound. The magically-reinforced manacles wouldn't break under demigod strength. She'd still be able to magic away, but I could at least bind her first.

A trapped breath buoyed me as I released the branch to drop through the air. My feet landed right where I planned.

On her back.

She toppled with a cry of pain and we crashed into the water together. The jostle threw me to the side, but the vine prevented me from crashing into the lake. I grabbed her arm, snapped the first manacle on her wrist, and yanked. The metal clanked shut as she jerked out of the water, sputtering.

I grabbed her hair and yanked back.

"Branch!" I called.

The closest tree bent all the way over, extending a long branch my way. I grabbed it, yanked farther, and slammed the manacle shut around a juncture between two limbs.

Hold firm, I said.

We protect you, replied the low-toned voice of the tree.

The demigod gasped; I ducked. Her wild, hopeful punch would have slammed into my ribs, throwing me into the nearest tree trunk. Instead, the forest peeled me away with shocking speed. The female's hand drove forward, skimmed my breast-bone, and slammed into the branch. Wood splintered and cracked. She shouted, wrenching back. Blood trickled over her pale knuckles.

"Where are you, amulet-breaker?" she hissed. "It must be you. I've never heard of a witch so involved in everything."

Her animosity would have been flattering in different circumstances. I hovered just out of reach while she struggled against her manacle. This temporary entrapment would expire soon. She'd figure out how to get out of the manacle—or she'd just go back to Alaysia *with* the tree.

Gratefully invisible, I scrambled out of reach of her flailing arm. The slosh of water around my ankles whipped her head around to stare right at me. She couldn't see me, but I *felt* her livid fire. She threw a wide kick. I dodged, stepped behind her, and grabbed the amulet. With a yank, the chain cracked and gave way.

She gasped, reaching for her neck.

"Now!" I cried.

The tree branch straightened. The demigod screamed, yanked into the air with the branch. Her wild shout faded in sound as the tree swept her higher into the canopy.

A guttural yell, and the hard *whack* of something firm ramming my side, shoved me into the water. It sloshed over my head, enveloping me. My lungs were paralyzed and my head swam. A hand fisted in my hair held me down. I struggled, flailing against unusual strength to no avail.

The blow scattered my mind. I attempted to conjure a spell, but the magic didn't slide together. Transportation magic wouldn't work while someone touched me—unless I wanted to transport them. The power and concentration such a feat required was outside my abilities with my instincts screaming.

Fear clouded my mind. I tried to ease it away, but it was impossible to stay calm when the chilly grip of the water encircled my body. The stolen amulet brushed against my wrist, like a shock. An electric force. A reminder.

With a jolt, I forced my mind to work. A spell transported the amulet to Baxter—I couldn't hold onto it. All would be wasted. My chest began to burn. Accomplishing one thing gave me a mental stance again.

I calmed.

The mortal shifted his weight, allowing me to orient his body in the water. I slammed a foot out, approximating where his knee should be.

A crack, then a bellow, came next.

He hobbled, but didn't release. The urgency to breathe forced me to let go of a gasp of air. The mortal held tighter, fingers clamped around my neck now. Water filled my ears, trickled into my mouth.

Arborra!

The mortal disappeared.

I surfaced with a gasp. Rain, thunder, and the distinct sound of a fist hitting flesh filled my ears. I scrambled to my feet, whirled around. Through sheets of rain, I could just make out a broad-shouldered figure standing over the mortal. A flash of red hair followed behind the first figure, and the mortal slumped over. He slid beneath the water, neck canted at an unusual angle.

"Papa!" I called, sputtering.

Papa slogged over, grabbed my arm, and pulled me to my feet as I coughed.

"We have to go!" he shouted.

Water drenched his hair. Regina stood just behind him, panting. Her white shirt clung to her shoulders beneath a dark vest.

"What happened?" I asked.

"Transport now, B!"

A strange sensation overcame me then. Trembling in my feet, my ankles, my knees. The water vibrated around us. Thunder sounded. No, not thunder . . . a sound like stampeding horses. I spun to the east and gasped. Trees dove from side to side as a titanic, dark force barreled this way.

The silence of the trees broke. In unison, they roared in pain, terror, death-cries. I froze, unable to think. Slicing pain, utter loss gripped me. All I could comprehend was the raging mudslide that raced out of the trees. It wiped out all life as it broke Letum Wood in half.

What, Arborra said in hoarse gasp, *magic is this?*

A wave of debris nearly knocked my legs out from under me. With the trees screaming, dying, gasping, shouting in my head, I couldn't use magic. I couldn't even summon the mind power to command it to take me away.

All I saw was destruction.

Loss.

My nightmares from Alaysia come to life.

Move, I told my body. *Move!*

Nothing happened.

Papa shouted. He attempted to slosh toward me through the water, but it swelled around his waist and carried him farther away. He dove, arms outstretched. Voices petaled through my mind in falling refrains.

It destroys.

We cannot fight.

We fall.

Mud slammed into my side. I stumbled, grasping for branches, vines, anything. As I fell, a pair of arms wrapped around me from behind. The smell of the forest surrounded me.

Merrick.

I gasped, let go.

Chapter Twenty-Two

My eyes flew open. Despite all odds, I still drew breath. A mountain of mud didn't entomb me. No demigod to attack. I sucked in a lungful of air. A pair of hands grabbed my shoulders, jostling me back to life.

"You all right, B?"

Merrick studied me, green eyes restless and frightened. We stood in a different part of Letum Wood. High ground, away from the flooding trees. Thunder crashed and wind gusted by, driving rain and hail into my skin like needles.

I grabbed his arms, anchored again.

"Fine. I mean, no. I'm not. I don't know. Where's Papa? Regina?"

He squeezed my shoulders. "They're all right, I'm sure. The good gods, what were you doing? I was with Baxter and an amulet appeared. I came to find you as soon as I saw it. I landed at your cottage, but it was . . . I couldn't see you. Then . . . the forest took me, I think . . . I figured . . ."

He paused, then shook his head as if nothing made sense. With a growl, he jerked me back into him. My hands shook as I wrapped my arms around his waist, let him hold me close. He pressed a kiss onto the top of my head.

"You've got to stop almost-dying," he muttered. "This isn't good for my heart."

Arborra? I inquired.

A tremulous voice replied. *The forest mourns.*

Silence followed.

Without livid demigods or racing mudslides, this area of the forest was oddly silent. The type of quiet that only comes after violence. My heart settled into a slow, steady plod again.

Reality descended too quickly. I gasped, shoved away.

"My cottage?"

Merrick put a hand on my cheek. Pain filled his eyes. "It's gone, B. A demigod conjured a landslide, from what I could tell. They . . . moved the land. All the trees are demolished."

"But her amulet. I took it. I—"

He shrugged. "I don't know how."

None of it made sense. The mortals disappeared unexpectedly, and the mud slide came *after* I had taken the amulet. Had there been a hidden demigod, perhaps? Such an animalistic force couldn't have been natural—someone had created that powerful mudslide.

"I want to see my cottage," I rasped.

"B—"

"I'll go with or without you."

He sighed. "Together, then. But prepare yourself. It's . . . well, you'll see."

With a firm hand on my arm, Merrick brought me back to the house. He transported us to the branch of a nearby tree—an old one hundreds of paces away and barely outside the devastation. He held me when my knees weakened.

Nothing remained.

No cottage.

No forest.

No life.

Goat and Other Goat's pen, the manulele hedges, my garden, the paths that created my internal map of my world. The one my heart knew forward and backward.

Gone.

A river of mud swept through. It hurried along now, swift as a torrential flood. The powerful wall that had punched a hole in Letum Wood oozed by with terrifying strength. Entire tree trunks bobbed out of it, like giant corks. More timbers crashed and fell as it continued to plunder the wood with a wide scar, a gash. The slide overtook my home and then some.

Numbness rippled through me from the inside out. I could only stare, uncomprehending. Merrick tightened his arm around me.

"Come. Let's go back to the castle. Your father just told me to meet him there."

* * *

Merrick remained glued to my side while we congregated at Grandfather's apartment, wearing half armor, his hair in a messy braid. Papa and Regina, slicked with drying mud and scratches, spoke quietly near the fire. They didn't touch, but Papa stood close enough to her that I knew they wanted to.

Grandfather handed out glasses of water, which they gulped, while he spoke with them on the other side of the room. I stared out the window, forehead pressed to the cool pane. The quiet gave me a chance to reorient, like a compass finding north again.

Darkness—and more rain—lingered beyond the glass panes. Also demigods and wrath and destruction and emptiness.

Arborra?

A moment passed.

We mourn.

Are there other demigods?

Yes, but we cannot see them. They are invisible to us right before the trees fall. They have learned.

More mudslides?

Yes.

I asked nothing more.

Maybe I'd been a fool all this time. Tontes and Ventis were gods that craved revenge. Who were witches to stop two gods?

My heart ached with a dozen prickling pangs when I pushed away from the window. Merrick eyed me, worry in his gaze. I tried to reassure him with a smile that turned into a grimace. Flashes of my cottage flapped like wild birds through my mind. My bed, Isadora's teacups, thick mantle, warm hearth.

Gone.

"All of the mortals escaped?" I asked.

Merrick nodded. "Your father reported that the trees appeared to try to stop the mortals. One mortal hung upside down, vines wrapped around his legs. A woman was pinned against a tree with a cage of branches, but she disappeared. The other one as well."

"Do you need to return to Baxter?"

"No. I'm staying."

Papa spoke from off to the side. "There were two demigods. It's the only explanation."

I whirled to find him standing a few paces away, arms folded over his chest. Fatigue tugged at his expression. Mud smeared his half-armor, saturating a filthy, sweat-stained shirt. His sword stuck out near his hip at his side. Regina stood there, her expression long with fatigue.

"You saw two demigods?" I asked.

Papa drove a hand through his hair, causing muddy strands to stick straight up.

"No, but it's the only explanation. We saw you fighting the female demigod. Tried to get there faster, but mortals swamped us. The moment we caught them, they'd disappear. Sometimes they returned, unless we injured them enough. Took awhile," he muttered, hand on his jaw. He worked it up and down with a grimace.

"Tontes has learned from past mistakes," Merrick said. "Had a decoy amulet awhile ago, now a hidden demigod to preserve his fighters, who appeared to be well-cared for. Not emaciated, the way you described, B. Not too shabby a plan, if you think about it."

My fingers closed in a fist. Only one amulet against the eight that we needed. Somehow, we had to locate seven more amulets *and* obtain them so that Ignis and Gelas could destroy them. Assuming that Baxter found Nicomedianthekus, of course.

With more mudslides and destruction, Letum Wood weakened every moment. I could *feel* the losses. Slashes across the heart. Paper cuts of pain on the soul. Minuscule, but mighty.

A piece of parchment popped into the air in front of me. I reached for it, unfolded the edges. Baxter's handwriting filled the interior.

Ignis reported that Tontes will make his final push tonight and confirmed that it will happen at the circle of the ancients.

Scarlett and Niko have been informed. If I don't find Nicomedianthekus, our plan will dissolve.

Get whatever amulets you can.

Buy me time.

I passed the note to Papa. Regina read it over his shoulder, then nodded to indicate she finished. Papa passed it to Grandfather. A somber expression rose as Grandfather comprehended the words. He passed it to Merrick with a frown.

"I need to report to Scarlett as well as Network delegations," Grandfather said, running a hand over his eyes. "Our defensive plan must go into effect immediately. Thank the goddesses that we have one, with Scarlett's pressing and cajoling other Networks to form one with her."

I glanced at him, amused by the catchphrase.

"Thank the goddesses?"

Grandfather smiled wryly. "Well, considering the state of the gods ..."

He trailed away and my hilarity faded. His gaze flickered to mine.

"Thank you for your guidance days back. Evidence of gathering mortals and demigods appears that you were right—the attack on Deasylva is happening at the circle of the ancients."

"You're going to report to Scarlett, but not the Council?" I asked.

He shook his head. "This is a matter of life-or-death, military might, and Guardian prowess. Scarlett will make these decisions herself. The Council will have to focus on keeping our witches as safe as possible while the Guardians focus on finding amulets. Forgive me, but I must leave immediately. Whatever you do, keep yourselves alive and available for messages. Once the gods directly attack, we're going to need all the help we can get."

* * *

Michelle, Sanna, and baby Isadora filled Leda's small apartment in Chatham Castle to bursting.

A bed of blankets near the fire held a sleeping Sanna, who snored softly, her full lips parted. Isadora dozed in a pulled-out drawer at the bottom of an armoire. She reminded me of a cocooned caterpillar in her rolled-up bundle of blankets. Candlelight illuminated the room just enough to reveal the distress in Michelle's downturned lips. She tapped her thumb against her palm and stared at the clock.

Leda was nowhere in sight, likely with Scarlett at the meeting of Network leadership. While Merrick changed clothes and grabbed something to eat, I found Michelle. Grandfather promised to send word on Scarlett's plan, which meant that all of Alkarra existed like a held breath. Paused. Life waiting. The world stilled.

The trees whispered about silence in the forest. Outside, the rain and wind paused. Mist crawled across the world.

"Where's Nicholas?"

My voice broke Michelle out of a trance. She shook her head, adjusted where she sat at the edge of the couch, and reached into a burlap bag of clothes. Based on the general wear-and-tear, the varying sizes, and the light scent of lavender, they'd come from Leda's mother. The mudslide would have wiped out everything Michelle owned as well, baby clothes included. A tightening sensation overcame my stomach at the thought.

"Nicholas is somewhere with the dragons, I think. He told me to leave once Reebis saw the mudslide coming. I grabbed the girls and came here. I could . . . I could hear it crashing through the trees." She shuddered. "The castle was the only place I could think of at the time. I just . . . left in a panic."

"You did great, and I'm sure Nicholas is fine."

"I sent him a note to tell him we were staying here. He didn't reply, but how would he? I . . . I'm not worried for him. Reebis will take care of him. I'm, well, worried for everything else."

I nodded, unable to say much more.

"Priscilla is in Scarlett's apartments," she continued, anticipating my next question. "Celia and Scarlett's butler, Marjorie, get along very well. Leda was so kind to give me her place to stay. I . . . I just couldn't bring myself to stay in the High Priestess's personal quarters, though Leda said that Scarlett offered."

A woman who lived in the forest her whole life, ate the same meals everyday, in the grand opulence of Scarlett's apartments, made no sense.

"I'm sure you'll be more comfortable here."

Michelle cast her gaze around, then nodded. She sank to the couch, her knees still trembling. A ripple of shock seemed to move through her as she reached for another small shirt with shaking hands. One fold at a time, she created a perfect square out of the garment.

I straightened. "You'll be safer here, too. The attacks are centered on Letum Wood so far. I haven't heard of any demigod sightings near the Castle."

Michelle said nothing. I wanted to ask her about Nicholas and the dragons, but I didn't know what to ask. How should I contact Reebis when we needed her? Would Nicholas come to our side as well? The words failed to materialize.

Instead, I let the silence ride.

A note popped into the air a handbreadth from my face. I frowned at the unfamiliar scrawl, tapped the edge. It rolled open.

Bianca,

Would you please join the Council in our meeting room? Immediately.

—Rosanna
Council Member of the Letum Wood Covens

After today, not much shocked me. Not even a summons from Council Member Rosanna. I sighed, and sent the scroll into the fire.

"I need to go find Merrick, then deal with something that just came up," I said. "I'm glad you're safe and I hope you see Nicholas soon."

My mouth opened to say the words, *everything is going to be fine,* but they wouldn't form. I didn't know that. Perhaps part of me didn't believe it would be fine, either. I could only say, "We're going to fight with everything we have."

Michelle met my gaze for the first time since I entered the room. Trepidation, terror, hope. I saw all of them at the same time. They faded back into a restless fear, haunting in their own quiet way.

"Thank you, Bianca. I know we will."

Chapter Twenty-Three

Assistants bustled around the Council Member room, faces lined with stress and anxiety.

Scrolls zipped around. Messages appeared at random intervals and varying heights. Water pitchers poured into crystal glasses, then soared overhead to lower in front of someone else.

Two Council Members stood behind tall-backed, velvet chairs in deep discussion. Another paced near the fire. The rest sat in varying stages of disarray and puzzlement as they beckoned Assistants, waved away messages, blinked back shock. Copies of the *Chatterer* littered the table top. Articles blinked in synchronized updates, like giant bugs opening and closing their eyes.

Outside the room, Chatham Castle bustled in greater uproar. Coven Leaders and Council Members had loaned their estates to witches uprooted by floods and lived out of their offices. Assistants slept in the halls. Fireboys ran constantly, attempting to find and ferry dry firewood.

A low-level hum of chaos thrived in the halls, lending more frantic energy to the air. In some way, it reminded me of the moments before the Battle of Chatham Castle more than three years ago now.

How I hated that it had returned.

On the other side of the table, Hiddleston looked up, saw me, and relaxed. He lifted a hand to draw my gaze, then beckoned me closer with a flap of fingers. Somewhat reluctantly, I obeyed. Breathless, arms stuffed full of paperwork, he tilted his head the other direction.

"With me," he said crisply. "Council Member Sia is waiting for you. You can stand by her. Trust me, you won't want to be near any of the others."

Sia ran the Ashleigh Covens. A formidable, stalwart woman with a firmness that reminded me a little of Mildred.

"Is Leda with Scarlett?" I asked.

"Yes. She asked me to watch here, just in case. I'm glad she did. I just heard that Rosanna messaged you. Sia told me. She's livid with Rosanna for getting you involved and demanded that she will see to your comfort."

"That bad?" I asked.

Hiddleston nodded.

With that ominous introduction, I followed him to the far edge of the table, near the spot Scarlett often occupied. Merrick followed close behind, invisible, though I expected Hiddleston to figure it out soon enough.

Chairs, makeshift desks cluttered with books and parchment, ringed the perimeter of the room. Council Member Sia looked up as I approached, lips pinched. She stood, fingertips pressed into the tabletop.

"Thank you, Miss Monroe. I'm sorry that you've been summoned. We'll try to make the best of this. Have a seat?"

"No, thank you. I prefer to stand."

A brush of fingertips across the small of my back confirmed that Merrick remained close. He'd retreat to the wall, not far away, to avoid a blunder with someone walking by. Having him near brought great comfort.

To the room Sia called, "This meeting has begun."

A gong rang from the corner. Silence fell, broken only by the scrape of Rosanna's chair as she stood. A lilac dress gave her a sallow appearance as she pushed her sleeves up to her elbow. When she spoke, she stared right at me.

"I understand that we don't need to relay to you the gravity of the situation that we're facing?"

I shook my head.

"Wonderful. Let us get right to the point. We've asked you here to support an idea that we've just developed together."

An ominous feeling crept over me. The Council conspiring outside of Scarlett's awareness could never be a good thing.

"Some of us," Sia called sharply. "Not all of us were included in this conversation."

Halifax, Council Member over the Tate Covens, tapped two fingers on the table in assent.

"You want *my* support?"

To Rosanna's credit, no disdain or annoyance lingered in her studious gaze. "You, Miss Monroe. As improbable as it seems."

"What is your idea?"

"Yesterday, while discussing our unfortunate situation with Talmund, he mentioned something that caught my attention. He said, '*If we must put the Network-wide plan that we've developed into motion, the demigods need something to distract them away from the forest while the Guardians get into position.*'" Rosanna's arms opened. "The Council can't help but agree, and this is where you come in. Allow us to show you what we're thinking?"

After a nod of assent, Rosanna waved to Massimo, a man with an overly-large, bristling mustache who ran the Eastern Covens. She ceded the floor to him. As she sat down, Massimo stood. He gestured to an empty portion of the wall straight ahead.

Glowing white lines appeared, squiggling around until they formed the shape of the Central Network. Green marks scrawled out a general form for Letum Wood, fading out into the edges of the wall where other Network boundaries came into play.

"We've come up with a strategic plan to protect the Central Network from an alleged god invasion by distracting the gods."

"You mean demigods?"

"No. We mean the gods."

Astonished, I could only stare at him. He continued, unbothered by my blank stare. "It's reasonable to assume that such an attack could be any moment now, so this plan would need to be enacted immediately."

The lines changed, narrowed into just the shape of Letum Wood. Known structures—like Chatham Castle—faded. Only the forest remained, a sprawling green blob against the stone backdrop. Brown slash marks indicated mudslides, other disasters. Ragged things that made me wince. I counted ten.

So many?

"We're seeing massive instability in the forest," Massimo continued. "Trees falling on homes on the outskirts of Chatham City, destabilizing landslides, washed out roads, bridges, etc. That is only reporting in our Network, as other Networks have fared worse due to the prolonged, severe weather. If the gods are attempting to soften Alkarra, it's working. Despite all this, we feel, and Talmund agrees, that the gods plan to focus their attack on Letum Wood. At least, that is what they're doing now."

He waved to me with a hand, eyebrow raised high in silent question.

"I agree."

"Scarlett is speaking with other Network delegations right now about a united approach. A plan to bring together Alkarran

Guardian forces, Protectors, and Masters to fight as one. We, on the Central Network Council, want to buy the Alkarran Guardians forces time to establish themselves in Letum Wood, where it's believed the battle will begin.

"We want to distract the gods from the forest while the Guardians set up, and see if we can't . . . delay them or head them off from the beginning of the attack."

Suspicion built in the back of my mind. I agreed with them. It would be an unexpected, strategic move to distract gods, but therein was half the battle. How to distract a god?

Yet, in the midst of this, something still wasn't right.

Georgette, Council Member over Chatham City, stood next. She remained behind the table, hands folded in front of her. "The Central Network Council supports the plan that Scarlett and the other delegations have come up with . . . except for one tenant."

Neither spoke.

I tilted my head to the side. My hand went to Viveet on instinct, aggravated by the look in Georgette's eyes.

"What tenant is that?" I asked.

Massimo and Georgette exchanged a glance before she spoke, staring hard at me. "Her plan doesn't accommodate any action that involves *you* at all. We think that *you* are a target for Tontes and Ventis. One that we can use strategically to our benefit."

"Me?"

Georgette nodded. A ripple ran through the room. I followed it, noting Halifax's livid stare, and Sia's white knuckles. Hiddleston's full lips had pressed into a furious line. Georgette's deliberate pause gave me a moment to absorb what this must mean. Once I did, my fists clenched at my side.

"You want me to be bait."

"No," Georgette countered coolly. "We want you to be a distraction so the Guardians from all Networks can move into position and protect Alkarra. We want you to take the fight away from the forest."

I sucked in a breath.

Bold.

The audacity nearly made me laugh. As if the gods could be plotted against, thwarted. The Council didn't know what sort of power they attempted to subvert. Not really. Though I'd been to Alaysia and a conduit for god magic and I knew more than anyone, Baxter aside, even I felt woefully inadequate to advise.

The cold, hard lines of her expression told me Georgette knew *exactly* what she was doing. They wanted to get me out of their hair as a potential unknown, yet allow the Guardians time to set up to fight. Should I be successful, all the better. For Alkarra, and for the Council, on whom this would reflect so positively.

She did all that by hitting me in my weak spot. The one place from which I couldn't back away. She *knew* I wouldn't refuse an opportunity to protect Letum Wood.

Take the fight away from the forest.

After what I had just seen in Letum Wood, there was nothing I wanted more. For the first time in my life, the Council and I had the same motivation.

"I see."

Silence.

Merrick put a hand on my shoulder, squeezed hard. The lightest whisper sounded next to my right ear, away from Sia.

"Don't do it."

All the eyes in the room stared hard at me. Despite my best efforts, I couldn't help the way my thoughts returned to the same words over and over again.

Take the fight away from the forest.

As if she sensed my weakening, Georgette continued.

"Letum Wood is sheltering witches from all over Alkarra.

Those witches are now dying from floods, landslides, mudslides, falling trees. Strategic windstorms fell trees wherever witches can be found. You can't tell me that taking the fight away from the forest will be a bad thing?"

"Say nothing," Merrick muttered, voice hard as flint. "They're sacrificing you as a distraction, a desperate attempt to do something, but it won't work."

Unfortunately, I couldn't say that I didn't share her observations. Letum Wood had become hazardous for a lot of different reasons. Desperate animals were now losing their homes, which would drive them farther from the heart of the forest. Creatures we didn't know existed might emerge, and not to great effect.

Letum Wood's last response haunted me.

We mourn.

Could the forest still fight? Hadn't the power of the gods shocked Arborra? A couple of hours ago, I would have emphatically said Letum Wood was ready. Now, reality dampened my enthusiasm. Hadn't Arborra been cowed by the power of god magic? The desecration of my home—and all the trees that surrounded it—left me an uncertain mess.

Trees couldn't fight thunder.

With that in mind, I asked, "What do you suggest for a plan?"

Massimo pointed to the drawing on the wall. "You draw Tontes or Ventis or both to the West."

The drawing on the wall panned out again. The green lines shrank, making room for the Central Network, with some of the Western Network blended into the border.

The outline of the West appeared in flaxen tops, like strings of sand curled together. A bright, red circle appeared in the West, not far from the borderlands and the river that split our Networks. Fortifications appeared on the map.

"The borderlands along the Western and Central Network would be an ideal place to draw the gods. The storms have dropped historic rainfall there, as well. The sand is thick and easier to use to build structures with magic. It's far from important places in our Network, and no witches live there."

Said sand would also be unstable and ever shifting. A joke against the most powerful god in Alaysia. Ventis alone could wear the structures down in a single breath of wind.

Images of buildings and bulwarks appeared on the stone wall, brightening with color. Sand pits. Ditches. Tent-like structures, made to pop up quickly and without much effort. Most of it could be done by magic. Exhaustive, but not impossible.

Also entirely foolhardy.

"These are structures that we could help you construct, if it would be helpful. We agree this is the best spot."

"Structures of sand?" I asked. "The best spot for what? How do you plan to use sand against a god?"

"That's for you to figure out. What we have here is a conglomeration of ideas that we've put together to assist you."

"In other words, you have no plan."

Massimo said nothing.

Council Members shifted. Assistants stood against the wall, eyes averted to the floor, the ceiling. Anywhere *but* me. Anxiety filled the air, yet no one spoke.

"You want me to distract the gods, yet you have no plan?"

"You *are* the plan."

I scoffed at the hypocrisy. The Council wouldn't give the Sisterhood the time of day—until my life benefited their purposes.

"We have come up against impossible foes," Georgette said quietly. "Dueling gods. Floods we cannot stop. What would you have us do, Miss Monroe?"

"Fight back."

"How?"

"Build support systems to get rid of the flooding waters. Use magic to support the forest."

"We have done that. Are doing that. But we cannot force the populace to go into dangerous conditions when they're attempting to save their families, and all Guardians are preparing for the battle of their lives."

I opened my mouth, closed it again.

"Maybe we could make it safer," I finally said, desperate now. "For witches to help. The younger trees are attempting to direct their roots down, while the older trees remain stable. They . . ."

Wanted to fight lingered on my lips, but I hesitated. If I took the fight somewhere else it could save Letum Wood . . .

No, this was all a waste of time. One path existed for getting out of this, and that had been clear from the moment Georgette started to talk.

"Fine," I snapped. "I'll figure out something, but only to buy us time and protect the forest and *not* because I'm a willing sacrifice for you. I do this for the Guardians who are about to die saving Alkarra. When we win this battle and you and I come head to head over something again, remember the witch that cared enough to *act*, not sacrifice."

Tense faces morphed into relief. Slumped shoulders. Quick sighs. Only Sia and Halifax and Clare betrayed deepening trouble. Halifax straightened. He glared at me through rheumy eyes, a cane pointed to my chest.

"Do *you* have a plan?" he asked, fury in his aged voice. "You might be wild, Bianca Monroe, but I've never known you to be a fool. No daughter of Derek Black would accept the errand of idiots."

I met his challenging stare.

"I always have a plan."

* * *

"You're insane."

Merrick's supportive words accompanied me through

Chatham Castle, toward Grandfather's apartments. I sped through the crowded halls, burdened by ideas, plans, precautions. A fireboy rushed past, tinder in hand. His scrawny legs peeled into another hallway just ahead.

"I know it sounds insane."

Merrick strode at my side, visible again, his steps long and sure. "You know I'm behind most of what you want to do, B, but the Council has asked you to complete a suicide mission. One doomed to fail. You can distract Tontes and Ventis, but to what end? They're gods. It would be better to work in conjunction *with* Scarlett and not waste your time on futile efforts."

"Scarlett is too busy to deal with this. As much as I hate it, I can't disagree with the Council. There's a way for us to help, and that is distracting the gods."

"You can hide behind that lie if you want, but I'll never believe it."

"It's not a lie!"

"You're doing this because you want to protect the forest. You don't trust Letum Wood to recover from what just happened."

I stopped. My hair spun as I whirled around to face him with a snarl. He set his hands on his hips, ready for my rebuttal. Blistering annoyance compelled me to open my mouth, but I stopped short.

What was there to say? Merrick was right. I sighed, an aggravated sound that caused him to lift an eyebrow.

"Yes, I do want to protect Letum Wood. Taking the fight away from the forest might be one way to do it. But there's more to it than that."

"What?"

I floundered, my tongue bound. In fact, there *was* nothing else. Nothing except terror. Fear. A blind sense of loyalty to a forest that had saved me from the lands and lives beyond this life.

When I offered nothing but befuddled silence, Merrick ran a hand through his hair.

"Does the forest know what you're doing?"

"No."

"Is *that* fair?"

My response faltered.

"According to your report, the forest helped you tonight, B. *Like Ignis,* you told me. Maybe you were meant to fight with the forest, not protect it. Deasylva may have given you equal power, just in a different way."

"This isn't like Ignis," I snapped. "This is different."

"How?"

"Because . . . that is . . . it just *is!*"

Merrick softened. He put a hand under my chin. "You lost your home tonight, B. Your trees, who are your greatest friends. Don't make a wild decision based on frantic emotions. What if you cripple your ability to truly help the Network by doing this? The Council is scared—bottom line. You're a wild card and they're hoping you land it, that's all. They didn't even have their own plan. These are witches that snubbed a nose at you right until you became the only option. Don't forget that."

Sorrow welled up in my throat, blocking my words. Tears prickled at the backs of my eyes, but I blinked them away. Now wasn't the time for emotion, Merrick was correct. I needed cold, hard facts. Logic and strategy.

Still, my heart curled away inside.

"Take away my cottage," I said. "Take away the overwhelming damage happening to Letum Wood with every moment that passes, and my fury at everything in general. Strip every emotion out of this situation. Look at the facts, Merrick.

"We have gods on the way. The only chance to stop those gods is to steal their amulets. To steal their amulets, we need as many witches ready to fight as possible. Ideally, those witches will be in Letum Wood, because we believe that the gods will attack Deasylva directly.

"The Guardians that have been training or planning to get said amulets have to move into position. If I can distract the gods while the Guardians position themselves for success, lives will be saved. More amulets will be won. Our chances of survival will increase. Right?"

He scowled. Pressing my advantage, I continued.

"You have to admit that distracting the gods would be a strategic maneuver to help us get our Guardians into place."

"Yes, but—"

"There's no buts. Yes or no?"

"Yes," he muttered.

"If the gods topple the ancients, which is the heart of Deasylva's power, the rest of the forest will fall. Do you agree?"

"Yes."

"He's already weakened—is weakening—Letum Wood. Not to mention putting in danger all the witches that are finding refuge there. That's another fact."

He glowered deeper. "Yes."

"Logic follows—again—that buying time makes sense. It helps us save the witches, the trees, the ancients, and by extension, Deasylva's power."

"Yes."

"Then this *is* a good path."

I schooled back dark amusement. It wasn't often I could best Merrick with facts, but when I did, it felt good. Even over the layers of despair.

"Sounds like you're trying to convince yourself, B."

I frowned.

He turned away, jaw tight, before I could formulate a response. "Fine, but know that I don't like it."

"I don't think Ventis and Tontes care what we like. Do you think any Guardians will be able to steal amulets?"

"They're *hoping* to. Whether an average Central Guard contingent could stand against god magic and demigods, I have my doubts. Matthais, Baxter, Talmund, and Scarlett have been working together with a plan to have the Protectors be involved. Big picture? Yes they can do it. Will amulets be taken from a prepared god who has been violently destructive and sneaky? Unlikely."

I pressed my palm to his hand. "Then let's try this path. We need every advantage we can get. If I fail to distract the gods away from Letum Wood, I'll be back in the forest immediately to help find amulets and cripple whomever I can."

"And if you don't make it back?"

"I will."

He stared at me, long and hard. Chatham Castle flowed around us. Busy maids, bustling witches, calling Assistants. No one paid attention to the couple pressed together in the hallway. Thunder punctured the air, rolling out for a full ten seconds before Merrick palmed my cheek in his hand.

Words wrenched out of him, his face split in pain.

"I'm afraid of losing you, B. You could present the most well-thought out plan with the best chance of success and survival, and I still wouldn't like it." He paused, swallowed hard. Horror filled his gaze. "I can't go through that again."

His husky voice teetered on an edge of desperation. Shocked, I could only blink, lips parted. The scrape of his fingers along my cheek as they curled into a fist sent a shiver down my neck. He leaned closer. The air between us charged with the force of his emotions. The power of his voice.

"You died, B. You died and I couldn't do anything about it. Your life drained away in front of me. Only sheer luck, and the right choice on *your* part, brought you back from the lands and lives beyond this life."

My bunched frustration loosened like a freed corset, a released sigh. My fingertips touched his stubbled, dirty cheek. I wrapped a hand around the back of his neck, pulled him closer. He closed his eyes, breathed in.

"I've survived the gods before."

"Barely."

"Letum Wood saved me then, it will save me again."

"This is different."

"How?"

"They're gods."

"They were gods months ago."

"You don't have Ignis protecting you anymore."

For a moment, I almost shared his fear. As imperfect as Ignis had been—still was—we had been a lethal match. Seamlessly integrated and with mighty power.

"Maybe not, but now I have Deasylva."

Skepticism showed on his face. Despite all proof to the contrary, I *felt* the words to my bones. She'd proven to be a quiet goddess. We hadn't interacted since the In-between, but I felt her hum in the background. The switch to knowing, irrevocably, that she existed changed everything.

"The forest is part of me, Merrick. If I can save it, I will. If Letum Wood has to fight? It will do that too. But, before that, I have to try. I'd never be able to live with myself if I didn't do everything in my power to prevent more destruction."

His stony expression didn't appear reassured, but slightly mollified. "If I can't stop you, at least let me join you?"

"Do you need to help Baxter?"

"I can't find him, and no. You're more important."

I smiled. "I wouldn't want anyone else at my side."

Relief finally showed in his wry smile. "Thank you, B. I'll be at your side forever, if you'll have me."

"I love you."

He pressed his forehead to mine. "Through the lands and lives beyond."

I closed my eyes, breathed him in. The harried air in

Chatham Castle faded as he held onto me. Our hearts mingled. Breath combined. The connection satisfied the terrified part of me orphaned by my once-safe cottage.

When I opened my eyes again, infused with new courage, he smiled.

"Well, little troublemaker. Shall we save Alkarra?"

"Follow me. Oh, and let me do the talking when we get to where we're going, all right? We're going to start with Tontes, since he's the most powerful. Also, do you happen to have a pencil on you? I need to send a quick message."

* * *

The Zamok Castle gardens were still visible despite advancing daytime hours. Zamok Castle lingered on the edge of Southern Network tundra, where lower, rolling mountains, carpeted with thick timbers, met wild grasses. The sun hovered in the lower sky, hugging the ground like pebbles over water.

This time of year brought a short sunset, a quick sunrise. The sun dipped below the horizon for only a few hours before returning to the sky in a loop of near-perpetual day. Darkness reigned in the Central Network, but the Southern Network clung to the edge of light here.

I turned my attention to the trees, listening. My experience with forests outside of Letum Wood was limited. Letum Wood began talking to me years ago, and I'd never thought of hearing another one. Today, low notes filled my mind like a gushing tide. Different. Gentle. Not so packed with power or adoration, yet familiar.

She comes to us.

All belong to her.

You are one of us.

I stood at the edge of a garden and peered out. Bands of darkness represented the forest that filled my mind. My heart drew out to it, swelling. I loved these trees, too. It wasn't just Letum Wood. Anything with Deasylva's influence drew me closer, a powerful vibrance.

You belong to me, I whispered.

Cries echoed, exultant things.

Merrick shuffled behind me. He kept one hand on his sword hilt, the other at his side. His gaze darted constantly, allowing me the space to focus on the trees in the distance. I blinked, coming back into my own head, and spun to face him.

"I hope she received the letter."

He nodded toward the castle, where torchlight illuminated the walls in rings of yellow. A woman stalked out of the castle and turned toward us, eyebrows knitted together in a wrathful expression.

"I think she did," he drawled.

Tipa arrived all at once, full of wrath and fire. Her eyes flashed. Her fists balled at her side. If I hadn't known her to be Gelas' daughter, I would have pegged her as a child of fire. Her amulet, Kibbukonialamonta, sparkled from a barrette in her hair.

"You are the maddest witch I have ever met!" she cried. Behind me, Merrick advanced. I could feel his warning glower, though I couldn't see his face. I stopped him with a hand at my side. He halted, but hovered close. Tipa skidded to a stop with a furious glare.

"What are you thinking?" she snapped.

"Merry meet, Tipa. Always a pleasure. My note arrived, I take it?"

"Are you mad? You must be." She held up a twisted piece of parchment, as if she'd crushed it. "This is a joke. Tell me that this is a joke."

I said nothing.

She snarled.

"Will you do it?" I asked gently.

"No!"

"Why not?"

Her eyes bugged out. "You want me to take you to Tontes' kingdom? *You* want to speak with Tontes? A servant of Deasylva?"

I nodded.

"You're mad!"

"Strategic. The two are very different. If you agree to hear me out, I'll tell you my plan. If you want to keep ranting and raving and wasting Alkarra's time, you can do that. If you don't take me, I'll find someone who will, but you're costing us time and lives. Your choice, Tipa."

Her ire stalled. Her mouth opened, then closed. She glanced at Merrick, frowned, then looked back at me.

"Explain," she spat.

As quickly as possible, I summarized the plan, the goal. The astonishment in her face altered into something like disbelief, then dubious uncertainty. That, I could work with.

"So I need you to take me to Tontes."

Merrick stood behind me, rigid as a sword. I hadn't told him the full extent of my idea until this moment. I could practically hear him silently ranting to me in his rolling Northern brogue.

Her rancor faded to astonishment. "You really think it'll work?" she asked.

"I have no idea."

Her brow came together in hesitant frustration. After a long pause, she rolled her eyes and muttered, "Fine."

"Really?"

"Only because I will do whatever it takes to help my father obtain this land without Tontes and Ventis destroying it. This has nothing to do with you!"

"Thanks. I think."

She glowered. "We go now," she muttered. "There's no guarantee that Tontes will be there, or hear you, or anything like it. We could be wasting both of our time."

"If we're in his circle of power, won't he be able to sense us?"

"He'll know we're there, but he might not care."

I grinned. "Then we have to *make* him care."

Chapter Twenty-Four

The thought of returning to Alaysia left my heart in my throat.

When visiting there with Baxter, I'd only been in Tontes' kingdom for an hour. Locked into a boggy marsh while I awaited judgment at the Heart of Alaysia. That hardly counted as a precursor for what to expect from my plan.

It certainly built a horrifying expectation, though.

Thanks to Tipa, god magic delivered us instantly. My stomach dropped all the way to my feet the moment my eyes opened.

"Jikes!" I cried under my breath.

My toes hung off the edge of a cliff only as wide as my hand. I leaned back, fingers scrambling for purchase against a flat shale wall.

"Tipa!" I shrieked.

We stood on the edge of a precipice. Merrick on my right, Tipa to my left. Thin, brittle cliffs soared above and below us with precarious height. Thunder rumbled. Lightning illuminated the sky, brightened slate clouds. A flat, sandy ground lingered hundreds of paces below.

A rise of nausea welled in my stomach. I tilted the back of my head against the cliff, pressed my spine more firmly on the uneven rocks behind me, and forced myself to breathe.

Merrick stood with his hands splayed out. He gazed around, less stiff or concerned than me or Tipa. His legs were braced, tense.

Tipa tightened next to me, shoulders drawn back. Her expression paled as she stared straight ahead, into the blooming fury of a thunderhead. We hovered so far off the distant ground, I felt as if I stared into the eyes of the storm.

"Great spot, Tipa," I hissed.

"I've never been here before," she muttered through gritted teeth. "I did the best I could."

"Where are we?"

"Tontes' kingdom," she snapped.

"His home?"

"Presumably."

Her amulet illuminated the hair behind her ear. Active god magic shifted the colors inside, with swirls of blue and strands of teal and silver. Despite myself, I couldn't help thinking of Ignis' kingdom: the unfurling rainforest, and the landscape dotted with volcanoes.

"Does Tontes have an actual habitation?"

Carefully, she cut me a sharp gaze. "Like a *Rostina*?"

"Yes."

"I wouldn't know. We tend to ignore the other gods and demigods when we can."

"Is there a top to these cliffs?"

Tipa swallowed. "Presumably, but it could be who-knows-how-high."

"Take us there?"

Tipa hesitated. A rock trickled down the mountainside from beneath her feet, crashing to the depths below. Her shoulders bunched near her ears, then eased down. Tendrils of vapor clung to her hair, saturating the strands from the humidity

"Fine."

The world faded, then reappeared. No terrifying cliffs in our new position. No vista to study. No billowing clouds over the ocean, stirring white caps and danger. Instead, we stood on top of a bunch of rocks with nothing but clouds. A soupy sky descended, thick enough to send shivers down my spine. Electricity crackled the air.

The shale, brittle rocks broke apart beneath my feet when I shuffled forward. The movement caused the fog nearest me to twirl. It parted to reveal a circle a hundred paces across, surrounded by walls of wisps.

No thunder.

No lightning.

Raindrops formed like crystals in the air, creating a glittering image that swept away in another swirl of vapor. Complicated mandalas formed in the clouds, layered with gray, silver, and black, rimmed in white. For three seconds the intricate patterns held their shape with depth, precision, and texture, then faded away. The depictions appeared here and there. Moving artistry.

Another formed in front of me. A tree, sprawling out with giant roots, long arms. The umber-and-emerald colors edged into darkness, then appeared again. The tree had fallen, rooted from the ground. Hints of red, like rivers of blood, stained the earth around it.

It faded into nothing.

Tipa's shoulders lowered as she gazed around, oblivious to the silent threat. Merrick studied all of it, gaze flicking from place to place.

"Welcome to the land of the gods," I muttered.

He scowled.

"Can you hear Matthais from here?"

Merrick paused, gaze distant and focused. Seconds later, he nodded. "I can. Barely. I have to strain to hear it."

"Really?"

He shrugged. Shock gave me a moment of pause. The Protector magic must be even stronger than I expected.

"What's happening over there?"

"The meeting of Network leaders has concluded. Guardians arrive in the forest from the other Networks to receive instructions from Talmund. They're going to transport into position near the circle of the ancients in an hour. No sign of demigods so far. Mudslides have slowed. The wind stopped, too."

"Tell them to make it fast. I don't know how long we'll last here."

He nodded.

The lack of movement in Alkarra gave us a narrow window of time, in addition to the unnerving sense of having no control. The gods could act at any moment. Why did they stall? What did they wait for?

Here is where it mattered most, so I brought my attention back to now. I turned to Tipa. The greenish expression had faded from her face, and she wobbled less. Tension still made her stiff as a board.

"Can Tontes hear me if I talk to him?"

"If you entered my father's circle, he would know. I assume the same for all the gods."

I drew in a deep breath. My plan was simple. Get Tontes' attention, distract him from Alkarra, then go from there. Yet, it lacked everything else, like certainty, back ups, and a grounding in reality.

"God of thunder," I called, "you have a lovely home."

A pause.

Silence.

Seconds ticked by like eternity. Tipa tensed, obscured by the miasma of clouds that swirled around us. The thickest fog I'd ever seen. When I walked a few steps one way, the clouds swirled back. If I went too far away, they would close me off from Tipa and Merrick.

"If you're too busy to talk, I understand, but I'd love to have a word with you. Before all of Alkarra goes to war and you lose to the goddess of the forest. You may not think me all that important, but as Deasylva's servant, I would disagree."

False bravado boosted my tone—I sounded far more confident than I felt. I had to push aside feelings of sheepishness. Speaking to a god in front of Tipa? Absurd. Her cagey, darting gaze didn't reassure me at all, either.

More quiet.

"No?" I called. "Very well. Proceed, if you dare. I've already stolen one of your amulets tonight, I figured you might want to chat before I take some more. With my hidden army."

Merrick sent me a questioning glance.

I shrugged.

A voice boomed.

Why have you returned, Lady-witch of Alkarra?

Merrick ducked. Tipa hissed through her teeth. It took all of my courage to affect a casual response.

"I prefer Lady-witch of Letum Wood, actually. That's the source of my power. You know, servant of Deasylva, and all. Figured we should be consistent."

You were annoying while you were here before, you continue to be so now.

"I could say the same."

Rolling thunder responded. The hair on the back of my neck stood up. Tipa rubbed her arms in the crackling discomfort, her gaze uneasy.

"I came to speak with you."

Then speak.

"Do you accept warnings?"

He laughed in billowing notes, like crashing drums.

A witch come to warn a god?

"Yes."

State your warning.

"You remember the *beelae*? When I worked with Ignis, I discovered that we had become a conduit to the power together? You should, because your children are the ones that attacked. I suppose I don't need to remind you what happened with Neel . . ."

Tipa shot me a glare.

I ignored it. Let the god of thunder get angry. Rash emotions could work to our advantage. Or disadvantage.

A growl followed, which I took as affirmative assent.

"That ability—that depth of magic—is not limited to only the gods. Did you realize that? I may have been a conduit for Ignis, but I access Deasylva's power as well. Since this is news to me, I thought I'd share."

You believe Deasylva could mimic the same?

"I know it."

The words came out steady, despite an underlying sense of uncertainty. Did I actually *know* it? No. I wondered about it, certainly. The facts added up to it a logical explanation that way. Letum Wood and I had shown strong promise together in various ways—every day seemed to uncover a new use to the magic, a new strength. Would my connection to Deasylva ever be as strong as it had been with Ignis?

I sincerely hoped so.

Do you know it?

His musing tone told me he hadn't bought my bluff. Just as well. The longer I kept him in conversation, the more time we gained. Assuming gods couldn't be in two places at once.

"Why else would Deasylva call me to be her servant? Trust me with her forest? When you war against Deasylva, you war against me. The magic will respond to the same. It rises with me, works to my command. Particularly in the forest."

Forgive me for not being frightened.

"It just means you're not paying attention."

And you seek to warn me so that I do pay attention? What an honorable witch. I imagine that I can now win the war thanks to your little visit, your attempt at distraction.

His biting sarcasm wasn't lost on me, but the *attempt at distraction* gave me reason to worry.

Uh oh.

You believe that I require such a warning? That I haven't planned for centuries for such a war? That I know so little of the machinations of the goddesses and gods that I wouldn't have readied myself for interference from Deasylva's . . . creatures?

My confidence began to shrivel away with his menacing tone. The only thing I had needed to accomplish here was delay, but I saw my success with that spiraling away already. His tone indicated he twirled toward a point. The slippery sense of falling down a precarious slope overcame me.

What did Tontes know?

Merrick stepped closer, his chest against my back. Tipa shuffled away, brow furrowed. I reached for Viveet as lightning broke with a *boom*, sending a sharp sensation over my skin. I grimaced at the pain that rolled with it.

Keep him talking, I thought. *Distraction is all.*

Our need for more time pushed me to action. The caterwauling saplings, Arborra's mournful tone. All of them brought me to this moment.

"You seem to require *something*, Tontes."

I'm not the only one with a requirement, witch.

Another mandala appeared. A swirling, complicated rendition of Nicomedianthekus, complete with crystal blue facets, a brilliant interior that moved like glaciers and waves. The mandala pivoted, like a shifting cloud constantly moving, but the amulet remained the same. Layers built on layers. The intricate magic created a stunning picture.

One I didn't want to see.

"Oh no," I murmured.

Tontes knew.

Of course he knew. What fool that planned his revenge for centuries would go into a battle without all the information? Tones must have known all along that we'd need Nicomedianthekus to fight back. One path existed toward our freedom— the amulets.

A dark feeling settled in my gut.

Admirable, that you would come so far to delay my attack on your land, but you have wasted time. Pointless. Your forest is going to fall, Lady-witch of Alkarra, regardless of what you do here. There is no way for you to find what you want. Your path is already lost.

"How do you know it's lost?" I asked weakly.

He laughed again, and the air trembled with power. Merrick reached forward, fingertips on my back. Tipa shuffled to the side, but there was nowhere to go. The vast emptiness of the air extended beyond the clouds that veiled where we stood. Everything about this kingdom felt . . . empty.

The sense of being on the verge of a truth pushed me farther. Surely, that was the breathless sensation in my chest. Not terror.

Not utter fear.

You assume that I don't know about Nicomedianthekus? That I wasn't there when all four gods formed this course for the magic? Witches are such fools. You always have been.

"I never said that."

Go home, Lady-witch, to what's left of it. I desire you to see the end, so I will allow you to live. I want you to suffer as the gods suffered. To see everything that you couldn't save fall to pieces. Deasylva will never be greater than me. Thunder doesn't quake at the sight of a forest.

His words replayed through my mind, looping in terror. The heady realization that we were utterly, tragically, outmatched paralyzed me. We'd only lasted minutes distracting the god.

Minutes.

There is no way for you to find what you seek. Your path is already lost.

"B," Merrick murmured. "We need to go *now*."

Understanding lingered just out of reach. A shadow beyond the ring of light. A realization so close . . .

I sucked in a breath.

"Wait."

Tontes would only say, *there is no way for you to find what you want,* if he knew where to find Nicomedianthekus.

If he *had* Nicomedianthekus.

The good gods. Tontes had been in control this whole time. We were scrambling around Alkarra, attempting to find something already in his possession. It's why Tontes acted with such bravado. Why he felt so certain about his victory in Alkarra.

Tontes held Nicomedianthekus.

I leaned back, felt Merrick behind me. He tightened a fist from my dress, pulling me closer.

"Take us back now, Tipa," I called.

Thunder growled. Static thickened the air. Any second now and a lightning bolt would strike.

A percussive *bang* split the air a moment before Tontes, and his kingdom, disappeared into darkness. We landed back in the Southern Network. I grabbed Tipa's shoulders, breathless.

"Bring Baxter here. I think I know where to find Nicomedianthekus."

Chapter Twenty-Five

For an agonizing ten minutes, Tipa was gone.

Merrick paced in front of a square, wooden arch with winding black flowers while I stared out at the tundra, heart thumping. The implications of what just happened with Tontes continued to circle my mind, like birds of prey about to dive for the kill.

What a fool I had been.

All this time I'd been attempting to protect Letum Wood, I'd really been cutting myself off from the most powerful source of magic that I had. The signs had been there all along. I'd bluffed with Tontes to buy time, but my suppositions had been true.

The way the forest spoke to me made our connection clear. We had worked seamlessly together against the demigods that had attacked my house. We hadn't saved my cottage, but we'd been effective in getting the amulet.

All this time, I hadn't seen my true power until I had to face Tontes.

The goddess magic had been growing inside of me for weeks now. Each day, a new advantage. More skill, more power.

Targeted and strategic. Though growth had been slow, it had been steady.

True.

The powerful connection I'd harbored with Ignis, I also had with Deasylva. I hadn't recognized it as the same until this moment. God magic had been bold, blatant. Powerful in ways that took my breath away, but it held a dark side. Goddess magic had been far more subtle. It required choice, not force, which meant I had to *want* it.

Now, I wanted it.

No, needed it.

Everything lay so bare—so pristinely clear in front of me. The power had been inside me all along, I just had to *trust* it.

"Dragons are reported to be flying over Chatham City," Merrick said.

He'd stopped pacing to stare out, lips turned down. His shoulders splayed wide against the dying light in the background, casting him in a dark silhouette.

"Demigods have been spotted in the forest. Witches continue to flee to the Southern Network from all over Alkarra. If they can't transport, though most can, others are transporting them."

"Are the borders closed in the North?"

"Geralyn tried. I'm not sure, though. Derek said something . . ."

"Are the demigods following the fleeing witches?"

Merrick paused. No doubt he received updates through the Protector magic. From a wily, ages-old Protector named Chi, most likely, as Chi had eyes and ears everywhere. What I'd give to be part of that exclusive circle—such quick and easy access to them would change the battle everywhere.

"No," he murmured. "The demigods are concentrated inside the forest. Foresters are spilling into Chatham City. They're saying that the demigods are cutting down trees, attempting to flood where they can."

"Is it working?"

"Sometimes, I think."

"Not surprising."

"The rain has stopped in the Central Network, but winds have picked up. Trees are falling in the flooded areas from the gusts. Some have fallen on homes." He broke, shook his head, then continued. "Forest lions are roaming villages, Chi says. Witches are saying they're unusually agitated. None have attacked any witches."

"The good gods," I whispered.

Letum Wood was bleeding like a severed artery. Creatures, trees, and panic spilling everywhere.

"The hurricane in the East is picking up speed," he continued, his voice low. He spoke methodically, relaying what someone else said. "It's turning into violent winds instead of rain. Tornadoes have broken out across marshes. Reports put the bulkhead of tornadoes as close as two hours from the eastern edge of Letum Wood."

"Not that far from the circle of the ancients."

"No. Dust devils are rampaging across the Western Network, too." He grimaced.

"There's only one way to stop this," I muttered.

With a touch of magic, I brought the forest to the front of my mind. Trees screamed. Saplings shrieked. I winced, closed my eyes, against the instant cacophony. With it came pain. The rending of soul with each lost tree. My heart felt like tattered fabric, almost torn to shreds. It palpitated inside me, an aching mass.

Tontes and Ventis had doubled their attacks in the wood. Saplings fell everywhere, but the older trees gave little indication of their status. Their silence reassured me only slightly.

Guilt followed.

With my heart, I reached out to them.

Arborra, I have more to tell.

Before Arborra could respond, I turned my heart to the magic. Our connection was enough that I felt as if I'd turned a microscope to my vulnerabilities. All lay bare before me now.

My insecurities. My deep-rooted fear of losing the forest. The decisions that led me to this point. All of my revelations to Arborra were tinged with desperation. A quiet hope of forgiveness summarized in two softly spoken words.

I'm sorry. We're . . . connected, I said to Arborra. *We're tied together. You're part of who I am.*

Part of you, they whispered, *but not* you.

Grandfather's words from what felt like so long ago resurrected in my mind.

You're so much bigger than that.

Ah, so *that* is what he meant. Had I tied myself too tightly into the forest? Had I too-closely aligned myself with Letum Wood? Yes.

But that wasn't real.

I'm afraid of losing you. The words rang, barren, even in my head. *Thousands of years of history came from this soil. It lives in you. I don't want to sacrifice your lives to the gods. Deasylva's power is rooted in the forest. If we lose you, we lose Alkarra.*

Arborra's voice strengthened. *Not if we fight together.*

Some trees will die.

Yes, and so will witches. It is the way of things.

With a wince, I turned away.

I've taken care of the forest for so long . . . I don't know if I can let you die, Arborra. I only wanted to protect you.

The admission crinkled inside of me like cold leaves. My heart shriveled. For a moment, time hung in the balance. The air stilled, time stopped. Arborra's words shook me to my center.

Your heart is known and understood and cherished. You have found your path, now allow us to have ours. Together, we will fight.

We can win. Only you can direct us. With you at the front, we can make our own destiny.

Other trees spoke at the same time, tripping over each other in their haste to be heard.

We will be your eyes.

She leads us.

We follow her.

Always.

Such unequivocal belief humbled me. A tear formed in my eyes as I pulled in a deep breath. Heat swelled in my chest. With it came a melody of voices. They gathered together, funneling into one voice that represented Arborra's steady, quiet tone.

We are one.

Truly now, I said. *We will do this together.*

We are here.

I trust you.

As we trust you.

A sense of release followed. Freedom, perhaps. The realization that the only true chance Alkarra had involved Letum Wood, and my ability to trust the trees to do what they must. Losses would happen.

I couldn't change that.

We face a hard path ahead, I said. *We will lose trees. The forest will have to fight for its life. I can't save all of you, but I will fight with you.*

Millions of responses followed.

It is all that we ask.

I drew in a deep breath, feeling as if I stood on solid ground for the first time. Uncertainty mixed with elation. With Letum Wood at my side, I would be a far more powerful force than Ignis could have ever been with me.

The forest *knew* me. In some ways, better than I knew myself. Our magic would be seamless and tremendous. Though Ventis rampaged the forest and knocked down trees, and Tontes moved closer to Deasylva's heart center, I knew I stood *exactly* where I belonged.

This time, Letum Wood was the conduit. It was always meant for this purpose.

I have a plan, I said with growing confidence. *It's a plan that has a chance. Are you ready to hear it?*

A pause. As I turned my mind over to Arborra, the trees responded in a denouement of sound. Silence prevailed in my soul, as oddly calm as the forest became on many occasions. In it, I gave my mind to the forest. Let them see my plan, hear my thoughts, and appreciate the path.

The noiseless moments continued until Arborra spoke again.

We see your plan.
Are you willing?
We are ready. Will the witches agree?
They won't know.

A humming resounded. Affirmation, as if Arborra agreed that subterfuge was best. The enacting of my plan would happen in conjunction with Scarlett and the Networks' plan. Mine relied on quiet, steady patience. On the witches who were prepared to make this happen—like the forest was prepared to fight for its life.

For Alkarra.

Together, I promised.

Always.

A rush of sound drew my head back up, out of my thoughts. Arborra's trailing whisper faded into the background as Tipa reappeared. With her usual purposeful stride, she moved toward me. Merrick paused, turned. Behind her, Baxter appeared. He was ragged, with bags under his eyes. Clothes wrinkled, a bit haggard. He saw me and a raised eyebrow followed. What felt like moments later, they stood in front of me.

"What's going on, Bianca?" he asked.

"Tontes has Nicomedianthekus," I said quickly. "I think I know where he's hiding it. I have two jobs for you. If you can do them, we have a chance of winning."

Baxter hesitated. His gaze searched mine. What he looked for there, he must have found, because he nodded.

With a hard swallow he said, "What do you need?"

* * *

Matthais blinked.

Talmund stared, face scrunched.

Merrick chewed on his bottom lip.

Total silence lay on the Gatehouse as I waited for all three of them to respond to my plan. Merrick stood a few paces away at my side, gaze intent on his leaders. I knew he wanted to be closer to me, but he stayed back so I could stand before Matthais on my own.

In the waiting quiet, clanking chains sounded from below as Guardians lowered the portcullis. Voices called from the lower Bailey, and a *thump thump thump* indicated a dragon soared right past the window. Flames burst, illuminating the sky for a moment. The chaos of Alkarra represented itself in the mayhem.

Moisture curled off the stones outside, filling the air with vapor. The rain had stopped, but the storm continued. Winds gusted past at intermittent intervals, rapidly changing direction. Their mischievous bursts, then falling power, lent a harried feeling to the air.

Talmund opened his mouth, then closed it. He straightened from where he'd leaned over the table to study my proposed attack strategy. With the heel of his hand, he rubbed his bloodshot eyes, a suppressed yawn tightened his jaw.

"It's a wild plan, Miss Monroe."

"It can work," I said.

He glanced at Matthais, who watched me with a glittering, studious gaze. I met his stare, tension all the way down my spine.

"*Could* is a far cry from *will*," Matthais murmured.

His gaze dropped to an open map on the table, filled with a grid-like structure of the forest. Chatham Castle lay to the left of the page. The rest of the forest rolled out like a skirt.

Colorful triangles indicated contingents from each Network. Emerald for the East. Amethyst for the North, who represented themselves through a witch named Nadira. Crimson for the Central Network. Mustard yellow for the Western Network.

West Guards would hover around the western edge of Letum Wood, as well as Chatham Castle. Each Network defended their own castle, except the East. Magnolia was too far underwater to need defense. They'd place their extra contingents along the eastern border, to escort witches to the Southern Network.

The room fell into utter stillness as I pointed to a spot on the map where I felt certain the circle of the ancients stood. The heart of Deasylva's power. Mapping out Letum Wood to any degree of exactness was like unwinding yarn, but I had a feeling my instincts in this matter were correct.

"The seat of Deasylva's power is around here. Tontes knows this—he's going to put his foremost attack at the circle. If I had a guess, I'd say that he'll concentrate all his most powerful demigods and mortals there. He *craves* this victory. More than anything, I'd wager."

Talmund frowned. "You think that's where the demigods will congregate, too? We assumed they'd spread their resources out in a wider net to destroy the forest while mortals fought at the circle. A few signs of mortals congregating there are already obvious."

"It seems most likely to me, because the circle is the real target. Ventis and Tontes are already destroying the forest—now they need to go for the throat, so to speak. After our meeting, I'll transport there. You can follow if you need to."

In a thought, I turned my mind back to the forest. Their collective whisperings resumed in the interior of my mind. Murmurs and thoughts whirled around. As if I could extend myself through the roots, my awareness raced all the way to the circle.

No demigods have revealed themselves here. They work elsewhere. Witches have begun to appear in greater numbers.

Could the demigods be invisible, Arborra?

Yes. We would not be aware.

I blinked, bringing my mind back to the room.

"Letum Wood will listen to me. The forest wants the amulets as much as we do. It will help wherever it can. The trees are good at anticipating what we might need."

My thoughts rippled to the dragons, creatures, saplings, undergrowth, and finally to a goddess who placed her trust in me. The magic had always been at my fingertips, but now it lay at my command. I was not Letum Wood's caretaker anymore.

I was their High Priestess.

"What does that mean?" Matthais asked.

"It means," I said with finality, "that we're going to take the gods by surprise."

"Your plan relies on the cooperation of trees," he murmured, voice rolling like thunder overhead.

"And a demigod that might be willing to double-cross us," Talmund added in a mutter.

Merrick stepped forward, the dull thud of his boot on wood reverberating. His expression was stern. "His name is Baxter," he said tightly, "and he's not *just* a demigod. I trust him. Baxter has already proven his loyalty."

Talmund's reluctance faded, only slightly. Matthais glanced at Merrick out of the corner of his eye, then back to me.

"You want to do this without telling Scarlett?"

"There's no reason to. It would only distract. The plan that the Networks came up with centers around the circle of the ancients anyway. We can work with their plan. The Guardians will give us some advantage as they fight the mortals."

"You're sneaking your plan on top of this one?"

"It's all we have time for."

Another pregnant pause.

Finally Talmund lifted one shoulder. "Fine. It's no skin off my back for you to try it, as it wouldn't alter the course for my Guardians. They're almost entirely into position. The answer lays with Matthais." Talmund slapped Matthais on the shoulder. "Update me as you are able. I'll keep the mortals as stressed and busy as I can while we try to find amulets."

With that, Talmund returned to the forest, leaving Matthais and Merrick and myself alone in the Gatehouse. Matthais widened his stance as lightning streaked across the sky. The bright flash of white faded back to utter darkness. A waiting pall enveloped Alkarra, as if the land knew that destruction awaited.

A thud rattled the door. I tightened, stopping myself just short of a gasp of surprise. Matthais disappeared.

"Come in," Merrick commanded.

A young boy stumbled into the room, drenched. His hair dropped down his brow in saturated curls, pasted to his skin. Water collected in a puddle beneath him as he doubled over, gasping. Matthais reappeared by the door. He braced his fingers against it and closed it with a thud.

"What is it, Nate?" he asked.

"Demigods at the edge of the castle," the boy gasped. "Mortals, too. They're gathering around all the entrances and exits. They're about to attack! A butler sent me to tell the Protectors. I don't know anything else."

Matthais held up a hand to indicate they should wait, then gazed off into the distance. Moments later, he turned back to the lad, hand returning to his side.

"Talmund just left. He said he's assigning a contingent to come back to the castle and support the one already here. Run to your butler, tell him that."

"Forgive me," Nate squeaked, "but there are so many demigods! More than a contingent can handle."

Merrick growled.

Arborra, can the trees nearest the castle see the mortals and demigods amassing outside?

A pause, then, *Yes.*

Tell the trees to get rid of them. I don't want a single demigod or mortal near the castle.

A thrill infused Arborra's reply.

As you command.

"It will be taken care of," I said to the boy.

Matthais lifted an inquiring eyebrow. "Will it?"

Already, the voices of trees rose in my mind with promises of protection and revenge. A thirst for justice drove them to action, I felt it stirring my blood. Overhead, a screech, then a burst of dragonfire, headed that direction.

I couldn't see what the trees or the dragons did, but exclamations, discussions, and cries from the saplings indicated some level of success already.

"Go, Nate." I nodded toward the door. "See for yourself."

Nate turned to Matthais, who relented with a nod. The boy scampered back outside, disappearing with a crackle of lightning. Thunder flowed next, lasting for several long moments.

"You're serious?" Matthais murmured.

"Quite."

"The trees just . . . obey you?"

"They want to fight for Alkarra. I simply . . . guide. It's the power I've been given."

"By the goddess?"

"Yes."

He let out a controlled breath. "All right."

"With the forest, we can save the Network, but we need the Protectors help getting the amulets. The trees can't fight forever, and the only way to stop the gods is to destroy the amulets."

"Baxter hasn't found Nicomedianthekus."

"He will have, shortly. If Baxter does his job well," I replied, "we'll only have one god to deal with. He's going to find Nicomedianthekus, return it to Gelas, and distract Ventis until we've found and destroyed at least eight amulets. We have seven left."

My confidence didn't waver. Tontes had inadvertently revealed himself, and my trip to Alaysia made it almost glaringly obvious where the amulet could be hidden. If Baxter drew his father's attention away, we'd have one less god to grapple with.

Hopefully.

Matthais pulled in a breath, his nostrils widening, then shrinking. The intensity of his gaze hadn't waned as he considered the rudimentary steps of my plan. Breath rushed out of him. He nodded once.

"Fine. You have my support, on one condition." He paused, lifted a finger. "Rognvald, Chi, and myself are involved. Derek is on his way. I'll brief him and Regina."

"Agreed. I expect the six of you to take an amulet each. That will amount to seven. I'll find one myself, which makes eight."

"What's our backup plan?" Merrick asked. "In case someone doesn't get an amulet."

I grinned.

"The forest. Once you find an amulet, the forest will take it from there. It can send them to Ignis and Gelas more safely than we could without Baxter here. Ready to get started?"

Matthais stopped me with a gentle hand on my shoulder.

"Wait."

I froze, startled by the contact. He dropped his arm back to his side. Both eyebrows crashed together, wrinkling the skin between them.

"I wanted you to know that the Brotherhood is proud to work with the Sisterhood."

Heat welled up in my throat. Relief. Pride. Joy. Matthais continued seamlessly, as if the words didn't cost him a thing to say.

"You've done well, Bianca." His gaze darted to Merrick, then back to me. "I love my Brothers like my sons, and I hope one day to say the same about the Sisterhood. Let's go amulet-hunting, shall we?"

My lips curled into a slow grin. I nodded.

"Oh, one more thing."

His hand reached back out, settled on my shoulder. He murmured under his breath, full lips moving fast and steady. Heat welled up in his palm, slipped into my body. Magic darted from my shoulder to my mind like streaks of fire. I gasped, shuddered. A shift occurred, like a breaking within. My mind opened to fireworks of bursting light.

Matthais stared at me, gaze tapered. His lips didn't move, but I heard his voice all the same.

Welcome to the magic of the Brotherhood.

A thrill shot all the way through my body, lifting goosebumps on my arms. The Brotherhood magic. As powerful an acceptance as I could ask for. No more sending written messages to Papa or wondering when Merrick would reply. The Brotherhood had access to me, and I to them, in an unprecedented, clever way.

Matthais had given me the gift of arriving.

Joy infused me. Courage. Readiness. I smiled. Matthais returned it, however briefly. Within moments, he sobered again.

"I'm going to find your father," he said with a step back. "Give him and my other Protectors updates and assignments. Merrick, stay with Bianca. Chi, Derek, Regina, Rognvald, and myself will meet you both at the rendezvous point at the circle of the ancients."

At my side, Merrick grinned. He clapped a hand on my shoulder, squeezed. *Let's go, little troublemaker,* he said in my mind. *We've got the Network to save again.*

An intentional thought sent my reply.

We have one more witch to find.

* * *

Guided by a darting blue light, Merrick and I sprinted through Letum Wood.

Muddy ground squelched between my toes as I ran, grateful to find higher ground. My chest burned as I hurried past freshly-fallen trees. Some propped against other trees, like a sick friend. Saplings filled the forest floor. Fading cries issued from them as I soared past. Moisture soaked us in moments as we splashed through puddles, wading through swollen streams trickling downhill.

With each footstep, cerulean light appeared beneath me. I trailed my fingers along the trees, grabbed vines. Brilliance lingered with each touch. Voices spoke with each caress.

We are yours.

You belong to us.

We protect each other.

I trust you, I said. My mind lay open to the forest, broadcasting my thoughts, my commands. Tree branches stirred. Limp bushes straightened, as if finding courage again. In the distance, the roar of forest lions could be heard.

Magic reared up inside me, a prickling, ferocious power. A beacon of light and ability, so much greater than Ignis and I ever shared. My heart stirred with restless regard to the potential sitting in my chest. I poked and prodded the power to life, allowing the full extent of abilities to make itself known. The magic stood up, willing to respond.

To the trees, I continued my refrains.

You follow me.
I lead you.
We fight together.
You take care of yourself.

The whispers responded with growing volume, increasing measure.

We follow you.
We fight together.
We fight.
We take care of ourselves.

A building thrum followed their words—so similar, yet different—to what I'd always heard. Their growing courage spurred me to move faster. My heart slammed in my ribcage. Thunder growled overhead. My feet slapped mud, pressed past rocks. Lightning flashed at every other moment. Wind gusted by in wrathful surges.

Still, we plowed through the forest, spreading my message. More voices crowded my mind, my connection broadened to welcome all. Agitation accompanied the forest response. Deeper, similar, but distinctly different at the same time.

At once, I knew it to be the forest dragons.

Their deep-seated annoyance and thriving frustration gave them away. This deluge of rain threatened their heat. They tolerated moisture, according to Nicholas, because it maintained the foliage in which they hid. Such copious amounts would be outright torturous.

Good.

A prickly hoard of dragons could be *just* what the Network needed.

The farther I ran, the deeper the angst. Wings flapped overhead. Penumbras shifted in the forest next to me. I glanced to the side to find galloping bodies, furled wings, snarling teeth. The dragons ran *with* us now.

A bellow of fire came from up ahead. I skidded to a stop.

Mud slipped all the way up my calves, caking my legs to my knees. My hand reached for purchase and a branch appeared. I grabbed it, kept upright by its gentle guidance. Merrick halted behind me, chest heaving.

I stopped, tilted my head back, and stared into a familiar pair of enraged yellow eyes.

"Reebis."

You have returned.

"We need you. I came to ask the dragons to fight with us tonight. The gods are advancing."

A body shifted, stepping to the side just behind the dragon. My breath caught as Nicholas moved into view. His hair was askew, eyes wide, lips down. He stalked, his heavy feet stamping through water until he stood a few paces away. My heaving shoulders slowed.

"Nicholas."

He nodded once, face hard as stone. "The dragons are ready to fight."

Chapter Twenty-Six

Nothing stirred in Deasylva's circle.

The wide spaces that lay between each ancient tree could hold hundreds of witches, yet nothing moved. Not a light, not a voice. Only endless, vapid darkness. A mask, given by the trees. Black night so complete it looked like a dark hole had overtaken the world.

Instinctively, I shied away from such utter shadow. Letum Wood was poised for this moment. Deasylva made certain of it.

Merrick reached out, held my arm. Though I knew the trees would keep me safe, I felt better with him at my side. Somewhere to the left lay the abandoned Dragonmaster village, a testament to hundreds of years of history. My right hand extended into the dark until the tips of my fingers met a hard, porous substance.

Bark.

Blue light bolted through the tree, climbing higher. The momentary flash illuminated Merrick's face, the space around us, then faded. I had enough time to see that we stood in between the roots of Arborra, at the foot of the giant tree.

Chatter from the Brotherhood had been minimal. Hardly anyone spoke unless something pertinent happened. Updates from different parts of Alkarra, changes in weather that had significance. Increasing rain, lightning concentrated in an area.

"The Guardians are out there?" I asked.

Merrick made a noise in his throat. "Twenty Central Network contingents are in position here at the circle. Ten Southern Network, plus a couple of Western, too."

"So few?"

"For now."

"How many total contingents do we have available?"

"Hundreds. They'll come in as needed. The Eastern Network is ready as a second wave. They're somewhere else, with orders to transport in at certain spots."

With only ten to thirteen witches per contingent, Network leadership were starting with low numbers. Darkness this vapid likely meant they'd want to test the battle first, see how many mortals advanced.

Protect the witches, Arborra?

Arborra's voice came with unwavering confidence. *The saplings join together to form barriers. The darkness is complete.*

"Can demigods see in the dark?"

I felt Merrick shrug. "Not sure. Probably?"

We'll have to assume so, I said through the Protector magic. A deathlike pall had fallen over the forest that I didn't want to break again. Despite more than a hundred Guardians in position in Letum Wood, not a sound stirred.

No sough of wind.

No sigh of witch.

Silence.

The hair on the back of my arms stood up. A crack, then a bang, crashed overhead. The *plink plink plink* of rain followed, pattering my shoulders. It pinged off of Merrick's half armor, a reminder that the gods had only just begun. This battle would be a struggle with war, destruction, and survival.

Updates from the Guardians? Matthais asked. His voice

moved through my mind like a ripple. Merrick's head turned, as if he was looking off to the side. Matthais must have sent it to all the Brotherhood.

To my surprise, Talmund replied. *The initial wave of Guardians is in position, with orders to sow chaos and discord, destroying as many mortals and demigods as they can manage. More remain ready to transport in for support when needed. If possible, all Guardians will try to get an amulet. They've been instructed to assist any Protector if asked.*

Any idea how many demigods to expect? Papa asked.

No, I said. *Ventis has less than ten children that might be willing to fight—we aren't sure which of his daughters would volunteer. Tontes has an unknown number, but guesses have varied from twenty to seventy-five to over a hundred demigod children.*

Busy man, Papa muttered.

Despite myself, I chuckled. Rognvald cut through my amusement. *Any sign of the enemy?*

Only the rain, Talmund said.

Any other leaders with you, Talmund? Matthais asked.

Niko Aldana commands his forces. Alina is here as well, protected by a demigod named Tipa. When the battle starts, Tipa will take her to the Arck in the Western Network, where Scarlett, Aldred, Lana, and a Council Member from the North are commanding the strategy.

Neither report startled me, but I frowned all the same. Having Network leaders in the battle complicated our potential losses, particularly in the Southern Network, as Alina hadn't named the new High Priest yet. I couldn't worry about that now. That was Talmund's business.

Trust, Grandfather reminded me.

The gods were out there, somewhere. *That* was my only focus. The rest would have to work itself out. Merrick tightened. I swung around, startled by a distinct and ringing sound in the emptiness.

Whispers.

Hushed voices. A chattering language, not our own. The lilting accent, flowing words, immediately swept me back to Alaysia. Cloud cover packed the sky, preventing moonlight from giving us more visual aid. I cupped my hands around my ears to hear better. A spell amplified the voices.

Undeniably Alaysian.

They came from the other side of Arborra, to my right. A few at first, then more soft sounds followed. Did the demigods use magic to bring the mortals here a few at a time? I could imagine no other way they'd get them here. Unless Ventis or Tontes did it themselves and all at once.

Arborra's footprint spanned so wide I could barely hear the voices. I pattered closer, winced when mud squelched beneath my feet.

Mortals have arrived, I said to the Protectors. *Around the northernmost ancient. They're coming around both sides of Arborra, ancient number one.*

Understood, Talmund replied.

The quiet returned. Only a shuffle betrayed them.

Hold to the plan, Merrick said just to me, as if he could sense my anticipation to get the mortals out of here.

The trees are ready, I said to everyone.

Merrick gripped my shoulder, squeezed. The reassuring motion quelled my rising uncertainty and fear.

Mortals to the south and southeast corners, came Chi's low, steady voice. *Near ancient number six and five.*

Confirmed on the east, Rognvald said, *near ancient three.*

Papa's voice filled my head felt like a comforting hug. *Confirmed on the west, between ancients eight, nine, and ten. I believe we're surrounded, gentlemen,* he said brightly.

And lady, I said.

A laugh filled Papa's voice when he replied. *Welcome, Sisterhood. We're pleased to have you.*

In the darkness, I grinned. No matter what happened tonight, Papa fought with us. We faced the best possible chances with all these witches working together.

Awaiting orders from the mission leader, Matthais said. The open sound of his voice, as if it reverberated through stone halls, made it clear he'd said it to all the Protectors. Such a comment meant they waited on me.

I turned to the magic, feeling the forest out.

Hold your positions, I said after a moment.

To Arborra, I asked, *Is it time to start the plan?*

A faint tension filled my chest, then faded.

It is time.

With a shoulder-expanding breath, I spoke into the magic. *Initiate the mission, starting with the southern edge. All of you have your assignments. Find an amulet, the trees will take it from there. Good luck.*

Like a curtain drawn away, moonlight fell into the circle. The forest removed the magic they'd hidden behind, starting along the southern edge. Shadows peeled away in a sheet. Bruised light appeared, illuminating the forest. The stalwart ancients stood as black sentinels. A greenish forest floor, mostly coated in night, came next. The wink of armor, a glint of sword, a hint of weak torchlight, scattered here and there.

Hushed voices followed.

Surprise.

Shock.

With the dissipating darkness came movement. Trees skidded across the landscape. Along the southern edge of the circle, the ground churned. Roots sprayed clods of dirt that landed with heavy *thuds*. Like wild snakes, the roots plunged back into the soil, grabbed onto something below the dirt, then pulled. Some of the saplings, unable to pull themselves from the ground, would be sacrificed in the attempt.

They groaned with the herculean effort of moving through

the heavy mud, forming a screen along the inside of the circle that lessened the battlefield area. It would force mortals to fight in a more dispersed way, drawing them out.

As the trees drove closer together, the barricade tightened in a braid of branches, impenetrable by anything bigger than an arrow.

Victorious songs rang in the back of my mind, exultant as the forest changed.

We fight.

We conquer.

We defeat.

I nearly giggled at their exultant song. The trees uprooted themselves with surprising joy. Another burst of wind swept through the leaves overhead, but none stirred my hair.

Guardians to reveal themselves in five, Talmund said.

Silently, I counted backwards.

Two . . .

One . . .

Hundreds of Guardians came into view, massed around the edges of the circle the saplings had just formed. Torches sprang to life with them, sending beams of buttery light onto the sodden ground.

Their half armor had a dull shine in the muted blaze, bouncing with the flow of flames. Each Guardian stood tensed, ready. Contingents blurred into each other, standing close.

Sword in hand, Merrick leaned forward, legs braced. I wrapped my left hand around Viveet, but kept her in the sheath.

The mortals stood just beyond the light cast from the Guardians, visible only as vague shapes that moved here and there. Witches paused, barely stirred. The trees calmed, silent as a tomb.

A cry rang from the mortals.

They advanced.

Bodies flooded the area. As one, they came upon the circle.

Gritted teeth. Flexed arms. Gleaming weapons. Running legs. Several hundred immediately rushed at the witches. For mortals, they were shockingly hale and hearty. A brute force of people with as much reason to fight as us.

With grunts and shouts, the mortals threw themselves as one against the Guardian forces, pressed tight against the circle of trees.

The Guardians disappeared.

Like popping bubbles, they exploded. A spell, all of it. Only the torches remained, flickering in the inky night. The mortals stumbled, collapsed on top of each other. Those at the back of the advance tripped over falling bodies as they attempted to keep their feet. Their battle fury stalled into sheer confusion.

Guardians incoming again, Talmund said in the dry tone of a battlefield leader. *We estimate five hundred mortals on their initial attack. New contingents activated. We'll match their numbers.*

A voice rose above the others, off to the left. I swung around to look that way, spotted what had to be a demigod. Underneath a dark-sleeved shirt came a subtle gleam. What appeared to be a working amulet wrapped the wrist.

From this distance, I confirmed they were a demigod with a touch of their allure, and listened to the instinct that believed it true.

Demigod to the west, I said to Rognvald. *Take that one, please. He has long hair in braids, around his shoulders.*

Understood.

Another voice shouted from the east. I reached higher up the bark, felt for a grip, and used my legs to push to a better position. Another presumed demigod that way, though no visible amulet.

Chi, a potential demigod to the east. He's wearing a black vest over what appears to be a brown shirt. Not confirmed, but he has a touch of allure and I don't think his eyes are golden. Amulet location is unknown.

Understood.

Mortals shoved back to their feet, whirled around. Two other potential demigods appeared to the south, too far away for me to be certain. An assignment to Papa and Regina would take care of them.

Four assigned.

Tontes had sixteen amulets. Papa had captured one at the Gimsteinar mine months ago, and I had stolen one near my cottage tonight, which left fourteen at large. Ventis had an unknown number of amulets floating out there. Arguably, at *least* ten, if not more, though Letum Wood had taken one days ago.

Finally, the mortals seemed to have gathered themselves back together. They stood near the trees, eyes darting around. A moment of quiet followed.

Then a roar.

Guardians advanced from the dark band of trees all at once. Hundreds transported into position and charged, swords flashing, half armor glinting. More torches appeared, flooding the circle with greater light.

Archers stepped out of hidden spots higher in the bark of the ancients, loosing arrows on the mortals. Heavy *thwacks* of arrows hitting flesh, snapping ribs, followed. Screams filled the air. Blood spurted. Whenever a mortal fell, they disappeared.

Unharmed mortals scurried away from the Guardians. Trees bound together, attempting to keep them inside the circle. Demigods countered by ripping the trees in half, yanking them out of the earth with god magic. Entire saplings were uprooted and flung through the air like cabers. Half a contingent of Guardians fell when a flying tree slammed into them. Groans issued over the sound of increasing raindrops and wind.

Commands shouted back and forth in Alkarran and Alaysian, in between splashes of bodies falling in the mud. Chaos reigned.

I ignored it.

Matthais, I called. *Confirmed demigod to the northwest. Blonde hair, female, slender body, with a blue blazer. The amulet is on her left hand in a ring. It's a purple one named Alasparin, and it's known as a more powerful Tontes amulet, so be wary.*

Understood.

Five amulets assigned.

Three to go.

I climbed higher, disguising myself under an invisibility spell. The bark provided ample handholds as I scaled.

Merrick?

Here.

Head to the southeast. There might be three demigods speaking together, in between ancients seven and eight. One of them used magic to stop a Guardian advance. I'm not sure of the other two. Proceed carefully, I'm not sure if a leader is amongst them.

Is *there a leader over the demigods?*

"I hope so," I muttered to myself.

Not a clear one yet, I said to Merrick.

Understood.

Guardians continued to advance from the forest. Within the darkness, more mortals appeared, as if both sides had an ever-populating army. When a mortal fell, magic took them away, which meant that demigods must be watching. A constant flow of magic would also mean that the power of their amulets would expire eventually.

Unless Ventis or Tontes worked here.

Arborra, any demigods in the trees?

We observe none.

Remove them immediately if they attempt to climb.

As you command.

If you see an opportunity to help Guardians?

We shall.

Slightly mollified, I climbed higher. We had three amulets

left to assign out and the battle had only been waging for fourteen, maybe fifteen minutes. So far, so good. Yet I couldn't count on anything in the battle going according to plan. I pushed myself to climb higher. Our success relied on finding the amulets immediately.

A familiar flash of purple caught my eye from the other side of the circle as Guardians backed away. Mortals moved to the middle in a circular formation. Their chests heaved. Blood stained their shirts, their skin. Guardians lay on the ground between the two forces. Vines crawled through the melee, wrapped around injured Guardian ankles, and pulled them to safety. Guardians chugged water as the bodies cleared. Mortals glared.

I straightened.

That amulet color . . .

Across the way, familiar white-and-gray hair moved into sight. The demigod female that destroyed my house wove through mortals standing off to the side, panting. Others flowed in her wake, jogging to keep up with her long strides. She commanded respect on such a backdrop. My cottage flipped through my mind.

My home.

I tightened my grip on the tree. Arborra spoke, as if it sensed my distress.

The ill-fated return.

"She has another amulet. She's the same demigod that commanded the mudslides that destroyed my house. Shall we obtain it together?"

A vine wrapped my waist, tightening in a reassuring squeeze.

We shall.

* * *

While I crept through the forest, avoiding the goriest parts of battle along the edge of the circle, battlefield conversations flowed through my mind.

There doesn't seem to be any organization between demigods and mortals, Papa said to the Protectors. *From what I can tell, the mortals aren't following an individual demigod. The fighting mortals seem to work together, apart from the demigods.*

The mortals are moved with magic when they are in harm's way, or injured, Chi said next. *But I also cannot decide if it is done by demigods, or something else.*

Confirmed three amulets, Merrick said. *Two of them split away. I tracked them toward ancient number ten.*

Will follow, Chi said. *Mine disappeared.*

I'll remain on this one, Merrick said.

So few amulets means they're holding more in reserve, Matthais muttered, his voice dark. *Let's just get this done.*

Our reality sent a chill all the way through my bones. Indeed. A wise god would hold some of his amulets in reserve. Observations of the battlefield further painted a bleak picture. Unknowns and questions populated everywhere, intensifying my impatience.

Despite the importance of strategic attack and observation, I wanted another amulet already. A win to keep us going to the next one.

Panicked saplings called from the back of my mind, but older trees calmed them. Guidance, discussion ensued. I mentally set them aside. The trees would care for each other now. The saplings were not my responsibility in the same way as before.

The urge to know what was happening with Baxter distracted me too much as I invisibly worked toward the moving female. Did he find Nicomedianthekus? Was all of this for nothing? I shoved aside that question for now.

Baxter would come through.

On this side of the circle, Guardians and mortals had separated; each sized the other up from opposite sides. Brawny mortals at the back spoke rapidly. Heads nodded. Teeth were bared. New plans, no doubt. The battle continued on the other side.

With a curse, I realized too late that we should have asked Baxter to put god magic on Merrick so he could understand Alaysian.

A flash of familiar dark hair drew my gaze across the circle, to the other side of the ancients. Niko stood in front of several contingents of East Guards. He wore armor, carried a sword with a long, gleaming blade. His lips moved. Concentration tightened his face into the hard angles of a leader. Dutiful Guardians remained at his side. Priscilla would be undeniably proud of him when she heard of this.

I silently wished him well, and pressed on.

The demigod female appeared at random intervals; her new amulet was a large gem instead of a collection of several smaller. She stood out of the main circle, but not far enough. I followed as best I could, barely able to keep her in sight.

I'm going after amulet number seven, I said to the Brotherhood. *With the three amulets Merrick confirmed, and the others I assigned, we have enough in this circle to hunt. We still only have two Tontes amulets captured and need at least six more, seven to be safe. Let me know when you have obtained one and given it to the forest.*

A chorus of *Understood* followed.

I climbed a root from the next ancient over to give myself a better vantage point. Mortals attempted to fan out, sneaking into the trees. If the occasional glint of silver in the darkness meant anything, the Guardians anticipated such a move.

A cry resounded over the field.

Another charge.

Mortals hurtled across the circle, running fast as their sturdy legs would carry them. Guardians transported in their midst, slashing with swords. Screams and gurgles followed. One Guardian grabbed a mortal by the arm, attempted to stab between the ribs.

Both vanished.

The female demigod had stopped to watch the battle. She stood two hundred paces away, her lower half hidden in a root well. Silver hair cascaded down her shoulders, near her elbow. With her arms, she gestured higher. Battlecries and clashes covered background thunder. Lightning illuminated the distant forest, momentarily brightening the floor. Her hair flashed white, then faded.

She stood too far away to rush her, even invisibly. Historically, she moved too often. Mortals surrounded her, as well. If I transported to her side, I'd throw myself into the middle of a bigger problem and not come out with an amulet.

On instinct, I reached out to the tree. Light bloomed beneath my touch, sinking deep into the wood.

What's your name? I asked.

Balooma, the ancient whispered.

"Will you help me?"

We protect you.

The deep voice, steady and keen, reminded me of Arborra, though distinctly different in tone. I smiled, comforted by a surge of affection that followed. I switched to thinking through the magic so Balooma could understand my plans.

Tell me your thoughts, Balooma.

We surprise them.

How?

Where they don't expect you.

My forehead ruffled. Where *wouldn't* they expect me?

Dirt trembled beneath my feet. I stepped back. A brown circle began to form in the thick earth. Clods of soil danced on top, like beads of oil across a hot pan. Solid ground gave way, rolling back to form a hole. The little pit deepened as loam pressed to the side, wide and deep. A handbreadth at a time, the hole burrowed into the earth, as if invisible arms scooped it away.

With a gasp, I realized what Balooma meant.

You want me to go underneath?

I save you, it said.

Without words or images, I understood what the tree meant. The hole was just wide enough for my shoulders and body to shuffle through. I gazed around, but no one seemed to have noticed. All mortals kept their attention on the battle. The female demigod shifted to the side, stepping with her right foot.

No time to waste—she would be on the move soon.

Thank you.

Balooma said nothing as I ducked into the hole. Darkness, thick with loam and clay, left a dank tinge to the air. The claustrophobic hole wrapped around me like a close embrace as I hurried on my hands and knees. Mud slaked each wall, the ground saturated from the rains. Dirt and debris oozed between my fingers. Viveet's sheath scraped the ground, collecting grime along her edge as I scurried along.

The burrowing gnomes at my cottage came to mind. Had they survived?

I hoped so.

My first attempt for the amulet failed, Rognvald growled. *They're fast and seem to be anticipating our moves.*

Third attempt failed here, Matthais said. *The first one I grabbed was fake.*

Their magic is thought-based, I said. *If you can't take them by surprise, try to confuse them. Cloud their mind. If you can force them to focus on something else, it will be too hard for them to channel their intent into magic.*

Understood, stated four other voices.

I kept going.

A hint of color appeared ahead of me, a faint blush of navy blue against sheer darkness. Mud trickled down my neck, coating my hair. I ignored it as I slipped back into an invisibility spell and emerged out the other side.

Once I crawled free, the hole disappeared.

The demigod stood in the same spot as I gained my feet and reassessed. A simple touch and I'd be able to grab the chain around her neck, but I wouldn't fall for that again. The real amulet had to be somewhere on her body.

She turned, giving me a view of her profile, as she spoke to a mortal. Blood streaked his lips from where it poured out his nose. The edges dried to a darker crimson.

My gaze darted down her body. No hair accoutrements. No bracelet. No rings. No other obvious jewelry or suspicious bumps in the fabric.

Balooma, can you detect magic?

Yes.

God magic?

No.

I scowled. Her amulet must be somewhere under her dress, a gray piece with sleeves all the way to the wrists, skirts to the ground. My gaze tapered. She could make the amulet invisible with magic, of course . . .

Her left arm twitched. Her other hand moved to touch it, then stopped. She stiffened slightly, then forced herself to relax. She peered out, arms folded loosely across her middle, eyes narrowed into thin slits. Her lips pursed in deepest disapproval.

I straightened.

Interesting.

Nothing was visible on her left wrist or hand. Her dress gave no errant hints of light that indicated the god magic was in use from an amulet. Nor her other wrist or what I could see of her ankles.

On my command, Letum ivy sprang to life at my feet. Quick

as a lizard, it crawled ahead. The ivy scooted over, dancing above a fallen body, and plunged beneath her skirt.

My heart pounded.

Can you feel an amulet on her ankles? It may not be visible, but it should be felt.

Not here, said Balooma.

Try the wrists.

The female glanced down, brow wrinkled. She shook her head and stepped back, as if searching for something. I dodged a mortal as they hurried by, almost knocking me off my feet.

It is on her wrist, Balooma said.

Grab it!

A squeak came from the female. She reached for her left wrist, where a hint of green showed from beneath the sleeve. I threw myself at the demigod to distract her. She fell beneath me as the vine disappeared.

It is obtained, Balooma murmured.

The vine retracted.

Send it to Gelas!

As you say.

I dodged a blow from the female. A vine fell, wrapping her free wrist as I gained my feet and slid Viveet from her sheath. The invisibility magic slipped away, revealing me as I pressed a smoldering Viveet to her neck.

She tensed, chin tilted back to avoid the cobalt fire, hissing. Her upper lip curled over her teeth.

"You destroyed my home," I growled.

She snapped with her jaw, as if to bite me. I pressed the blade harder into her neck.

"You'll never win, amulet-breaker!"

"Amulet-stealer would be more appropriate in this case. I think we could give the title of amulet-breaker to Gelas, if you were so inclined. He now has two amulets from you, thank you very much."

Her gaze dropped to her left wrist. She circled it with her right fingers, then glared at me with resolute hatred. A feral cry came from deep in her throat. Her gleaming teeth bared, she snapped at me again, like a wild thing.

"Are you animal or demigod?"

"Alkarra is for the gods!" she shrieked.

"Then come and take it!" I shouted.

With greater strength than mine, she shoved to her feet. The force threw me back, slamming my spine into a root. Teeth gritted, I forced myself to stand.

The demigod advanced. Viveet slashed in a circle, tearing her dress open at the waist. A bright line of blood bubbled to the surface. She screamed, reached for me, but Viveet's flames leapt to life. With a squeal of pain, she twirled away. The scent of burnt flesh lay acrid in the air.

I twirled into guard, Viveet between us.

With a scowl, she tilted her head back.

"Take me away!"

A smirk and she vanished.

Two men crashing together shoved me from behind. I scuttled out of sight, pressed closer to the trees, as I hurriedly resheathed Viveet. Protector voices poured through my head as I skirted the edge of the circle. Clashes continued throughout the interior, where the coppery scent of blood lay thick in the air. In the distance, I thought I saw Apothecaries bustling around witches.

Amulet obtained, I said.

My amulet not *obtained,* Rognvald cried. *More mortals are coming.*

Demigods pushing hard on the western flank, Chi said. *I count four new demigods over here. The two recently-seen amulets are red, not gray or purple. The demigods attached to them are focusing away from the battle, looking at the trees.*

Rain sprinted down now, turning everything slippery.

Mortals and Guardians fell over each other in the middle, amidst the saplings that still formed an interior circle to lessen the battlefield space.

Screams rang out. Mortals that had fallen before returned to the fracas, completely healed. Silvery scars glittered on their bodies, but no blood.

There were two demigods over here, Merrick said, his voice broken, as if he panted. *Can only find one. The other left, the first is hard to track. She leaves without a trace, there's no way to follow. I keep losing her.*

Papa responded. *Mine has retreated as well.*

Mine is also missing, Matthais said.

A dark sensation overtook my chest. For *all* the demigods to fade away around the same time meant . . . something.

Attempts to keep the Brotherhood straight in my head were almost met with failure. Chi had started on the eastern edge and had to push to the western edge? Ignis' rebellious demigods were here now. To preserve Ventis' and Tontes', I'd wager.

Mortals spilling in from the north, Papa said with grim certainty. *I estimate four hundred in a new wave.*

South, too, Merrick said.

By my calculation, Talmund should anticipate a thousand new mortals en masse, Rognvald muttered.

Understood, Talmund said.

The forbidding reports overwhelmed me. Where were these mortals *coming* from? Tontes? Ventis? A combination? They could still have thousands of mortals between the two of them, for all I knew.

The plan from the Network leadership is to send in the second wave of Guardians, Talmund said. *Fresh ones from the East and the North, but no one planned on this many mortals to fight. We won't be able to stand long against their opposition. We'll have to pull from our third wave, which will cripple us later tonight. Scar-*

lett, Marten, Alina, and Lana are attempting to come up with another plan.

Our Guardians and Letum Wood had held the initial attack at bay, but we clearly weren't prepared to support a brute force battle much longer. The losses had been greater than anticipated, if the frantic Apothecaries meant anything.

I tilted my head back to regard the rain.

We hadn't lost yet.

It's time to call the dragons, I said to the Protectors.

Quiet fell.

Talmund broke it in astonishment. *What did she just say?*

The magic shuffled inside me, as if it knew what to do. I felt it click into position, shifting my mind away from the Brotherhood. Reebis' attention, her fury, connected with me like a tower of fire. I let the magic enter my blood with passion and rage. A scream, then a plume of flames, illuminated the night sky overhead.

Reebis? I called.

We are ready, Lady-witch of Letum Wood.

Happy hunting.

The dragons descended.

Chapter Twenty-Seven

The ground trembled.

The stampede-like vibration made my teeth clack together in painful ways as I sprinted to the closest tree. Torches had long extinguished, leaving the forest more black than not. Only a few flickered here and there near the interior of the battle, illuminating grisly scenes.

When the dragons arrived, sweeps of fire landed over the top of the gathered mortals. Blankets of smoldering red fell in rampant destruction. Screams, sizzles, grunts. At least ten dragons appeared immediately after my call.

Wind burst through the sky, barely audible over the thud of dragon wings that sprawled like snapping leather blankets. The supple scales, flickering tails, disappeared into the canopy. Their fire cast strange shadows and a shifting reality over the world.

Get any amulet! I cried to the Protectors. *Use the distraction you have. Forget your assignments, go for whatever you can find. The demigods and mortals will try to bring down the dragons with god magic, which will illuminate the amulets. Watch for them to reveal themselves, then attack. We have five amulets left to obtain.*

The expected plethora of voices replied.

Understood.

I climbed higher up the closest ancient. Slippery hand holds in the bark led me up, but precariously so. A vine appeared, wrapping my waist. It caught me when my bare foot slid out of a hole and prevented my plunge to the mud-soaked earth.

"Thank you," I whispered.

Twenty paces higher, I stopped to peer over my shoulder. Torchlight dotted the darkness, kept alive only by incantations in the midst of the downpour. Smoke sizzled from extinguished areas, where mortals fled the hot breath of advancing dragons. Amulets illuminated the night here and there, like fireflies. Dragons swung their heads and giant necks around, eyes glittering like full moons as they assessed their next target.

Who is on the eastern side? I asked. *Near ancients three and four?*

No response.

Anyone?

I don't know where I am, Merrick muttered. *I'm away from the circle, chasing another demigod.*

West, Matthais said. *By ancients nine and ten.*

No response from Papa or Chi. With a growl, I transported to the other side, right where I'd seen the amulet. Chaos met me. Screaming mortals. Fighting Guardians. A sword slid right over my head, a finger's-breadth away from chopping my ear off. I ducked a breath early. The Guardian and mortal grappled away, shouting.

Dark shadows burst from the circle as a giant dragon glided through the air. Light gray washed through ebony scales in ribbons of slate. Behind it, a familiar red-and-black dragon, carrying the silhouette of a burly witch.

Reebis and Nicholas.

Despite the sprawling lizards, mortals continued to pour

into the circle, injured or not. Their ferocity had an animalistic quality.

The mortals and demigods are pouring something like acid on the roots of the ancients, Papa said, panting. *It's eating away at the bark. They're digging tunnels, or creating them out of magic, and pouring it down.*

Matthais spoke next. *The mortals are here to distract us, then, from the true purpose of killing the ancient trees.*

Arborra? I whispered.

The magic gave Arborra the words Papa had just said, which meant I didn't have to repeat their horrible sounds. My heart squeezed painfully while I waited for its response.

This is true.

Will you die?

We will fight.

That's not an answer, I growled.

We will fight.

Any word from Baxter? Chi asked, his voice low and quiet.

Helplessly I whispered, *No.*

Talons scored the earth as dragons reached for racing mortals, wings unfurled, their giant bodies taking to the sky. Mortals screamed, skin seared from the hot dragon talons.

Can you sense god magic? I asked Reebis as she winged overhead.

It is everywhere.

You can't find individual amulets?

There is too much here. It blinds us.

Frustration zipped through me as I ran to another tree, uselessly searching. Elis, the largest dragon—a massive, elegant beast with dark gray rippling through his scales—screamed when a spear pierced his wing. The translucent, webbing-like skin bled. A demigod must have used magic, for the spear wrenched down. The wing tore with another scream of pain. The dragon's head lashed around, fire bursting in bright plumes of white and yellow.

Reebis cried out with an anguished scream.

Elis!

The mighty dragon twisted in the air, fire spraying all around him.

He fell.

The crash of his body into the earth sent a shudder through the ground. Witches peeled away, shouting. Through the chaos, I thought I heard Chi say in deepest frustration, *the demigod has escaped me again. I cannot track them or the amulets. This is impossible.*

Mortals rampaged over tired Guardians, who couldn't transport to safety fast enough. Bodies littered the ground, welling in puddles of blood and mud. Rain thickened in a foggy haze, turning to sharp pieces of hail. Another crash of thunder boomed through the forest. A reminder of whom we *really* fought.

The deluge thickened. Dragons peeled away, unable to navigate with the weight of rain on their wings.

We cannot stay in the air, Reebis said. *It is too much. We will fight on the ground.*

Behind the ancients, a groan. A crackle. The *pop* of breaking wood, and a shout. Mortals and witches scattered as a tree behind the ancients toppled with a groan. Pain tore through me, like a dragon talon across my chest, as it plummeted to the ground. I gasped from the force of it.

Tontes boomed, his audible voice breaking across the midnight sky.

"Witches of Alkarra, your land is mine."

* * *

We're not going to make it.

I said the words to Arborra, because Tontes made it impossible to think into the Protector magic. Concentrated thunder descended on the forest in waves so thick it hurt. Wind drove the rain into my skin with painful bursts. My teeth ground together, my brain ached. The booms didn't stop, undulating between rapid raindrops and painful pebbles of hail that smacked my face. Surges of wind worsened the hysteria.

All around the circle of the ancients, disorder prevailed. Mortals advanced, witches fell back with grimaces and shouts that no one heard. Feet splashed through growing puddles the size of ponds. All the while, cries of pain and fear came from the forest to rend me from the inside out.

Arborra's strange silence told me there was more to fear than I wanted to acknowledge.

Increasingly foreboding updates streamed through my head from the Protectors.

No amulet.

Can't see anything.

Demigods have taken off.

They're hiding their amulets well.

All of us fight, Arborra said, *to the end. I shall call the others.*

A tap on my shoulder caused me to tilt my head, look up. While witches raced past, getting out of the way of a growing mudslide, I stared into the high canopy. My arm lifted to protect my eyes, enabling me to see just beyond the pouring moisture.

A vine hovered over me. It retracted, drawing back until it stopped at the closest branch. I blinked, peering right into the yellow-moon eyes of a forest lion.

Once I made eye contact with it, it snarled. White, pearly teeth appeared in a flash. I blinked back a bolt of terror.

Forest lions?

We all fight, Arborra whispered. *To the end.*

All?

Trust us. Save your witches. This is all we have to give.

During a break from the wild thunder, I turned back to the Protector magic. *Talmund, recall all the Guardians. Have them retreat out of the circle. They shouldn't leave, but tell them to stop fighting.*

A moment of astonished silence, then, *What?*

Trust me.

Ten seconds later, shouts rippled through the amassed Guardians. They began to fall back, like departing stars. Mortals chased them, then stopped to cheer. The sheer number of them congregated in the middle of the circle took my breath away.

How were there so many?

More savvy mortals lingered along the edges, weapons in hand, shoulders taut and ready for the next wave. Their weapons startled me. Morning stars, maces, spears. A curved sword with two pointed tips, another spear with a dagger tied to each end. Throwing stars filled the hands of another mortal, who crouched, head tilted back. Water poured down their faces, dripped off crude armor.

All are clear, Talmund muttered what felt like an eternity later. Exhaustion filled his voice. How much time had passed, anyway? Minutes? Hours? Would the sun ever rise again through such thick clouds?

The forest provides, I said to the Protectors. *It's our last chance to find the amulets.*

A strange stillness had overtaken the air. It wavered, then shattered when a distant, guttural shriek broke through the night. My shoulders lifted, bunched around my ears, when a second high-pitched, screeching sound zipped past me.

"Eeeeeee!"

Explosions of brilliant colors filled the air, like thrown confetti. Thousands of fairies freckled the darkened night sky with glowing bodies, elegant dresses, and bared fangs. Mortals recoiled, staring at the tiny bodies in astonishment.

I eyed one fairy in particular. She sped around, darting from mortal to mortal, with so much attitude I would have known her Networks away.

Dafina, the fairy that helped me escape Mabel's clutches in the Western Network. Dafina and her pack had overtaken the Witchery, a turret that my friends and I shared while living at Chatham Castle, for far too long after we departed it.

Mortals screamed as the flying fairies stabbed at eyes, poked holes into necks, issued guttural bellows as they swooped down to bite swollen flesh.

While the bitty warriors distracted the mortals, forest lions slinked out of the shadows on the ground. Out of utter darkness, they raced past witches, lean bodies lithe and powerful, and leapt. Entire packs appeared from the darkness, moving silently.

The screaming intensified.

Mortals collapsed under giant lion paws. Others swatted at fairies. A few mortals were utterly overtaken, stabbed to death by the fairies' sharp spears. A thump, and a splinter of wood, drew my gaze higher. I stepped away from the tree.

From behind shingles of bark emerged blue-gray creatures with wide shoulders, thick arms, and forearms like clubs. They were eyeless, with translucent skin, staggered teeth, and purple spittle that foamed from wide mouths.

Beluas.

The horrible creatures smelled like sulfur and never touched the ground. They burrowed holes into trees, created nests, and had babies in the heights. I rarely saw them from where I remained on the forest floor. Their fists alone were deadly foes.

Ten emerged.

Twenty.

Falling gnomes dropped from branches, screaming as they fell. They whacked mortals on the top of their heads with hammer-like weapons. One mortal dropped, out cold. Another shouted as ten gnomes swarmed him, stabbing with their sharp little knives.

Burrowing gnomes popped out of the ground with shrieks, biting ankles, tripping others. They attacked passing mortals by slicing at bare calves with every opportunity, aiming for the tendon at the back of the leg.

Mortegas approached, sharp antlers ready as they ran into the melee.

Owls swooped down, scoring faces with broad talons.

Dragons fought from the ground, using their secundum to wipe out mortals or obvious leaders. Just beyond the vague light in the circle, a *thud, thud, thud* walked by. Shadows tall as the trees shifted by. My heart leapt into my throat.

A troll?

A . . . something?

All of Letum Wood had come to protect Alkarra. Their sacrifice snapped me out of my shock.

Five amulets left! I cried to the Protector magic.

Merrick's voice came to my mind. It sounded closed off, which seemed to indicate he spoke only to me.

Any word from Baxter?

I ducked an attacking mortal and swung Viveet around to fend off an advance. The mortal skidded to a stop, rushed back to his comrades, running from a dragon whelp that chased him with a mouthful of fire.

No.

Where are you?

To the north-northwest, between ancients ten and eleven.

Merrick appeared twenty paces away. He whirled around. Our eyes connected and relief showed there. He strode over, grabbed my face, pulled me into a kiss. Passion, fear, terror, relief. I felt it all in the grip of his hand on my jaw, the desperate searching of his lips against mine.

He pulled away. A scratch crossed his cheek, smearing blood all the way to his jaw. "If we're going to be in another battle at the same time," he muttered. "We're going to do it together, all right?"

"Always."

A wry smile crossed his face as he readjusted his grip. "I'm behind by two amulets, if my count is correct."

I opened my mouth to reply, but stalled. Reports poured into my mind from the Protectors. Miniature surges of hope against raging evil and torrents of god magic that we couldn't stop.

I'm on the tail of a demigod that's stuck in a belua's hand, Matthais said, his voice strained. *Should have an amulet in a minute.*

I see you, Rognvald called. *I'll intercept from the north. We'll close in together.*

Chi's quiet purr followed. *I stalk another trapped against a tree by a mortega. Will update.*

A stillness in the air drew my attention. I tilted my head back, looked around. Not a branch shifted. No breeze.

No wind.

"Merrick?"

"What?"

"There's no more wind."

He whirled in a circle. "What does it mean?"

"I have no idea, but it's . . . gone."

"Think Baxter is distracting his father?"

"I hope so," I murmured.

Lightning illuminated the distant fog, drawing my gaze outside the circle, to the left. In the strobes of light, a dark, shadowed profile appeared. Flares of electricity illuminated from different angles, revealing a thick, broad-shouldered man with what appeared to be long hair. He stood fifty paces away, facing me. I knew him the moment I saw him.

Tontes.

My throat turned dry as a desert.

I grabbed Merrick's arm and spun him to face me before he also spotted the god of thunder. "Go help Chi," I commanded. "We need the amulets more than anything else."

"B—"

"Now!"

"What about you?"

"I have something else to deal with."

My firm tone left no room for questions. He hesitated, but I shoved against his shoulders. Tears filled my eyes, but I blinked them back. No, I couldn't think about another parting now. I'd faced the gods once, I could do it again.

"Go! If we don't get the amulets, all of this was for nothing. Merrick, do it now! I'll see you once this is all over, all right? Help Chi make this happen. We've only found two! We need six more at a minimum."

He growled, tightened his hold on his sword, and transported away. The fury in his face made it clear he would not be happy about this later.

Another illumination brought Tontes back into view. He stared hard at me, brow heavy with a scowl. I headed toward him against a sea of screaming gnomes throwing rocks at approaching mortals. They left me alone as I veered through, closer to the place of crackling, dark energy.

Right to Tontes.

* * *

"Lady-witch of Letum Wood," Tontes drawled. "You and your forest provide an admirable fight."

Another flash brightened the same cloud. Up close, his profile was more daunting than I'd thought. Shoulders the size of boulders. Hair to his neck, unbound. Thighs that could crush. Everything about Tontes exuded power—and I only saw his silhouette.

Thoughts of Papa, Merrick, Leda, my home, propelled me to close the distance between us. According to Baxter, Tontes loved a game. He loved a *big* victory, not just a little one. Let him have his fun with me while the rest of Alkarra fought for our lives.

"Thank you."

I slowed my approach. We stood ten paces away from one another now, on the edge of the circle of ancients, not far from Arborra. The battle continued around us, as if he shielded us from it somehow.

"I thought the dragons were a nice touch."

"I accept your surrender."

"I haven't given it."

"Then why do you approach?"

"Same reason you did."

Amusement rippled through his tone. "To personally watch you fall?"

I smiled, not entirely certain he could see me.

"To make sure *you* do."

The clouds grumbled overhead, but I couldn't tell if they held annoyance or mirth. The fog in which he stood had thickened, his profile disappeared. It lent an oddly exposed feeling, and the unnerving sense that I'd already lost track of him.

His voice came from behind. "Summon your creatures, if you wish, Lady-witch, but they will also die. You waste precious life that I would rather make good use of when I take over Alkarra. Call them back, preserve their lives, and surrender yourself."

"I'll pass."

He laughed. "In another circumstance, perhaps I might have liked you."

"The feeling is not mutual."

Another voice spoke to me, this from without. The distant quality, far away, hid pain. Desperation. Gasping breath. The sound of Baxter's reeling voice left me feeling cold.

I found it, he gasped. *Gelas has it.*

I opened my mouth to reply, but stopped. He wouldn't hear me. I couldn't god-magic a reply to him.

Grimacing, I turned away.

Gelas has Nicomedianthekus, I said to the Protectors.

A chorus of, *Understood,* followed.

Tontes reappeared a few steps away. Instead of a silhouette, I caught a glimpse of shadow on skin. Wavy hair rustling in the wind.

I gripped Viveet.

Fight a god with me, I said to Arborra.

We are with you.

This is our purpose, I said. *We were created to be mighty.*

The ancients rose in my mind, careful voices, steady with intention. I crouched, bracing myself. Magic welled at my feet. It climbed higher, a warm feeling. Shared power. Rampant ability. The chance to save all that I loved. With the heady exultation of raw magic came a familiar voice.

Deasylva.

You and the forest as one have access to my power. Save my land, daughter of the forest, and you save yourself.

The magic surged past my heart, into my head. Undeniable capacity filled me. Again a conduit to raw power, I touched the brilliant-white magic in my mind and felt no edge.

A flash-bang brought me firmly out. Vines wrapped around my arms at the same moment, yanking me back. They moved more quickly than made sense, definitely propelled by magic. I flew back a second before lightning slammed into the ground at my feet.

Heat singed the air. The smell of sparks and burnt leaves filled my nostrils. I tumbled back, gained my feet. Bushes straightened nearby. Tree branches lowered. Vines congregated at my back.

Move, Arborra commanded.

I dove to the left. Lightning crackled at the spot I stood

before. Another dive took me just out of reach of a third consecutive bolt. My shoulder slammed into a log as I rolled across the mud-strewn earth. I winced through the pain.

Amulet obtained, Papa cried, his words broken. *Letum Wood took it. That means we've taken four.*

Five down, called Chi. *I have given it to the forest. The demigods seem to be losing power. The mortals are not disappearing and healing anymore.*

A vine grabbed my waist, jerked me back, as another bolt of lightning attempted to score me. I sprinted away, slipped behind a trunk. Lightning crackled as it burst against the wood. My touch lingered, sending blue fire into the grains.

I'm sorry.

We protect you, the tree whispered.

All I must do to truly cripple my sister, Tontes sang in my head, *is kill the Lady-witch of Letum Wood. I've been a fool for not realizing that before. You're like an annoying gnat, you know? You keep coming back. You're harmless in the broad scheme of things, but you think you're not.*

Drop, Arborra said.

Saplings bent over me as I slid across a bed of old leaves, skidding on my side. Thunder percussed. Lightning struck, but the trees absorbed the initial shock. I gritted my teeth through the crackling electricity left in the air. The hair on the back of my arms sparked with the force of it.

Can we attack him? I asked Arborra.

The god cannot die.

Frustration rushed through me.

Then how do we fight?

We distract.

Grim-faced, I steeled myself. Survival was the game until Gelas and the Protectors came through. Letum Wood whisked me away mid step. Behind me, another bolt split into the ground with a terrific crash. Instinctively, I hurtled deeper into the forest, away from the circle.

Tontes followed.

Fog crawled along the ground at my back, tripling at a stunning rate. The profile of a striding man illuminated by the flashes of lightning within the cloud. I tripped over a fallen tree, glanced over my shoulder, then shot back to my feet. Fast as a blink, vines yanked me into the air as gnarled electricity sped along the ground, hungry for me.

I whirled into a mid-air somersault. The vine tossed me to another one, which wrapped around my arms, then gently lowered me behind another giant tree. There, I pressed my back to the trunk and panted. We had wandered away from the torches. Darkness would aid—or cripple—me now.

Obtained another one, Matthais cried, exultant. *The storm is relenting, which is increasing visibility. That's six.*

Our count stands at six amulets, Merrick said. *We have two left for a minimum, but Baxter wants seven total amulets if we can. Just to be safe. I'm on the tail of a waning demigod. She appears confused. The beluas have her pinned to a spot.*

Regina has eyes on another one, Papa said. Confidence filled his voice again with a sturdy timbre. *I see another. We'll proceed. The more amulets, the merrier. Let us continue, Protectors. Sisterhood.*

Tontes interrupted their steady, bolstering flow.

You can't hide from me forever, little witch. I can do this all night.

Tontes' singsong voice sickened me. He *truly* enjoyed this far too much.

"You've been here all night?" I called.

You think I would trust demigods to lead the advance? To bring all the mortals as one? To heal the falling bodies?

Well, that explained a lot. The gods had been watching everything. They had removed the injured mortals, healed them, and sent them back. Who knew what else they'd participated in tonight, which explained the definitive edge they held from the beginning of the battle.

"So you do have a soft spot for mortals."

Only for what they provide. Necessary manpower.

I whirled around. Running through the forest was about to expire as an option. My fingers flexed at my hip as I hurried through alternate plans, all-too-aware that a god chased me through these dark acres.

Arborra, I whispered. *Can we hold him off in different ways? This is what I'm thinking.*

I see your thoughts. Yes, we can.

Building power thickened the air, a sure sign lightning was about to hit yet again.

Then get ready!

I ducked, throwing an arm in front of me. Earth flew in the air, bubbling higher in an instant wall. Roots, boulders, and old bones rose with the mound of dirt. The lightning struck it, fizzling out.

On a thought, Letum ivy raced across the ground, heading toward Tontes. I might not be able to kill him, but I could *trap* him. The green shoots wrapped his ankles. I opened my hand, commanding them to me with a thought, just like god magic.

The ends of the ivy sprang into my hand. Tontes glanced down, gaze on his ankles.

I yanked.

The ivy tightened around his calves, upending him where he stood. Feet flew into the air. Instead of slamming into the ground, Tontes twisted. He rose higher, breaking through the Letum ivy. It jerked out of my hand as he landed back on his feet in a crouch. The clouds dissipated around him.

He snarled.

My heart shriveled.

His giant shoulders sprawled out, tensed. Legs tight, braced, his back bent over in a ready position. He growled, upper lip curled over perfectly white teeth, nostrils wide with indignation. I shuffled back a step, startled by the intensity in his gaze.

"What is this?" he asked in a gentle purr. "Is the Lady-witch of Letum Wood finally frightened of something?"

"No."

The wobbly lie didn't convince him. Ebony strands of hair dropped down his back in gleaming waves. Equally inky tattoos trailed across the top of his shoulders, decorating the broad planes of his back to his bare waist in unbroken designs. He wore a pair of loose, flowing pants, all the way to bare feet. At his full height, he reminded me of Tiberius. A giant, hulking man.

"You're a terrible liar."

"I'm not as frightened of you as you think," I managed to say with a little more strength.

He lifted an eyebrow.

I licked my lips and continued. Each second pulsed by, a promise of more time. More hope.

A chance.

"It's the havoc you leave in your wake that I'm more worried about than you," I called. "The god of thunder has a great reputation for desecration."

"What a compliment."

"Take it as such, if you like."

"I shall."

In the quiet that followed, not a sound could be heard. Had I run so far from the circle? No rain dribbled on me here. No wind. Nothing but abject stillness in the heart of the wood.

"I've heard you like to toy with your prey, too," I sidled back a step. He shuffled forward one.

Gelas's insight into Tontes was the only weapon I had left. *Tontes loves a good hunt. He toys with his prey. He likes to come out on top after a long and challenging struggle.*

"Hunting is only fun if it's difficult," Tontes said in a

musing voice. He stalked toward me. For every pace forward, I slipped one back. Arborra guided my steps around obstacles so I moved smooth as a wraith.

"What is it about the chase you love?"

His eyes gleamed. "The end."

When the hair on the back of my arms stood up, I leapt. Vines reached for me, faster than comprehension again. They yanked me away at the last millisecond before the lightning exploded at my feet. The vine unrolled from around me, gently depositing me back to the ground. I froze behind a tree.

When I peered around the side, Tontes strode through the smoke with an arrogant grin, gaze intent on me.

Amulets? I asked the Protectors. My attempt to hide my desperation failed. The word came out as a gasp. *We only need two more.*

No response.

The sky rumbled, a distinct sound that sounded just like . . . laughter. Tontes' gleaming teeth were visible in the murky night.

Act weak, Arborra said.

What does that mean?

Be what you aren't.

The cryptic message made no sense. A root snaked behind my foot, tripped me. I landed with an *oomph.* Tontes slowed. His lazy smirk meant he enjoyed every second of the stalk. Twigs and branches scraped my hands as I scrambled back, out of reach.

Stop, Arborra commanded.

I obeyed.

My gaze locked on Tontes. He used magic to put himself right in front of me, his foot a pace from mine. I held my breath, stared at him. His cold eyes. Angry tattoos. Chiseled expression twisted with malcontent and a gleam of pleasure.

Another! Papa cried. *Regina was successful.*

One left, Matthais called.

Hope surged within. Tontes crouched next to me, so close

that I could feel magic emanating from him. He crackled like lightning, difficult to bear with so fulsome a presence.

He smiled. A hand reached out, touched my skin. I jerked back. His touch sizzled, too hot to tolerate. Electricity fizzled under my skin where his fingers trailed, harrowing and bright. I was locked in position, unable to move. My head swam.

Trust us, Arborra whispered.

Always.

"Lady-witch of Letum Wood. How appropriate for you to die here, of all places. Now of all times." He leaned closer, until only a handspan separated us. "I am going to destroy Deasylva one tree at a time until I stand on the flooded and charred remains of her power. I will think of you while I'm doing it."

His finger trailed down my cheek.

I swallowed.

The demigods are disappearing, Rognvald said. *All of them are leaving.*

Low level panic infused Papa's voice, though he held it steady. *I can't find any demigods. The mortals are confused. They're scrambling around, in chaos. The attack has stopped.*

We need one more amulet to end this, Matthais growled.

Terror filled me.

"They know," I whispered. The sound of my own voice shocked me. I sucked in a breath, wondering why I'd said it aloud.

Tontes' head tilted to the side. "Who knows?"

A shaft of moonlight canted through the trees, falling for the first time in weeks. It landed on my hand, gentle as a moonbeam.

Moonlight meant no clouds.

Beneath me, the forest floor shifted. Trembled. Dirt broke apart in gaping cracks.

"Your demigods. They know."

"What do they know?"

I leaned closer. "That you're about to lose."

Tontes frowned. His gaze became distant, as if he just clued into something beyond here.

Amulet obtained! Merrick cried. *Leda just showed up with it. I . . . I have no idea how. The forest has taken it.*

I blinked.

Of his sixteen amulets, we'd stolen eight. We'd crippled Tontes power.

We did it.

Tontes' shoulders tensed, teeth bared. Clouds moved away from the moon, revealing greater light. He tilted his head back, gaze narrowed. Hidden shadows dissipated, brightening the forest to a dark blue instead of sheer black. Trunks, bushes, became visible.

Arborra?

Hold on, Arborra whispered.

All at once, the ground gave way. A vine snaked out, wrapping my wrist. I gripped it as the earth slid away from beneath me, opening into a giant chasm fathoms deep. Tontes dropped with a shout.

The sides of a sinkhole crumbled away as my body fell into the hole. The vine snaked down my leg, holding me firm. I gasped in a lungful of dirt, then coughed as the vine pulled me back to the top. My shoulder bumped earth. I scrabbled for purchase, scrambling out of the dank soil with one free hand. Clumps of grass gave me leverage to pull myself to the forest floor.

I rolled onto my back with a gasp.

The canopy towered overhead, a false darkness in its heights. Just beyond, the moon shone. Stars glittered. I shot to my feet, woozy.

Merrick?

Where are you? he asked.

I . . . I'm not sure.

To Arborra, I pled, *Bring Merrick, please?*

Moments later, Merrick appeared. Mud covered his left arm and leg. Blood smeared his right ear and cheek, and a split lip was swollen on the bottom. He swung around, my name on his lips, then paused when he saw me. Relief replaced the terror.

With a cry, I rushed to him. He caught me in his strong arms, pressed a kiss to the top of my head, raked his hands through my hair.

"We did it, B. The demigods have left. Mortals are disappearing or dying. Tipa returned, said that Gelas declared it done. The final amulet has been destroyed by Ignis and Gelas."

Papa appeared across the way, near Regina. Matthais, Chi, and Rognvald followed, only a few paces back. Brought by the forest, no doubt.

Upon seeing me, Papa exhaled in relief. Regina's shoulders slumped as she put a shaky hand on his shoulder. Half her hair had been singed off on one side, it stopped at her ear. A burn mark coated her cheek in blistering skin.

Their solemn expressions, panting shoulders, testified to the horrifying night. I stared at them with pride.

"You did it."

Merrick's gaze darted around until he saw the sinkhole not far away. His eyes widened. The depths already started to fill back in. Dirt rushed into the giant hole.

"What happened?" he asked.

"Tontes."

Papa frowned. "Excuse me?"

Too late, I remembered that no one knew what I had been doing.

"I . . . uh . . ."

Papa glowered at me. "You were dealing with the *god*?"

Before I could defend myself, a shimmering cloud appeared between us. On instinct, I stumbled back and shoved Merrick away. Lightning cracked right in the middle of the cloud, breaking it apart. Protectors flew back, jolted by the power.

Earth sprang up in front of me, protecting me from the blast. The barrier crumpled.

Tontes stood in the middle of a scorched circle, glowering. His skin had a pale, sickly tone. His nostrils flared. He grimaced, as if pained. Thunder curled quietly, a long distance away.

"You win the battle, Lady-witch of Letum Wood, but Deasylva will never win the war. This is eternity for us."

Merrick tried to step in front of me, but I put a hand on his arm to stop him.

Tontes hunched.

"This is not over, witch," he growled.

The Protectors dropped into battle-ready positions. Swords glimmered. Matthais side-stepped closer to me and Merrick, dagger in hand. Papa advanced one step, then two. Regina hovered at his side.

"Go home, Tontes. Enjoy reforging your power."

His gaze flickered from me to Merrick, and back again. He straightened, shoulders back to their expansive norm.

"Failure hurts," he murmured with unnerving calm. "Cleverness can only save so much. Instead of killing you and ending your agony, may you suffer for the rest of your life, as I will for the next several centuries."

Electricity charged the air.

Everything thickened, even as it slowed. All at once, I knew what he intended to do. My heart did a painful double-thump as I spun on my heel.

Time stopped.

I lunged.

A scream of, "Merrick!" whipped off my lips just as the flash-bang followed. The blast of lightning hit too close, too quick. Not even Letum Wood could save me from the strike. Sheer electric power shoved me back.

Darkness swept over my mind like a veil.

Chapter Twenty-Eight

Lucidity hovered on the edges.

Vaguely, I felt my body land in dirt, skidding several paces through rocks and soil. Pain ricocheted through my exhausted muscles, but it kept me from letting go entirely.

With all my tenacity, I held onto consciousness, attempting to wrestle it back to my mind through sheer force. My head bobbed on my neck, lolling to the side. I screamed in my mind, unable to make my brain work as I struggled to gain my bearings.

Merrick! I wanted to scream. *Merrick!*

Fingers dug into the earth, aching beneath the nail beds. The pain zipped through me in a reminder.

I arched my back, forced my sluggish eyelids open. Blackness attempted to drag me under, but I fought. With all my power, I attempted to open my eyes, to right my head.

Fuzzy darkness.

I blinked once.

Twice.

Three times.

From the edges out, the picture began to clarify. I threw an arm across my chest to build momentum. My body rolled with it, pushing me onto my side. Dull, painful heartbeats reverberated through my chest, my temples, as I shoved myself upright to my hands, then on to my knees.

Vines reached beneath my arms, gently pulling me higher. I stumbled on barely-working feet, but pressed on. The darkness ebbed out of my vision, clarifying a dark night. Tontes had left. No sign of him remained.

"Merrick? Merrick!"

Burning wood filled my nostrils. Singed hair, the smell of charred skin, and death. With a sob, I rushed across the sodden ground. Mud caked my toes, my legs as I fell. The vines tightened, holding me in the air before I smacked my face on a rock.

A body lay on the ground, thrown back. Limp. Scorched black. Smoke rose from the destroyed half-armor.

I sobbed, threw myself across the space. Letum Wood bore me the rest of the way, until I landed on my knees on the soft earth.

"Merrick!"

I reared back with a gasp.

Not Merrick.

Matthais.

Shock rendered me incapable of movement for several long moments. A black, charred area covered Matthais' chest. The leather of his remaining half-armor smoldered. Fire chewed away at the pieces, crumbling it to ash. The metal had melted from the blast, fused to his body. His neck, blackened, was limp, his face turned away.

Slack.

A sob broke free.

"Matthais!"

A moan drew my attention. I whirled around. Merrick lay sprawled outside the blackened circle, on his side. With a cry, I hurried over, dropped to my knees. Tears blurred my eyes, so thick I couldn't see.

My palm pressed his face.

"Hey."

His green eyes opened onto mine.

"B?"

"Are you all right? You're alive?"

"Fine. I . . . Matthais." He choked, shoved back to his knees. "Matthais pushed me. Where is he? I—"

I put a hand on his shoulder to slow him down.

"Merrick, stop."

He ignored me, back on his feet now. Dazed, he blinked. For a moment he tottered, woozy. I straightened up next to him. Finally, his gaze stopped on Matthais' body. His tortured expression went slack. Helpless, I could only watch through hot tears.

Silence reigned in the forest. The questions cleared from his eyes. A gradual dawning registered on his face, his features, until he understood what I couldn't say. His lips pressed, nostrils flared.

"The gods," he whispered.

When a tear dropped down his filthy cheek, a fisted hand covered his heart.

"My brother."

Papa leaned over Matthais, closed his half-open eyes. Rognvald dropped to a knee on Matthais' left, his bushy beard matted with blood, half-armor nearly torn off. Chi materialized from the darkness next to Rognvald, a slight witch with wiry arms and a bald head.

"Brother," each of them whispered.

A tear dropped from Papa's cheek and onto Matthais. Regina stepped up to Papa's side as he crouched. Her hand went to his shoulder, squeezed.

Papa stood. He went willingly into her arms, clutching her

in tight fists. He shook. Regina closed her eyes. Tears trickled down her cheeks as she whispered something, fingers in his hair.

I turned away, because now I understood. Papa had who he needed. Regina could hold him through this—walk him through the darkness—in ways that I never could. In ways that Mama couldn't have either.

In a strange sense, Regina completed Papa. Seeing them together helped me comprehend what Papa couldn't say all along.

Regina *fit*.

Merrick startled when I reached up, cradled his cheek in my hand. Wretchedness filled his watery eyes. He blinked, and a tear dropped.

"B . . ."

"He saved you, Merrick. Saved Alkarra. We will never forget."

Gradually, the horror faded from his expression. He nodded once, jaw tight. I curled my fingers in his hair, then let my hand drop. Rognvald shuffled back, sat on a fallen tree with a staggering shock. Chi disappeared.

Merrick's hand found my shoulder, squeezed. He pulled me close. "B," he murmured against my hair. "I love you."

I curled up against him and wept. For the forest, for the Guardians, for the Protectors. Vines wound through the air, spiraling around my ankles, my wrists. A soothing balm whispered through me, releasing the pain. Peace flowed down my body in languid, ready torrents.

I cried for Matthais.

For Alkarra.

* * *

Hours later, my hands wouldn't stop shaking.

I sat against the Wall, in the lower Bailey and stared at my cup of tea as it trembled. Waves rippled from the outside in, never calm. Always agitated. A reflection of my mind.

A clear sky unfurled overhead with littering stars and swoops of fresh air. The damp humidity of the last several days cleared away, swept out with a soft breeze. Across my shoulders lay a heavy blanket.

Guardians groaned from litters in front of me. Some called out, others snored, drugged by sleeping potions. Near me, injured Guardians that could walk sat against the wall, waiting for their turn with an exhausted Apothecary.

I shouldn't be here. Not *here*. I could just as easily go to Scarlett's office. The Gatehouse. Grandfather's apartment. Anywhere but this spot. Certainly not home because my cottage didn't exist.

There was no home.

Tears welled up in my eyes, dropped down my cheeks. In vain, I cast a spell to stop my hands from shaking, but nothing happened. My magic had depleted. Not even a trickle left. Everything felt hollow.

Spent.

Gone.

Matthais's blank face, lost in death, intruded on my thoughts. I welcomed it, my heart an empty pit inside. Papa would be looking for me by now. At least an hour had passed since I made an excuse to find some water and left. Merrick would be searching for me, too, once he returned from checking on his family. Scarlett. Leda. Nicholas. So many witches would want to speak with me about the battle.

I couldn't face them.

Not any of them.

Not yet.

Tears dribbled down my cheeks. I told myself to set the tea aside, but my hands didn't listen. Just quaked in my lap, as if detached from my mind. Who had even brought me the cup? I couldn't remember . . .

A body lowered to the bench next to me. The heavy arm around my shoulder pulled me close, tucked me into their side. A sob broke free as Grandfather's comforting scent wrapped me in safety.

"Cry, my girl," he murmured. "Sometimes, it's the only release we have."

Relief came.

Shuddering, deep sobs flowed free. Grandfather took the tea cup, set it aside. He stood, guiding me elsewhere. I followed blindly, too wrapped in the quaking emotions to stop him. The torchlight from the Bailey faded as he tucked us into an alcove and embraced me.

I cried into his chest until all the emotions swept away. The expense left me wrung out. Ragged. Empty in a way I'd never felt before. All the hollow spots that were once vibrant trees ached now. The rampant destruction. My lost home.

The narrow odds.

For minutes, Grandfather held me close. When the shuddering cries slowed, he squeezed my shoulder. I peered up at him through burning eyes.

"Grandfather, I . . ."

He put a palm on my tear-stained cheek. "I know."

Tears blurred the comforting vision of him. He did know. He knew everything I couldn't wrap in words. I didn't understand how, but felt as if he saw me perfectly, even when I didn't. He wiped the tears free with a gentle thumb.

"What do you need?"

"Quiet."

"Food? Water?"

I nodded.

"Come to my apartment," he murmured. "I'll keep everyone

else at bay until you can replenish yourself, though I can't promise anything about Leda."

I snorted. "Good luck trying."

"My home is yours."

Relieved, I leaned into him again. He held me tight, a broken whisper on his lips.

"I love you, Bianca. I'm so glad to hold you alive in my arm again."

Chapter Twenty-Nine

Sunlight streamed into the High Priestess' office.

Not another soul occupied the room with us. Not Leda, Hiddleston, the Underassistants, nor the journalists from the *Chatterer* that had almost taken up residence the last week. Dust motes stirred in the air as Scarlett regarded me, motherly concern filling her soulful eyes.

"Bianca Monroe," she muttered in exasperation. "You are a handful."

For the first time in days, I found a smile.

She returned it.

With a wave, she motioned me into a chair. After she lowered into her seat, I followed. A moment of silence passed while Scarlett mentally searched for where to start in all that we had to say. I let her guide it, grateful not to be in charge.

"Well, I'll just come right out and say it," she said resolutely. "*I* was right from the beginning, but *you* saved Alkarra."

A light-hearted chuckle escaped me. The burden of grief alleviated for just a moment, and the levity felt good.

"Yes, Your Highness, you were right. Letum Wood ended up being the most clever way to fight the gods."

"I take little joy in being right this time." True sorrow threaded her tone. "You lost so much."

"We all lost so much."

Her gaze slipped off to the side, where three paintings stood near the hearth. The first showed Matthais, on a stand populated with flowers. A small, metallic shield with a sword through it lay beneath his portrait—the sign of the Brotherhood.

Next to it stood a similar image—Niko.

My throat tightened at the sight of him, surrounded by Magnolia flowers. A deep ache beat inside me, in tune with my heart. It rose and fell like the waves, expanding and contracting at will. No matter how many days I had to get used to news of Niko's death, comprehension eluded me.

Niko, the heroic High Priest of the Eastern Network, would never see his son grow up. Tomas would never know his father. Niko intentionally distracted a demigod, which allowed Papa to steal one of the final amulets.

Then Niko died.

Already, the upper and lower Baileys were packed with witches waiting to honor Niko, Matthais, and Aldred, their deceased High Priest.

Leda had been preparing for the shared memorial service all morning. All three would be recognized by the Central Network this afternoon, along with the Guardians, Captains, and others who died in the Battle of Letum Wood. Delegations across Alkarra planned to attend, including Nadira, Highest Witch of the Northern Network. The general mending of bridges felt like new ground between the Northern Network and all the others.

Leda spoke of rumors of demigods in the castle, Hiddleston and Leda teaming up, and a rare show of strength from Aldred, Ava, and Protector-hopeful Tysen. Thanks to the High Priest, they captured an amulet and showed up at the last minute to defeat the gods.

Heroes, all of them.

Prickles rushed through my body when I regarded Aldred's solemn expression in the final painting. I turned my attention back to Scarlett. I wouldn't miss him, but I mourned that he had to die in such a way. Without him, I may have never trusted my forest. When it mattered most, Aldred had been the right witch for the job, and I honored his sacrifice.

"Lost much," Scarlett murmured, "saved more. Without the advantage that Letum Wood gave to us, we would never have won. I want to thank you, personally, for what you did. For the changes you were willing to make. The . . . battles you took on."

I nodded.

Her intent gaze told me she knew exactly what I'd given up. My home. My control. Almost lost Merrick. But no matter how much perished during the war of the gods, my life remained.

"The Network will move on, as we have before," Scarlett continued with the duly bright tone of a leader who knew her next step. "I have little doubt that repairs will take some time, as they always do. The Central Network has weathered wars before, we shall do it again. As always, witches prove resilient. We know more now than we ever have before. I have faith in us."

"I share your trust, High Priestess. It's who we are."

Warmth stole over her features in a rare moment of softness. Instead of a bun, she wore her hair down on her shoulders today. It felt like an admission of grief, a vulnerable change. She appeared ten years younger for it, particularly with her affectionate smile.

"Several new Council Members are on the way. Many of our old Council have stepped down to enjoy retirement or allow new Council Members to help us through a time of healing."

"Halifax?"

"Amongst others, like Rafe, Rosanna, Massimo."

"Georgette?"

Scarlett chuckled. "You're not that lucky. I plan to take some time to select the right candidates. A rigorous qualification process that we're putting into place for one, to exempt Council Members attaining position from political favors."

My amusement settled. "Your new High Priest will help you choose the right ones, I have no doubt."

"We are most lucky to have him, aren't we?"

"Grandfather has been preparing for this role his whole life, I think. He'll be an excellent High Priest, particularly after working with Mildred for so long. Being confined to an office, instead of transporting all over Alkarra, will be easier on him."

"I certainly hope so. Taking such a high position seems to be a family tradition," she quipped with a smile. "Please, don't tell me that you have any motivations to—"

"No."

My firm response sent a frisson of amusement through her. "I thought not and am glad to hear it. At any rate, Marten will be the ideal High Priest to get us through this time. I'm grateful he accepted my invitation."

Hope swelled in my heart at the thought. Grandfather as High Priest, Scarlett as Highest Witch. With a new Council, the Central Network faced bigger ideas. Better ones, I hoped. A fresh start everywhere.

Scarlett folded her hands in her lap, peering at me in deepening curiosity.

"And the Sisterhood?"

"What about it?"

"Do you plan to continue?"

My turn to be amused. "Yes, High Priestess. My plans have only strengthened. I am aware of a few more areas where I could benefit from greater training. I plan to focus on those, find mentors, hone my skills. I have hope that the Brotherhood and the Sisterhood may one day work together again, with greater consistency."

"Rognvald is more progressive than he seems. He'll be open minded as the Head of Protectors, if you ask me."

"I hope so. It certainly doesn't hurt that we've already worked together, and with great effect."

"Has he allowed you to remain in the magic of the Brotherhood?"

I smiled quietly. "So far. I haven't said anything, so I'm not sure he remembers."

She nodded, seeming pleased. "I stand ready to support you in whatever ways you need. I have a feeling, after all that occurred with the Battle of Letum Wood, that opportunities will be open for you."

"I'm here, High Priestess, for you first and always."

"You shall be called on, first and always. You have finally found your place in the Network, Bianca. I hope you realize that. Now, shall we go down to the memorial together? I'm to arrive a few minutes early for Leda's sake, and I happen to know she's saved you a seat next to her. Your best friend feared for you prodigiously. I promise to give her time to spend with you soon. For now, she's helping me piece the Network back together, one meeting at a time."

* * *

Trampled, razed earth stood before me.

Well-known paths had been obliterated. My friendly, humble cottage reduced to piles of mud, splinters, and rocks. I stood on flat ground, devoid of trees, with a hollow pit in my stomach. The place where I started as the Lady-witch of Letum Wood had been lost.

Gone.

Forever.

A warm hand weighed on my shoulder. "I'm sorry, B."

"Me too," I whispered.

I leaned into Merrick's steady chest. His solid warmth. Not for the first time, a cold chill shuddered through me. I'd almost lost him. If Matthais hadn't understood what was about to happen, I would have. Instead, Matthais had thrown himself in the path of death in lieu of Merrick.

The ultimate Protector.

Seeing the devastation by the light of day forced me to feel all the frustration again. The depths of grief, already so hollow inside.

"What will you do?" he asked.

I paused. Until this moment, I hadn't given it much thought. In an odd twist of fate, Grandfather had moved into Papa's old apartment, and I'd inherited my old room until I could figure out where to go next. A place I'd never thought to live in again.

Reeves positively glowed.

The thought brought a smile to my face. It faded as quickly as it came.

"I don't know," I murmured. "I have a feeling it will involve Papa and me building our separate houses at the same time, though."

Both his arms came around me, closing the space between us. I leaned my head on his shoulder, grateful in new and deeper ways for his reassurance.

"We can always rebuild," he said.

"We will."

"Where?"

"Wherever Arborra tells me."

His neck tightened as he smiled. "The forest always takes care of you, B. This is the beginning of something new and better. It will be your cottage now. Your home. If you want, we'll make it together, one piece at a time."

"We can steal all of Papa's tools," I quipped.

Merrick laughed. The delightful sound made my heart patter. I turned in his arms, grateful to twine my hands around his neck. He felt solid and certain beneath me, reassuring in the deepest way. I reached up, brushed a lock of hair out of his eyes.

"I love you, Merrick."

He pressed our foreheads together.

"To the lands and lives beyond."

The chasmic emotions in his eyes told me I didn't need to say another word. Like the forest, like Grandfather, we both understood. His arms tightened around me, gaze glittering.

"By the way, where is Goat and Other Goat?"

I laughed, unable to help myself. "I found them in a tree, at the top of the branches, after the battle. Letum Wood had kept them there, with all the manulele birds, safe from the waters. Priscilla and Ava are caring for all of them at the school."

He chortled.

A cracking twig came from behind. Merrick glanced up. A perplexed half-smile appeared there.

"Regina?"

I whirled around to find Regina standing several paces away. She held herself coiled, like an uncertain mortega about to spring free. Her hair had been pulled out of her face in a low, braided bun. Magically fixed after losing half of it, I assumed. A few tendrils escaped to dance around her temples. Sunlight dappled her shoulders, the top of her head, which glowed in reddish strands.

Apart from a few hours after the War of the Networks, when Regina had given me a few basic lessons and a tour of her life in the Masters, I'd had little-to-no interaction with her. Admired her from afar, certainly, but had no other claim on her as a friend. Now that Papa had fallen for her, much would change.

My tension bled away. "It's good to see you, Regina," I called. The strange air fractured. I smiled to banish the rest of the lingering malady.

Regina advanced a step with a careful smile. Merrick released me to shuffle back.

"Well," he drawled, "I have a few things to discuss with Rognvald. I'll see you at my place for dinner, B?"

"Yes, thank you."

With a wink to me, and a nod to Regina, he left. Regina stared at me with soulful green eyes. She swallowed hard, the sound audible. Her neck tightened a little, the white lines set against a cream-colored shirt. She gestured around with a swing of her hand.

"I'm so sorry for what happened. I would love to help you build again, should you decide to."

"I would appreciate the help."

"From what I hear of it, it was cozy and a place of love. I'm sure you'll be able to rebuild."

"It will be an interesting challenge," I said with a chuckle.

"Derek told me that he mentioned . . ." She paused, appeared mildly confused, then pressed on. ". . . the way we feel about each other. I just wanted you to know that I respect your father. He is the best of witches and I've long admired him."

Her words, earnestly and hastily spoken at the same time, softened something inside of me. Regina always held her composure so thoroughly. To see her undone, harried, and nervous made her so . . . real.

I couldn't deny the light in Papa's eyes when he spoke about Regina. A glimmer of something that I hadn't seen . . . since Mama died.

The frustration of anyone but Mama causing that in him welled back up, then faded to nothing. In the wake of almost losing Merrick, seeing the way Regina soothed Papa at the end of Matthais' life, I understood better the empty chasm of Papa's life without her.

What a stunning, terrifying time it would be.

What would give him purpose if not the Protectors? Where better to invest his time, his depth of caring, than in someone that would give the same back?

Who *else* but someone who, for all intents and purposes, needed him as much as he needed her?

Mama, I thought. *I know you'd want this for him.*

A gentle burst of wind rustled by, a caress on my cheek. Aquamarine light slipped up a nearby tree, just within sight. Taking it as an affirmation, I gave Regina my warmest smile.

"I can tell that he truly cares for you as well. I'm glad for a chance to talk about it together."

Her lips twitched. "Thank you for saying that. He's infuriating," she said with a wry smile, "but amazing. I . . . I want you to talk to me, should you have questions or concerns or need anything."

"Thank you."

A delicate tension remained between us, easily stifled this time. Regina opened her mouth, then closed it again. Her brow furrowed. She canted to the side a little, gazing away.

"The last several weeks have been an interesting time for the Sisterhood," I said as I kicked at a rock on the ground. It scampered away. Something about admitting weakness in front of Regina made me itch under my skin.

"Oh?"

"I've learned that I have some work to do. Some . . . soft spots to work on. I'm entirely too dependent on one weapon, haven't picked up magical detection, and continue to allow details to elude me."

"Och," she laughed a little. "How well I understand that list."

"You struggled with those?"

"In the beginning? Constantly. Dillon was always harping after me to figure out magical detection. It was a true sore spot for years."

"Now?"

"One of my greatest strengths."

Relief coursed through me. "I'm happy to hear that. Would

you be open to the idea of . . . helping me? I've heard that you've been reinstituted as Head of Masters in the North, and I'm sure that will keep you busy."

"I am the Head of Masters, but not in the same way. I'm . . . part-time, I suppose you could say. My replacement, Jacob, is beginning his transition into Head of Masters. I'll ensure they're in a good place, then back slowly away."

"Oh."

"My time will be my own within the next couple of months. I'd be happy to help you with whatever I can. Though," she added with another quick smile, "I have promised your father extensive help on his house. He's a puppy sometimes, you know."

A laugh bubbled out of me.

Regina would be just right.

* * *

You belong to us.

We save ourselves.

The goddess returns.

The trees continued their reports as I darted through the forest. Joy kept me running faster than I intended, the late summer air hot in my chest.

Fallen saplings littered the forest floor, impeding my progress. Torn bushes. Dead leaves. Fallen branches. River-wide flows cut through the forest like missing arms. Over the top of it sprouted new growth. Hints of green. Shoots of tree tops. I skirted each gentle life with careful steps.

For every one I passed, I whispered encouragement.

You belong to me.

You are powerful.

You take care of yourself.

All around me, trees hummed. Brightness filled the forest in a new way, banishing the dark canopy that had prevailed for so long. The new sunshine coaxed fresh growth from the ground.

A shimmering of greater magic lay over the wood. For all we'd lost, Deasylva compensated. Greater magic infused the ground, speeding the recovery process. Years would pass before the new trees had true height and growth again, but the bushes would restore by next year. The blank spaces would fill in.

Letum Wood continued, as always.

With each breath, my thoughts ran rampant in the back of my mind. A tree called out to me, pleading with me to stop. I slowed, skidding to a halt on dry ground in front of it. When I pressed my hand to the trunk, it thrilled.

The goddess awaits.

She shall speak.

I tilted my head back in surprise. Deasylva? I scoured the trunk, waited for the scripted, blue handwriting to appear the way it had before. The trunk remained as brown and empty as before, edged with umber shadows and little hairs. I frowned, head tilted to the side.

"Where are you?" I asked.

No words appeared, but a familiar voice answered.

With some convincing, you have accepted your place within my creations. I am proud of you, as I have always been.

Relief swept through me, accompanied by an abiding familiarity. Her voice recalled a denizen of memories, most of them good. The In-between. Mama. For a moment, I felt the serenity of the In-between again. All frustration had been erased, buoyed in memories of better. Never had I regretted my choice to return to this side of life, but the peacefulness of that place provided a constant draw.

"I understand now. If Letum Wood takes care of itself, I can better run the Sisterhood. I won't be beholden to the trees."

Amusement lined her response. *You do understand.*

My fingertips dropped from where they pressed into the

tree, as if I could tether myself to the goddess. My thirst to connect with her again took me by surprise. It felt like a different hunger.

Deeper.

Harder to satisfy, longer to crave, deeper to cherish.

"You hold more faith in me than I hold in myself. I . . . I guess I was afraid. I wanted the best for the forest. I was afraid to trust and lose again."

What is best for us isn't what we think at first. With time, all becomes clear. The question is whether you *are ready for what awaits. My trees have prepared. They are ready to stand on their own now. Are you?*

"That depends on what awaits," I muttered.

A low chuckle.

That is not for you to know.

My brow wrinkled as I peered into the forest. "Are you going to make me stand on my own out there?"

Do the trees truly stand alone?

"No."

Have you abandoned them?

"No, I just . . . I know they can do hard things."

Do you think that you *will truly stand alone?*

The pause in which I contemplated the question lasted for several minutes.

"No," I finally said.

You are never truly alone.

Letum Ivy wound around my ankle in a tiny squeeze. Heat flooded my skin, washed up my body in flows of light. A bright, ethereal, otherworldly calm flooded me.

My absence from the forest will not be long as I recover my energy, my daughter. You have done well. Continue to do so, for much awaits you.

* * *

After Deasylva departed, I sprinted through the forest. My legs flew, arms pumped, heart soared. Trees sang in tune with the steady flow of blood. I soared on the wings of trees, like dragons, and threw myself into the depths of wild places.

Come, the magic whispered, stirring up my heart. *For you belong to us.*

THE END

Coming up next . . . .

After a story like that, you probably have some questions.

Let's see if these sound familiar:

"Where did Baxter find Nicomedianthekus?"
"What happened in the North with Geralyn?"
"Niko *died*? How?"
"Is Priscilla going to be all right?"
"What about Alina in the Southern Network?"
"How did Leda get an amulet?"
"What happened when Aldred died?"
"Where was Prana in all this?!"

Well, no worries.

I have all those answers for you, and more.

In the following pages, you're going to hear an upcoming sneak peek from THE FINALES. It's a 70,000+ word novel (for comparison, WAR OF THE GODS is 94,000 words) that encompasses the individual stories for Baxter, Regina, Derek, Ava, Leda, Hiddleston, Aldred, and Alina, during the final fight for Alkarra.

Get all the deets that you couldn't see from Bianca's perspective.
And trust me.
You. Want. These. Deets.
Keep reading!

CHAPTER ONE

Gelas, god of ice, reminded Baxter of a cool summer morning.

Hints of warmth littered his bearing, riddled with bursts of something chilly during the unexpected moments. Like a cold front moving ahead of a thunderstorm.

His glittering eyes weren't as glacial as the ice floes he cherished, but they weren't warm. Dark black hair, streaked with white, all the way to his shoulders, provided a strange dichotomy to the driven snow constantly around him.

An empty spot next to Gelas drew Baxter's gaze. Bianca had been standing there only a moment before. Baxter drove his fingers through his hair as he let out a long breath.

With Derek Black on the prowl and no longer confined to the Protectors, one never knew who might listen in.

Baxter mentally switched back to the Alaysian language when he said, "Bianca's gone. You can tell me the full truth of what you expect for Alkarra now that Tontes and Ventis are going to attack."

Amusement flittered across Gelas's face. He cast a sidelong glance in Baxter's direction.

"I *was* being honest, Baxter. My assessment of the situation as I presented it to the Lady-witch is wholly true. Prospects are bleak. We must find Nicomedianthekus, and she must bring me the amulets as they arrive."

The tension in Baxter's chest loosened. He'd prepared himself for a sucker punch. Layers and details that Gelas might have held back because Bianca lacked the full context of Alaysia and the land of the gods.

Yet he wasn't excited about the truth, either.

"You really think Alkarra stands a chance?"

Gelas lifted one shoulder in a non-committed shrug. "A chance."

"Not a great one?"

"Not with Ignis as weak as he is. He may have enough amulets to remain functional for now, but that doesn't make him powerful. He's using what time and energy he has to figure out how to destroy amulets."

"You have all *your* amulets."

"Save one," he murmured.

The lost Gelas amulet, Nicomedianthekus, drove a spike of desperation through the conversation. The giant amulet—the first to be forged when the gods decided to harness magic in a new way—had been missing for centuries.

"Seems like a wild chance that Nicomedianthekus would be in Alkarra," Baxter said.

"Where else?"

"I don't know. Anywhere but here makes more sense. The gods haven't been on this land for thousands of years."

Gelas shuffled forward a few steps, hands on his hips as he peered out on the tundra. Summer swept away the local ice, but it was a cooler summer than usual. Gelas' doing, most likely, though the witches wouldn't realize it. In winter, Gelas truly stepped into his world.

"I've been looking for my amulet all that time. It's nowhere to be found."

"Prana?"

"Not even there. Mermaids, sea dragons, you name it, they've searched. They've watched Prana's bounty and hidden treasures. I don't believe my sister has it."

"The ocean floor is massive."

"So is the length of centuries, if you think about it."

"Could Deasylva have it?"

"How?"

Baxter shook his head. The goddess of the forest had no connection that would easily bring the lost amulet to her. Sarena, goddess of the desert, had land that backed the ocean—but that supposition was a far cry, too.

"Everything you told Bianca was true, but you haven't told her *everything*, have you?"

Gelas's neck twitched. Several long moments before he shook his head.

"No."

"What's really going on? Witches might believe that Deasylva wants help to defeat Ventis and Tontes because she doesn't want Sarena involved, but that doesn't make any sense."

"I know."

"The witches are buying into it because their lack of understanding about god and goddess life allows them to accept that as a plausible explanation. Sarena loves Alkarra as much as the gods. She wouldn't want to destroy it."

"But she could."

"Doesn't mean she *would*."

Gelas cast him a wry glance. "You know so much, do you, pup?"

Baxter fought off a scowl. The condescending nickname hadn't been necessary. "It's not that hard to figure out."

A scoff escaped the god, who folded his arms across his chest. His legs braced, teeth sank into his bottom lip. Several moments of contemplation passed before Gelas let out a long breath. Something stirred in his expression that gave Baxter pause.

"I've spoken with the goddesses."

"All of them?"

Gelas waved a hand. "Yes. Deasylva and Sarena, mostly. Prana lurked in the background, I think, but she's a hard one to track when she doesn't want to be seen."

"And how did it go?"

The lines on Gelas' face deepened. He blinked, shook his head, and sighed. "Unexpectedly. It's been thousands of years since I've seen any of them face-to-face together. Deasylva and I have had limited discussions during the past couple of eons, but rarely, and not for long."

"Selsay wasn't there?"

"She remained in her mountains," he said lightly. An under-tone thrived in the words that Baxter couldn't hope to understand.

"Are you glad you met with them?"

"I don't regret it. We call ourselves siblings, you know, but it's not exactly that straightforward. It's the easiest delineation for witches to understand."

His musing tone sidetracked Baxter for a moment. The gods and goddesses weren't strict siblings, which seemed to lessen obligation or affection in cases such as these.

"Anyway," Gelas continued, "The goddesses were unusually open with me, and revealed more of what's at play."

"So there *is* something else."

Gelas nodded, held the silence, and finally continued after a long minute. "You're correct. Not everything is as it seems. I'll agree to tell you more about Deasylva and Sarena—not every-thing, but something—as long as the information doesn't extend beyond us. Not to witches, not your father."

The piercing glare that followed sealed the promise of retribution should Baxter betray him.

"I agree."

"I don't desire Sarena's wrath, which is bounteous, so I will only tell you that I found out the full extent of the truth myself after the Lady-witch nearly died in Alaysia."

"What is it?"

"Sarena has great reason to need a little more . . . protection . . . than usual. Deasylva is shielding Sarena from Ventis and Tontes, not the opposite."

"But Sarena is the eldest goddess."

"Yes."

"Historically, the most powerful. Why would she need protection?"

"History changes." Gelas turned to meet Baxter's gaze. "Unprecedented measures drove Sarena out of her desert for the last several hundred years. Deasylva's expanding power in her ridiculously overgrown forest has been strategic for several reasons, and Sarena has been taking advantage of the protection offered by Deasylva's presence. When Ventis and Tontes attack, Deasylva hopes that witches will be enough to cripple them without her help."

"Because she'll be protecting Sarena?"

Gelas nodded.

Astonishment quelled Baxter's rising questions. They stuck in his throat, thick as cold honey. What could force the most powerful goddess into hiding?

"Will you tell me why?" he asked.

"No."

Gelas's firm response didn't surprise him, but the leaden weight did. Whatever secrets the goddesses harbored would remain hidden—potentially for centuries. Eternities. Silence filled the space for several minutes, allowing Baxter's shoulders to unwind again.

Gelas lifted a hand. "All I can offer you is this: Sarena has her secrets, and Deasylva is helping her keep them. There is much more at stake than I imagined, and that's all you need to know. If we don't win this war, it will create dark days, indeed."

"Can we do it? With Nicomedianthekus, can the witches be a strong enough force for Deasylva?"

"Deasylva says she's seen it and that the possibilities for success are possible. She didn't say *likely.* It depends on the Lady-witch extending a little trust and being clever, but . . . isn't that always the case for most living things?"

"I wouldn't know."

A laugh rolled out of Gelas. "You're right, you wouldn't. I forget you don't exist in eternity."

The conversation dwindled, leaving Baxter with another swamp of doubts. The fault was his own. He'd asked the questions, Gelas had answered. Now, he needed time to sort through all the strings and oddities that lay jumbled in the aftermath. He shoved questions of goddesses aside for later.

Or never.

He had an amulet to find, and by extension, an entire world to save. Baxter shoved a hand in his pocket, cleared his mind, and faced Gelas.

"Alkarra is a big place. I'm assuming you have some idea where the amulet might be?"

"Some."

"Then where do you want me to start?"

Gelas frowned. "It could be anywhere, as you know, but I'm inclined to think it'll be in a cold, snowy place."

"There are lots of those."

"Then I suggest you start with the obvious." Gelas glanced at Zamok Castle in the background, then to him again. "The Southern Network has always loved their gems. If there's any place to verify whether or not the amulet is hidden in a secret horde scrabbled away by jealous witches, you're standing on it."

* * *

If you're ready to read more, visit my website to purchase your paperback copy!

THE FINALES is a 70,000+ word novel that encompasses the individual stories for Baxter, Regina, Derek, Ava, Leda, Hiddleston, Aldred, and Alina, is only available at www. katiecrossbooks.com.

Acknowledgments

Ah, here we are.

The most difficult part of a book. Particularly a series-closer, when so much of my heart and soul is on the floor at the finish line.

(As it should be.)

First and foremost, to my team at KCW, what would I do without you? Samantha, Kaley, Mike, Kerri, Evan, Carol, Laila, Louise, Gemma, Darcee, Debbie, and Kim.

What would I do without you?

Beta reading. Proofing. Editing. Advance-listening. Dealing with my plethora of ideas. Thank you for all you are to me.

To my readers, an **extra special** thank you this time! Your ideas for amulet names were inspiring! I loved all the submissions *and* all the winners.

Artemis, JoLynn, J'net, the "Secret Alkarran Northern Network Master" Dean Webb, Kim, Ami Journey Gallier, Jule Webster, and Veronique. Thank you being part of Alkarra and my world. I'm grateful for your creativity with amulet names!

To my family, friends, dogs, and the mountains that deal with my incessant story ideas.

I love you all.

Now, let's get back to Alkarra with more fantastic tales!

—Katie Cross

Join Other Witches

Merry meet!

There is more epic magic and wild places waiting for you.

If you want to stay in-the-know about new releases, get awesome discounts (IE—more books, less money), and have free novels and short stories land in your lap, I've got your back.

Go to www.katiecrossbooks.com to join the other witches on my email list, where you get exclusive, can't-find-anywhere-else kind of stuff.

(In fact, I'll send you some free stories right away—first email!)

Or you can go to The Witchery, which is my Facebook group of other readers just like you. Please visit www.facebook.com/groups/thenetworkseries to learn more!

There, you'll see more images of Alkarra, join all your witchy friends, and go to lunch with me on my weekly Coffee With Katie calls.

(No, seriously. I will Uber-Eats you lunch!)

Can't wait to see you there!

—Katie

Also by Katie Cross

The Dragonmaster Trilogy

FLAME

Chronicles of the Dragonmasters (short story collection)

FLIGHT

The Ronan Scrolls (novella)

FREEDOM

The Dragonmaster Trilogy Collection

The Network Series

Mildred's Resistance (prequel)

Miss Mabel's School for Girls

Alkarra Awakening

The High Priest's Daughter

War of the Networks

The Network Series Complete Collection

The Isadora Interviews (novella)

Short Stories from Miss Mabel's

Short Stories from the Network Series

Hazel (short story)

The Network Saga Suggested Reading Order

1. The Parting (novella #1)

2. The Lost Magic (full-length novel)

3. The Lamplighter's Daughter (novella #2)

4. Merrick (novella #3)

5. The Rise of the Demigods (full-length novel)

6. Priscilla (novella #4)

7. Viveet (novella #5)

8. Prana (novella #6)

9. Derek (novella #7)

10. The Forgotten Gods (full-length novel)

11. The Returning (novella #8)

12. Regina (novella #9)

13. Leda (novella #10)

14. The Sister (prequel to WOTG #1)

15. The School (prequel to WOTG #2)

16. The Council (prequel to WOTG #3)

17. The Goddess (prequel to WOTG #4)

18. War of the Gods (full-length novel)

19. The Finales (a collection of novellas)

20. Marten (novella #11)

The Historical Collection

The High Priestess

The Swordmaker

The Advocate

The Reader Request Series

The Gods

The Plummet

About the Author

Katie Cross is ALL ABOUT writing epic magic and wild places. Creating new fantasy worlds is her jam.

When she's not hiking or chasing her two littles through the Montana mountains, you can find her curled up reading a book or arguing with her husband over the best kind of sushi.

Visit her at www.katiecrossbooks.com for free short stories, extra savings on all her books (and some you can't buy on the retailers), and so much more.